SEASPARROW

Ian Schoenherr

SEASPARROW

KRISTIN CASHORE

DUTTON BOOKS

DUTTON BOOKS
An imprint of Penguin Random House LLC, New York

First published in the United States of America by Dutton Books,
an imprint of Penguin Random House LLC, 2022

Copyright © 2022 by Kristin Cashore
Interior illustrations copyright © 2022 by Ian Schoenherr

Dutton is a registered trademark of Penguin Random House LLC.

Visit us online at penguinrandomhouse.com.

Library of Congress Cataloging-in-Publication Data is available.

Book manufactured in Canada

ISBN 9781984816672 (HARDCOVER)
1   3   5   7   9   10   8   6   4   2

ISBN 9780593616031 (INTERNATIONAL EDITION)
1   3   5   7   9   10   8   6   4   2

FRI
Text set in Adobe Garamond Pro

for Marie Rutkoski,
wonderful writer
and dear friend

A NOTE TO THE READER

IT'S DOUBTFUL THAT the worlds of my fantasy novels have a method of date-keeping equivalent to our Gregorian calendar or our seven days of the week. When I use our months and weekdays while relating this story, consider it a friendly translation I'm providing for you, from their world to ours. I want your mind to be free to enter these characters' lives—not tangled up in confusion about what day or month it is.

Please note that this story contains brief references to sexual assault and sexual abuse witnessed or experienced by characters before the action of the story.

Also, in case it is helpful: There is a cast of characters at the end of this book.

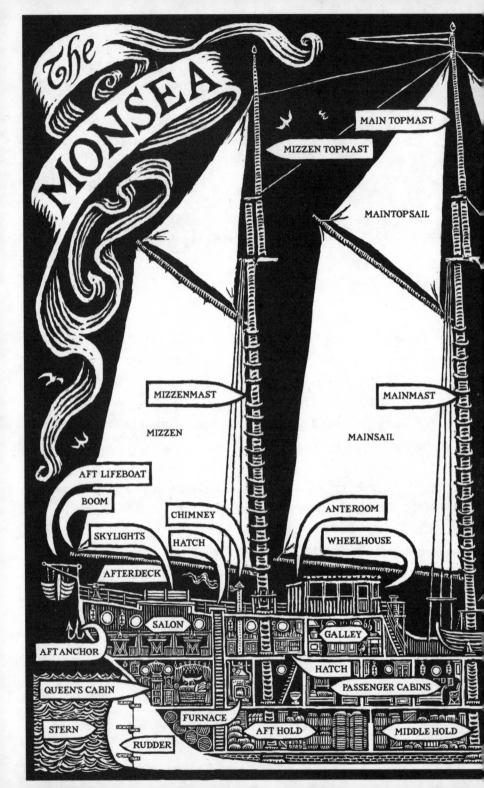

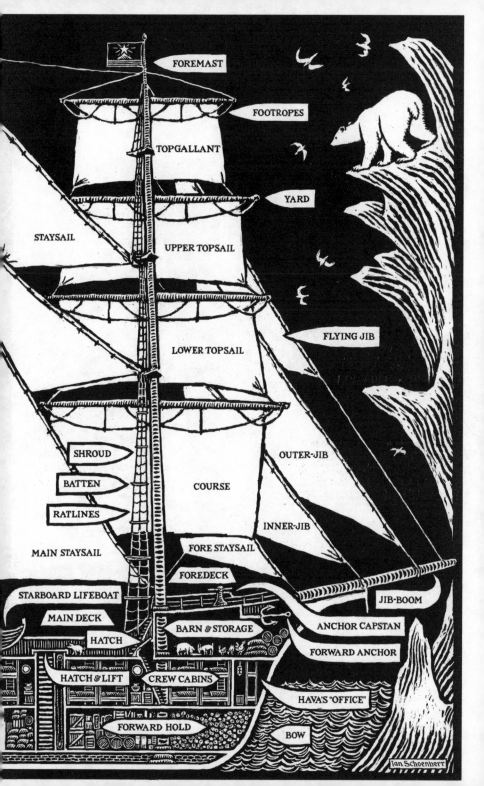

PART ONE

1.

IF YOU COULD eavesdrop without anyone knowing—if you could turn yourself into a barrel, or a coil of lines, or a clump of canvas on deck where two people are standing together, whispering secrets to each other—are you sure you wouldn't?

EAVESDROP. I WONDER where that word comes from. Did people used to climb into the eaves of a house and snoop on conversations? Then drop? Then what? Yell "Surprise!" and watch people jump and throw their papers around?

That would be funny. I've never done that.

I asked Giddon his opinion, but he had no ideas about *eavesdrop*. He said he's fond of the word *snow*drop, and he's right; it's a good word. It snows almost every day now here at sea, so it's nice to imagine white petals drifting down onto my face. But it doesn't help me with *eavesdrop*.

He said it aloud, "Snowdrop," as we stood on the foredeck of the *Monsea*, where the plunge of the prow into each wave is more extreme than anywhere else on the ship. I like it there on the foredeck. It feels like exciting things are going to happen.

Then he said, "Foxglove, that's a nice word too. Moonflower," he added, staring across the gray water like he was having a revelation. Giddon is big and tall and handsome in a noble sort of way, with a neat dark beard and pale skin like mine, and he has a fire inside him that he reserves for Bitterblue. I could see him mentally picking a bouquet for her. "Larkspur," he said, so I said, "Skunk cabbage," because I was getting tired of Giddon.

"Skunk cabbage?" he said, turning a look of indignation upon me. "Of course not."

"Impatiens," I said significantly, but he wandered down to the main deck with a dreamy expression on his face, and I wished, as I've wished many times, that Giddon and Bitterblue, who's the Queen of Monsea and secretly my half sister, would confess their newfound romantic relationship to me. I'm not stupid. I'm a spy. It's my job to figure things out. And she's my family, even if hardly anyone knows that. They should tell me.

I'll ask Teddy about *eavesdrop* when we get home. Teddy's part of Bitterblue's Ministry of Education. He's clever with words, cleverer than Giddon. My mother once told me, in a moment of lucidity, to keep a list of cherished qualities I would like in a friend. I never have. It's not like people line up for me to choose from, with their qualities listed on their chests. But if I did keep a list, maybe "Clever with Words" would be on it.

Not that Giddon lacks good qualities. He would tear off the head of anyone who hurt my sister.

I used to jump out and surprise my mother, actually, now that I consider it. I would hide myself from her, then make myself visible suddenly. Reach for her, arms outstretched, laughing. One time, when I did that, she screamed in such terror that the king, my father, came running. So I hid quickly, and never did that again. It wasn't safe to startle my mother. Too often, she wasn't in her strong mind.

ANYWAY, MY POINT is, I don't have to climb into the eaves to eavesdrop.

I can stand right in front of you, plain as plain, do a trick on your brain, and you see something else. It's my Grace. Are you in a room now? Look around. I could be right there and your eyes slide over me and see a coat on a hook instead, or a potted tree that you would realize is vaguely person-shaped if you only looked harder, but you won't. Is there some part of the room that's especially boring to you, some corner you don't seem to want to focus on? That could be me. It's not your fault. I'm discouraging your attention, and changing what you think you see.

Anyway, it was just an example. I wouldn't do it as a trick. In fact, I'm not supposed to do it at all, not without Bitterblue's permission, and only on official queen's business. Of course, seeing as I'm a spy, one could argue that I'm always on official queen's business. It's my job to keep her safe. I do that by hiding and snooping. By not trusting people. And by having adventures; I've sailed to the other side of the world and crossed the sky in a flying machine. I've talked to silbercows in the sea and pulled a pin that made a bomb explode. I've stolen formulas for weapons that will make my sister powerful. I've been to Winterkeep, and now we're going home again.

2.

LIVING ON A ship is like nothing else.

Every morning I'm rocked awake by the same crashes and creaks that soothed me to sleep the night before. I run upstairs as quickly as I can, eager to see what kind of day it is—the kind with snow dropping from a low, gray sky or the kind with a sunrise blasting beams of gold through cracks in the clouds.

If I stand in the bow, the wind drives through me. The plunge into every wave is a promise of a day ahead more thrilling than any day on land. When I turn back around and see the ship, I want to whoop, because I don't understand everything about how this ship works yet, but I will. There are things in our world we can't understand, like why I was born with a Grace and Giddon and Bitterblue weren't. Then there are riddles with answers. A ship crosses water because of the principles of physics. I will master them.

Today when I turned back around, Kera, the first mate, was standing right behind me, poking at a big metal something-or-other that sits on the foredeck, cylindrical, wrapped in chains. I jumped in surprise, which was embarrassing, but she didn't seem to notice. Kera is always sunk inside herself. Her skin is clear and pale and she has a mass of auburn hair she shoves up under a black knit hat. This morning, a little cone of snow sat atop her hat, like a mountaintop.

"Kera?" I said. "Good morning. What is that thing?"

"Anchor capstan," she said, half-distracted.

"What?"

"Sorry," she said, seeming to wake up, looking into my eyes. "Hava. Good morning. The anchor capstan is a wheel that holds the anchor chain. See this chain here? And these are the handles. We turn the capstan to drop or raise the anchor. Here, come look," she said, leading me to the rail with a steady hand and pointing to a massive anchor that was tied to the side of the ship. A fat chain from that anchor stretched over the rail to the capstan. "Careful," she said, her grip tightening as I leaned out. I guess I appreciated the gesture. Bitterblue fell overboard during our journey to Winterkeep. We didn't know she'd fallen in. I was sleeping; Giddon thought *she* was sleeping too. We left her behind. Then the people who plucked her out of the water kidnapped her. Opportunists will always try to hurt a queen. That's why she needs me.

But I'm not going to fall in.

"I didn't realize that anchor was there," I said.

"There's an anchor in the stern too."

"Why are you poking at the capstan? Is something wrong?"

"There's a pin that keeps it locked, so it doesn't spontaneously drop the anchor. See this pin here?" she said, leading me back to the capstan. "Annet says it's slipping. Water gets trapped under it and freezes."

"Oh," I said, happily breathing this in. Would she have to fix it, I asked next. Do Keepish and Dellian ships have the same mechanism? Why does it matter if the anchor drops? If the anchors are so heavy, do they unbalance the ship?

"Good questions," she said. "Has anyone told you about the ballast in the hold?"

No one had told me about the ballast in the hold, but I know all about it now. It's made of sacks of sand and stone that the sailors shift wherever they're needed, to balance the weight of the ship and make her just the right level of buoyant.

I now think that *buoyant* is one of my favorite words. It sounds like bubbles of air traveling from the depths of the sea to the surface. I like that we hauled a lot of useless, heavy stuff aboard, just to give the *Monsea* the right sorts of foundations for a house on the water.

"Coming to breakfast?" said Kera.

3.

IN THE SALON at breakfast—and at every other meal—I eat like I might never see food again. One of the Monsean sailors, Jacky, asks after my tapeworm whenever he sits down.

This morning he chose a place catty-corner to me—the sailors often position themselves at my edges, as if they want to be polite but aren't entirely sure of me—glanced at my full plate, and reminded me that the food's delicious because this is a royal ship.

"It's not like this on a *real* ship, with *real* sailors," he said, not seeming to notice that his jab at me was also an insult to himself. That's how important it is to Jacky to make me feel like I'm missing out on an authentic experience. He's one of those giant, muscly people who's around my age but seems younger, because he's always trying to prove something. I guess he's good-looking, pink cheeked with wavy dark hair and a pert mouth always about to smile, or maybe just mock me. I make a point of ignoring him.

Next, Jacky's friend Linny, who's Dellian, sat down across from me next to Jacky. Sometimes I think Jacky is afraid of me and Linny isn't. In fact, I catch Linny watching me with a look on his face like I'm a wild horse he's trying to figure out how not to startle, and I want to tell him he's directing that at the wrong person, because I don't startle easily.

Often Linny eats, then gets up and piles his plate with seconds, then raises his eyebrows at me to ask me if I want some. When I give him a curt nod, he slides seconds onto my plate so I don't have to get up. I've never asked him for this, he just does it. He gets it right too; he seems to know what I want more of. I haven't figured out whether to put a stop to this or just pretend it's fine. I hid myself from him once on the deck while he coiled lines, so I could watch him and look for signs, like strange-colored eyes or hair, that he's a Graceling or a monster or anyone with powers. He's not. His eyes matched each other, amber in daylight, pretty, but normal, especially for a Dellian. His hair is a normal dark color, straight, and always sliding down onto his forehead. His skin is brown. He's not interfering with my mind. He just knows what I like to eat.

Linny looks like a girl to me, actually, with a delicate, fine-boned face, but he has a wiry boy's body. I've seen him and Jacky bathe in the sea, stark naked in view of everyone, though I try not to stare. A lot of the sailors, men and women, bathe in the sea, unconcerned about their naked bodies. I bathe in the cabin I share with Bitterblue. Linny is one of the sailors who fills the copper tub for us, mixing cold water with water that burns if it splashes you. Jacky remarks on the luxury of it, as on all our luxuries, teasing me about my soft life. Linny doesn't remark at all.

Sometimes when they talk about it together on deck, when they don't know I can hear, Jacky has an edge to his voice that cuts the teasing away. Jacky doesn't like being a queen's servant. He wants to work on a ship with fishers, whalers, and merchants, not queens—or anyway, he thinks he does. Linny, who's been a sailor longer, tells him about frostbite and eating moldy food on the fishing ships, over-crowding, sickness. Then Linny cocks his head sideways as if he hears something, and I worry he knows I'm there.

Anyway. Annet, who's the captain, says I'm eating so much because of the cold. She says December is always cold in this part of the Brumal Sea, but this year it's colder than usual, and cold makes a person hungry. This morning at breakfast there was something in the eggs that gave them such a savory softness that I piled mounds of them onto my bread and shoved them into my mouth like I was starving. Our cook, Liel, is a genius. He climbs down into the hold through a hatch on the main deck and comes up again with vegetables and sauces and flour kept cold by the frozen sea, then collects eggs from the chickens, then carries it all into the galley and performs miracles for the benefit of everyone on board.

We are twenty-one people, one cat, one goat, four pigs, assorted chickens, and one blue fox, on a three-masted ship. We left the port of Ledra, which is the capital of Winterkeep, in early December, three and a half weeks ago. The *Monsea* is a barquentine, which means that only one mast, our foremast, carries square sails. The other two masts have fore-and-aft rigged sails, an arrangement that allows us to sail close to the wind with a small crew. I don't actually know what that means yet. But I heard Annet say it to Giddon once. It sounded thrilling. The big front sails are squares, the rest of the sails are triangles, and the *Monsea* is beautiful. That's all you really need to know. Her hull is teal against the gray of the sea and her sails are like wings. Queens have to name royal ships boring, patriotic things, which is why ours is named the *Monsea*, but I think I'd call her something to do with a bird in winter. The *Snowy Owl*, or the *Brumal Tern*. The *Osprey*. She flies across the water. Imagine a ship turning into a bird.

Of the twenty-one people on the *Monsea*, eight are court people and thirteen are ship people.

The court people are: me; Giddon; the queen; the queen's two guards, Ranin and Mart; and three of her advisers, Froggatt, Barra, and Coran. Coran's also a doctor, and Ranin and Mart double as sailors. All eight of us are Monsean, except Giddon, who isn't really any nationality. He's from the Middluns, where he used to be a lord. Then his king burned his estate to the ground and banished him because he's a revolutionary who helps people the world over rebel against tyrannical kings. He and his rabble-rousing friends call themselves the Council, and they're infamous lawbreakers. Maybe it's a conflict of interest for the queen's lover to travel the world dismantling monarchies? Could such a person really be a queen's consort?

Consort is a funny word. CONsort. ConSORT. On this ship, I prefer to consort with sailors rather than with court people. They have more to teach me.

The sailors are: Annet, the captain, who's Monsean, of course. The captain of the Monsean queen's ship has to be Monsean. Kera, the first mate (also Monsean, not that it matters, but I feel I should continue what I started). (Kera's the one with the auburn hair in the black hat who was poking at the anchor capstan, remember?) Navi, the second mate, who's Keepish. Jacky (Monsean) and Linny (Dellian). Ozul, Sorit, Noa, and Lisa, who are all Keepish women. Alzar and Riz, a Kamassarian woman and man who married each other only a week ago. (Coran, our doctor, married them on the foredeck. Apparently doctors can marry people. It seemed like weird timing for a wedding, but whatever.) Liel, the cook, who's Monsean. And Olivan (Ollie), the youngest, everyone's helper, who's Lienid and has a way of making me smile.

Anyway. Every morning after breakfast it's my solitary job to consort with some boring papers in a tiny cabin in the bow, which is the cold end of the ship, farthest from the furnace. So, stuffed to my nose with eggs, I left the salon and poked my head into the galley, where Liel is king. I caught him feeding eggs to his cat, Tulip, who's the size of a bull terrier and I guess I know why.

When he saw me, he reached for a thermos standing at the base of the stove, wrapped it in a cloth, and handed it to me without comment. Liel, who's tall and thin like a pole, is a man of shy, bright blue eyes and few words. But he sends me off to my chilly exile every morning with a thermos of hot tea.

4.

In my tiny workroom in the nose of the ship, I have no porthole, no privy, no room to lie down on the floor if I wanted to, which I don't, but my point is, it's dark and small. The wall across from the door curves to accommodate the shape of the prow. Three bunks—too short for anyone to stretch out on—are stacked against that curved wall. When Bitterblue asked Annet for a private spot I could use, this is what Annet offered, probably because it was the only thing available. There's no wasted space on a ship.

The crew sleeps in the bow of the ship. I don't know if this is what all their cabins are like or if this one is empty because it's considered unlivable. But it's different from the cabin I share with the queen, which has two portholes to let in light, a privy with its own porthole, wooden shelves and moldings carved with pictures of whales and octopuses, silver stars painted on a dark blue ceiling, and a copper tub hanging on hooks above. Oh, and heat. The queen's cabin is below the salon and next to the furnace room, where sailors keep the stove packed with wood that creates heat that gets piped first into the areas where the queen and her people spend their time. Comfort is caused by expansive hot air infiltrating dense cold air. Maybe Jacky's resentments can also be explained by the principles of physics?

Annet, or someone, found an unused door, brought it into this cabin, and laid it across the bottom bunk to make a kind of writing surface for me. Someone else found me a crate to use as a chair. I sit at my "desk" with my forehead banging against the middle bunk, a lantern casting dim light onto page after page of Keepish writing that I'm meant to translate into Lingian, which is the Monsean language.

While we were in Winterkeep, we discovered that a Keepish politician was making explosive weapons out of zilfium. He planned to sell them to Estill, which is the hostile nation to Monsea's north.

That politician is in prison now, and his weapons have been deactivated. The scientist who invented them, Linta Massera, is dead. I caused an explosion that killed her. It also threw me into a cavern, where I was trapped, until Giddon did the manly, heroic thing and rescued me. Coran took the cast off my leg only ten days ago. That skin feels cold all the time now, from the strangeness of being touched by air. I still have a wobbly ankle and an ache in my chest, from that blast some seven weeks ago.

Guess what else I have? Linta Massera's formulas for building the zilfium weapon. I stole her notebooks before she and her workplace exploded. I copied them, symbol for symbol, picture for picture, and Keepish word for Keepish word, then set the originals on fire so the Keepish police would think they'd been obliterated from existence. Then I gave the copies to my sister as a gift. My sister's mountains in Monsea are rich with zilfium, you see.

Now she's asked me to translate the formulas, which is no easy job. I'm good at languages and I'm fluent in all the world's alphabets, but I've never studied chemistry, at least not the way you'd need to in order to understand these formulas. When I was young, living in the Monsean court during the reign of my father, I could get pretty creative about where I hid. Sometimes I hid in a room in the castle where the wife of one of King Leck's advisers taught her children grammar, music, math. Systems of order, all three, with three different symbol sets: words, notes, numbers. But chemistry is a system I never got to spy much upon, not in all my childhood hunts for safe places.

These formulas are full of drawings and labels I don't understand. Diagrams of bulbous apparatuses, glass containers shaped like onions and eggplants and squash, sketches that remind me of drawings I saw once when I was hiding in the royal library and pulled down a book that showed the many stomachs of a cow. Also, there are names of compounds and procedures that I don't know how to translate into Lingian, plus Linta's shorthand symbols. There are asides where she's coming to conclusions I don't understand. Maybe there are concepts here that I *might* know the equivalents of in Lingian if I only had the first idea what anything meant, but I don't, because it's chemistry. Should I translate the words I know and precisely copy the diagrams (again)? Will it start to make more sense as I move forward, the way a cipher starts to reveal itself halfway through? I remember, from when I copied Linta's originals before, that it changes at some point. Linta had a colleague, called LV, and I think eventually she starts reporting some of their conversations, which are less technical. Will that part be easier? How long till I get there?

My sister has assigned me this job. She's the queen. So I'm trying to muddle through.

This morning I was shivering and cursing the dim, swaying lamp when the door behind me burst open.

I turned, draping my arm across my papers casually, the way you might do when it's imperative to hide something while also seeming like you don't care. Jacky and Linny stood in the doorway, poking their heads in sideways one above the other, like the opening of a clown act.

"Heard of knocking?" I said, speaking Lingian. Linny speaks Lingian better than Jacky speaks Dellian, so their default when they're together is Lingian. "What can you possibly want?"

"We need to get to the lamp oil in the floor," said Jacky.

"Don't you keep lamp oil anywhere else?"

"Move," said Jacky, "and we'll be out of your way sooner."

So I moved, pushing my papers to the back of my "desk" and shoving my crate in on top of them, just as if my only motive were to get the crate out of their way, not to cover up my work.

"What are you doing in here anyway?" Jacky said, once the door was open and they were both cramming themselves into the room with me. They're both so physical. I think it's a sailor thing; sailors inhabit their bodies more fully than other people do. Jacky mostly hurls a sense of power and noise at me, accompanied by smirking, whereas now that Linny was pressed up against me, I noticed he smelled like salt and cold and was just my height. My same shoulder breadth too, and slender like me. My sailor twin. But prettier than me with that delicate face, and with those eyes lit like a honey jar sitting in a window. And with more of a presence in the room than I had, which annoyed me. It's *my* room.

"I'm writing letters," I said.

"Who do you think's going to deliver your letters?" Jacky said. "An albatross?"

"I'm writing letters to my cousin in Lienid about how annoying you are," I said, making up a cousin I don't have. "I'm going to mail the whole batch when we land. By then, it'll be the epic tale of how annoying you are."

"Sounds repetitive."

"You have the power to change the story."

"Ha ha."

While we talked, Linny bent down to a ring in the floor. "Move," he said, waving us aside with a vague hand that didn't provide much guidance about where we were supposed to go. With limited options, I chose the middle bunk while Jacky climbed onto the top one.

Linny opened a trapdoor to reveal a cavity in the floor containing four large metal cylinders with handles on top. Lamp oil. I knew it was there, of course, because I'm a snoop. There's storage everywhere on a ship. Bitterblue and I have a compartment like this in the floor of the cabin we share. Also, sometimes when we're sitting in the salon at a meal, Liel needs us to move so he can open the floor and pull out grains, beans, tea.

With a small grunt, Linny hauled one of the cylinders up into the room. "Thanks for your help," he said to Jacky, his Dellian accent softening the words.

Jacky dropped down from his bunk. Balancing partly on the floor, partly on the rims of the cylinders still stored in the compartment, he grabbed the cylinder, hefted it up by one hand, then carried it easily into the passageway. "Smartass," he said.

Linny closed the trapdoor, so I climbed out of my bunk. As we straightened together, he looked into my face, his eyes exactly at my level. He spoke in Dellian. "Are you a chemist?"

He'd startled me. I used my Grace to pretend I was staring blankly back at him, but my eyes flicked to my papers. I saw what he saw: one of those incomprehensible cow stomach diagrams, sticking out from under my crate.

"A little," I said nonchalantly. "I dabble. It calms my mind."

"What does *chemist* mean?" I heard Jacky ask from the passageway, speaking the word in Dellian, as Linny had.

"Have a nice day," I said to Linny, reaching behind him for the door in a way that effectively shouldered him into the passageway. I closed the door on them firmly. As they walked away, I heard Linny explaining about elemental substances, reactions between them, theories about the building blocks of matter, until Jacky got it and said, "Oh, a chemist!" in Lingian. "Is she a chemist?"

Great.

I scowled at the edge of paper that had betrayed me. It contained a rough diagram of some liquid—water? Gravy? Slime?—moving step by step through one glass apparatus after another, with scattered Keepish letters and numbers labeling the steps.

I wonder: Why would Linny—a Dellian and a sailor—recognize Keepish chemistry?

5.

AFTER A COUPLE hours of translating, I've usually had enough. I mean, my desk is bucking, the lamp is swinging, the water's crashing against the walls, and my handwriting requires a massive display of fine motor control. Every wave is a reminder that I could be somewhere else, doing something a hundred times more exciting.

I tuck the papers into their sealskin wrapping. I secure them inside my Keepish fur coat, pulling my belt tight. Then I go out on deck to see what's happening.

Tulip often sits on his gigantic rump outside the galley next to the rain barrels, surveying his surroundings. He's one of those patchy cats, twenty different browns. Today he ignored me as I passed, but if I were Giddon, he'd jump up and launch himself at my feet. Cats love Giddon. Probably they recognize an intellectual equal.

Outside I found the second mate, Navi, at the rail of the main deck, warming her hands around a steaming mug of something. The sailors work gloveless, scarves wrapped around their ears and throats. Navi wears a red silk scarf threaded with iridescent gold, but no hat. I can always spot Navi because of the flash of red at her throat. She's Keepish, her skin deep brown. Her curly black hair is tied messily back, and if you look close, she has a scatter of dark freckles across her nose.

"Did you know that your name has boat-meanings in Lingian?" I said, going to stand beside her. The cold air filled my lungs, pushing the stupid chemistry out of my body. "Like the word *naval*," I said, "and *navigation*."

Navi lifted dark eyes from her cup when I told her this, raising her gaze to the sky, measuring the thick clouds. Then her tiny smile came, pinching her mouth. It always feels like a reward.

"Maybe I was meant to be a sailor," she said in her deep voice, speaking Keepish. My Keepish is better than her Lingian, so we speak Keepish together. Generally I speak to people in their own languages.

"Maybe," I said. "Have you always been one?"

"Oh, yes," she said. "I grew up on Keepish ships."

"Annet and Kera are teaching me the Lingian words for ship things. Will you teach me the Keepish words?"

"Sure," she said. "And I can tell you about Keepish ships too. Ours tend to be squatter than this, and thicker-hulled. Designed for stability over speed, since Keepish winds are so ferocious."

"Thicker-hulled?"

"We sail through ice more often than you do, I suspect. Speaking of names in other languages, did you know that a *habpva* is a Keepish bird?"

"HOB-puh-vuh?" I said.

She spelled it for me, in Keepish.

"That's a mouthful," I said.

"Yes, you spend a moment on all those letters in the middle."

"That requires slowing down."

That earned me another tiny smile. "Not something that comes naturally to you?" she said. "But it's a remarkable coincidence, really, because of how a habpva looks."

"Why, how does it look?"

"Like a lot of the birds in its family," she said. "Small, gray, squat—"

"Sounds like a sparrow," I said, wanting a habpva to be a kind of sparrow, because we have sparrows in the courtyards of my sister's castle, and I like them.

"Maybe a sparrow," she said, shrugging at the Lingian word. "But this sparrow is different from the other small gray birds who live in Ledra year-round. Every summer, the habpvas throw themselves out to sea. The wind currents hurl them north to Kamassar. You can see them blasting across the sky from your ship."

"Oh!" I said. "Is it safe?"

"They seem to come back to the city every fall," she said, her mouth pinching into that smile again. "But I haven't told you the nice part yet. They're gray and squat, but they have these bright patches of red and copper on their heads!"

I use my Grace more often than people realize, to hide a wary or confused expression.

"I didn't know that," I said. "Well, see you later."

6.

To reach the cabin I share with Bitterblue, you drop into a hole (called a hatch), descend a steep staircase (called a ladder), and slip through narrow corridors (passageways), almost as if our own cabin is a hidden storage space.

I wound there quietly, passing no one I had to decide whether to hide from. Inside our cabin, I sat on my bed in the wavering light.

My left iris is copper-colored and my right iris is red. Gracelings have unmatching eyes. Some Graceling eyes are beautiful, but mine are not. My eyes shock people. Some Graces are beautiful too, but mine makes people distrust me. I'm not used to people alluding to my eyes unless they're being cruel.

There aren't many Gracelings in Winterkeep; the Keepish don't know what's cruel. Navi had not meant to be cruel.

She was not being intentionally cruel, I told myself, repeating it a few times to see what I thought of it. A Keepish bird, adventurous and plain, with flashes of color like my eyes and a name like mine? She'd meant the word *habpva* as a gift. The sting I felt was from her not knowing, not from any hatred she bore for me. I didn't like the sting. But it was safe to keep wanting to be Navi's friend.

Safe too to think about habpvas, which sounded nice to me, as long as no one was mocking me with them.

A lumpy form lay on the bed beside mine, covered with blankets.

Bitterblue sleeps a lot on ships, waiting for it to end. The Keepish tea she drinks, called rauha, is a comfort. It smells like licorice, takes the dizziness away, and restores her appetite. It also makes her silly, though, so on rauha days, she isn't much of a queen.

She can't drink rauha every day, because it's addictive. Yesterday was a rauha day, so today and tomorrow she'll have to do without. Today and tomorrow, she'll be serious and effective and debate topics like the animosity of the nation of Estill with Giddon, and occasionally she'll throw up. I'm beginning to develop an association between Estill and vomit. "That's fair," Giddon said when I told him.

I touched my sister's shoulder. I can do that from my bed. We have the biggest cabin on the *Monsea*, but everything is close on a ship.

She moaned, a quiet, soft noise. A grateful, ironic noise. Even when Bitterblue is sick, she laughs at herself. "Hava?"

"Do you need anything?" I said.

"A promise that we're closer to home than we were yesterday," she said.

"I do so promise."

"How are you, Hava?" she said.

"Fine."

"How's the translation coming along?"

"The same. Slowly."

"Mmph," she said, turning over and curling into a tighter ball.

"We need a chemist," I said, after a long pause.

No answer.

"Giddon has stripped to his underclothes. He's standing on the jib boom like a figurehead," I said.

No answer. Convinced she was asleep, I reached under my blankets to the cavity I've created inside my mattress. I know how to hide things. Under a mattress isn't good enough, because everyone looks there. Inside a mattress is better, because no one remembers it exists.

Extricating my formulas and translations from my coat, I slid them into the cavity. Then I pulled out something else I keep in there, a bundle of small, sharp objects wrapped in a piece of tattered silk that was once a scarf belonging to Bitterblue's mother.

In my lap, I unwrapped the tattered scarf, pale gray and soft like Bitterblue's eyes.

My own mother was a sculptor. The king forced himself on her and made her pregnant with me. He also made her sculpt things, but he never liked what she made, for her sculptures contained too much truth. She couldn't help it. It was the only way she could sculpt.

One day he killed her, because he was too weak to coexist with things he couldn't control.

Before that, she hid me from him. Every day it was difficult, for he had a Grace too, one of telling lies that people believed. His Grace made him powerful and persuasive and confusing. But she hid me so I would be safe from him, she hid my entire existence, except at the very end of her life, when we were sitting together one day and I was handing her tools for her work and he came in unexpectedly and I wasn't hiding and he saw us together. I was eight.

BUT NEVER MIND that.

Before that day, she made stone figures for me. Small, so I could hide them. Sharp, so I could press them into my palm and clear my mind of his lies.

They are tiny sculptures of me turning into things. That's what she always sculpted, though on a larger scale: people, mostly women, turning into strong, ferocious things. For example, a sculpture stands in the castle library at home. It's my sister as a little girl, turning into a fortress. Her upstretched arm has become a brick tower with little archers at its top instead of fingers, protecting her. "Sculpt my daughter, Princess Bitterblue," the king said. My mother sculpted an untouchable girl. You understand why her sculptures always made him angry?

She made those sculptures for the king, who hated them, but kept asking for more. These tiny sculptures, she made for me. They're white, with veins of red and copper. I don't know if she chose those colors for me on purpose. It was hard to have lucid conversations with my mother.

In one of them, I'm a girl with claws and whiskers, a long tail and long teeth. I'm turning into a mountain lion. In another, the face is recognizably me but I have fur on my haunches, padded feet, a broad strong back, and a wide-open jaw with teeth like blades: I'm turning into a bear. In another, I have fins and flippers, a long smooth torso, and a very surprised look on my face. I'm turning into a porpoise.

In another—my favorite—my fingers are sharp and curved and my arms are thick with feathers, outstretched like wings. I'm turning into a bird. It's my favorite, because a bird can fly right off the earth. She can be alone, touching nothing, preyed upon by no one; if she likes, she can never come back.

Habpva, I thought to myself, cradling the Hava-bird in my palm and imagining a sparrow riding the winds of the sea. Touching the figurine to the bridge of my nose, between my strange eyes. Sparrows aren't seabirds. But my Hava-bird can be whatever I imagine.

My sister moaned and stirred.

Then a small shape separated itself and crawled out of her blankets: her Keepish blue fox. The queen's new spy, a better spy than I, because Keepish blue foxes can communicate telepathically and read minds. They lie too, about how powerful they are; humans in Winterkeep don't realize just how easily the foxes are reading their minds. Bitterblue's fox has confessed all his powers to her, supposedly. In consequence, Bitterblue has shared some of our secrets with him. For example, he's the only being on this ship besides Bitterblue and Giddon who knows that the queen is my sister. Bitterblue has also forbidden him to spy on anyone, read anyone's mind, or communicate with anyone without that person's express permission. I think he's doing what he's told. I've tried to bribe him into disobeying, with food. He acts insulted that I could imagine him capable of defying her. He's like Giddon. He thinks my sister hung the moon.

Rumpled and gray like a storm cloud, he blinked at me, gold eyes gleaming. He reached his nose toward the sharp little shapes in my hand.

Spying on me? I thought at him.

Just curious, I felt him say in my mind, like a bubble that swelled, then popped. *Those things are pretty.*

They're private, I said.

I understand, he said. Then he sniffed primly, dropped onto the floor with soft feet, and scurried out of the room.

The cat's at the top of the steps, I called after him, because even though I don't like him, that doesn't mean I want him to be murdered by Tulip, his archnemesis.

I wrapped my sculptures in their stolen silk and slipped them back into my mattress.

Then I went upstairs again, because I can never resist the outdoors for long. On deck, Annet shouted, sailors grunted, the lines creaked, and the sails snapped. I like being outside when they're adjusting the sails. It isn't that I don't get dizzy sometimes; I do. But the dizziness thrills me to my fingertips. It's hard to worry about big, stupid problems, like how to defend your sister from greedy, violent nations, when your house is bucking its way across the sea. I wish I could always live in a house that's moving.

I said that to Annet once. She smiled and said she understood.

Then she added, "But wherever you go, you take the weather with you," which is silly. When you're moving, you can skirt the weather. You can decide which weather to steer into, and which to avoid.

I went up onto the afterdeck, behind the wheelhouse, where there are usually fewer people to notice me, and where it smells nice, from the woodsmoke that pours out of the chimney. Kera, the first mate in the black hat, was in the stern, holding her glass to her eye, aiming it at the clouds behind us. I wondered if she'd fixed the pin in the anchor capstan yet from this morning, but I didn't ask, because I didn't want to interrupt her. She's our weather expert. Maybe she was reading something significant in the colors of the sky: oyster, pewter, and lead.

The wind threw words back to me from the voices of the sailors hauling lines on the mainmast, which is the middle mast and the tallest of the three. I heard my name. I heard the word *chemistry*.

Seems to me these sailors don't have enough stuff of their own to talk about.

7.

I DECIDED SOME SNOOPING would be worthwhile. It's always good to know the gossip, especially if it's about you.

The *Monsea* has three lifeboats, one sitting on either side of the main deck and one suspended on a davit over the stern. I lie on my back inside one of the main deck boats sometimes, when the crew is setting sails. From there, the ship is made of white triangles shooting into the sky.

On the best days, a perfect wind blows from behind us, we drop the square sails down on the foremast, and the ship flies with the breath of the earth blasting us straight home. We haven't had many best days lately, but today, Linny climbed the foremast and unlooped the gaskets that hold the square sails closed tight against the yards. Annet's voice rang out happily, calling up to him to climb higher, loosen the next one. Annet is like a mother full of love and pride in her child. Her child is the ship. "The topgallant too!" she yelled. "It's going to be a beautiful afternoon!"

Linny moved around up there as if it were easy, safe; as if his gloveless fingers weren't frozen and he couldn't conceivably fall. As he pulled himself onto the highest yard, it occurred to me that he must be very strong. He's my sailor twin, but I can't picture myself moving effortlessly like that. The mast swayed back and forth with the ship, sharply left, sharply right, Linny's legs wrapped around the yard and his breath blowing steam.

I heard one of the pigs grunting on the deck nearby. Their pen is under the foredeck but they're allowed to graze the main deck some-times. I'm not used to being so close to my future food. Ollie, the youngest sailor, the one who's Lienid, feeds the animals and cleans up after them, and I hear him talking to them in baby voices, calling them names like Curly Tail and Pink Bottom. Then, at breakfast, he digs into his ham with delight. People are strange.

Far above me, Linny shifted, working a knot loose. When a rope swung free, snow cascaded onto me, disturbed from its perch.

Linny shouted something down, possibly at me. I couldn't hear.

"He says you're in the way," Jacky said, looking into my boat. "You should move."

"Our habpva is not in the way, and that's not what Linny said," Annet responded, glancing in at me with laughter in her voice. Annet has straight blond hair she ties back in a tail, and clear, gray eyes behind wire glasses. She has straight shoulders too, and a calm pink face. "Jacky likes to tease. You stay there as long as you like, Hava."

"Or you could be useful and haul a line or two," said Jacky, who was also laughing.

"The square sails drop down from above," said Annet, "instead of us pulling them up from below. Gravity. We don't need extra hands for this, as Jacky well knows."

I believe in Annet's laughter. I haven't decided yet if I believe in Jacky's.

I stayed where I was.

Later, I heard a soft, scraping sound that didn't have the broken rhythm of a pig. I peeked out of the boat. Linny was crouched nearby, drawing something in the snow of the deck with his finger, his breath still steaming. I watched him, briefly, not sure what to do or say. I can never get a read on him.

I decided to sit up.

The thing he was drawing looked like one of my chemistry diagrams, lines and symbols stretching out from a central point like the legs of a spider.

It was as if he was provoking me.

"How do you know how to recognize Keepish chemistry?" I asked.

He wiped his picture away. "I didn't know it was Keepish."

Well. He knew now, thanks to me being an idiot.

"I didn't get a good look," he added, glancing up at me with a quick flash of amber. Linny's eyes are very clear. "But I bet chemistry looks the same everywhere. I'm sorry I blabbed it in front of Jacky. I was just so surprised."

Every time he opens his mouth, he knocks me off the top of our conversation. Why was he apologizing? Was he that concerned for my privacy?

"You didn't answer my question," I said. "How do you know chemistry?"

He shrugged, his face quiet, soft. Unreadable. "I was raised on the estate of a Dellian lord. My mother was one of his maids. He took an interest in me and taught me things."

Which probably meant that Linny was the illegitimate son of a Dellian lord. One whose magnanimity only extended so far, though, if Linny was a common sailor now.

"How do you know chemistry?" he asked. "Is it something people learn at the Monsean court?"

I couldn't exactly tell him I didn't know chemistry. "Yes," I said. "Are you good at chemistry?"

He shrugged again. "I enjoyed it when I was learning it. Why do you ask?"

"What's it like up there on the mast?" I said, deciding it was time to change the subject.

"Do people usually answer your questions," he said, "even when you don't answer theirs?"

His tone contained no aggression, nor any particular offense. But there was something. A kind of mild, yet friendly, resistance to me pushing him around. And again I was unsure of my place in the conversation.

I decided to resort to honesty. "Sometimes, yes," I said. "Usually it just annoys people."

His face cracked into a surprised grin. "I'm glad you answered that one. Want to climb the mast? See for yourself?"

That was an easy one. "Would you show me how to climb? Really?"

He wrote a word in the snow. *Yes.*

"Why are you writing instead of speaking?"

"I'm not sure," he said. "Sometimes I like to see my ideas big. What word would you write, if you were writing in the snow?"

I studied his expression again, looking for mockery. Finding none. *Not* yes, I thought. *Not* eavesdrop. *Not* consort. *Nothing from inside me.*

"*Cold,*" I said, because it gave nothing away.

8.

A WORKING DAY AT sea is divided into sections called watches.

On the *Monsea*, watches are either two or four hours long and the schedule rotates regularly so that no sailor gets stuck working any particular watch permanently. A chart hangs in the wheelhouse window so the sailors can remind themselves when they're on duty and when they're allowed to rest. I memorize it regularly so I can always know who'll be where.

In the afternoon, standing at the rail, I watched Ozul, Sorit, Noa, and Lisa, all Keepish girls, patching the ratlines on the port foremast. Definitions: (1) The foremast is the mast at the front of the ship. (2) *Port* means "left," so they were working on the left side of the foremast. (3) The ratlines, pronounced RAT-lins, are the short, tight ropes that form a kind of ladder to the top of a mast, so sailors can climb up into the rigging. (4) The rigging is every part of the ship's web: the fixed system of ropes that support the masts, and all the ropes that move to control the sails.

Keepish girls climb and swear, carry knives unhidden, wear pants, walk straight-shouldered, don't hide. I know some women like that from home, but they're exceptions. People call them masculine. It's not usually meant nicely.

I've wanted to ask Sorit, Ozul, Noa, and Lisa about it, but I haven't figured out what to say. I've asked Navi about it, because she's

Keepish too and she's older, so I mind a little less if our differences make me feel like a child.

There's not much she's been able to tell me, though. "It's just the way we are," she said.

"Are Keepish girls given knives?"

"Keepish sailors are given knives."

"Are Keepish girls encouraged to be sailors?"

"Of course. Aren't Monsean girls encouraged to be sailors? Annet rose all the way to captain."

"Annet is unusual."

"Are you sure?" said Navi, wrinkling her forehead, looking doubtful. There's something nice about Navi when she's thoughtful. Concern touches her features gently, while strands of dark hair blow across her scarlet scarf and her cheeks.

"Annet and Kera are the only female sailors from the Seven Nations I've ever met," I said. "I think there are more in the Dells and Pikkia. But not on our side of the mountains."

"I'm really surprised to hear that," Navi said. "I'm going to ask Annet about it."

Today, Ozul, Sorit, Noa, and Lisa worked together, tying new rope-rungs to the shrouds, pulling them tight, knotting them with bare hands, slicing the ends. Cutting the old ratlines away, throwing the frayed pieces down to the deck. Working without much talking. Talking in Keepish, of course, when they did. Bursting out with laughter now and then that made me feel like I might as well not be a girl, so little am I a part of them.

Heavy feet clapped down beside me. Ozul, who's taller than me and broad, with a pretty, deep brown face.

"Want to learn now?" she asked me, in Keepish. Ozul wears her hair in braids and has a lot of different scarves. Today a gold scarf with purple threads woven through was wrapped many times around her neck.

"Learn what?" I said.

"The captain said you wanted to climb the mast," she said. "You told Linny?"

"I—" *I thought Linny would show me.* "Is now when I'm supposed to do it?" I asked, then hated myself for sounding so infantile. With my Grace, I made my expression look cold, uninterested.

"You don't have to," she said, shrugging. "But we fixed a few of the ratlines so it's safer for you. Sorit and I have some time now. Want to try?"

"Yes," I said, because "No" would have been too humiliating.

"I'll get the harness," Sorit said, behind me. Where did she even come from? I felt crowded, rushed.

"You don't wear a harness," I said to Sorit, to prove I wasn't scared. "Why should I?"

"I wore one when I was learning," said Sorit. "The boards are slippery and the ropes are wet. I think you'll be able to relax more with the harness."

Sorit said it with kindness, as if the sting in my tone was lost on her. Then she left and came back with a strappy thing. She crouched down with it, showing me how to step in. Sorit is as tiny as Bitterblue, with a quick grin, short black hair, golden-brown skin, and a cute nose. Sorit and Noa are a couple. They're not married like Alzar and Riz. In Winterkeep, where the laws aren't as unkind as some of the laws on my continent, women are allowed to marry women, so that's not why; I think they're just young. Ozul's maybe twenty-five, but I doubt Sorit, Noa, and Lisa are even twenty—no older than I am really.

I leaned on Sorit's shoulder and stepped into the harness, feeling like an unfriendly giant.

Sorit tightened the straps on my legs and shoulders, the belt at my waist. She unclipped a pair of hooks from the belt and explained how to hook myself onto the ship as I climbed, one hook at a time, so that I was always attached somewhere.

"You don't have to do this," she said, which was when I realized I looked sick and anxious.

"I'm not scared," I said hotly, which was and wasn't true. I wasn't scared of climbing, not with the harness. But maybe I was scared of Sorit and her grin, Ozul and her strength. Scared of shaming myself. Of not being a strong enough girl. Of Linny and Jacky, everyone, coming on deck and seeing.

I flickered, once, into a stone sculpture of myself. I do that sometimes, accidentally, when I most wish I could be invisible.

Ozul and Sorit both jumped back. Ozul put her hand to her gold scarf and formed her mouth in the shape of an O.

"Sorry," I said, fighting to show them my real body.

"It's—all right," said Sorit, while Ozul continued to stare. "We understand that it's your Grace."

"It doesn't mean anything," I said.

"Come to the rail," she said. "I'll show you how to get started."

Is there any part of the ship more like a stage than the rigging of the foremast?

PRESS THE LEFT pin. Open the left hook. Reach up with the hook, stretch, stretch, tiptoes. Snag the hook onto the highest bit of metal you can find, close the hook, climb, step up, step up. Feel the sway of the ship, watch the prow push through walls of water. Steady your wobbly ankle. Ignore the ache of your once-broken rib. Glance at the dark clouds at the stern, feel a bolt of lightning sear its imprint into the back of your eyes. Look ahead, to white clouds so stretched out and thin that you can almost see the blue behind them. The sky is so big up here.

Press the right pin, open the right hook, reach up, tiptoes, ankle, rib, stretch, stretch, ignore the voices. Ignore the faces craned to watch, all the sailors, the fox, Liel the cook, who've come out for this show. Push back the urge to hide behind your Grace. You're alone on this mast at the front of this ship.

Once, I looked down because I heard the deep timbre of a voice that made me feel less exposed. Giddon, a person who might understand how I was feeling. I saw his pale, bearded face turned up to mine, smiling and proud, and I let him see my lack of delight. Someone yelled encouraging words—Jacky's voice, "Go, Hava!"— and I let Giddon see the way the words made me scowl.

Soon, most of my audience had cleared away, only Ozul and Sorit remaining on deck, plus Navi and Annet watching through the glass windows of the wheelhouse. Much better. I knew Giddon had made it happen and that he'd probably used some handsome, gracious method of shooing everyone away that, if he explained it to me later, would not embarrass me. Giddon is stuffed full of manners and elegance when he needs to be.

Breathing more easily, I continued to climb.

The rungs made of slats of wood instead of rope—called battens— were slippery to step on. The ratlines, made of good, rough rope, were preferable. My hands had never been more cold or stiff in my life, and I was even wearing gloves. When I reached the first platform, I found it to be a wide, flat ledge of wood above my head blocking my way, and couldn't figure out how I was supposed to get onto it. Ozul scrambled up. Ozul talked me through the necessary contortions. It took a lot of arm strength. Then she scrambled back down again.

After a rest atop the first platform, I kept climbing. When my head hit the second platform, I considered whether my frozen hands, my tired, aching forearms could pull me onto it. I needed to save enough strength for the downward climb, but it's hard to stop when you've started something.

I was so high that I could see over the wheelhouse to the afterdeck behind it. There, holding a lantern in one hand, Kera was opening a hatch in the deck and stepping inside. She peered around her as if to see who was nearby and it seemed funny to me that she never looked up, toward the foremast, where I was watching.

A thrill of exhilaration ran through me. Once I become comfortable with this climb, it'll be a new place for me to hide and spy.

But not yet. Exhausted, I began to climb down.

"You did great," Ozul said, a year later, when my feet hit the deck. She clapped me on the shoulder and I thought I might fall over. My wobbly ankle was trembling.

"I didn't make it onto the second platform," I said.

"You will next time," she said, tugging at the straps of my harness, helping me out. "Before you know it, you'll be sitting on the third platform."

I tried to swallow the words down, but I couldn't stop myself. "You're very encouraging," I said. "Don't you think you're unusually encouraging?"

She laughed. "I guess I learned it from the uncle who raised me. My big sister too. And my first captain." She laughed again. "I guess I had a lot of people teaching me. Didn't you?"

How could I explain it to her? In my childhood, only one person knew I existed. And the only thing she ever taught me to do was disappear.

"There was nothing to climb where I grew up," I said, pretending to misunderstand the question.

9.

THERE ARE TIMES when I'd like to eat dinner alone, with my thoughts to myself. But no one gets the salon to themselves at mealtimes.

At dinner, Jacky called down the table from three seats away to demand why I like to lie on the floors of the lifeboats.

"It's a good place for thinking," I said, not wanting him to know about the view of triangles shooting into the sky and squares dropping down. That's mine.

"What do you need to think about?" he asked.

"Plans to take over the world."

He grinned, surprising me with dimples. He looked like a giant, harmless, pink baby. "I heard you're Queen Bitterblue's spy," he said. "Is it true?"

"Would I tell you if it was?"

That made him laugh. "Why did the captain call you *our habpva* today?"

I shrugged. I'd noticed, of course, when the word had fallen from Annet's lips. It had to be because Navi had told Annet about the Keepish bird. I get the impression Navi tells Annet most things. I don't think they're a couple, exactly, just yet? Maybe things like that are complicated, with Annet in charge? But maybe Navi tucked a hot drink into Annet's hands, then wanted an excuse to stand with her for ten seconds before going away. Maybe in that moment, I walked by, and Navi said, "That reminds me."

"I guess the captain has my name wrong," I said.

"She called you Hava in the next breath," said Jacky.

"Beats me. Ask her," I said, knowing that the sailors on the *Monsea* don't bother their captain with idle questions.

"Hava made it to the second platform today," said Ozul, who was sitting catty-corner to me and wearing a different scarf now, black and iridescent silver. Linny sat across from me again, eating quietly. "Did everyone see?"

"I made it to the spot below the platform," I amended. "Not onto the platform."

"Did you do any good spying up there?" said Jacky. "Come up with any master plans?"

"A few," I said noncommittally, not really in the mood for Jacky's teasing. "Where are you from in Monsea, Jacky?"

"Monport," he said, which made sense, for a sailor. Monport is our biggest port city, on the southern coast. "You?" he added.

"Castle-born."

"Fancy."

"What about you, Kera?" I said to the first mate on Linny's other side, speaking over whatever cutting thing Jacky was about to say about my soft life.

Kera was eating her dinner with focused attention, using a piece of bread to sop up the juices of a potpie. "Southeast," she said, not looking at me. "High in the mountains, up above the silver mines. There's a town up there. You won't have heard of it."

"What's it called?"

"Hawkery."

"And how does a person from up in the mountains become a sailor?"

She shrugged. "There's not a lot of work there. I have a sick husband." Her eyes rose to mine, pale gray. "And a child to support," she said, something flashing through her as she said it. Like that moment of sharp surprise when a cat scratches you hard and you're trying to keep from showing how much it hurts.

Then she turned back to her plate, bent her head to her food, so that all I could see was her black knit hat. It was clear the conversation was over.

But I kept my eye on her for the rest of the meal, while using my Grace to pretend not to, because she'd surprised me.

I've been to Hawkery. In fact, I've been to every corner in Monsea no one's ever heard of. I was four when I first left my mother behind in the castle and started wandering the city. Eight when my mother left me and I struck out across the countryside alone. If it sounds unlikely for a child so young to take care of herself and not get lost, well, I did get lost. I learned not to. Anyway, it was safer to be lost in the city or the countryside than in the castle, where the king might find me.

The point is, I know Hawkery. The people who live there number only a couple dozen. Their view, over a mountain that's been ravaged for silver, is ugly in the foreground. Beyond the seams of the mines the rock drops to a lush green valley with a winding river dotted with the houses and farms of people less isolated and cold, less strange. Hawkery is insular. I didn't stay long. It's harder to hide and steal when everyone knows everything about everyone, down to how many potatoes they've stashed away for the winter. The people have pale, clear-skinned faces there like Kera, and they're quiet, deliberate, slow. The same way Kera is quiet, deliberate, slow.

So why don't I believe that Kera is from Hawkery? Is it because so few people live there and I don't remember any stories about a woman going to sea? Is it because there *is* work there, always, in the mines?

Kera is lying about something. The sick husband? Maybe.

I don't think she's lying about the child.

10.

IN THE MORNING, when I went out on deck, the eastern sky glowed ashy gray and the water around us was specked with chunks of ice. The wind pressed sideways against the triangle sails on the mainmast, the ship bucking.

Sometimes it's hard to tell whether we're moving fast across this ocean, or just stuck in a lot of wind and rushing water. I wonder if the sailors stand on deck, feel the power under their feet, and know exactly what we look like from above?

My ankle was sore and stiff from climbing yesterday. I stood at the rail, doing a few of the stretches the Keepish doctors taught me, watching the ice. An escaped chicken was clucking around the foredeck. The chickens aren't allowed to graze, because birds of prey dive out of the sky and try to eat them, or so Ollie's told me. I believe him, because I saw one of them almost snatch Bitterblue's fox once. It was an osprey. It dropped like a boulder, landing so close to my feet I almost screamed. The fox ran off, shrieking at me that I should have warned him.

How was I supposed to know? I shouted back. *I don't walk around looking up at the sky!*

I can sense their minds! he yelled at me. *I can make a point of watching out for them! But am I likely to, if no one has informed me they exist?*

Do you seriously not know about birds?

THAT BIRD WAS THE SIZE OF A HORSE!

All right, I said. *Got it. There are sharks in the water. Don't jump in.*

He sent me a feeling of withering disdain, to which I responded with one of disgust. But I think it scared us both.

Remembering the osprey, I walked up to the foredeck to grab the chicken. Holding it awkwardly in both hands while it struggled and shed feathers and screamed bloody murder, I carried it back down to the main deck, where the coop is. Coran, my sister's adviser—the one who's also a doctor—lurched toward me, grabbing the rail as the deck rolled. I considered telling him to try bending his knees a little when he walked. His face, peeking out of a hat of gray fur, was wild with alarm. All three of Bitterblue's advisers look like that, pallid and anxious.

"I saw you on that mast yesterday," he said, shivering. Coran is always shivering. "From the wheelhouse. I was getting an update on our progress from the captain."

"Were you?" I said, because he seemed to be waiting for me to say something. "Do you mind excusing me while I figure out what to do with this chicken?"

He eyed the chicken, which was trying to flap itself out of my grip. "Cook it for dinner, I should think. Does the queen know about your new hobby?"

"Rescuing chickens?"

"Risking life and limb pretending to be a sailor."

I used my Grace to hide my facial expression. I didn't need a lecture from Coran about how I spend my time. "How is our progress?" I asked, changing the subject deliberately.

"How does it seem to you?"

"What does it matter how it seems to me? You just said yourself I'm not a sailor. What does Annet say?"

"The captain is happy with our progress," Coran announced, in a tone that told me something else. That he didn't believe her; that the very idea made him indignant.

"But you're not happy?"

"It's much rockier than it was on the way to Winterkeep."

"It's December!" I said. "Annet can't control the size of the waves for your benefit!"

With a scornful noise, he left me, pulling himself hand over hand along the rail that led toward the door, then lunging at it, grabbing on to the doorframe. I watched him haul himself inside. My sister's advisers are scared of everything. How does she put up with them?

Ollie stood outside the hatch to the crew quarters, rubbing sleep out of his eyes. He yawned, the Lienid gold in his ears flashing. I shoved the chicken at him. He thanked me politely, as if a surprise chicken pass was a normal start to his day.

Then I went inside to breakfast and ate everything in sight.

11.

Next, translating.

In my tiny office in the bow, chunks of ice tap against the wall as I work. It reminds me where I am. I might forget otherwise that the ocean is on the other side of my walls. For all I know, there's a whale out there, gliding along beside us, living a life with its own problems that have nothing to do with mine.

I've gotten to the part with Linta Massera's colleague LV, and I was right: This section is easier going. Less technical. It's also interesting, because I'm pretty sure Linta was secretly using her employer's money to fund experiments of her own that had nothing to do with building zilfium explosives. Of course, this means that maybe I shouldn't be wasting the queen's time translating them. Bitterblue needs the weapon formulas, not Linta Massera's personal research. But I'm not going to skip over the only parts of this job I actually like.

Listen to this: She writes that she convinced her employer to fly her and LV up in his airship, far higher than I think airships are meant to go, maybe even higher than humans are meant to go. (She and LV got terrible headaches.) While she was up there, she took measurements of air pressure, temperature, humidity. She collected samples of air in her glass apparatuses. She told her employer she needed to do this so she could learn the effects of "different kinds of air" on a zilfium explosion, and maybe that's true. But she also calls him names in her notes, all the time. Keepish words that I translate as *naive* or *gullible*, or, my favorite, *dopey*.

Today I translated: "He'll do anything if I tell him it's for the weapon. And I must tell him so, because he's too dopey to appreciate the quest for a theory of indivisible particles. It has to blow up, or he doesn't care. But my experiments both with various gases at the moment of the weapon's explosion and with various gases at different elevations are demonstrating proportional changes in volume depending on temperature and pressure. Proportional changes!"

I sort of understand what she's talking about there. Not the proportional changes thing, but the rest of it—well enough for my purposes, anyway. "Theory of indivisible particles" is my best translation for this theory I don't remember the name of in Lingian, but that I've heard Bann and Prince Raffin talk about. Bann and Prince Raffin are part of Giddon's renegade Council, but they're also chemists, and they talk a lot. Apparently, every single thing in the world is made of tiny, indivisible particles. Like, if I took the ink I write with and started dividing it, and dividing it, and dividing it, eventually I would divide it into these teeny, tiny, essential particles that are the building blocks of ink. I wouldn't be able to divide it any more. It wouldn't be ink anymore, either.

It's not something I get excited about, but chemists do. I think the idea is that everything in the world, even the air, is made up of these tiny, invisible, indivisible particles, and there are lots of kinds of particles, they have different properties and different purposes, they respond differently to different experiments ("Proportional changes!"), and chemists think they're the most thrilling thing ever.

Whatever. What I like is that Linta was giving herself headaches and lying to her employer. I hope her employer got a headache too.

"LV made a joke about the heads of Keepish politicians expanding proportionally, based on the pressure of their own hypocrisy," she writes. "I coughed my tea into one of my solutions and had to start over."

In the section I translated today, she did eventually get back to the weapon formulas, at which point, the work again became really difficult for me. I gather that Linta Massera worried about someone finding her notes. Her employer had guards who were always lurking around her workshop, coming in when she wasn't there, refusing to tell her why. (I think I know why. We know a lot about what Linta's employer was doing back then, besides building explosives. He was murdering people, imprisoning people, with the help of his guards. Linta seems mostly in the dark.) Anyway, I get the sense that she didn't *want* the formulas for an explosive to be written out plainly for anyone to find. And it seems LV had a good memory for numbers, so Linta asked LV to store some of the particulars mentally, instead of writing them down. I translated: "Ask LV for the quantity here." Then later: "Refer to LV for proportions."

And of course Linta was right to be cautious. Someone *did* sneak into her workshop and find her notes: me.

Here are my two takeaways from today's translating: (1) The weapon formulas contain intentional holes. (2) It would behoove us to identify LV, who's presumably still out in the world somewhere. I met plenty of people in Winterkeep, but none with those initials.

No, three takeaways.

(3) I will never know if the weapon formulas are of any value for Bitterblue until I get the help of someone who understands how to read them.

Linny?

I think I need to talk to Bitterblue and Giddon.

12.

EVERY DAY, I try to get through one page. Two, if there are a lot of diagrams I can't do anything with. I've worked every day since we set sail from Ledra about twenty-five days ago. There are sixty-three pages of notes.

That should give you an idea of how much longer I'm doomed to suffocate in this teeny cabin. I sure hope there are more pranks on Linta's employer ahead.

Today, as soon as I finished, I went out on deck, wanting to climb again. Go higher. Make it to the second platform at least.

I was lucky, because there weren't too many people around. Navi came down from the wheelhouse, helped me strap the harness tight, and gave me the go-ahead.

"I'll leave you to it, habpva," she said.

I said nothing, just watched her climb back up to the wheelhouse. Something fills my throat when people use that name. It's not a bad feeling, exactly. But I can't respond.

I'd had it in my mind that I'd scurry up the mast so quickly that no one would notice or care, like Linny does. Well, that was unrealistic. There's no scurrying when it's *my* frozen muscles pushing *me* straight up into the air.

But at least it was less scary this time. The hooks that attached me to the ship were cold as ice and a little too wide for my hands, but I trusted them.

When I hauled myself onto the first platform unassisted, I was so proud that I almost hoped someone had been watching. I sat on the platform for a long time, taking huge breaths, feeling the ship's sway, recovering. When I glanced once at the wheelhouse, I caught sight of Navi's scarlet scarf. Then she raised her hand, and though I couldn't see her expression through the glass, I imagined her giving me that rare smile.

Next, upward. As I climbed my way to the second platform, a funny thing happened: I forgot about everyone else. The sounds below me faded. I heard instead the rigging as it stretched and creaked, the mad flapping of a torn corner of canvas.

Above me, a wheeling bird screamed, so I sent my sister's fox a message.

Wherever you are, Fox, don't get eaten.

Hava? he said, his voice coming to me faintly. *Is that you?*

I'm flying, I said to him. *With the birds.*

Have you been drinking your sister's rauha?

No, but I am high.

If a fox can produce a sensation of snorting inside one's mind, that's what happened next. *Let me guess: You're climbing the mast again? Don't fall.*

Does this mean you care about me, Fox?

Your sister cares about you. And by the way, I have a name.

I have to go now, I said, leaving his scorn behind, climbing until my head was butting against the second platform.

To get onto these platforms, you have to do a kind of gymnastics during which you're not balanced over your legs. You're tipping back, holding your weight with your arms, grabbing with numb, cold fingers.

I hauled myself onto the second platform.

"Ha!" I shouted.

Chest heaving, I stared at the sky behind us. It was knit with ugly clouds that flashed a peculiar orange brown whenever lightning struck. I wondered if that storm on our tail would follow us all the way to land, then break against us as we crossed the Dells on Dellian horses, riding through forests thick as fur, to the tunnels that take us to Monsea. I prefer a ship to a caravan of horses. A ship doesn't hurt my back and my neck, my legs and my bottom. A ship smells like woodsmoke and snow and salt. And it has masts I can climb.

Far below me, Linny and Jacky came on deck, then started testing the davits that hold the lifeboats in place. They always seem to be on watch together; I've noticed the patterns. At least a few of the Keepish girls, Ozul, Sorit, Noa, and Lisa, also tend to be on duty together. The Kamassarian sailors, Alzar and Riz, now married to each other, function as a unit. Ranin and Mart, Bitterblue's guards, do too. Ollie has a more predictable schedule than everyone else's, because he takes care of the animals and assists Liel the cook. Then there's Annet, Kera, and Navi, who alternate being in charge.

I'm going to have to do some more detailed reconnoitering if I want to figure out the best time to climb without an audience. (*Reconnoitering*: That's a word I've always liked, maybe because it's something I'm good at.) I can learn the watch schedule, but that doesn't mean I'll know what the sailors on watch will be doing. Sometimes they're shoveling snow into the sea. Sometimes they're in the rigging. Sometimes they're chopping wood on the foredeck, or feeding the fire in the furnace room, or hauling water up from the hold. Sometimes they're having a quick, warm drink in the salon, talking about their families or the weather. Sometimes, if it's night, they're in the bow with a light, straining their eyes for great bobbing blocks of ice so whoever's at the wheel can steer around them.

As I sat there catching my breath, I saw Kera on the afterdeck again, opening that same hatch in the floor. Again, she held a lantern in one hand, and again she peered around her. She wasn't wearing her usual black knit cap. I was surprised by the river of auburn hair cascading down her back.

This time, she thought to glance up in my direction. I don't know why, but I turned myself into a wisp of fog. It wasn't a very good wisp of fog—if she'd looked hard, she would've noticed that it was girl-shaped, and not moving the way fog up high on a windy mast is likely to move. But there wasn't anything else I could think of that would believably sit on a platform on the foremast, and anyway, part of the power of my Grace is that unless people see the change happen, their eyes slide over me. I blur their attention and blend into whatever's around. Kera didn't seem to be on the lookout for girl-shaped fog.

But she was on the lookout for something. Her eyes, quick and hot, were shooting across the ship, stern to bow.

Then she climbed into the hatch and disappeared.

13.

Interesting. Isn't it?

When my feet hit the deck, Jacky was nearby, sweeping slush overboard with a broom.

Wanting to investigate that hatch, I tried to slip past him.

He blocked me, big and grinning. "Good job with all the climbing, habpva," he said.

If people are going to start calling me that, I don't want Jacky to be one of them. Annet and Navi, maybe, but not Jacky. I don't know or care if he's learned that it's a Keepish sparrowlike bird with spots of red and copper; I need it to stop.

"Do you know that *habpva* means 'beloved' in Mantiperan?" I said.

He wrinkled his nose. "You speak Mantiperan?"

"I'm good at languages."

"That's true," said Linny, coming alongside us, speaking Lingian, like us. I saw again how level his gaze is with mine and tried not to eye his body up and down while wondering how he can climb so easily. Maybe it's not actually easy? Maybe he's dying inside?

"Hava's Dellian is almost as good as mine," said Linny.

"But Mantiper is on the other side of the world," said Jacky grouchily.

That's why I chose it, of course. Fewer people to refute me when I make things up. I highly doubt that *habpva* means anything in Mantiperan, but there are no Mantiperans on this ship for Jacky to ask.

"I study all the languages," I said.

"Because you're a spy for the Queen of Monsea?" said Jacky, showing his dimples again.

"Maybe it's because I assassinate foreigners for her," I said, which I don't, in case you're wondering.

"What's the Mantiperan word for *annoying*?" asked Jacky.

"*Dardya*," I said, which is the Mantiperan word for *brave*. I do study all the languages. And it *is* because I'm my sister's spy, but it's also because languages are like a blanket you can crawl into and be warm. And words are like pebbles you can throw.

"See you later, dardya," he said, walking away with a glow in his face like he was clever.

I'm pretty pleased with how that went.

14.

ON BITTERBLUE'S BAD days—so, most days—Giddon comes to
our cabin after dinner.

He brings her food and sits on the bed with her, patient and
serene, while she chokes it down. He knows the foods that are easier
for her: bread, if the butter is salty. Meat, if it's soft and savory. Broth,
or anything she can drink. There's nothing he'd rather be doing than
cheering her on while she eats a crumb. If I'm ever that fawningly
devoted to someone, I hope someone will put me out of my misery.

"Any news?" she asked him tonight, propped against his side
with eyes closed, her first time sitting up since yesterday. Bitterblue's
mother, Ashen, was Lienid. Bitterblue has her mother's coloring,
gray eyes and dark hair, pale brown skin. She looks younger than her
twenty-three years. She's small, with gold rings crowding too-skinny
fingers. She lost weight during her kidnapping. I try not to notice.

"Froggatt thinks that if Monsea develops airship technology, then
makes it known that you're using your zilfium to build explosives,"
Giddon said, "you'll be able to keep your zilfium safe from invaders."

"I see," she said dryly. "And does he imagine that would make the
world safe?"

"He thinks that since no one else has as much zilfium," Giddon
said, "no one will incite you to war."

"No one else has as much zilfium *that we know of*," she corrected.

"What happens when Estill or Sunder look closer at their own mountains and find zilfium buried deep? Or some other fuel with some other capability?"

"I asked him that," said Giddon. "Froggatt thinks that the idea of any nation dropping explosives from airships is so terrifying that no one would ever risk war."

"Froggatt has his head up his ass," said Bitterblue, suddenly angry. "Froggatt is conveniently forgetting who our neighbors are and the wars they've already risked. The attempts Estill has already made to purchase this weapon. Who my father was, and what would happen if someone with a Grace like his was ever born again. *What people are!*" she almost shouted. Then she made that resigned face that means she's about to vomit and Giddon handed her a basin, pulled her hair back, murmured soothing noises. I hate this part. I don't have Giddon's superhuman patience, maybe because I've spent most of my life watching my sister suffer. I'm done with it. It makes me want to yell and break things.

"Wait," Bitterblue said to Giddon, after retching. "Did you strip down yesterday and stand on the jib boom, like a figurehead?"

Giddon's breath caught on a small, disbelieving noise. "I do that every day," he said, "don't you remember?"

Bitterblue giggle-snorted. "Did I dream that? Or did Hava put it into my head?"

Both of them turned to me. "I never," I said innocently.

"If you weren't with us, Hava," my sister said, "I would never laugh." Then she started to retch again and I had to leave, even though I hadn't talked to them yet about Linny.

I went upstairs, out into the dark of the main deck, where I can breathe. I can always breathe out there, under the sky.

Above me, golden lamps lit the wheelhouse, turning it into a small glowing box. I could see Kera's auburn hair bent over some papers at the table.

I climbed the ladder and glided past her, deciding to do some reconnoitering. As I approached the mystery hatch in the afterdeck floor, it swung open. Then Ollie began to emerge, a lamp in one hand and a sack of something on his shoulder.

"What's down there?" I said casually.

"Oh!" said Ollie, lifting his lamp to me, startled. "Hi, Hava. Just the hold."

"I thought you accessed the hold from the main deck."

The studs in his ears glimmered. All the Lienid people I've ever met wear gold. "There are a couple entrances," he said. "The hold's as long as the ship. You access the forward hold from the main deck and the aft hold from here."

"Tell me," I said as he emerged the rest of the way, "how do you climb a ladder while carrying a lamp in one hand and a sack on the other shoulder?"

His grin flashed at me. "I was born climbing," he said. "You'll get the hang of it."

Then he left me, no doubt to deliver that sack to Liel, who'll use its contents to make us some wonder for breakfast.

I glided past the wheelhouse again, climbed down to the main deck, turned, and promptly crashed into Linny.

He grabbed my arms to steady us, then quickly let me go. "Oh," he said. "Sorry. Hi."

I could barely see him, but I felt trapped anyway. "Hi."

"You . . . getting some air?"

I didn't want to explain myself to Linny, or anyone. "What are *you* doing?" I said, then realized I was replacing his questions with my own again. "I mean, never mind."

"Hava," he said, choking over my name with a kind of amusement that made me bristle. But when he spoke again, his voice was even and friendly; he didn't sound like he was laughing at me.

"I just like to be alone sometimes," he said.

"Oh," I said. "Me too."

"I'll let you get to it, then," he said, moving around me, starting up the ladder to the afterdeck. He faded away, leaving me stewing. When you're being unfriendly, and a person comes along being thoughtful, and it's not Giddon or Bitterblue—the people this usually happens with—it's unnerving. I mean, I'd really just wanted to be alone. It hadn't seemed like a polite thing to say out loud. But then he'd found a polite way to say it to me, without laughing at me or implying I was a jerk.

I found a lifeboat and lay down inside it, thinking about how I was a jerk. It wasn't a new revelation, but it was new in relation to Linny, who keeps drawing me into conversations where I'm not sure of my footing. In my lifeboat, it was freezing, the boat's floor like ice all along my body. The square sails were tied up. Annet must have lost her good wind. I watched the yards swaying against the inky sky.

Maybe I could make a point of not being a jerk the next time I saw him?

I wondered why it was always so easy to talk to Ollie. Was it because he's only thirteen, and small, nonthreatening?

And then I thought of my sister retching. *If you weren't with us, Hava,* she'd said, *I would never laugh.*

That puts a lot on me. You know?

My sister is some two years older than I am. Until she was eighteen and I sixteen—five-ish years ago—she didn't know I existed. That's how well I'd learned to hide.

But I knew she existed; oh, how I knew. I lived on the outskirts of her life, watching her mother try to protect her from our father just as my mother tried to protect me from him too, but differently, because Bitterblue was allowed to exist and I was not. Her life was a story that took place in the light. She was a princess and an heir. She had rooms made of marble, glass, and silk; lessons at a burnished oak table, with pens that glided across smooth paper; baths of warm water and sweet-smelling soap; and a mother who wrapped her in a towel, held her and crooned to her while she dried. When someone wraps you in a towel, you can feel your own edges. You can begin to learn who you are.

My mother hid me in closets and chests. My baths were few and rushed and I learned to sleep alone, breathing the stuffy air of a wardrobe or a cabinet. Sometimes she would fly into a panic and hide me even when Leck was nowhere near. It wasn't her fault. She could get confused. But I learned to sneak away, hide from my own mother. Obscuring myself with my Grace in the corners of my sister's rooms, I learned who Bitterblue was. When she was angry or scared, I tried those feelings on, and understood. When she cried, I shed tears. When she bathed, I breathed the smells. On the rare occasions she laughed, I felt myself wanting something so badly, but not knowing what it was.

Our father forced himself on both our mothers. He—

Wait. Why do I couch it that way?

Our father raped both our mothers. He manipulated both our mothers' minds, over and over again, with his Graced lies. Our mothers both fought against the power of his Grace, each to protect her own daughter from him. He murdered our mothers too, mine first, then Bitterblue's. We have lived the same life. But when Bitterblue looks in her mirror, she sees herself, and when I look in mine, I'm not sure which of us I see. Sometimes I wish I had stronger barriers against whatever she's feeling. I'm porous. Her feelings invade mine and I disappear. Does this happen to other people? Is it because she's a queen, and the most important woman in the world? Maybe everyone around her experiences this?

I lay on my back in the boat while the snow floated down. As a child, I used to press myself against the edges of the fountains in the courtyards and hide myself. I used to look up at the squares of glass in the ceiling and imagine them falling, slashing Leck with their jagged edges, crushing him with their weight. I used to watch snow blow against the glass panes and feel like I was trapped in a box.

I'm free of that now. Aren't I? Here on the ship, there's nothing between me and the snow. It touches my face. In the quiet moments, when the ship hangs at the crest of a wave, before it crashes down again, I can hear ice tapping on my skin.

15.

THE NEXT MORNING was a rauha morning.

On rauha mornings, Liel brings us hot water, tapping on our door so early that often even I'm still asleep. Sometimes I open the door while I'm still in bed and he waits in the corridor, tall and shy, until I'm on my feet. I wonder when Liel sleeps?

I light a lamp and brew the tea for Bitterblue with one of the sachets we keep in the tin on the shelves at the foot of her bed.

Then she sits with her back to the curved wall and takes sips, her hair messy, her eyes closed, and her small shoulders stiff with patience, waiting for release from her suffering.

"How are you, Hava?" she said this morning. "Is there anything I can do for you while I'm well?"

"What would you think if I asked Linny for some basic chemistry lessons?" I said. "Help me with some of the main concepts?"

She breathed slowly, seeming to consider. The sharp, licorice smell of her tea tinged the air, making me want my breakfast.

"Why does Linny know chemistry?" she finally asked. "And how will you learn what you need from him without revealing what you need it for?"

"He grew up on the estate of a Dellian lord who taught him," I said. "And I doubt I can, because it's possible the entire ship already knows what I'm doing."

Bitterblue opened her gray eyes and narrowed them on me. "How did that happen?"

"He and Jacky barged in one day while I was working. They needed some oil that was stored in the floor."

"I see. And now the entire ship knows?"

"I expect that's thanks to Jacky, not Linny."

"But you don't know that for sure."

"I'd bet a lot."

"Linny is Dellian, not Monsean."

"The Dellians are our allies."

"That's true," she said thoughtfully, "though it's an alliance that's never been tested. I don't know, Hava. Doesn't it seem safest for you to continue working on your own?"

"Sure," I said, "as long as you don't actually want to know how to make zilfium explosives."

Bitterblue gave me a puzzled look. She was sitting up straighter; I think the tea was starting to do its job. "Will you tell me more about Linny?" she said. "Why do you trust him? I know you're not quick to trust, Hava, so it means something if you trust him."

"I don't trust him," I said. "It's not like I want to show him any part of the actual notes. I just want to understand chemistry diagrams and notations."

"But, Hava, I find it hard to believe you would suggest this if you didn't trust him."

I wished she would stop saying that. "Fine," I said. "Accuse me of lying."

Be respectful, came another voice, this one like pinpricks in my mind.

I glared at the lumpy mounds of my sister's blankets, not sure which one was the fox. *Bootlicker,* I shot at him.

"Hava," said Bitterblue, "can we start over? I think this conversation has gone astray." Then she blinked, and hiccuped, and suddenly giggled. "I like the way Linny's hair falls into his face when he's working. He has a very nice mouth, and nice shoulders. Is *that* why you trust him?"

When Bitterblue gets silly, the tea is working. Which means she has no further need of me.

I went to breakfast.

16.

Outside, the snow was thick, the clouds a low, ashy blanket. After breakfast, when I closed myself in my workroom, it felt like a burial. And why not? At least if I'm buried, I'm alone, which means no one can expect me to justify every little thing I do.

In the bucking nose of the ship, I shaped Linta Massera's Keepish words and sentences into Lingian while fantasizing about building zilfium explosives with Linny, then using them to save Monsea from Estill. Imagine the moment when my sister realizes how wrong she's been to question me. Imagine Giddon in the scene too, looking stricken and regretful in the background. Can you see it?

Then a knock came on the door and Linny himself stuck his head in.

This time I was ready with an innocuous page of scribbles, which I slid over my work. That doesn't mean I was happy to be invaded, though. "You can't possibly need more lamp oil already!"

"I don't," he said, "but I need to put the can back into storage."

"Always at this hour?" I said. "When you know I'm in here?"

"I'm following orders, Hava," he said. "I don't think Annet's thinking about where you are."

I remembered, then, my intention not to be a jerk.

"Sorry," I said. "I—overreacted."

He curved his lips into a tiny smile. Then, as he reached down to the oil can, his hair fell into his face and I jumped up, instantly embarrassed on his behalf because of something Bitterblue had said that he knew nothing about.

"Okay, come in," I said, moving my crate to the tabletop, then squeezing myself against the wall, wanting to be out of the way.

He lugged the cylindrical can into the room, opened the trapdoor, and lowered it back into place, his movements smooth and easy. "Thanks," he said, straightening. And then, plain as day, he turned and looked directly at my papers. Then at me.

"Distilling," he said.

"What?" I said, glancing at the papers in alarm. Only my formless scribbles were visible.

"You're working with diagrams about distilling," he said. "I can say something like that to everyone, if you like. Shut down the rumors about what you're doing in here."

"You want to shut down the rumors?" I said in confusion.

"It's my fault," he said. "I asked you about chemistry in Jacky's hearing and now everyone has theories about what you're doing in here. But last time, I thought I maybe saw you drawing pictures of the distillation process." He grimaced. "It's the sort of thing you might do if you were interested in winemaking. I can tell everyone so. Would that help, or make things worse?"

I studied him, trying to get a read on him. All I saw were those clear amber eyes, sitting in his quiet face. Why can I never get a read on Linny? I mean, I was being honest when I told Bitterblue I didn't trust him, but that's because I don't trust anyone. Was there something about Linny I didn't *not* trust?

This was ridiculous. "What are the rumors?"

He took a moment to consider the question. "That you stole the plans for an explosive weapon from a Keepish chemist, then killed her," he said. "That the plans supposedly burned up in a fire, but now you're doing chemistry in secret, so maybe you memorized them before they burned."

"I see."

"I think people are a little bit . . . fascinated by the whole thing," he said.

I wondered if that was a polite way to say they were "fascinated" by me, except actually wary of me. Of my Grace, my weird eyes, and that detail about me killing someone.

"I haven't told anyone the other thing you said," he added. "That it's Keepish chemistry."

"Why not?"

He shrugged. "I'm interested too. I admit it. But I don't like rumors. I like facts."

"Yet you'll tell everyone it looks like I'm studying how to distill wine?"

He shrugged again. "Arguably, it did."

"Okay," I said. "You can tell people that."

"You're welcome," he said, with a twist of irony to his lips that was probably meant to shame me into thanking him. I didn't. Like I said, I don't trust him. When one person is working with secrets, another person could have all kinds of motives for wanting to seem helpful.

But as he turned to go, I said, "I didn't kill her on purpose," because for some reason, I wanted him to know that.

He glanced back. "You didn't?"

"No."

"I mean, it's none of my business."

"I've killed people on purpose," I said. "To save the queen's life. I didn't kill that woman on purpose."

He watched me with high eyebrows, studying my face. I guess he doesn't know the pointlessness of trusting any expression on my face, because he said, "Obviously I don't know much about what a person in your position needs to do. But I believe you."

Still, it's the truth, whether Linny actually believes me or not. I didn't kill Linta Massera on purpose. I didn't realize that thing was an explosive when I pulled out that pin. There was a Keepish girl with me. She knew. She snatched the thing from my hands and threw it, which certainly saved my life, and hers. It landed near Linta Massera. Then, when the world flew apart, no one was more surprised than I.

17.

I'M PLEASED TO report that Linta Massera and LV seem to be continuing their unauthorized experiments. There's one here involving a very expensive rare gas (paid for by Linta's employer) that makes Linta's voice sound high-pitched when she inhales it. She's doing some kind of test with it that requires light, and a lens, and a prism. I don't understand the experiment, but I'm 95 percent sure it's about the theory of indivisible particles again, not the zilfium weapon.

I translated this: "On a whim, asked LV for a dynamic image. 'What!' was LV's response. 'Any dynamic image,' I said. 'The sillier, the better.' LV said: 'Okay, a silbercow chasing its own tailfin.' I thought about it a bit, then asked for another. LV said: 'A blue fox playing kick-the-ball with a piece of chocolate.'

"It got us imagining particles spinning in on themselves, and particles bumping against each other. Moving things along.

"I'm trying to expand our ways of thinking about how particles change."

I remember enough about what I copied my first time through to know that Linta Massera never reaches any amazing scientific revelations, aside from building the zilfium explosive, of course. The first time through, that was a little disappointing. Don't scientists live for revelations?

Reading it now, though, the main thing I'm noticing is that they seem to be having fun.

AFTER I WAS done my translating for the day, I went out on deck. Bitterblue and Giddon were at the portside rail, leaning together, tiny and big, watching snow dive into the sea.

Whatever Giddon was saying, it was sending Bitterblue into fits of laughter, a sound so rare and beautiful that even when I'm annoyed at her, it makes me float. Everyone in Bitterblue's entourage is lighter on her rauha days. You can watch the pinched faces of her advisers relax. Ranin and Mart, her guards, smile and tell jokes while they work. Giddon is especially ridiculous, all demonstrative happiness, like a puppy.

Annet came down the ladder from the wheelhouse and went to them, a broad, tired smile on her face.

"How do you feel, Lady Queen?" she said.

"I feel like a daisy," Bitterblue said, her voice warm, no pain hiding in her breath. "I feel like the nose on a snowman. I feel like eating a carrot dipped in honey icing."

"Liel could probably make you one of those," said Annet.

"I'm going to eat just like a rabbit all day!" said Bitterblue. "Slow-roasted rabbit," she added, then seemed to enter a reverie. "Yum."

"I don't think rabbits eat slow-roasted rabbit," said Giddon. When Bitterblue laughed, he looked so pleased with himself that I rolled my eyes hard enough that they may have gotten stuck in the back of my head. Bitterblue and Giddon make themselves stupid, the way they adore each other. I wish they'd just admit to me that they're a couple now. I'm sure it started in Winterkeep. Feigning ignorance is beginning to strain my patience.

Then Giddon turned and saw me sitting on the edge of one of

the lifeboats. He joined me, reaching into a pocket. He handed me a tiny, slender nail with a head shaped like a five-pointed star.

"What's this?" I said, twirling it between finger and thumb. It was cute. I like small things.

"It's for you."

"But, why do you have a little nail with a star on it?"

"It fell out of my bootheel."

"You wear star boots?"

"Is there some reason I shouldn't wear star boots?"

"Don't you need this nail for your bootheel?"

"Seems fine," he said. "Take it, if you like it."

I had an image of myself nailing it to the top of the foremast, when I got there someday. A mark of my achievement.

Then I heard Bitterblue say, "Balls, my neck is sore from always being curled in on myself. I want a bath today!"

I left before their good moods ruined my grouchy one.

18.

WHEN BITTERBLUE'S UP and about, our cabin becomes my fortress. I sit on my bed, all alone, listening to the footfalls passing overhead. The pigs root around above me; I can hear them snorting. I love ship noises. Something's always happening somewhere, reminding me of what kind of house this is; that there's a deck above my ceiling with pigs, and above them, sky.

I'd just pulled my bundle of sculptures into my lap when someone knocked, then pushed the door open without waiting for a response.

I jammed my sculptures back into the secret hole inside my mattress. When one thudded to the floor, I kicked it under the bed with my foot.

Ollie appeared, carrying a mountain of sheets.

"Ollie!" I said. "You can't just push into the cabin of a queen!"

"The queen's on deck," he said. "I saw her."

"Nonetheless, this is her private space!"

"I think you're worried about your own privacy," he said. "Not the queen's."

"Go away," I said, half grinning.

"So, I shouldn't give the queen some nice new sheets?" he said impishly.

It's a mystery why some people's teasing makes me laugh and others' doesn't. Again, this easiness with Ollie. He's Lienid, so he looks like my sister. Is that it?

"Oh, fine," I said, then got up and tugged at Bitterblue's tangled bedclothes in an effort to help. When the fox popped out, squealing, I said, *You! Am I never alone?*

I'm not talking to you, he said, leveling a glare at me through golden eyes. *You call me names!*

Then Jacky and Linny were suddenly beside me, making me jump. Together they reached up to the ceiling and removed the queen's copper tub from its hooks.

"Never, ever come into the queen's room without knocking!" I said.

"Ollie was in here already," Jacky said, "and the door was open."

"Ollie knocked!"

"Oh, come off it, Princess Dardya," said Jacky.

"Listen," I said, "I don't mind. But *she* might, and her fox is in here, watching everything you do."

"Oh," said Jacky, disconcerted, then with a resentful edge. "Of course we meant nothing by it. We'll knock next time. Right, Linny?"

"Sure," said Linny, but smiling to himself a little, as if he wasn't paying attention.

Then Kera tapped on the doorframe, holding a steaming kettle. I know this routine. Sailors tromp in and out for a while, setting up the bath, hauling water.

The fox stood. Braced on his four skinny legs, he glowered around the room like a small, rumpled king. Then he dropped to the floor and marched out, like he couldn't stand it anymore. Or maybe I was projecting.

I did the same.

OF COURSE I was back again not long after, because Bitterblue always lets me take the first bath.

She says it's too hot for her, but I don't believe that's her real reason. Once, when she asked me about my life as a child in the castle, I told her more than I should have. She knows now that weeks would go by sometimes before it was safe enough or my mother was well enough to help me wash. Near the end of those weeks, it became harder to use my Grace, because people might not be able to see me, but they could smell an unwashed body nearby. Sometimes I would try to wash in the courtyard fountains in the middle of the night.

Anyway, she knows how much I love a bath now.

And a ship bath is the best kind of bath, because it's funny to sit in a tub full of water that's adjusting to a room swaying one way, then another. It's always a sloshy bath, you get pushed all around, and it's hard not to get dunked. When I rub soap through my pale hair and submerge myself to rinse it, it's equally hard to stay under. It's like trying to bathe inside a rolling barrel.

After my bath today, I put on clean socks and underwear, pulling them from the small chest against the wall that smells like a cloud of mint when we open it. I dressed in my usual clothes, then spent more time drying the floor than I spent drying myself, so that my sister wouldn't slip.

As I ran my towel across the burnished wooden boards, I considered mint. Most people raised in the castle don't learn about growing things. But after my mother died—was murdered—I saw the rest of Monsea.

Beside a pool where I would bathe when I was staying in Hawkery, the town Kera says she's from, there was a carpet of mint. It grew wild along every sunny creek bed in Hawkery. It was summer. I stayed a couple weeks, sleeping in a hillside cave and stealing food from the people's gardens, sometimes their kitchens. Every night I fell asleep to the clean, bright scent of mint, and woke to it in the morning.

One dawn I woke to giggles and murmurs and crept down to my pool. There, in the water, two young people not much older than I were washing each other. They began kissing. Then more than kissing, reaching for each other with light touches that became more insistent. Finally pleasuring each other, with gasps and cries.

I recognized them. One had an older sister who made delicious tarts from the berries that grew against the walls of their house and the other had a father who was sick in his lungs, like many of the miners seemed to be. They were maybe fourteen, too young to be miners themselves yet, but they would be soon. I'd heard their families, both of them, talking about it. I don't think their families knew about them coming to the pool like this, though.

Their bodies, moving together, crushed the mint at the edge of the pool and sent the smell of it up the slope to me where I watched. A mountain lion could have walked past them to drink in the pool and they wouldn't have noticed. How can people trust each other that much, and have that much abandon? I've never been able to fathom it. Whenever I remember the smell of mint, that moment comes back to me, and with it, the anxiety I felt for them then, that they would be discovered. That someone would intrude, and stop them, and ruin their happiness. I wanted them to be happy.

I guess I've watched a lot of people have a lot of different kinds of sex, though I haven't always wished for them to be happy. I stabbed a man in the behind with a knife once, in the castle. He was trying to rape a maid in the laundry. I was only there to steal some clothes, but I wasn't going to do nothing when I saw his hand cover her mouth and his heavy weight push her against a mountain of sheets. He screamed when I stabbed him, and I hid again. He tried to accuse her of stabbing him and I got worried for her again, so I appeared, waving my bloody knife, making myself look like a (very small) castle guard. When people came running in, I escaped, but not before seeing him handcuffed, ashamed and yelling, making a fool of himself, his pants down, blood running from his wound. I was seven. He deserved it. I'd do it again.

Anyway. The kids by the pool had both wanted what they were doing, and they'd wanted to please each other. I remember that.

When the floor in our cabin was dry, I groped under my bed until my fingers found my fallen figurine, pressed against the far wall. It was the one of me turning into a bear. I examined it for chips, but it seemed unharmed. I've dropped my sculptures before and they never break. My mother made them out of something indestructible.

When I reached for the bundle in the mattress, I found my other figurines sliding out of their scarf. Tucking the bear in with the others, I folded the scarf tightly around them. Then I reached in past them until my fingers touched my translations, just to confirm they were there. Linta and her secrets. Stay safe in there, Linta.

Through the side wall, I heard voices. My sister's advisers, Froggatt, Barra, and Coran, share the cabin next door, but they're not exactly lively neighbors, to put it mildly. They're all the same, all three of them: thin, dry, dusty, and drab, like scuttling leaves in November. Never a spark of light in their eyes. So I was surprised they had the lung power to be heard through the wall.

I glanced once at my sister's bed, reassuring myself that the sheets were tidy, flat, and fox-free. I wanted to spy without being spied upon.

Then I slid across the floor between our beds and put my ear to the wall. It was Barra and the doctor, Coran, their voices pitched with urgency, which was interesting.

"Navi was right," Coran said. "We should have waited for a more favorable season."

"Calm down," said Barra. "A captain knows more about sailing than her second mate does. Kera also urged departure, and she's the first mate, and the expert. She's been shipwrecked before! She doesn't take unnecessary risks."

"Froggatt agrees with me, not you," said Coran.

"Froggatt has a pregnant wife. He's upset because he's realizing he won't be home in time for the birth. I sympathize, but it has no bearing on our safety."

"Go to the wheelhouse and ask Annet if we should turn back," said Coran. "Ask her! She'll say we should stay the course, but she'll say it with a sick look on her face."

The wall to which I held my ear felt different suddenly. My bed, screwed to the moving floor, seemed balanced atop water that was very deep and cold.

Upstairs, I found my sister at the rail and told her her bath was waiting.

Then I went to the wheelhouse.

19.

OUR WHEELHOUSE IS a little wooden box with glass windows all around.

When I stepped into it, Kera had her nose to a chart on the table, a strand of auburn hair spilling out of her black hat. An unlit lamp hanging from the ceiling swung and clanged, swung and clanged.

"Kera?" I said. "Where's Annet?"

She didn't even look up. "Off duty."

"Oh. Do you know where she is?"

"No idea. Try the salon."

"Okay, thanks. The queen sent me to ask after our progress," I added. "Do you have anything to report?"

"Nothing since she asked me this morning," said Kera, squinting up at me doubtfully. "Didn't she drink rauha today? It's not supposed to make her anxious."

"It's probably just making her forgetful."

"Hmph," she said, studying my dripping hair. "Put a hat on your head if you're planning to climb. You'll get sick if your hair freezes."

"Thanks," I said. "I just bathed. I feel fresh as a patch of mint."

She grunted again, already reabsorbed in her charts.

"Mint?" I said.

"What?" she said, glancing up at me, distracted.

"Mint," I said. "It's a beautiful scent."

"Is it?"

"How old is your child?" I said.

With those words, I had her attention. In fact, suddenly I could see through her eyes into her heart, open and raw.

"She's eight," she said. "Turned eight in September."

"What's her name?"

"Sera."

"Like Kera."

"But sweeter," said Kera, then cleared her throat. "Why do you ask?"

"Just curious," I said. "I miss my mother."

Kera snorted. "I don't miss my mother." Then she spoke in a softer tone. "But I miss my child."

"We'll be home soon."

"Yes," she said, turning back to her charts. "Put on a hat, Hava."

I found Annet in the stern.

She was standing by herself, looking out at the clouds, glasses glinting, one hand braced on the lifeboat that hangs there. I don't know why, but I stopped, watching her for a minute. She reminded me of a solitary bird in the sky.

"Annet?" I said, going to stand beside her. "Have you considered whether we should turn back?"

She swung her face to me, surprise plainly written there. "Turn back?" Then, taking in my expression, her own softened. "Habpva?" she said. "Have you been listening to rumors?"

The nickname brought a rush of warmth to my neck and ears. All those letters in the middle of *habpva* make people linger on the word—on me—in a way that feels like I'm being touched, or something.

"Yes," I admitted.

"A ship is quite a breeding ground for rumors," she said. "Too many people, too little space, too little news from the outside world. I've been hearing some rumors too, but I apply a healthy skepticism."

"Oh?" I said, wondering how much Annet knows about my work in the bow.

"Maybe you've heard questions about whether we set out from Winterkeep too soon?"

"Yes."

The clear steel of Annet's eyes is like the clear steel of my sister's eyes. Her shoulders are always straight, her pale hair always tied neatly back. Right now it was shoved under a furry band around her ears and her hand on the lifeboat was tough, strong-looking.

"Habpva," she said again. "We would not have embarked when we did if it had been a reckless thing to do. Our progress west is slow, and we're taking a more northerly route than we would with better winds, but everything's within the range of what's acceptable. I promise you, I've sailed in seas much worse than these."

"Okay," I said, wanting to believe her.

"As far as turning back goes," she said, "surely you've noticed what's behind us? Here." She reached into a pocket and held out a long, shiny brass tube. "Take a closer peek, but only if impressive weather won't make you worry more. We're keeping ahead of it. I think you'll agree that turning back would be unpleasant."

I studied her for a moment, understanding how wrong Coran was, for there was no sick look upon her face.

Then I took the glass and held it to my eye, peering at the blanket of black clouds behind our ship. A bolt of lightning shot across it, so bright, it burned its imprint into my retinas.

"That's supposed to make me feel better?" I said.

Annet chuckled. "Maybe you have to be a sailor."

I had a flash of memory then, of a time I'd spied on Bitterblue and her mother. Bitterblue had been little, maybe seven or eight. She'd wanted—insisted—on reading the journals of a legendary mountain climber named Grella who'd died trying to cross the mountains from Monsea into Sunder by a route no one had ever survived. That was Grella's thing. If he saw a mountain, he wanted to climb it, before anyone else did. Later, several members of the team who tried to retrieve his body also died. They never found him. But they found his journals, buried under a tower of rock by a man who knew what was coming.

"Are you sure you want to read this, love?" Bitterblue's mother, Ashen, kept saying, as Grella described chilblains, frostbite, hands that couldn't grip. Failing to find wood, failing to build a fire. "Isn't it scary? You remember how it ends, don't you?"

"But it makes me feel so warm and safe," Bitterblue said, wrapped in a blanket in her mother's arms, beside a roaring fire. "We're here, Mama."

I'm here, with Annet. The deck of the *Monsea* is solid beneath our feet. That storm is way, way out there; we're racing along ahead of it.

Maybe I am part sailor. I handed the glass back to Annet, feeling better. "I don't need to worry?"

"No. She's sound," Annet said, with her slow smile that made me trust our ship again.

20.

I'VE BEEN THINKING that maybe nightfall is my best bet, for climbing without an audience.

Tonight Annet had the first night watch, so she joined me on the foredeck as I strapped myself into my harness. We stood together, tilting left, tilting right—I should say port and starboard—while fat snowflakes fell around us.

"How does the climbing feel?" she asked me.

"It's moving a lot up there," I said. "I'm trying to improve my balance, so I haven't gotten past the second platform yet. I've learned I need to reserve enough strength to come back down again, or I'll be sorry."

"You're a thinker, habpva," Annet said. "You consider all the factors. A good quality in a sailor."

I was glad for the darkness, to hide my flush. I don't use my Grace around Annet. I'm not sure why; it's just something I decided at some point, a small promise she doesn't know about.

I CAN NOW report that I like night climbing. The cold and the dark force me into a narrow zone of focus and I don't think about the hard deck below, or the ocean. I don't think about the mast stretching above. I don't think about any of the sailors, or the storm on our tail, or Linta Massera's secrets. The lamp on the main deck casts just enough light to show me the rigging as I climb and I think about the ratline I'm standing on, the section of the shrouds I'm hooked to; the ratline I'm climbing to next, and the section of the shrouds I'll hook to next. Every step is my whole world.

Below me, Giddon emerged on deck, then noticed my movements above. He was standing near the lamp; I watched him separate my shape from the rigging.

Surprise crossed his face, then anxiety, then outrage. Then anxiety about his outrage. He does try not to be patronizing, even if he doesn't always succeed.

I watched him fight with himself, waiting to see where his decision would fall.

"Hello, Hava," he finally called up to me.

"Hello."

"What are you doing?"

"What does it look like I'm doing?"

"It looks like you're climbing the rigging," he said, "in the pitch dark, completely by yourself."

"Annet's on watch."

He struggled with that one for a while. "Do you always let someone know?" he finally said. "Before you risk life and limb?"

"Why do you ask?" I said. "Do I need your permission?"

"Why, indeed," he said. "Please remember you have my life in your hands, because if you kill yourself, Bitterblue is going to kill me."

"I'm comfortable with that."

"Brat."

"Bully."

Giddon was chuckling. It made me laugh, which was bad for my focus. "Go away," I said. "I'm trying to concentrate."

"Take care up there, Hava," he said. "We would be lost without you."

EVEN THOUGH I'M not thinking about any of the sailors while I climb the mast, I'm *feeling* about them. Opening myself to my instincts, the same way I'm opening myself to the swaying and the wind.

I know when someone's trustworthy and when they're not. I just do. Kera is lying about something. She just *is*.

What? Her origin? Some detail about her daughter? Why?

Below me, I heard Ozul and Sorit laughing as they crossed the main deck. My climbing teachers. Noa was there too, holding Sorit's hand, her smile flashing. Noa is average-sized but her smile is outsized, and beautiful. She looks plain, until she smiles.

I stilled my movements, even though they never glanced my way. Riz and Alzar went by next, the newlywed Kamassarians, Riz big, Alzar small. They were holding hands too, not talking.

When I made it to the second platform, I considered the mast disappearing into the darkness above me and decided I'd done enough for one night. I sat for a while, touching the breast pocket of my coat, where I keep my little star-topped nail, feeling the snow tickle my face. Watching Annet in the shining box of the wheelhouse.

Navi came out on deck, climbed the ladder, entered the wheelhouse's glow. She handed Annet a steaming cup of something that Annet accepted with both hands and a smile. Then Navi stayed, even though she wasn't on watch. Leaning an elbow on the ledge in front of the big wheel that controls our rudder, she stared through the window glass idly, her face dark and quiet above her crimson scarf.

They hardly interacted, yet some invisible thread connected them. At one point, Annet held something out for Navi to read and Navi turned back and took it, sat down at the table, began writing on it. Said something that made Annet look up and smile again. From my perch outside, I could see the comfort with which they shared company. It's a thing I only feel if I'm using my Grace and the other person doesn't know I'm there.

I watched them for a long time.

21.

THE NEXT MORNING, my sister returned to her usual seasick self, of course. This is our routine.

I stopped in after breakfast and found Giddon with her, giving her moral support while she tried to eat a few bites of oatmeal mixed with dried cherries. He tricks her into getting a range of nutrients that way, like when you give a cat medicine by sticking it into a chunk of raw meat.

Hearing the name *Trina* as I opened the door, I sharpened my voice.

"What about Trina?" I said. Trina is a Monsean Graceling I met in Winterkeep. She is not our friend.

"She set out for home before we did," Giddon said, turning his patient face to me. "I was just wondering whether she got stuck in this weather too, or if she's back in Monsea now. And if she's back in Monsea, whom she's talked to."

"And what she's said," Bitterblue added thickly. "And whether our letters preceded her, so our friends will know to tread cautiously around her."

Trina has the Grace of finding things. Like, if you bring her into your house and say, "Where's my missing green wool sock?" she'll stand there for a moment feeling the air with her hands, then she'll cross into the next room, reach into a knothole in your floorboards, and pull your green wool sock out of the nest a mouse has been building. Or, if you stand her in front of a seam of mountain rock, she'll be able to say to you, "Yes, this mountain contains zilfium." She was born in Estill, where Gracelings aren't free. With the aid of Giddon and his revolutionary friends on the Council, she escaped to Monsea, where Gracelings *are* free. And then, with her new-found freedom, she helped some Keepish traders swindle Bitterblue into selling zilfium that Bitterblue didn't even know her mountains contained, for far too little money. Zilfium from the silver mines near Hawkery, where Kera is lying about being from. Everyone likes to lie.

Now Giddon imagines that Trina can be reformed and work on the side of the Council. You can probably guess what I think of that idea.

"I wrote letters too," I said.

Over the bowl she'd hardly touched, Bitterblue rested her gray eyes on me. They were grim, but I knew that was about her breakfast. "Good," she said. "What kind of letters?"

"To Po, Katsa, Raffin, and Bann," I said, naming the other members of Giddon's Council. "I wrote two letters about Trina to each of them and sent each letter on a different ship."

Now they were both staring at me with mouths slightly open.

"What?" I said. "You send letters in duplicate too, in case a ship goes down."

"Yes, though I've never sent *eight*," said Bitterblue.

"Two ships can go down," I said. "Three ships can go down. Eight is unlikely. They need to know the truth about what she did to you. Anyway, what else was I supposed to do while my leg was in a cast? I wrote one letter about her treachery, then I wrote seven more."

Bitterblue and Giddon snuck an amused glance at each other,

which annoyed me. "Incidentally," I added, my voice barbed now, "Kera isn't from where she says she's from."

"She isn't?" said Bitterblue. "How do you know?"

"I see it in her face when she talks."

"Okay. What does that mean?"

"Do you doubt my instincts?"

"Of course not, Hava!"

"Tell your fox to spy on her if you don't believe me," I said.

"Hava, it's not that I don't believe you! I'm trying to understand, that's all!"

"You could just trust me," I said, looking at both of them hard, both of them with their stupid secret, their private glances, even though they're supposed to be my two closest friends.

Bitterblue shut her eyes and took a deep, clearly nauseated breath, which made me feel like the brat Giddon calls me.

"Hava," Giddon began, in a voice so gentle that all my hackles rose. I'm not some delicate flower that needs a light touch.

"Everything I do is because I'm trying to keep you from getting hurt," I said to my sister. Then I left the room.

22.

THERE'S A BIG wooden block on the foredeck in the bow, for splitting logs. I found Linny there with the ax, chopping wood as easily as he climbs the rigging.

About every third log he placed on the block tipped over from the motion of the ship before he could strike it, but he seemed less ruffled about it than I would be. He just kept grabbing them up and balancing them again serenely, whereas I imagined myself flinging them overboard while screaming.

He lowered his ax as I approached, his hair falling into his eyes. "Morning, Hava," he said, with a small smile that made him look sweet, in an early-morning, sleepy kind of way.

"Morning," I said. "Where do the logs come from?"

He smiled bigger, and this time it felt different, like he was teasing me.

"What?" I demanded.

"Oh, nothing," he said. "Has anyone ever told you your conversation style is highly interrogative?"

"Not specifically, but everyone sure likes to give me unsolicited feedback."

Now his smile was lighting the entire foredeck. "The logs come from the hold."

I thought of Kera's strange sneaking. "Who gets them out of the hold?"

"Whoever needs them," he said. "Why? Building a bunker?"

Then Jacky arrived, emerging through a hatch in the main deck, carrying a mountain of wood that he lugged up to us on the foredeck.

"G'morning, Princess Dardya," he said cheerily, dumping the wood at our feet, then walking back down to the hatch and disappearing inside.

I was trying to remember not to leave Linny's questions hanging. "No bunker," I said to him. "I'm just curious. I've never been in the hold."

"Not much to it," he said. "Dark and smelly."

"What does it smell like?"

"Depends where you are," he said, lining a piece of wood up on the block. "Oil, food, bilgewater." He turned a shoulder to me as he lifted his ax. "Careful," he said. "Flying wood."

It was considerate, but I was annoyed he wasn't inviting me into the hold the way he'd invited me onto the mast (and then passed that job on to someone else). Am I going to have to reconnoiter the hold myself?

"My chemistry is rusty," I said.

Arresting his movement, he looked over his shoulder at me. "What?"

"I wondered if you could help me remember what some of the equations mean," I said.

His surprise was plain. "*What?*"

"You seemed to understand that diagram immediately," I said, "with just a glance."

"Hava," he said, lowering his ax and facing me. "Are you asking me for help with the secret work you're doing in that cabin?"

"No," I said. "Not really. Just a little chemistry help."

"For that work," he reiterated.

"To refresh my chemistry."

"So you can do that *work*," he said.

"Well, yes," I said, with an edge of irritation. "Why? What's the problem?"

He was studying my face so closely now, his own expression quiet and intent, that I didn't think I could use my Grace without him catching on. I wanted to look confident and impatient, but he was rattling me.

Then he said, "Don't take this the wrong way, but I'm not sure I want to contribute to that work."

For a moment, I was too stung for words. "What do you imagine I'm doing?" I said. "You said yourself it looked like I was distilling wine."

"I offered to tell the others that," he said, "as a kindness."

"But what? In fact, you think I'm doing something terrible? Like I'm some kind of villain?"

"Of course not," he said. "I know you're not. But you work for the Queen of Monsea."

"She's not a villain either!"

"Of course she's not! But whatever you're doing, it's probably important. Not something small, but something with consequences."

"And what? You're Dellian?"

He was looking at me so hard that I flickered into a sculpture, just once, for the tiniest fraction of a second. He blinked, then opened his eyes wide. Then he said, "Well, yes, but that's not it either."

"Then what is it?"

"Hava, isn't it obvious?" he said in patent perplexity, rubbing his hand back and forth across his hair, so it stuck out in funny directions. He has a cowlick, I noticed, at the edge of one temple. "Why would I agree to help you with something big and important when you're not even telling me what it's for? Tell me, and then I can decide. Or does everyone truly always do whatever you ask?"

Usually I don't ask. Usually I just make things happen. "You're a sailor on the queen's ship," I said. "If she tells you to help with something, you'll do it whether you want to or not."

Shutters closed in his face. I knew he wasn't closing them against the queen. And now, as he lifted his ax again, I did feel his unfriendliness.

"I doubt I remember much chemistry anyway," he said, plainly lying and not trying to hide it. "That was a long time ago, in a different life."

As he positioned his log and swung, Jacky came up from the hold once more, hauling another mountain of wood. No doubt he was climbing that ladder hands-free, despite the weight of his load. He was gloveless as usual, as was Linny. I guess splinters don't bother them.

"What's wrong, Princess Dardya?" Jacky said, grinning into my face. "Cold? Don't you see us chopping wood for your own personal furnace?"

The queen's furnace, I wanted to say. *I don't care if I'm cold.* But I know better than to assert my independence from her a moment after I've tried to use my association with her to bully someone.

Ignoring him, I turned and went to my workroom.

23.

So. LINTA MASSERA convinced her employer to fly her up high again, and then she had a terrible headache that lasted two days.

It's too bad, because when she's headachy, she works on the zilfium explosive instead of the theory of indivisible particles, and translating becomes a drag again. Today she wrote, "As long as I feel miserable, I may as well do the work that I enjoy less, and that LV doesn't like at all."

I think I understand why she loves her theory work so much that she's willing to give herself headaches. It reminds me of a kind of excitement I've seen before. Like Teddy's love of words. Or my mother sometimes, when the sculpture she was creating would surprise her. Or maybe even the thrill that runs down my own legs to my toes whenever I understand something new about how the wind propels the *Monsea*.

What I'm not sure I understand is why she works for a man who wants to blow people up.

Not that I'm so super great at understanding people anyway, considering all the things I miss that are right in front of my nose.

Why am I so surprised that Linny has a mind of his own?

Because I *am* surprised. People usually *do* do what I ask, because they assume I'm an agent of the queen. People like Linny anyway, who's her employee. Even Annet has to do what Bitterblue asks, and

Annet is the captain. If Annet asks Linny to do something, he certainly does it.

So who does Linny think he is, talking to me like that? He talked to me the way Giddon talks to me, freely, like anything goes. Linny is no Giddon.

In between one of those cow stomach diagrams—showing the distillation process? Is that what it's a diagram of? What exactly *is* distillation, anyway?—and an incomprehensible string of symbols, I hit a big, fat block of text. I took it line by line.

"We are limited to water tests of the explosions," I translated, "which is a problem, but my employer won't allow me to test explosives in the forest or the caves. People will hear, he says, but who he imagines hearing anything in this forsaken corner of the world is beyond me. I tried to explain that a water test of an explosion has limited value, since water, especially water high in salt like seawater, almost certainly alters the results. The effects the explosives have on fish, whales, and silbercows do not predict the effects it would have on humans. I tell him that the chemical agent sticks and burns in water as he's requested, but that does not ensure it would do so on land. I tell him that if this is the effect he wants, then I need a field and a pig. But as I've long observed, he's incapable of appreciating even the most basic principles of science."

There was more, but I needed some air.

Outside, Ollie was on the main deck scratching one of the pigs behind its ears. As I pushed past him, I heard him cooing nonsense. "World's cutest porker!" he said.

Up on the foredeck, I stared out at the grayish-yellow clouds, taking big breaths. I was trying to clear my mind, but an image kept intruding: Ollie and the pig, standing in a field together while some invisible thing in the atmosphere began to burn away their skin.

What is wrong with you, Linta Massera? I thought to myself. *You say you like the explosives work less, but I'm not exactly picking up on any regret when you talk about it. Why do you care about the tiny particles that make up the precious things of our world, if you're only going to tear those things apart?*

And of course Linny is right that there's villainy here, which only makes me more angry. Although I guess *villainy* was my word, not his. His word was *consequences*. He's right that there'll be consequences to me translating these formulas, consequences of one kind or another.

But Linny's wrong if he thinks there's a right or wrong to helping or not helping. His decision is about his own comfort, nothing else. His freedom to choose is a luxury. These formulas exist in the world. A horrible Keepish person who likes the thought of chemicals that harm pigs and people employed a scientist who brought them into being. Why? To sell them to Estill, Monsea's neighbor to the north. My sister is the Queen of Monsea. She's powerful, but she does not have the power to stop a nightmarish weapon from having already been invented. Nor does she have the power to stop her neighbors from wanting such a weapon. What she has is the formulas. To the best of our knowledge, no one else has the formulas, but (1) we can't know that for sure, and (2) even if we did, it would not be responsible for us to try to bury them, when we live in a world where such things can exist. We need to *understand* them, so that she can be prepared for whatever comes next.

So Linny can just get off his moral high horse.

In daylight, with the pigs snorting below, I decided to climb the mast, even though anyone on deck would be able to see me. Indignation gave me fuel.

24.

As usual, once I was up on the second platform, my perspective changed.

What is it about this mast? It's like when my feet are on the ground, my thoughts are tied in a hard little knot. But if I can only rise to a place where I can see that we're on a tiny wooden ship in a massive ocean, then the knot comes loose and my thoughts can fly.

Linny doesn't know any of the details I know. He doesn't know my mental calculations about the weapon, and it's not his fault if he doesn't appreciate all the reasons I can't tell them to him. I was rude about that. And bossy.

Also, Linny never said he had the moral high ground. I'm the one who put him up there. What he said was that he wanted to know what I was doing before deciding whether to help. He wanted a *fair* exchange, like he always does. That's all.

And who did he think he was, talking to me that way?

I'm beginning to have the sinking feeling that he thought he was my friend.

Well. He probably doesn't have that thought anymore.

25.

IN THE EVENING, I lay in one of the lifeboats, shivering in the dark, watching clouds swallow stars. Thinking, wondering. How do people become friends? *Why* do people become friends?

Nearby, the hatch to the crew quarters creaked open. Someone lurched toward my boat and looked in.

"Hey there, Princess Dardya," said Jacky. "Having a nap?"

"Yes," I said, hoping it would encourage him to go away.

"I'd like a nap," he said. "Can I come in?"

"Huh?" I said, startled. He burst into laughter. I guess he'd meant it as a joke, then? I'm not sure if I was more relieved or annoyed.

"Linny thinks you have hidden depths," he said, "but I think you're just shy." And now I hated him a little. It isn't shyness that stops me from wanting a nap with Jacky. He laughed again, the fog of his breath hitting my face. I smelled the licorice sweetness of rauha tea, which isn't just a medicine. Some people drink it on purpose to get high. It's expensive, though. Not sailor fare.

"Are you drinking rauha?" I asked, surprised.

"Of course not," he said.

"Okay," I said, making my voice bland.

"Anyway, I'm off duty now. I'm not on watch till morning. The night is mine, to drink whatever I like. Want to come play cards with me and Linny and Ozul?"

In all our weeks on the ship, Jacky has never invited me to do anything. Never motioned me toward the crew quarters like this with an open face and an eager, waving hand; never admitted outright to wanting to be in my presence.

Rauha does that.

"Will you share some of your rauha if I do?" I asked.

"No," he said, "because I don't have any rauha. Haven't you heard of raffrara? Stop being a dardya. Come play cards."

Raffrara is another powerful Keepish tea. It makes people quiet and content, but kind of stupid. It's far less expensive than rauha, and pretty popular among Keepish sailors, but it smells earthy and sour, like rotting leaves.

"Sorry," I said. "I'm playing cards with Giddon and the queen."

"Sure. Have fun with your fancy friends," he said, shaking his head and chuckling.

After he left, I went to my cabin to check on my sister's rauha supply.

26.

First, I made sure Bitterblue was asleep.

"Giddon's waiting for you in the furnace room," I said to the lump on her bed, "wearing nothing but a sock on his you-know-what."

She made a noise that was half a murmur, half a snore. Asleep.

Next, the fox. *Are you in here, Fox? Are you watching?*

The answer came faintly. *I'm in the furnace room. I don't spy on you. Also, my name is Adventure. Stop calling me Fox.*

Yes, his name is Adventure; it's too silly to bear. Technically, his name is the Keepish word for *Adventure*, but foxes aren't fussy about which language you use. Their communication is more about intentions and meaning.

Is Giddon in there, wearing nothing but a sock? I said.

You ask the most bizarre questions.

I went to my sister's row of wooden shelves carved with fish and seahorses and whales, each shelf with soft, velvet insides to provide cushioning, and with a high lip to prevent things crashing to the floor. I saw that the tin that contains her rauha sat open.

When the Keepish doctor gave Bitterblue enough rauha to last this voyage, she'd said, "I've calibrated the sachets to your size, Lady Queen. Taking too much too often risks addiction. You may have one sachet every three days. Do you understand?"

We all understood, and I volunteered to keep track of the

schedule. If that makes me sound wonderfully sisterly and responsible, you may as well know that it was a preemptive strike designed to keep Coran, the adviser-doctor, from butting into our cabin more often than he already does. So I took the sachets and counted them. I put them in a tin. Then I told my sister that if I found her ingesting more than one every three days, I would throw the whole batch into the sea.

"Your bedside manner needs work," she said. Then she stood on her toes, kissed me on the cheek, and thanked me for my care of her, which was mortifying.

Anyway, the point is that I know how many sachets of rauha we started this voyage with, and how many she's used so far. I stood at her shelves, touching the spot on my cheek where she'd kissed me, counting.

Three sachets were missing.

Absently, I sat on my bed, feeling the slight bump of my figurines in their hiding place beneath my butt. I was remembering the night Jacky and the others filled our copper tub. I'd left while they were working. What had happened after that? I imagined Jacky's hand reaching into my sister's rauha tin, the tin that's her only relief from an abject misery. My sister is a *queen*. Who steals from a queen? I watched the scene in my mind, over and over, because I enjoyed the pleasure of my rising contempt.

What about Ollie, though? What about Linny? Were they there when it happened? Had they protested? Or had they laughed? The thought of Linny laughing as Jacky stole from my sister made something sick twist inside me. The thought of Ollie laughing was terrible too.

But I was getting carried away.

My sister sighed in her sleep. "Giddon?"

I didn't answer.

"Hava?" she said next.

"Yes?"

"What are you doing?"

"Nothing. Counting your tea sachets."

I could hear the smile in her response. "To ensure my good behavior?"

"To ensure your health," I said, smoothing the sharpness out of my voice with an effort.

A moment passed, then she snored.

I solve my sister's problems, in the background of her life. That's the job of a queen's spy, or anyway, that's my interpretation. A sailor stealing the queen's rauha is a small problem. But it's mine to handle.

I reached for my figurines, wanting occupation for my hands while I considered what to do. I like to stroke each figurine on its back with a finger. I like to examine the face of each, mirroring its expression. I always focus on them in a certain order: Mountain lion–girl. Bear-girl. Porpoise-girl. Bird-girl. A mountain lion can tear gashes with its claws and a bear can bite and smash. A porpoise can swim away so fast, no one can catch her. A bird can hide in unreachable places, watch from above, fly away forever if she wants to.

I didn't start my careful order tonight, though, for there were only three figurines in my lap. The bird-girl was gone.

27.

OF COURSE, SHE couldn't *really* be gone. Right?

I shoved my hand back into my mattress, looking for the bird-girl. I plunged my fingers into every cranny, feeling around Linta's notes, forcing myself to be careful and slow. I pulled the formula papers out and checked that they were all accounted for. I felt under the mattress. I riffled through all of my sheets.

"What's going on?" Bitterblue said sleepily, waking again.

"I lost something," I said. "Something small and stone. A figurine. Have you seen it?"

"No. I'll ask Giddon," she said, as if Giddon is the solution to every problem.

I lay on my stomach and swept my hand across every part of the floor under my bed. I searched the floor under my sister's bed; I searched all of the floor. I even looked in the minty chest, where it couldn't possibly be.

I forced myself to think. I'd been interrupted by Ollie. I'd shoved them into my mattress. One, the bear, had fallen; I'd nudged it out of sight with my foot. Jacky and Linny had arrived. Kera had arrived. I'd gone away. I'd come back and found my figurines messy and disturbed.

I searched the bed and the floor again. Nothing. Someone had found them. Someone had taken one, my favorite one. Someone knew about my hiding place too; someone had gotten awfully close to Linta's formulas.

Well. I knew which of the sailors on this ship was a thief.

I launched myself out of the room.

28.

I THREW OPEN THE hatch to the crew's quarters, climbed down the ladder, and pounded on a random door. I didn't know whose cabin it was, and I didn't care.

Jacky pulled open the door, smiling big and bright when he saw me. Pushing past him into the cabin, I saw Linny, Ollie, and Ozul sitting on a tiny patch of floor around a game of cards. The room had four bunks. It was cold, dimly lit by a lamp hanging from the ceiling, and smelled like sweat and rauha.

Linny, Ollie, and Ozul stared up at me with shocked faces and I realized I was changing—into a sculpture, then back into myself, then back into a sculpture. Not just any sculpture. A life-sized sculpture of my bird-girl.

"Hava?" said Linny, pushing to his feet. "What's wrong?"

I ignored him. "Where's my figurine?" I yelled at Jacky.

"What?" he cried.

"You know," I said. "I'll kill you."

"Dardya!" he said. "Relax!"

I saw four shelves arranged one above the other on the wall between the bunks. "Which shelf is yours?" I said. "Tell me, so I don't have to tear all four apart."

"You're wild! You're crazy!" said Jacky.

I surged toward the shelves. "His is the bottom one," Ollie said in a small, strangled voice.

I began to pull things down from the bottom shelf and throw them onto the floor. A shirt, a hat, a scarf that caught on something and tore.

"Hey!" Jacky said. "My sister made that!"

"Hava!" said Linny. "You need to stop it!"

I grabbed at a pile of letters that went cascading across the room. Jacky kept trying to reach for my arms, kept trying to block me, but whenever I turned into a sculpture, it alarmed him so much that he backed away.

I grabbed at a chunky glass bottle with sloshing gold liquid inside.

"That's my father's liqueur," Jacky said.

I looked him straight in the eyes, lifted the bottle above my head, and smashed it down onto the floor. Glass shattered and liquid splashed everywhere.

After that, he left me alone. The others did too, backing against the far wall, quiet, watching. Linny looked sick. I guess I was sickening. I pulled down the rest of Jacky's belongings and threw them. More letters, clothing, a book.

Inside that book, I found my sister's two remaining sachets of rauha. I held them up to show Jacky, blazing with my own righteousness. I put them into my pocket.

I did not find my figurine on that shelf.

I turned to the group. "Which bunk is Jacky's?" I said.

"What are you even looking for?" Jacky squealed. "You found your tea!"

"Which bunk?"

Jacky pointed to one of the lower bunks. I tore it apart. But my bird-girl wasn't there either, not in his sheets or his mattress, not in the spaces between the mattress and its frame.

Tears were running down my face. I wasn't even sure anymore

what they saw; I looked like a sculpture to them, whirling around the room, tearing things apart, or I looked like an ugly, crying girl.

I turned on him and grabbed at his pockets.

"Hey!" he yelled in outrage, pushing my hands away. "Enough!"

I looked him straight in the face. "Never talk to me again," I said. "Never look at me again. You don't exist."

I left the room. I clambered up the ladder to the main deck. I found my harness, strapped it on, went to the mast, and climbed. I was careful with every hook. I climbed all the way to the third platform and dragged myself, gasping, onto its surface.

There, all alone with the stars making pale pricks of light above me, I cried for a long time.

29.

Above the third platform, a dozen or so ratlines create a path to the tippy top of the foremast. A horizontal beam is attached to the mast there. I've mentioned it before; it's called a yard. The highest square sail, the topgallant, hangs from it.

Sometime after I'd cried myself out, I decided to climb up there in the dark. I wanted to perform a ceremony with Giddon's little star nail.

It's actually only ten more ratlines—I counted—and yet, it was the hardest stretch of climbing I'd ever done. It was the cold and my fumbling as I attached each hook to a barely visible part of the shrouds; it was the ache in my ankle, or the one in my chest; or it was the emptiness inside me, giving me no fuel from which to draw. I was probably doing something I shouldn't. Annet would tell me to wait until daylight, and Giddon would have a personal crisis about it. With stiff, frozen fingers, I pushed on, my eyes streaming from the wind.

I felt no triumph when I reached the top. I felt nothing. When it occurred to me that of course you can't drive a nail into a mast without a hammer, a sudden passion whipped through me and I hurled the nail out to sea. The wind thwarted me, blasting it back toward the foremast. I heard it ding against some piece of metal in the rigging below, then it was gone. Giddon will probably find it on deck tomorrow and recognize it as evidence of my tantrum. "Brat," he'll say, teasing, but not really.

It's too cold that high up. I started down, my hands so numb, they were nearly useless; I hooked my elbows around the shrouds. At the third platform, I paused again briefly, warming my fists inside my armpits. A flash of light on the afterdeck caught my eye.

It's not easy to spy when you're at the top of the swaying mast with a fierce wind in your face and your eyes swollen from crying, but it helps if what you're looking at is something you've seen before. On the afterdeck, a lantern erupted into flame as Kera, her gaze sweeping the decks surreptitiously, disappeared into the hold.

30.

IN THE NIGHT, the sea was rough. Water pounded against the walls of our cabin, the wood creaking and straining, and the wind roared from every direction. I don't remember it ever being quite like that before.

Bitterblue gasped occasionally, holding on to her fox, afraid of falling out of bed. She stretched her fingers out to me once and I reached across the space between us and grasped her hand. It soothed a raw place inside me, where I worry sometimes about whether my sister thinks she needs me, and whether I'm any use at all.

I made myself a new hiding place. At the end of Bitterblue's bed, I pushed her sheets aside and sliced a cavity into her mattress, then pulled out some of the stuffing without her even noticing. It was at the bottom end where her feet don't reach, at the edge against the wall. I tucked Linta's papers and my figurines into the hole I created, satisfied. I don't think she'll find it. Our shelves and things are at the foot of her bed, so I can pretend I'm doing something with our supplies when I need to get in there. It doesn't show unless you're looking for it. And no thief is going to steal something out from under a sleeping queen.

At one point I struggled upstairs and peeked out onto the main deck. It seemed like every sailor was there, yelling, working together on the lines. Giddon and Kera were fighting with a halyard nearby.

Once it was secure, Giddon saw me and lurched over to me, water dripping from his hair, his beard.

"Should I be out there helping?" I shouted.

"Would you stay with Bitterblue?" he shouted back. "Make sure she's safe?"

"Okay. Let me know if you need more hands," I said, but he was gone, staggering away, before I'd even finished. I spent the night sitting on my bunk with my back to the wall and my feet braced against my mattress frame. I watched Bitterblue's attempts at sleep, and planned my approach for how I was going to spy on Kera in the hold.

31.

WE'VE REACHED CALMER waters.

It happened around dawn, the world around us relaxing its wild swing, the screeching walls of our wooden house settling into a contented murmur.

When I went up on deck, the surface of the sea was frozen around us, thin sheets like panes of glass that bent and flexed as the waves passed under them, then shattered as our hull sliced through.

When Annet found me standing at the rail, staring down at the sea ice, she came to me and said, "This is normal, habpva."

"I wasn't worried," I said, which was a lie, in case you're wondering.

"I'm glad to hear it," she said. "The temperature's dropped, as you can see. But this isn't a part of the ocean that freezes in earnest. We'll probably see a lot of this type of ice."

"It's beautiful," I said, which was true, even if it was also an attempt to hide my disorganized feelings.

I skipped breakfast, seeing as the likelihood was high of at least one person who'd witnessed my fury last night being in the salon. Instead I went straight to Liel in the galley and begged some snacks.

He gave me a harried look over a bowl of whisked eggs.

"It's for the queen," I said (another lie, if you're keeping count), at which point he practically threw his eggs aside and assembled a beautiful array of fruit, cheese, and breadsticks on a high-lipped plate.

Tulip blinked at me steadily from a stepping stool while I waited. I had to keep reminding myself that he's just a cat, not a fox capable of suspicion.

I carried the plate to the passageway outside my cabin, then shoved the food into my pockets. Inside, I slipped the plate under my mattress and grabbed a lantern, glancing once at my sister's bed, wondering if one of those lumps was her sleeping fox. There's nothing I can do to keep him from figuring out where I'm going today, if he decides to try to find me.

Out on deck again, I waited a few minutes until Navi arrived at the wheelhouse to take over Annet's watch. When they seemed focused on each other, I climbed the ladder to the afterdeck. There, I swept the decks with cautious eyes, just like Kera always does. I could hear Ollie on the main deck feeding the chickens, who were squawking with excitement. Riz and Alzar were shouting across the foredeck to each other, something about the jibs. But the wheelhouse blocked their view of me, and through the wheelhouse glass, Annet and Navi were turned away from me.

Maybe I wasn't lying when I told Liel the food is for the queen. It's for me to eat, sure, but that's because I need fuel for this mission, and this mission is for the queen. I need to know that whatever Kera's up to, it isn't something dangerous.

I opened the hatch to the hold and slipped down the ladder.

32.

I CAN NOW SAY that the darkest place I've ever been is the hold, and I've been in a lot of dark places.

It took forever to climb down the shaft, which seemed bizarrely long. Was I climbing to the ocean floor? My inability to see anything was disorienting, my grip awkward while also grasping an unlit lamp in one hand. (How do they do it? While carrying an armload of logs!)

When I reached the particular, inky black of the hold, the air changed. Now I was being swallowed by a cave. I groped for the floor with my feet, then crouched with my back braced against the ladder while the room heaved around me and I tried to light the lamp by feel. A lurch threw me off balance. Landing on my side with a yelp, I heard the lamp crash over and roll away.

In dark places, it's possible to explore with your ears, nose, hands. I have visceral memories of the dusty wooden smell of my mother's wardrobe. The scratchy feel of the unfinished wood at its back. But it turns out that this is harder when you're in a ship plunging into the trough of every wave. I did my best, patting the air around me, taking cautious steps, mostly crawling. It was a thick, stuffy darkness, with ever-changing smells and the explosive thud of water, and a soft, scratching noise that made me remember something I'd heard once about a ship's stores swarming with rats. I couldn't find the lamp. The constant movement began to make me dizzy.

That was when nausea crept upon me. A surprise visitor. Is sight what keeps me from seasickness? Is this how my sister feels all the time? I decided to try crawling back toward the ladder, but I couldn't find that either. Then I bumped into something soft, cold, and wet that wrapped itself around my face and tried to smother me as I rolled with it, certain I was fighting with a slime beast that had made its way in from the sea.

My head knocked against something sharp. My lamp! I flailed, grabbed for it, managed to set it upright and light it with shaking fingers, then discovered that I was tangled in a bedsheet.

Above me, more sheets hung on lines, looking just like the view of the sails when I lie on my back in the lifeboats. Beside me, barrels strained against a cord that held them in place and crates climbed in stacks to the ceiling. I saw the base of the mizzenmast, planted in the middle of the floor like a leaning tree. I saw mountains and valleys of objects filling this room, then a hatch in the wall, presumably leading into another room full of more objects; and just like that, my disorientation shifted into coziness.

I extricated myself from the damp bedsheet and did my best to return it to one of the drying lines. Then I began to explore.

A SHIP'S HOLD is a perfect hiding place.

Containers of all shapes and sizes loomed wherever I raised my lamp. I could identify treasures by smell. Salted fish here, cheese there, olives, mace.

As I explored, some of the smells I encountered were old, like moldy must, clinging to the insides of my nose and throat. Some were categorically putrid and brought a word of Linny's flying into my mind: *bilgewater*. What's bilgewater? I think it's water that gets trapped inside the bottom of a ship and grows increasingly filthy and disgusting. Some were fresh smells, like flour in dusty sacks.

Like molasses, like dried herbs that cut through my nausea. I wondered which containers held ballast. My lamp caught the scurrying of a small animal with a long tail, but I wasn't bothered anymore. Rats are inevitable. If I'm ever captain of a ship, I'll fill it with gigantic cats. Problem solved. *Sorry, Fox,* I thought, but to myself, not to him.

Captain of a ship, I thought, wondering where that idea had come from.

It was a magnificent room. A room I could live in, surrounded by the regular thud of the hull against water and the darkness trying to swallow my circle of light. Cold, though, as cold as the ice room that abuts the castle kitchens, where I learned not to hide as a child, after one time when I got locked in overnight.

When I passed through the hatch, I entered a new part of the ship's bowels. It was a room resembling the previous room, except that it was smaller and had no ladder and no hanging sheets. The base of a second mast rose from the floor, the mainmast this time. Barrels, sacks, trunks, and crates made mountains and hills around the mast, along with ropes, canvas, and wood . . . I was standing in a rocking Monsean landscape.

Another hatch stood in the opposite wall. I opened that hatch and peeked into a third room—the forward hold? Didn't Ollie use that term? It was longer than the other rooms, but similarly arranged. The foremast was planted in its floor some distance from me. Behind it, stacks of firewood climbed so high that someone must've thrown them up there. Closer to me, a ladder rose to the ceiling, wider than the ladder in the aft, and equipped with a lift—a sort of platform attached to a rig of long ropes—for hauling supplies above. Maybe Jacky didn't climb with all that wood?

I chose the small central room as my hideout. It was most removed from the ladders, making it the best room for anyone who was keeping a secret. I hoped that if Kera came in, she'd overlook the girl-shaped sack sitting in a shadowy corner.

I extinguished my lamp, then tucked it behind some crates. Quickly, I ate some of the snacks in my pockets, then set in to wait.

I'm good at waiting. It's the sister of hiding. When I hid as a child, I was waiting for my mother to return. Waiting for the king to go away. Waiting for a part of the castle to empty so I could sneak through without being seen. Tucking myself in some corner somewhere in plain sight but hidden with my Grace, waiting for someone to walk by, or people to speak, or something to happen to break the monotony.

When I'm waiting, I make my focus small and particular. Listening for the creak of an opening hatch. Watching for a flash of light. Small changes and surprises are the only things that matter. I can turn everything else off, tune everything out. Waiting is a way of making yourself as empty, small, nonexistent, and safe as possible.

I waited.

33.

WELL, THIS IS a puzzler.

I didn't wait long. Maybe an hour, ninety minutes? Then the hatch from the aft hold opened and light flooded the room, Kera pushing in behind it with a lamp and a purposeful expression. She was wearing her dark knit cap and exhaling fog. She never glanced my way. Maybe my Grace wasn't even necessary.

She marched across the room, put her lamp down, and shuffled some crates around quickly. The smell of stinky cheese filled my nostrils, almost making me sneeze. Extracting a crate that was smaller than the others, she set it on the floor beside her lamp.

She opened the crate. I couldn't see what was inside or what she was doing from my place in the shadows, but when she opened that crate, new smells assaulted me. Confusing smells. Urine. Feces. Infection and sickness. I had to breathe through my mouth, shallow and slow, to suppress my gag reflex.

Kera pulled a cloth out of her pocket, unwrapped it, and revealed a glass syringe. She positioned it in one hand. Then she stuck both hands into the crate and I cringed, knowing that there must be something alive in there, receiving that needle's sharp end.

She did something inside the crate with the cloth, then wrapped the syringe again and put it back into her pocket. She fitted the lid back onto the crate.

I memorized her movements as she returned all the crates to their original positions. I did my best to build a replica of the crate mountain in my mind.

And it's good I did, for once she left and I carried my own lamp to the crates, it took me a while to find that smaller crate.

It was light, weighing practically nothing. Before I opened it, I found a handkerchief in my pocket and tied it around my nose and mouth. I also decided which part of the floor was the best to vomit upon, just in case.

Then I told myself that I was a person who didn't care about anyone or anything. I was hard, cold, feelingless, not really a person at all. A collector of information. A spy.

I opened the lid.

It was a fox.

Tears began running down my face. It was a tiny blue fox, skin and bones, curled around its own swollen belly, its fur clumped and missing in patches, its skin bleeding wherever its fur was missing. It lay in straw caked with feces and reeking of the ammonia of urine.

I think I cried out. I think I gagged. It was like I was looking at all the suffering I'd ever seen, right there in that box. The king used to hurt animals. It was one of his joys. He kept them in cages in the castle gardens. I was never able to rescue them, but I used to bring them food. When I could, I brought them drugs to end their lives.

Anyway. Anyway. I could rescue this one.

Wiping my tears on my sleeve, I tried to figure out what to do. It was so small. I guess a fox is mostly fur. I guess a fox who's been starved is little bigger than a newborn kitten. It would be wrong somehow to say it was sleeping. It looked dead. I held the lamp very close to its body before I was able to perceive the slow swelling of its chest as it breathed.

I lifted its tiny, hollow-feeling body from the crate. It was a she.

When her head hung limply, I cupped it in the palm of my hand and held her to my chest, wanting to press her into my body heat. I slid her inside my long, warm, Keepish fur coat, tightening the belt at my waist so she would be secure, cradling her gently. Already, this was more than I'd ever been able to do for the king's animals. I could not stop crying.

Fighting with my stupid tears, I returned the crate to its usual place, stacking the other crates in their proper positions around it. If Kera found the empty crate, let her worry about what to think. Let her imagine that the fox somehow escaped; let her jump in paranoia with every person who approached her, wondering if this was the person who knew what she'd done. Let *her* feel danger and fear.

I went back to my hiding place and sat on the floor for a while, my hands cradling the lump in my coat, trying not to clutch her too hard, trying to calm myself down. I pushed at my thoughts. I needed to understand, and I needed a plan. Think!

This was essentially kidnapping. Right? True, I could imagine benevolent reasons someone might sneak a fox out of Winterkeep. As I've mentioned before, blue foxes in Winterkeep have a culture of lying to humans. My sister's fox says it works like this: Foxes pretend they can only communicate telepathically with one single human, the one they're bonded to, and they also pretend loyalty to that human, for as long as that human is alive. If that human dies, then they can bond to a new human. But in fact, blue foxes can read and influence the minds of any unguarded humans they like, and they're not always loyal. Fox culture in Winterkeep is a culture of secrets and lies perpetuated against humans. If a fox didn't want to be a part of that anymore—or if she got caught in a lie—maybe it made sense for a Monsean human to help that fox sneak out of Winterkeep.

But that fox could also just walk aboard a ship and sail away. Right?

Regardless, no benevolent plan involved keeping a fox, or any creature, drugged, sleeping in its own filth, starving, with infections growing on its skin, in a bitterly cold room, trapped in total darkness.

Kera was stealing this fox. Kidnapping it, and treating it horribly.

Why? Something to do with Hawkery? Something about her daughter?

Whatever the specifics, the essential answer was probably money. It usually is, and anyway, everything Keepish is valuable on the Royal Continent markets, especially the black markets. I don't know of a black market for blue foxes, but why wouldn't there be one? People will do anything for money. Someone on the Royal Continent might pay for a telepathic fox, imagining her as a loyal pet, and buyable. Not understanding that in Keepish culture, foxes aren't pets and they themselves choose whether to "bond" to a human; not caring that abducting them is cruel.

If Kera were involved in an illegal fox trade, she would need to hide the fox from her shipmates, in a place like the hold.

It occurred to me suddenly that she'd also need to hide the fox from the other blue fox on board, who would certainly sense a fellow fox's presence. That was why Kera was drugging her. So her consciousness would remain undetectable to the queen's fox.

Fox? I said, reaching out tentatively to my sister's fox.

My name is Adventure! he responded instantly. He felt very far away.

Are there any other foxes on board?

Why? So you can be rude and call them bootlickers?

So, no then?

Of course there are no other foxes on board, he said haughtily. *Leave me alone. I'm talking to the queen.*

Okay then. The drugs were to hide this fox from the other fox. And maybe Kera wasn't keeping the fox in her own filth on purpose;

maybe she didn't have time to do better. Maybe she wasn't starving her on purpose either. Maybe it was hard to feed a fox who was always unconscious.

But this fox's belly, swollen with hunger, made me care little about Kera's reasons. The single most basic thing all creatures deserve is food.

And water! Did she need water?

I lurched to my feet and returned to the aft hold. Then, the fox snugly positioned inside my coat, I climbed the ladder and emerged into the light of day.

34.

DEPENDING ON WHAT you need and whom you need it from, it is, or it isn't, convenient to be the roommate of the queen.

I needed hot water and a basin. So I went to the galley, used my Grace to erase Liel's perception of my puffy eyes and the lump in my coat, and said to him, "I'm sorry for disturbing you again, but we need a kettle of hot water and a basin."

I've never demanded things from Liel before today. No one does; he's king of the galley. But "we" means the queen, when I'm the one saying it.

An instant later, he placed a large, steaming kettle into a metal basin, then passed the basin into my hands.

"Will these do?" he said gruffly.

"Yes. Thank you," I said, and was gone.

I brought them to Giddon's cabin, since he has one to himself and he's hardly ever in it. Finding it empty as expected, I set my basin on the floor. Then I ran to the cabin shared by my sister's advisers.

Coran, the doctor, answered my knock, which was a small blessing.

"Yes?" he said, peering out at me with a disgruntled expression.

I used my Grace to hide my eyes and the lump in my coat from him too. "I need a disinfecting ointment," I said. "And bandages."

"What's happened?" he said in sharp alarm. "Has the queen been injured?"

"No," I said, prepared for this. "It's for me."

He looked me up and down. "You look fine. Is the queen well?"

"She's fine!"

"Then why—"

"You may ask her if she's fine if you don't believe me," I said, "but the reason I've come straight to you is that I don't want to worry her. She's having a bad day. If you insist on troubling her about my health, give me ten minutes to prepare her for your intrusion."

He humphed. "Well? What's happened to you?"

"It's private."

He reached a hand toward me. I turned into a sculpture of myself. When I turned back again, he was clutching his temples with his eyes screwed shut. Watching me change is hard on some people.

"Please don't make me get the queen out of bed to command you to help me," I said.

"Very well!" he said, fumbling behind him for his medical bag. "But I wish you understood that I only want your well-being, Hava. Your health and welfare are my responsibility, and discretion is part of my creed."

Blah, blah. Next, I slipped into my own cabin and unearthed the boiled cloths my sister and I use for our monthly bleedings. I also took my sister's small water barrel. We have fresh water in our cabin all the time, since she's the queen.

Her fox watched me struggle with the heavy barrel from the bed. *What are you doing?*

My Grace doesn't work on foxes, so I couldn't hide the bulge in my coat. *Nothing you need to know about.*

The queen will want to know why you took her things, he said, cocking his ear at the unmoving lump on the bed.

Then tell her I'm thirsty and menstruating, I said. *She'll be riveted.*

What's in your coat? he said, his gold eyes glinting.

It's private, I said. *Hasn't the queen told you not to spy on me?*

Humph, he said, sending me a blip of irritation.

I staggered out the door with my supplies. Once I reached Giddon's cabin, I locked myself in.

ON GIDDON'S FLOOR, I mixed warm water in the basin. I found soap on the shelves, next to a tin of some familiar, bitter-smelling tea I couldn't place at first. Then I remembered it's the Keepish tea for preventing pregnancy. Those two are hiding their sex tea from me.

That's fine. I can hide things too.

I bathed the little fox. The soap helped. First I scrubbed my own hands, so I wouldn't make her infections worse. Then I submerged her to her face and slid soapy fingers over her matted fur, loosening the clumps as gently as I could. I did my best to clean the wounds on her skin. I held her head above the water and watched the grime and blood lift from her body. I checked her breathing with anxious frequency, afraid to find that it had stopped, hoping I was doing everything right.

I also dribbled cold water over her lips repeatedly. It was hard to tell if any was going in, or how else to feed her. Once, I thought I saw her swallow. I dribbled with extra enthusiasm after that, but it didn't happen again. So I stopped, frightened of drowning her.

Finding a soft towel hanging on Giddon's wall, I wrapped her in it, trying, gently, to blot the water from her fur. She didn't react. It was like ministering tenderly to a floppy-headed doll.

Briefly I left her in Giddon's room, in the middle of his bed, tucked into her towel, while I ran the basin of mucky water down the passageway and poured it out in the head.

When I returned, she hadn't moved. Nor did she move while I applied the disinfecting ointment. In addition to sores on her skin where her own urine and feces had soaked her, she had a series of angry welts across her shoulders and back, where Kera had stuck her with needles.

Next I made her a diaper out of bandages and my bleeding cloths. Then I found a clean shirt on Giddon's shelf and wrapped her in it. Sorry, Giddon. I was having some trouble with my own snot and tears, because something about how drugged she was and the way her head dangled; something about her sores, her diaper, her missing fur, kept my stupid tears flowing. Her ears were enormous, much bigger than her head. They accentuated her gauntness. I blew my nose into one of my own cloths and commanded myself to narrow my focus. One thing at a time.

I tucked her back into my coat. When was she going to wake up? Eyeing my supplies on the floor—the basin and kettle, Giddon's soap, his towel now blotted with blood, the jar of ointment, the bandages, the bleeding cloths—I consolidated everything into the basin, shoved it under his bed, and left it there. I pushed my sister's water barrel against the wall, where it was hidden behind hanging clothing. It all seemed difficult to return or explain, without advertising that I was doing something unusual. Giddon would be puzzled the next time he came to his cabin, assuming he found any of it, but Giddon is the type to try to figure something out rather than make a fuss about it. I would explain when I could.

I checked that the fox was warm and breathing inside my coat.

Then I hardened my mouth, squared my shoulders, and went to spy on Kera.

35.

ALL DAY, I made myself invisible. I skipped meals, snacking on the food in my pockets. It was the simplest plan, since on top of everything else, I didn't want to have to deal with the social aftermath of the scene I'd made last night.

From the afterdeck, I watched Kera working in the wheelhouse. Then she disappeared into the crew quarters for a while and I went to my office, where I did very little translating and mostly just strained my ears for the sound of her leaving her cabin. I'd finally stopped crying. While I waited for something to happen, I dribbled water over the fox's mouth from a cup I'd stolen from the salon. It was hard to know what to plan for. I kept the fox safe and thought it through.

Linta Massera? I asked the pages. *Do you have any answers?*

But Linta was merely performing a series of tedious zilfium-related calculations while waiting for the arrival of LV, who'd gone out. "WHEN will LV return and rescue me from my boredom?" she wrote, which made me wonder who LV was really. Just a colleague, or also a friend? A relation? How old? Man, woman? Where was LV the day I caused the explosion that killed Linta? Did I leave behind someone who's now grieving?

Finally, Kera went on deck again. I followed her, slipping onto the afterdeck once more. A coil of fat rope sits near the rail there, called the dock line. When the ship's at port, the dock line secures her to the dock. I can pretend to be a second coil of slightly girl-shaped dock line, as long as no one pays too close attention.

Finally, in midafternoon, Kera climbed the ladder to the afterdeck with a lamp. As always, she raked the decks with her gaze. Then she snuck down into the hold.

I considered following her, confronting her, but it seemed unwise. Not in the hold, in the dark. Not alone. I waited on the afterdeck for her return.

She came out again looking agitated, her expression sharp and alarmed. I hid from her, still pretending to be dock line, so I wouldn't be the first person her eyes touched with suspicion.

But then I joined her on the main deck a few minutes later, approaching her carefully, because she was yanking lines from their pins, unraveling them, then winding them up again, with ferocity, as if correcting some outrage of slovenliness.

"Do you need help?" I asked.

"I can't bear sloppy work," she said, not even looking at me. "This is the ship of a queen!"

The lines she was tearing apart looked neat enough to me. "It might be my fault," I said. "I'm just learning, and I might be the one who wound them wrong," which was a lie. I hadn't been winding any lines. I wanted to see if I could touch her conscience.

"Oh," she said, slowing in her work. She looked into my face; I saw regret there. "I'm sorry, Hava. I didn't know that." Then her eyes slid down to the lump in my coat, which I wasn't hiding from her. Briefly, she froze. Then continued working.

"What's that in your coat?" she asked casually.

"It's the queen's fox," I said. "Sometimes he likes my company."

"Oh? Can I see him?" she said, just as if that was a normal thing to ask anyone ever.

"Um, sure, I guess," I said, sliding my top coat buttons open and leaning toward her. "He's half-asleep."

She peered in. I knew she couldn't see anything. My breasts aren't much, but they're enough to hide an emaciated fox. "Very nice of you," she said stiffly, leaning back.

"Thanks," I said. "Could I try again with these lines?"

"Certainly," she said, then deposited a heavy coil of rope onto my arm and sped away with her mouth twisted hard. I wondered if she had any idea how strangely she was behaving. Sometimes guilty people panic and lose perspective.

It made me wonder what else she might do.

Fox? I called out.

Yes? he responded after a moment, grumpily. *Hava? What do you want? You feel anxious.*

Did I wake you?

Why are you anxious? You may always wake me for matters pertaining to the queen's safety.

Stuffy little fox. *What about for matters pertaining to* your *safety?*

Sure, those too.

Stay away from Kera today, I said.

Why?

Just do it, I said. *Don't let her see you.*

I insist that you tell me why.

I will, eventually, I said.

It's not reasonable to be both dictatorial and secretive.

Don't you ever keep secrets from anyone in the course of your duty to protect the queen?

He grumbled, which felt like noisy, popping bubbles in my brain. *I keep secrets from those I can't trust. You can trust me.*

I'm still figuring out what's going on, I said. *And I'm working out what to tell everyone.* Then I stopped, annoyed at my own instinct to justify things. *I'm trying to keep you safe,* I added hotly, which was true. Kera harms foxes.

There are people you can trust, Hava, he said.

Sure, like a mind-reading fox who reports to my sister. *I'll explain soon.* Or someone will, I added to myself, for the fox in my coat was going to wake up eventually. After that, concealment would be beyond my control. I hoped she would explain some things to me. I hoped she would trust me, let me help. But I didn't know what she was going to do. And once she woke up, her secret would no longer be mine.

36.

GIDDON FOUND ME on the afterdeck after dinner.

"Hava?" he said, marching right up to my clever dock line disguise. "What's going on?"

"Nothing," I said, revealing myself, but hiding the lump in my coat.

"Nothing! Why is there a basin full of bandages sliding around the floor of my cabin? And why is my towel bloody? Are you hurt?"

"No."

He made a noise of exasperation. "You expect me to believe that, when it looks like you performed surgery on yourself in my cabin, you've been missing all day, *and* you're hiding your abdomen from me this very moment? Are you really okay?"

I rose to my feet, then jumped up and down and slapped my hands against my abdomen, to either side of the little fox. "If I had an injured abdomen," I said, "could I do this? While looking happy?" I added, giving him a big, toothy smile.

"Stop it!" he said. "Tell me what's going on!"

"I'm fine, Giddon. You can see for yourself."

"You're hiding what I can see!"

"Bully!"

He didn't say "brat" back at me, which wasn't a good sign. Instead he turned and marched away, his mouth twisted with unhappiness. I suspected he'd go to my sister next, but I also suspected he wouldn't tell her about it, not wanting to burden her on one of her seasick days. Giddon is often an excellent unwilling ally.

Then, as I crouched down again, the little fox inside my coat stirred and stretched.

My heart leaped.

Fox? I said to her, eagerly, gently. *Are you all right?*

Thirsty, came a faint voice, a half-unconscious voice, reaching out with its need.

I rushed down to the main deck, then went inside and down the passenger ladder. I snuck to Giddon's cabin, slipped in, fumbled through darkness to the place on the floor where I'd left the water barrel, relieved to find it still hiding behind his things.

Then I opened my coat and cradled the little fox on my arm. She was floppy still, weak and helpless. I opened the nozzle at the bottom of the barrel, dribbling water into the palm of my hand. I held my hand to her mouth like a cup.

When the cold water touched her nose, she started. Then her tiny tongue emerged and lapped at the water in my hand and I began to cry again.

A few minutes later, I'd returned her to my coat and we were upstairs in the salon.

At the buffet, I scavenged for soft, filling foods, keeping my shoulder turned toward the tables where a few sailors ate. I heard Jacky's sharp voice and knew he meant me to notice. I ignored him. He's a thief who has my bird-girl.

Chocolate, she said, her voice a weak trickle in my mind. *Chocolate pie,* she said. *Chocolate cheesecake. Chocolate tart.*

I don't think there's any chocolate today, I tried to explain, but the fox kept naming chocolate things. Inside the cup of my own hand, I mixed some peas and some mashed potatoes, then went out on deck again.

Bad, she said, when I thrust my hand against her face. *Yuck.* But she ate it. Her tongue was rough against my palm.

Are you warm enough? I asked, feeling inside my coat to confirm that her fur had dried from her bath. She did feel warm to me, and dry.

Warm, she said.

Are you scared of heights?

Heights.

Are you just repeating what I say?

Say.

I decided to climb the mast with her inside my coat. It was the one place where I could think, and figure out what on earth to do.

HER COHERENCE DID not improve.

Do you understand that you're safe? I asked her, over and over.

Safe, she would respond. Her thoughts were faint breaths in my mind.

Can you tell me what happened?

Happened, she would respond.

And then, finally, after a long time of this, she paused when I asked that question. Then she said, *No.*

You can't tell me what happened?

No.

Okay. Are you warm enough?

Yes.

Is there anything you need?

Another pause. Then, instead of words, I was awash in the sea of her sadness and confusion. *Who,* she said. *Where. No more pain. Tired. Stop. Hurts. I hate you!*

You're safe now, I said. *I promise. No more pain.*

Her words disappeared again. The sea of confusion remained. Then she seemed to fall asleep.

IT WAS A black, starless, moonless night. I sat in the dark, at the top of the highest platform.

With my back to the mast and my knees propped up to shield my stomach, and with my arms wrapped around my knees, she was protected from the wind. She breathed evenly, sleeping as we swayed. One of the hooks of my harness dinged against its metal shroud every time we tipped toward starboard, like a bell chiming.

I wondered, was there something wrong with me if I was very, very happy?

Also, is there something wrong with me if my happiness, when it comes, brings with it a tidal wave of grief?

I don't cry much anymore. I used to, in the time before I started working for my sister, which was about five years ago, when I was sixteen. I was at loose ends then. Few living people knew I existed, certainly not Bitterblue. I moved around the kingdom, watched other people's lives, as I'd always done. I stole what I needed. Sometimes I was like Trina and hired out my Grace, sneaking on someone else's behalf, if the job was interesting and they offered me enough money.

Then I did a job for a lord from central Monsea whom I should've known better than to trust. Lord Danzhol. He told me he wanted to rescue Queen Bitterblue from her life of drudgery, but what he actually did was put a knife to her throat and try to kidnap her. In fact, he almost killed her. When I realized what I'd helped him to do, I went through a stretch during which the very sight of my sister, the very sound of her voice, would choke me up with crying. She sought me out where I hid in her sculpture gallery, among my mother's sculptures. She guessed who my father was. When I begged her to keep that a secret, she agreed. She understood that I wanted nothing of titles or royalty, that I couldn't bear the attention. She forgave me, and gave me a home. I grew useful. I stopped crying.

Now I seem to have turned into Giddon, who cries at the drop of a hat.

Hava? came the voice of my sister's fox, from somewhere far away. He startled me.

What? I said, steeling myself.

He took a moment to answer. His voice was tentative, confused. *Earlier today, why did you ask me if there were any other foxes on board?*

That was it, then. He was beginning to sense her consciousness. I closed my mind, shut him out, refused to answer. I was not—I am not—ready for this.

For a few more dings of my hook against metal, I held on to the fox, keeping her safe, still crying.

And then, of course, I began to understand.

Whatever Kera is doing with this fox, it's too bizarre—and too criminal—for me to handle alone. So why am I sneaking around, keeping her secret?

It's because I want her in my coat. I want to be the one saving her. I want to nurse her back to health, be needed by her, avenge her myself.

I'm serving myself. And I'm risking her safety. It's time to tell the queen and the captain what Kera has done.

It's strange, how much clearer my thoughts are up here.

I began to climb slowly down.

As I passed below the second platform, the lantern on the main deck went out.

37.

It's surprising, the difference between a dim light and no light. I've never credited that lamp with helping much. Now I realize how it makes the sails glow gray, orienting my position, while the lines and boards trace dark patterns against the sky.

In darkness, I descended by feel. With every step, my feet swam below me, trying to find ratlines.

Was I prepared for what happened when I reached the deck? I think my instincts were, because I touched down lightly and listened hard. Some intuition told me to reposition the fox inside my coat and harness, pushing her little body to my right hip so I could shield her with my right arm. Some other impulse told me to confirm I was alone. I stretched out my left hand.

Someone seized my wrist and pulled.

"What have you done?" Kera's voice demanded, low and harsh.

Everything inside me surged; I was ready. "What do you mean?" I cried, trying to reach the knife I wear in a holster in my boot. I couldn't get to it. "What's wrong? You're hurting me!"

"Don't play stupid," she said, twisting my arm behind me in that way that makes you feel like your shoulder's going to explode. "I heard Giddon asking Coran why there were bloody medical supplies in his room!"

"So?" I cried. "Is that a reason to pull my arm off?"

"Where is she?" she said. "What did you do with her?"

She reached around me to feel my front. I let her grope at my flat belly, then decided it was time to go wild.

"What is wrong with you? Let me go!" I screamed, twisting, punching, kicking. Kera was startled. When she tried to take hold of my arms again, she got a fist in her mouth for her troubles.

Shouting in surprise, she seized me by my harness and hoisted me over her shoulder. Scared the fox would be crushed, I scrabbled at Kera, tried to grab her throat. She carried me to the rail. Understanding, I let her, for I was hoping she didn't know what I knew, that the harness was still attached by one hook to the shrouds.

She threw me over the side. The harness jerked tight, then unwound its short, bundled length of rope, the way it's supposed to do if you slip in the rigging.

The rope stopped my fall, shocking me with its sudden jerk. Then the roll of the ship slammed me against the portside hull, the sharp frame of a porthole stabbing into my face. In absolute darkness, I grabbed on to the porthole's protruding screws, and it's good that I did, because it turned out Kera did know. The tension of my harness suddenly eased, then my hook appeared, smashing into the bridge of my nose.

My eyes streaming with tears, I pounded my head on the porthole. I had no free hands.

Nothing happened. All I heard was water below me, moving fast. I could see nothing. I pounded harder, the pain in my forehead sharp and bright.

Then the porthole creaked open. As I grabbed for its edge, Linny stared out at me with eyes the size of saucers.

"What the—" he cried.

It was the room I'd trashed, which might have been funny, in different circumstances. The porthole was too small for me to fit through and the ship was rolling back in the other direction. I was going to fall off.

"Grab my arm!" I whispered. "Quick!"

With his help levering my arm inside the porthole, I groped inside my coat, snatched the fox, and shoved her at Linny.

"What the—" Linny repeated, holding the fox to his chest with one hand as Jacky came up looming behind him, gaping at me in astonishment.

"What are you doing out there, dardya?" Jacky said.

"Take this," I said, grabbing the rope attached to my harness, shoving it in at them, "quick, and find the end. Hold on to it. Then thread the rope out here again and close the porthole on it. Quick! No questions!" I said as they both babbled and stared. "Do it! Faster!" I hissed as Linny passed the fox to Jacky and fumbled with the rope, finding the hook at the end. "Then, as soon as you can, go out on deck and help me back on board, but get rid of Kera first! Don't let her see!"

After what seemed like a year, Linny pushed the rest of the rope back out through the porthole. He grabbed at me, flustered, confused. Fighting him off, I levered myself outside again, clinging to the screws of the porthole's frame.

"Now close the porthole on the rope!" I said, but Linny seemed incapable.

"Your face is bleeding!" he said, as if that mattered.

"Do it!" I cried.

With grim satisfaction, Jacky stepped forward and closed the porthole.

Alone in the darkness, clinging to the screws, I waited, looking up at the rail. Because I knew Kera was coming back. She would light the lamp and sweep it along the side of the ship. She would confirm I was gone, like any self-respecting murderer would do. And my Grace doesn't trick people if there's nothing believable to turn into, or if they already know I'm there. So I needed to hide for real.

I saw a glow approaching.

When it got close, I let go and dropped down into the sea.

38.

Have you ever been so cold that you felt like your body was made of stabbing?

Have you ever had to suppress a desperate urge to inhale, knowing it would kill you, while not inhaling kills you too, just slower?

Have you ever had to hold yourself underwater in freezing darkness, dragged by a ship, waiting for a glow of light above the surface to recede, frightened that a homicidal maniac will see the rope attaching you to a porthole?

These are ridiculous questions. Sorry. It was a ridiculous experience.

Come on, Linny, I kept thinking, over and over. *Come on, Jacky. Come on, Linny. Come get me.*

Why would they come get me?

The glow of light above receded. All I wanted to do was pull on my rope and explode above the surface, but some smart, desperate part of my brain forced me to rise slowly, so Kera wouldn't notice or hear. Then it huddled me, gasping, against the ship's hull, where there was nothing but my rope to cling to. I knew I needed to get all the way above the water. Cold water kills. With everything I had left, I tried to climb higher on the rope.

I can climb a rope. It's a thing I learned long ago, in Monsea. But it turns out I cannot climb a freezing, wet rope with freezing wet hands and wooden feet while a tipping, sliding ship drags me, and my body grows more and more numb from the cold of the Brumal Sea.

I held on, mostly submerged. Refusing to give up. Fighting to think. At least I'd saved the fox. That was something, right? Then I heard voices, cries. I heard Jacky shouting.

I must have lost consciousness, for when lights appeared and someone began to haul me up by my rope, I couldn't tell who it was, and I certainly couldn't help. Was this my rescue from the cavern in Winterkeep? Had I just caused an explosion, and killed Linta Massera? But then why was I so cold?

Someone was beside me on a metal ladder that hadn't been there before and I couldn't understand where it had come from. Linny. Linny was beside me, and his arm was around me, lifting me. This wasn't Winterkeep. Hands reached for me from above, but when they grabbed hold, I couldn't feel them on my body. I flopped over the rail onto the deck of the *Monsea*, caught by more hands. Someone bent over me and, teeth chattering, I looked into the face of Ozul.

She seemed calm, certain of what to do. "We'll bring her to our cabin," she said. Sorit and Noa appeared to either side of me, lifting and supporting me. Behind them was a commotion: Kera was thrashing in Navi's and Lisa's grip and screaming, while Jacky yelled expletives in her face. Whatever. Sorit and Noa carried me, more or less, across the deck to the hatch that led to the crew quarters, then got me down the ladder and into their cabin. They shut the boys out—Linny and Ollie were hovering—and stripped me of my wet things. Then Ozul and Noa put me in bed between them, under blankets, and held on to me tight. Sorit leaned over us, saying things I couldn't understand because she was speaking in Keepish and I seemed to have lost my Keepish. I focused, hard. It was something about how they mustn't warm me too fast, or the cold blood in my fingers and toes would rush to my heart and shock me to death.

I began to be able to feel my arms and legs.

After that, everything hurt so much that I knew I must be dying. It's ridiculous, how many times you can think you're dying and you're not. It makes me wonder what dying actually feels like.

I wish I could say that I fell asleep while they warmed me, but I didn't. I was awake for every stab and ache of my body coming back to life. Was this what it was like for Bitterblue, when her kidnappers fished her out of the Brumal Sea? Was anyone who rescued her kind? For a long time, Noa and Ozul held on to me while Sorit made me drink water, pouring it into me just as I'd tried to pour it into the fox, then wiping my face of water, snot, and tears. She cleaned the cut on the bridge of my nose and one on my forehead, bandaged them, and rubbed my hands and feet between her hands, which were hot as fire on my skin. *It hurts,* I thought. *It hurts.* Then I realized Sorit was saying, "Yes, I know it does, sweetie, I'm sorry," which meant I was speaking aloud.

"Can you tell us what happened?" Ozul asked in my ear, which made me laugh a little, with a laugh that sounded like a bleat. I'd asked the fox the same thing. Her answer had been *No.*

"Yes," I managed to say, in Keepish. "I will." But first, I asked if my fox was okay.

"We don't know anything about a fox," Ozul said.

"You have to find her!" I cried, then asked if the queen was okay. Why would I even ask that? What could possibly be wrong with Bitterblue now? They told me that everyone was okay except Kera, who was being held prisoner, though none of them had a clear idea why, so it would be helpful if I could explain what had happened.

"She tried to kill me," I said. "She threw me into the sea."

At that, they all went quiet, glancing at each other with big eyes.

"She's been keeping a blue fox drugged in the hold," I shot at them, convinced they didn't believe me. "I found the fox. Then Kera tried to kill me. You have to find the fox before Kera does. Can you ask Jacky? Linny gave her to Jacky!"

"We'll ask Jacky," said Ozul soothingly, the way you talk to an illogical person you don't believe. "It's okay, Hava. Here. Let's get you into some warm clothes."

She gave me a scarlet knit sweater and a pair of rough trousers that were long enough for me, but too wide. She helped me dress. She wound one of her scarves around my neck (gold) and wrapped me up in blankets, her hands so warm every time she touched me. Then there was a knock at the door and Linny, Jacky, and Ollie crammed themselves in, asking questions, hovering over me, taking up my air and my space. "What is wrong with you, dardya?" Jacky was saying. "If Kera was after you, why didn't you just let her see that we were helping you and the jig was up? Why didn't you send one of us on deck to stop her? Why did you have to be so dramatic and half drown yourself?"

Then I realized that Linny was crouched beside my bed, cradling the sleeping fox in his arms. I reached out for her and he passed her to me. His hands were warm too, his eyes soft and amber, and he smelled like salt. The fox smelled like soap. Tears began to trickle down my face, and then I started laughing, because Jacky's questions were funny. Of course he was right. I could've done either of those things. But I bet Jacky's never watched a cruel person do something irrational and deadly, just to get what he wants. Kera wanted me dead. The safest escape from someone like that is to pretend you're already dead.

There was another knock. This time, Bitterblue, Annet, and Giddon appeared, which sent everyone else flying out of the room.

"You stay here, Ozul," Annet said, so Ozul stayed, receding into the background.

Bitterblue rushed to me and climbed onto my bed, touching my wet hair, making noises of distress about my plight. "Hava!" she kept saying. "Oh, Hava." Pretty quickly, her noises turned to moans about the swaying of the ship. I pulled her to me with one arm, as I've seen Giddon do many times. She allowed this, resting her head on my chest. I had my fox safe in one arm and my sister safe in the other and it seemed possible to begin to believe the worst was over.

My story, once I started it, produced absolute silence. Annet watched me intently and Giddon, propping a hand on the bunk above, grew paler and more lock-jawed as I spoke. When I explained what it had been like to find the fox in her crate, I choked. Bitterblue's arms came around me. When I told about Kera picking me up and throwing me overboard, her arms tightened, becoming sure and strong.

"She will be punished," she said.

"Where is she now?" I said.

"Navi, Ranin, and Mart are guarding her in the wheelhouse," said Annet crisply. "You say she carried a glass syringe?"

"Yes," I said. "Do you believe my story?"

"I believe you, habpva."

The pressure in my chest lessened. She wouldn't use that name if she disbelieved me.

"How did you meet Kera?" Giddon asked Annet. "Why did you hire her?"

"She came to me in Ledra," said Annet. "Told me she was a Monsean sailor who'd worked mainly on trade ships. She had good references, and shipwreck experience too. I wanted a weather and survival expert."

"I don't think she's from where she says she's from," I said.

"Yes," said Bitterblue softly. "You told us so, Hava."

"We'll find out why she was hurting that fox," said Annet. "And we're about to lose our first mate for the duration of the voyage, so I'm promoting Navi. Ozul," she said, turning clear but troubled eyes to the tall young woman who was standing against the opposite bunk, pushing her braids out of her face. "You're our new second mate."

Ozul looked like the sun was shining from inside her body. "Thank you, Captain," she said.

Annet nodded, then adjusted her glasses. "Now, Hava," she said. "We'll be keeping Kera imprisoned. As captain, it's my duty to inform her of the charges we're pressing against her. She kidnapped and tortured a Keepish blue fox. She assaulted you and tried to kill you. Am I forgetting anything?"

"Yes," I said thickly. "She almost killed the fox too. She didn't know I had her in my coat, but that doesn't mean it wasn't her fault."

"Very well," said Annet. "I'll think about what charge is appropriate. Now, let's get you back to your own cabin and into your own bed. Do you need help?"

"No," I said quickly, before Giddon could become the noble hero and try to carry me anywhere. "But could I—could I have our cabin to myself for a few minutes, Bitterblue?"

"Of course," she said.

I made it into my bed before I started sobbing, desperate, breathless, choking cries that wracked my body. I took care not to hold the fox too tightly. I was afraid of hurting her in my grief.

Then I must've fallen asleep, because I can't remember anything after that.

39.

ONCE, A LONG time ago, I got it in my mind to kill the king.

It was after he killed my mother. I was going to pretend I was one of the sculptures in his art gallery, wait for him to turn his back to me, then stab him in the heart from behind. I was eight. Can you imagine? I would've had to stand on tiptoe to reach his heart.

But then, the next time he visited the gallery, he wasn't alone. He was with Bitterblue's mother, Queen Ashen. In my hearing, while they admired my mother's sculptures, he told Ashen lies about my mother. About what a bad woman she'd been, about how she'd deserved to die. He told Ashen true things too: about how he'd discovered that my mother had been hiding *me* from him. He made Ashen understand that I existed, and that she must find me for him.

His Grace was too strong for me. Believing that I must be found, I faltered, and turned back into myself.

Ashen saw me. Her face went blank with shock and she reached out to me behind his back, I don't know whether to save me, or to deliver me to him. Her eyes were wild, frightened, and frightening; she waved her hand as if to shoo me away; I turned back into a sculpture.

Bewildered, shaken, I stayed where I was. He began to do things to her. I had to watch him hurt her, hear her confused noises as he told her she was enjoying it. I did nothing to stop him. It was awful. I try not to remember it. I've never told Bitterblue anything about it.

Finally, he left her there, huddled against a hanging on the wall. After a while, when I felt able, I crawled away, found the exit. I left her there alone, mute and crying against the wall. I'd meant to revenge my mother and instead failed even to help my sister's mother.

WHEN I WOKE the next morning in my bed on the *Monsea*, Bitterblue was snoring softly nearby. I hadn't drowned. She hadn't drowned. I watched her for a moment, confirming it.

Beside my head, my fox was still sleeping. Shyly, I touched her fur. Her hide was patchy and uneven, her distended belly awkward-looking on such a tiny body. I wondered how long I would sleep, if I were kept drugged and starved in a box for weeks and weeks.

A movement on Bitterblue's bed caught my attention. The golden eyes of her fox glowed in the faint morning light.

Is she okay? my sister's fox asked, in an awed voice I'd never heard him use before. A sad voice that made me curious how much of the story Bitterblue had told him.

I hope so, I said.

Has she told you her name?

She's barely told me anything.

I hope she wakes up soon, he said. *I want to meet her.*

It'll be nice for her to have you to talk to, I admitted.

Kera is locked in the anteroom to the wheelhouse, he said. *The queen has given me permission to spy on her. She's cold and miserable, in case that gives you any satisfaction.*

It does give me satisfaction.

I never saw my father punished for all the things he did. But I will get my revenge on Kera.

40.

WHEN I WOKE again, the bridge of my nose throbbed and someone was touching my hair.

It was Bitterblue, sitting on the edge of my bed, tending to me the way Giddon always tends to her. The pupils of her eyes were enormous.

"I missed Liel bringing the water?" I said.

"He was quiet."

"Who made your tea?"

"I can put a teabag and some boiling water into a cup, Hava," she said, smiling.

"Well, you shouldn't waste one of your rauha days like this."

"Don't tell a queen what to do. How do you feel?"

I felt like I could lie there forever while the ship slid from side to side and Bitterblue stroked my hair. "My hands and feet ache," I said. "The cut on my face aches. Everything hurts and I'm tired. But I'm fine."

"You did well," she said.

I steeled myself for the *but*. Just because my sister is drunk on rauha doesn't mean she won't lecture me about keeping secrets and always doing everything on my own.

But then there wasn't a *but*. Instead, she tucked her chin against her chest and said gently, "We know a little bit more about what

Kera's been up to, Hava. The drug she was giving the fox was strong. Navi found it among her things. Coran doesn't know its effects on foxes, but he said that if a human took it like that every day for weeks, he might expect a number of problems. Brain hemorrhage, nerve damage. Neurological damage generally."

My fox was a warm, soft pressure against my side. I reached my hand to touch her with a tender stroke as careful and deliberate as the knife I intend to pull across the soft skin at Kera's throat.

"What's the anteroom of the wheelhouse?" I said.

"It's basically a closet. It's behind the wheelhouse, on the afterdeck."

Yes, I've noticed that little door. I'm going to inject her with her own medicine every day, then taunt her, whenever she wakes, with the neurological damage it's doing. "Are her hands and feet restrained?"

"I have a sudden disinclination to answer these questions," my sister said. "We're to stay away from that room, Hava, you understand?"

"Of course," I said. "I don't really want to hurt her. I just like the thought of it."

She made a little noise of understanding, then nodded. I was silent, knowing I'd placated her. I'll wait until the afterdeck is empty, then go into Kera's closet, waking her with a shake of the shoulder, standing above her with a lamp and a syringe, giving her a smile that'll tell her what's coming.

A voice in my ear said, *Girl.*

No, not in my ear, but in my mind. My fantasy popped like a bubble. I felt empty, and sore, and sad.

Fox? I said. *Is that you?*

My girl, said the fox.

Does that mean me? I said as my foolish, embarrassing hope rose. *Am I your girl?*

Water, she said. *Chocolate.*

"My fox is hungry," I said to Bitterblue.

"Your fox?" said Bitterblue. "Is she talking to you? Has she offered to bond to you?"

"She's talking," I said, "but she hasn't said anything about bonding. She seems pretty confused."

I see," said Bitterblue. "Well, remember, most people on this ship believe foxes can only talk to one person. If her mind clears, this fox will think we think that. In the meantime, if you're known to be talking with her, people will assume you're bonded."

"Right."

"We can figure all that out later," said Bitterblue. "Adventure can help."

OZUL'S CLOTHES ARE all too wide for me, but she's lent me her coat till mine is dry. Her coat! She's bulked herself up in wool sweaters and more of her Keepish scarves and a lighter jacket I'm sure isn't warm enough, but she keeps insisting she's fine.

Her coat has a belt at the waist like mine, so I can tuck the fox inside, though she's swimming around in there. It's a thick Keepish wool smelling of the sea; warm, but not as warm as my own Keepish furs. A rich woman we knew in Winterkeep, a strange woman full of secrets and plans named Sara Varana, gave Keepish furs to me, Bitterblue, Giddon, and the advisers, as parting gifts. "If you must sail in midwinter," she said, "at least you'll be warm."

I don't think I appreciated Keepish generosity then. I'm a little overwhelmed by it now, as Ozul walks around coatless.

When I stepped into the galley, Liel put down the knife he was using to slice a chicken. Wiping his hands on his apron, he said, "What can I get you, Hava?"

"The fox keeps asking me for chocolate," I said.

He studied me with bright blue eyes. "I take it she's that lump in Ozul's coat?"

"Yes."

"Do you like chocolate?"

"Doesn't everyone like chocolate?"

"I'll make a chocolate cake at lunch," he said, seeming to decide it in that moment. "For now, go to that counter and open the small blue tin on the left."

When I brought a piece of chocolate into the salon, I found Giddon scribbling at a table. I sat near him, but not too near, because I didn't want him fussing at me. Extracting the fox from Ozul's coat and placing her on the bench beside me, I broke off pieces of chocolate and fed them to her, pieces so tiny that I thought of Linta's theory of indivisible particles. Then I tried to take the thought somewhere clever and metaphorical, about what we're all made of; then let it go. I'm too exhausted for Linta Massera today.

After a moment, Giddon said, "How are you feeling, Hava?"

"Better," I said, resting a piece of chocolate on the middle of my own tongue. "Fine. Sore," I said, speaking around it while its rich sweetness melted and turned my mouth to happiness.

He watched me for a moment with an uncertain expression, not saying anything. I could see the edges of my own bandage in my peripheral vision between my eyes. Is my face discolored and bruised now? Does it distract from the colors of my eyes, or accentuate them? *Do I look uglier than ever?* I asked the fox, who was eating piece after piece of chocolate, slowly, with closed eyes and an expression of intense concentration.

My girl, she said, not looking at me.

I focused on her, to make the silence stretching between me and Giddon less palpable. I wonder sometimes if he tries to bully me into talking by unnerving me with silence. Maybe he forgets how much of my time I spend in rooms with other people, pretending I don't exist.

The moment the fox finished her chocolate, I tucked her back into Ozul's coat, then stood.

Giddon's voice hit my shoulders as I turned to go. "Hava? Could we talk for a minute?"

I turned back carefully, my face blank. "About what?"

"Well," he said, his own expression even. "You left a bloodied towel in my cabin. I didn't know where it'd come from, so I asked Coran, and Kera overheard us. I feel like it's partly my fault she tried to kill you."

"Of course it's not your fault."

"Okay, but, Hava, if you're going to involve me, you need to *tell* me, you know? I could've helped. Or at least not made it worse. Imagine if you'd died!"

"I didn't die."

"But maybe if you'd told me what was going on, it wouldn't have happened at all."

I was beginning to wonder if this was less about Giddon's concern for me and more about him wanting to know things. "You mean because we're a team?" I said. "Do you tell me everything going on with you?"

"Well," he said, with a touch of exasperation. "I'm pretty sure I'd tell you if I thought someone on the ship might be going to attack me."

"Sure, because you'd want to use my Grace," I said. "Right? When it comes down to it, I'm a useful employee. Right? Bitterblue is my boss. Maybe you think you're my boss too?"

A rare flash of anger hardened Giddon's dark eyes. "Are you kidding me right now, Hava?" he said. "After all we've been through together?"

"Maybe I need your permission to use my Grace too, just like I'm supposed to get Bitterblue's?"

"What!" he cried. "Bitterblue doesn't expect you to come to her for permission!"

"I mean, I never do," I said scornfully. "But I'm supposed to."

"I'm certain she has no such expectation."

"What would you know about it?" I cried. "She told me it's her expectation! Like, five years ago!"

"Well, I'm certain it's not anymore! She's talked to me about it!"

He was puffed up and earnest and hurt, and I don't think he even noticed there was anything rotten in what he'd said. "She's talked to *you* about it?" I said, and suddenly I was shouting. "She's talked to *you*? Why hasn't she talked to *me*?"

"Hava," he called after me as I turned to go. "I care about you!" he said, which made me even angrier, because he cares about my sister, and she cares about him. How could they care about me? They don't know me. I don't exist.

I went out on deck, where I can always commune with the sails, the wind, and the sea, and know they aren't disappointed in me and my choices. I climbed to the afterdeck and sat on the dock line, cradling the lump inside Ozul's coat, studying the door to the anteroom that abutted the wheelhouse.

There's a thrill to knowing she's on the other side of that door. I can imagine her cold and cramped, weary of the dark. How often is she being fed? Would people in the wheelhouse be able to hear her yelling from the pain I caused her?

"Hava?" Annet called up from the main deck. "Do you feel well enough to climb?"

41.

I LEFT MY FOX with my sister's fox on deck, but don't imagine I was thrilled about that.

I'll make sure she stays warm, he told me eagerly, jumping into a lifeboat, then choosing a spot under one of the benches.

I tucked my fox next to him, on his lee side, to protect her from the wind. She opened her eyes once and closed them again, the first flash of gold I'd seen, which startled me. *Will you be all right, Fox?*

She's not as frail as you think, he said.

Okay, I said doubtfully, wishing I had time to find her a blanket.

Oh, just go! he said. *She's safer with me than with you! I'm telepathic and I have sharp teeth!*

All right, all right.

To my surprise, Annet wanted to climb with me. I've never seen her climb before; she went first and moved slowly. I think she could tell I was tired. We stopped often so she could "assess the sails and lines," or so she said.

My old ankle injury was hurting, kind of a lot. I think maybe it's not the best idea to climb the rigging the morning after you get bashed around and almost die of hypothermia. But some things are worth it.

"When you're carrying all sail for long stretches of time," she shouted down to me, "lines fray and the canvas tears. I could send someone up to tell me what needs to be done, but sometimes I like my own eyes on the details. There's no job on a ship a captain should be unwilling to do."

"Does 'carrying all sail' mean that all the sails are unfurled?" I shouted back.

"Yes, that's right. We've been taking full advantage of these southeasterly winds. What a beautiful stretch we've had!"

She stopped near the top of the course, which is the lowest sail on the foremast. Usually, my focus at this point is up, up, farther up, but Annet was looking out, along the yard the course hangs from.

"Aren't the winds ever plain-old easterly?" I asked.

"We're making progress west, habpva," she said, a smile lighting her face. "You don't need to fear."

"But we've gone farther north?"

"We'll enter a current soon that flows southwest, counteracting the wind. I've sailed this route before, as have many others. But yes. We've gone farther north."

"How far?"

"We'll be able to answer that question the next time the clouds clear. We've had no sun or stars for quite a few days, and we need them to determine our precise location. But it's never as simple as making a straight line west from Winterkeep, you know. Not with the winds and currents of the Brumal Sea."

"Southwest," I said.

"What?"

"Monsea is southwest of Winterkeep."

"Hava," said Annet, chuckling. "In fact, the Dells, our actual destination, is west-southwest of Winterkeep. Do you think I don't know where we're going?"

"I just want to understand," I said, but it's more than that. North means ice fields, and uncharted seas. It means water where, if someone fell in, the cold would kill them within minutes. It means Pikkia, the nation north of the Dells, where someone is always at war with someone else, or so I've been told. I've never been there. I don't want to go there. I'm tired of winter. It's been cold since we reached Winterkeep months ago, and it's only gotten colder.

"A sailor needs to learn to adjust the plan," Annet said. "Winds and currents are stronger and more stubborn than wood and canvas. When something out here pushes, we don't just push back. We learn it's more productive to give way a little. Do you understand that?"

"I guess so," I said doubtfully.

Annet looked out across the low sky, her glasses reflecting gray clouds. Her cheeks were rosy and her breath made puffs of steam. She shrugged. She looked so happy up here, sitting on a ratline while the boat swayed.

"It's a directive for setting the sails," she said, "but it's also an attitude. Flexibility, give-and-take. You seem to like the ship, habpva. You seem to like the challenges. I've watched you lie in that lifeboat, smiling at the sails. It could be that you have an aptitude for sailing. But it also requires a certain attitude."

Which I don't have?

She didn't say it, and there was no reproach in her tone. Still, I was stung. No one likes my attitude, not Giddon, not my sister, not my sister's fox. Not even Annet, who thinks I'm too rigid, too nervous about going north.

"I live on land," I said, trying to create a defense that wouldn't sound too defensive. "At the Monsean court. We don't have winds or currents there. It's made of glass and stone."

Annet was chuckling again. "Yes, I guess that's true. Do you see that bit of torn canvas?" she said, pointing to an edge of the course that was flapping free. "Do you want to learn how to climb along the yard, and do something useful?"

"Yes."

"Good. This is a trickier kind of climbing, more of a sideways shuffle along footropes. There are fewer places to hook in, and the footropes are looser than the ratlines. Ready?"

No, not really, not while weary and hurting. "Yes."

She sent me along the yard first, so that I could be the one to mend the sail when we got there. "If someone else is on the footropes before you," she said cheerfully, "call out to let them know you're stepping on!"

At first I clung tightly to the yard. A loose rope isn't much to balance on far above the deck, on a rocking ship, in a stiff wind. I can't believe Linny and Ozul and Sorit and all of them do this without a harness.

But I did have a harness, and I've learned a thing or two about balance. You can't be stiff and hard with fear. You can't let yourself think you're sure to fall. You have to loosen up, and pretend you're only a handspan above the ground. Why should you fall from the footrope, while you have nice lines to grab on to and the wind is pressing you against the nice, firm yard and you're only a handspan above the ground?

"Good," Annet shouted behind me. "I'm stepping on!"

Then the footrope bounced under me and I wobbled around, squeaking in alarm, clinging to the yard for dear life. She came alongside me. When she handed me a piece of thick thread on a fat needle, I stared at her, flabbergasted.

"What do you expect me to do with this?"

"Patch that tear," she said.

"Up here, while we're moving?"

"It's a small tear," she said. "I'm going to the starboard side to see what repairs are needed. Give a shout if you have questions."

Then the footropes bounced again as she moved away. I stared at the needle in my hand, aghast. I don't know how to sew. I know how to sneak, hide, steal, and press a knife into a man's throat. I used to watch Bitterblue's mother embroider the edges of sheet after sheet, wondering if she noticed her own bleeding fingertips. But I can't do what she could do. Especially with gloves on!

Knowing it was probably stupid to subject my hand to a cold wind the day after I almost died of hypothermia, I pulled my glove off anyway. The next problem was how to let go of my handholds without falling. How to reach down to a flapping piece of sail while balanced on rope.

I decided to try sitting on the footrope. Then I wound my arms through the lines around me like I'd watched Linny do once, as if his limbs were threads on a loom. I bumped my sore forehead on the yard, swore, and kept weaving myself into place. The stupid bandage on the bridge of my nose, hovering in my peripheral vision, was distracting, but I tried to forget about it. I wondered, if Jacky saw me now, would he acknowledge that I was having an authentic experience? No. He wouldn't acknowledge anything. He had my bird-girl and I'd broken his things.

Once I was wound in, I was able to lean out toward the tear in the canvas without feeling certain I was about to die. The tear was small, maybe two handspans long, and in fact, I don't think my lack of sewing experience put me at much of a disadvantage. Imagine a tailor, sewing a shirt. In the picture in your mind, are the pieces of shirt flapping wildly in a stiff wind while the tailor's nose drips into a frozen ocean far below? No? Is a sharp rope cutting into the tailor's bottom? Is she nearly upside down? Is she wearing a too-big coat that's not so warm? Is her seat pitching back and forth, making its best effort to throw her off?

That was what it was like, my first time sewing. It was the ugliest stitch job anyone's ever done, but I managed it, even thinking to tie little knots into each end of the thread so it wouldn't come loose.

It took me so long that Annet climbed the entire rigging and assessed every line and sail on the foremast while I worked. She was waiting for me on the shrouds when I finished. I slid back along the footropes, stiff with cold and exhaustion. She stayed near while I was climbing down. When my feet hit the deck, I was shaking.

"How was that?" she asked, stepping down beside me.

"Fine."

"Did you like it?"

"Yes."

"Hava," she said, unclipping my hooks for me, handing them to me gently. "Do you know you don't need to put on a brave face for me?"

"I'm not changing my face," I said. Then I noticed her surprised expression and realized she wasn't talking about my Grace.

"I liked it," I said, embarrassed, but speaking the truth. I like pleasing Annet, and I like caring for the ship.

"Good."

She left for the wheelhouse, where Navi was standing at the window, watching us.

And what about you? I said to my fox, who was still in the lifeboat, tucked against her friend. She didn't seem to have budged.

We had a very nice nap, my sister's fox said. *Despite my fears you might fall on us.*

I pulled at the straps of my harness with numb fingers, wanting her inside my coat again. Then Linny came down the ladder from the afterdeck. He stooped before me and grabbed my glove, which had fallen. "Good work up there," he said, handing it to me.

"Thanks," I said, doubting my efforts had looked like much. I wished I could ask him to help me out of my harness without seeming weak. I wished I could just leave the harness on and go to sleep.

"Do you need help?" he asked.

"No," I said, automatically.

"You're shaking."

"I'm fine."

Jacky ran down the ladder behind Linny, saw me, and spun away with a contemptuous expression.

Linny watched me as I fought with the harness. When I finally got free, I headed inside with my fox.

Then I crawled into bed and slept for a long time.

42.

I woke in the afternoon.

Giddon was in our cabin visiting Bitterblue, the two of them sitting on her bed, giggling together. Right. Rauha day. I kept still. I couldn't bear to be talked to, or yelled at, or pulled into some joke, or asked how I was.

I'm achy, okay? And tired. My face hurts and my bandages itch. I don't know how far north we are and I hate it. I missed breakfast, probably lunch too, and no one has brought me food the way Giddon always brings a stash for my sister. I could die of scurvy. Who would care?

I care, said the little fox, who'd apparently crawled out of my coat and was sleeping near my feet.

I blinked in surprise, unaware I'd been thinking those thoughts to her. Proud of her for making a sentence.

Then I saw her lying with her chin on her paws, her gold eyes open, watching me.

Oh! Hello! I said.

Hello, she said.

How are you feeling? Did you get enough sleep?

Sleep, she said.

I closed my eyes, feeling the tears rise again. I wanted her to be okay, her brain uninjured. I needed Kera to die. Also, my bed was too hot. I still wore Ozul's coat, my gloves, all my scarves. But there was no way to get comfortable without announcing that I was awake.

I sat up, bracing myself against whatever they had to say.

"Hava," said Giddon. "You slept through lunch. Would you like a chicken pot pie, a piece of chocolate cake, and an orange?"

"Also, Hava!" said Bitterblue. "Giddon told me I've never talked to you about that rule we had. Remember, in the beginning, you were feeling a little—however you were feeling," she said, flinging a hand in the air, "and I made that rule you couldn't use your Grace without my permission? It's been so long. I thought we'd both let it go. But I should've said something! I'm sorry."

She was high, her voice singsongy and her pupils enormous. But she was leaning toward me, gazing at me sympathetically. I could tell she was sincere.

And I did remember how it had happened, now that she reminded me. I'd hired my Grace out to that awful man, Lord Danzhol, who'd tried to hurt her. After that, a bad stretch had followed. I hadn't been sure of my own judgment; I'd want a check on my Grace. *I'd* asked Bitterblue for that rule, because at the time, I'd trusted her more than I trusted myself.

Shame bloomed inside me. "I remember," I said.

"Shall we officially dissolve the rule?" she said. "It's long overdue, right?"

"Yes."

"Oh!" said Giddon, who was uncovering some dishes on a tray. "I forgot there are two pieces of cake, Hava. Liel sent one for the fox."

It is utterly absurd, the things that make tears come to my eyes these days. I ate Giddon's stupid chicken pot pie, plus the chocolate cake Liel had made specially for me and the fox. It was soft and rich and dreamy. The fox ate almost her entire piece.

Then I checked my coat, hanging on a hook on the back of the door, and decided it was dry. When I pulled it on, it was like returning to my own skin. I tucked my fox inside and slung Ozul's coat over my shoulder.

"Goodbye, sweetie," said Bitterblue, watching me from her bed.

"Goodbye," I said. "I hope you enjoy the rest of your rauha day."

I went upstairs, peeling the orange. As I stepped out on deck, the thread I'd sewn into the course broke free, flying away on the wind.

43.

JUST BEFORE SUNSET, Annet sat me down with Ollie in the storage space under the foredeck and gave us piles of tattered canvas.

"Teach our habpva how to sew canvas, Ollie," she said.

The storage space adjoins the chicken coop and the pens for the pigs and the goat. It smells like a barn and sounds like squawking. The light was gray and low, not my first choice for a sewing lesson, but I guess at sea, you take whatever conditions you get.

I tried to ignore the cheerfully critical look Ollie was giving me. "How are you feeling?" he asked.

"Agh!" I said. "People keep asking me that. Do I look like I'm dying or something?"

"You look the same," said Ollie, grinning, "just more bandaged. You always look the same. But you could have died, you know. Someone tried to murder you."

"I feel fine," I said. "I feel like I don't want to talk about it."

"Do you always bite people's heads off when they express concern?"

I breathed a laugh. "Sorry," I said, wondering why it's easy to say that word to Ollie.

"Any idea why she did it?" he said, which immediately made me curious about the gossip on board. I knew Annet and Navi had asked Kera, and Kera wasn't talking.

"My best guess is money," I said. "Some sort of blue fox black market or something. Do you have a theory?"

"That's the only theory I've been able to come up with too," he said. "It's so cruel, though. The fox seems like a sweet little thing."

I glanced at the starboard lifeboat, where the two foxes were sitting together, peeking out at Alzar and Riz, who were adjusting the staysails (small, triangular sails at the front of the mainmast). The differences between the two foxes are pretty acute. Bitterblue's fox is so much bigger, his fur long and lustrous, his eyes focused and clever. My fox looks like a starved rat who's swallowed a globe and is dying from it. "Malnutrition can cause swelling," Coran said to me earlier today, finding me in the port lifeboat with the fox in my lap. He looked like he wanted to climb right in with us and inspect her, but he restrained himself, merely peering in at her, nodding. "Don't worry, Hava. Her belly will shrink as she recovers."

I said to Ollie, "She is sweet."

"And murdering you over some black-market scheme seems kind of excessive," he said. "Okay, watch this."

He showed me how to reinforce a tear in a sail with a strip of canvas, then stitch it neatly to make a nice, flat repair. "The most important part is the knot at the beginning and the end," he said. "See how I stitch it to itself?" I paid attention to that part, now that I understand that wind isn't just a fist that slams against things. It has nimble fingers too, untangling my work.

I think I might die of boredom stitching sheets in a room in a castle, and resent the ache in my neck. But everything is more interesting on a rocking ship, surrounded by shouts, creaks, the crash of water, and the snap of sails. Sometimes, while we worked, the all-hands bell dinged, weakly, pushed by the wind. I glanced at the foxes again. A ship is probably a surprising home to wake to. Most foxes I saw in Winterkeep lived fancy lives in luxurious Ledran houses. Cozy miniature beds on warm hearthstones, and humans who spoiled them with treats and affection. That's probably what she's used to. When her memory returns, she'll want that back.

I'll keep you safe, I called to her, anxious that it wouldn't be enough to content her.

44.

THE NEXT DAY, the sun came out.

I was in my tiny office doing translation when Annet sent for me. The translation work is less tedious, now that my fox keeps me company. She pokes around the cramped cabin, touching her nose to things and curling up in corners, blinking at me calmly. *My girl,* she says, and I read to her from my work.

"Linta Massera says here that 'what matters is what the world is MADE OF,'" I say. "She writes 'MADE OF' in capital letters, like she's shouting it. She gets excited like that sometimes. You'll see. Then she says, 'The way we learn what the world is MADE OF is by observing how particles CHANGE.' What do you think of that?"

Chocolate, she responds.

"You're very single-minded," I say, nodding. "Linta would approve. She says that for the next weapons experiment, we need 'small amounts of charcoal dust.' What do you think of that?"

Dust, she says, stretching her nose out to sniff a cobweb, then sneezing.

"Exactly," I say. "'The ingredients must be mixed in a vacuum, carefully apportioned. Ask LV for the precise procedure.' What do you think of that?"

Chocolate? she says, trying again.

I was crouched in the corner feeding her a piece of chocolate

when the knock came. It was Jacky, of all people. He stuck his head
into the room, glared at us, said, "The captain wants you," then
slammed the door and stomped off.

In the wheelhouse, Annet was smiling like the sun.

"Ah, Hava, good," she said. "Do you know how longitude and
latitude work?"

"Yes," I said.

"Do you know about chronometers and sextants?"

"Yes, but I've never used them."

"Would you like to learn how to identify your precise location at sea?"

Well, that was an easy one. "Is that why you wanted me? Will you
really show me?"

"Sit down, habpva," she said.

Then she put the most beautiful tool into my hand, heavy and
gold, with glowing knobs and smooth, tight hinges, shining glass
mirrors, and a nice wooden handhold. A sextant is like a fancy pro-
tractor that measures the angular distance of the sun or other stars
from the horizon, and from that, you can use charts to figure out
your latitude. She let me swing every hinge and turn every knob on
the sextant, while my fox sat on the table watching me. Then she
showed me how to run my fingers down lists of readings in the nautical tables. She showed me how to work with the chronometers too,
which are basically highly accurate clocks used to measure longitude.
She taught me the math I needed. She explained how I would go
about doing the same thing at night, using the stars instead of the
sun. Then she showed me how to put everything away safely. The
sextant and the chronometers have their own special wooden boxes,
beautifully carved with constellations. And the nautical tables are
kept in bags of sealskin, to ensure they stay dry.

I have a shaky understanding of how to fix our position now. If I were given an hour and allowed to take the measurements three or four times, I could do it.

Annet didn't say this, even when I asked her directly, but when we were done, I saw something in her face. I think we're farther north than she expected.

I hope this means we're going to change course.

45.

WHEN THE ALL-HANDS bell rang, I was lying in the port lifeboat with the foxes, who were curled up together out of the wind. Icicles have been growing under the wooden seats there recently. When I find them, I make a job of breaking them away and lobbing them into the sea.

When the bell clanged, I sat up. Annet, Navi, and Ozul stood together along the rail before the wheelhouse, looking out over the main deck like queens surveying their territory.

Once every sailor was on deck, Annet began shouting orders and Navi and Ozul ran down to help. I've always loved watching these moments from the boats, but this time, I felt silly. Visible, and useless. When you help with some things—sort of, and badly—it becomes clear when your help isn't wanted because you'd only be in the way.

I understand what they did, though, even if I don't understand how they did it. They shifted the yards so the wind in the square sails would push us more southwest than northwest. They shifted the booms so the wind in the mainsails, staysails, and mizzen would do the same. They turned our ship away from the north.

Since that moment, the sea has been rougher, for now we're moving at an angle against the waves and the wind. And I know this is going to mean harder work, longer watches, tireder sailors.

Sicker days for Bitterblue. But my breathing is smoother now. A tight cord has loosened in my chest, because we're finally aiming for home.

Isn't it nice, how much easier it is to have a flexible attitude when you're getting what you want?

46.

I WAS RIGHT. EVERYONE'S tireder now than they used to be, from fighting the wind. Everyone has an extra watch every day now too. So I've been trying to pick up skills and make myself useful.

I'm getting better at chopping wood. At first I was timid, because if I miss the logs, I hit the deck with the ax. It can't be inspiring for whoever's in the wheelhouse to look out and see a Monsean court girl on the foredeck, chopping up the ship.

I imagine the ax crashing through the floor and beheading one of the pigs, because their pen is below me. But I guess they're in for it anyway. At least that particular pig wouldn't see it coming. No anxious anticipation. Though I suppose it might give the other pigs nightmares.

Other pig, singular. There are only two left. After I had that thought about pigs having nightmares, I went down and counted them. I guess the ham I fed my fox this morning had to come from somewhere.

"What will we do when we run out of fresh meat?" I asked Annet.

"Eat salt meat," she said, "and go fishing." But before she said it, she gave me that look again, like she could see the catalog of worries behind my eyes.

"I was just curious," I said.

"Curiosity is encouraged," she said.

"Could I learn the lines sometime? So if you ever need an extra set of hands, I could understand your orders?"

"Yes," she said, with her happiest smile.

That woman is bonkers about sailing.

AT MEALS, MY fox props herself into an advantageous position inside my coat, curled onto her back with her mouth extended upward, to receive whatever tidbits I pass down.

It gives me a way to disappear when Jacky talks loudly near me but carefully excludes me. He never looks at me, never talks to me, never admits to hearing the words I say. It's deliberate. I don't think he's trying to hurt me, exactly. I think he's protecting himself.

So I turn to the fox, focus on feeding her, and pretend I'm not stung.

But then, maybe I think of Jacky's hands on my bird-girl. So I look up from the fox, staring him in the face. I let him see the anger in my ugly eyes. It makes his voice quieter. It makes him get up and go away.

Most of the others have been talking to me freely, ever since the incident with Kera. Not Linny, exactly. Linny isn't cold or hard, and he's perfectly polite, but any meaningful conversation is gone now. I use my Grace sometimes to look at him, and find a troubled expression on his face. I'm sorry about it. He's Jacky's friend, I guess, and, well. I was vile.

Anyway. The others talk to me. "Can't you just reconcile with him, Hava?" Ollie asked one day, after Jacky and Linny both left together.

"Maybe," I said, "when he gives me my things back."

"Didn't he help save your life?"

I remembered Jacky jumping forward to close that porthole. Shutting me out, with a malicious expression on his face.

"You all helped," I said.

Ollie raised an unimpressed eyebrow at me, but I didn't know why he would expect more. "I'll consider thanking him," I said, "when he gives me my things back."

"He says he doesn't even know what you lost," said Ollie. "He's not secretive, you know. He's more of a bragger. He bragged about stealing the rauha. Then he bragged about having to clean the heads, when Annet found out and punished him."

"That definitely sounds like something to brag about," I said dryly.

"What did he take from you, Hava?" asked Sorit.

I could not talk about the figurines my mother had made.

"Ask him," I said.

"I don't think he knows," said Ollie. "Truly."

I turned back to my fox, shoulders curled, face blank. I fed her some bits of ham from my greasy fingers, breaking them into smaller and smaller pieces. Wondering what you would find if you divided me into my indivisible parts. Little building blocks of suspicion and despair? If Ollie is right, then someone else has my bird-girl, and anyone on this ship could be my enemy. Even Ollie or Linny, who were both in my room the day the figurine went missing. I suppose Kera was in my room that day too. I could hope it was her.

Once others began to leave the table, I returned to my cabin. There, I did another search. Methodically, I examined every corner. I even patted the blankets around my sister, though I was careful not to draw her attention to my hiding place in her mattress.

"Still lost your thing?" she said vaguely.

"It's fine," I snapped at her. "Go back to sleep." Then I sat on my bed against the wall with my arms crossed.

My fox sat with me, pressed against my leg.

I'm moping, I said to her.

Moping, she said.

Are you hungry? I asked her.

No.

Do you want to help me find something?

Yes.

I showed her a picture of my bird-girl figurine, let her feel my feelings toward it. Just in case she ever sees it, and can recognize it, and tell me.

Looking for this, I said.

Chocolate?

What? No, this, I said, nudging the picture at her again.

This, she said. Then she touched my mind with a picture of chocolate and I couldn't tell if she wanted chocolate, or if she might actually be making a joke.

Maybe I should call you Chocolate, I said, making my own joke.

No, she said, with a gurgle of amusement. *Not Chocolate.*

Do you remember your name?

No.

Should I call you My Girl?

No.

Fox?

No.

Hungry?

No.

Sweet?

Chocolate, she said, with another gurgle of amusement. Definitely a joke. I like that we have a joke now.

All right, I said, pushing up from the bed. *Let's go find out if Kera stole my figurine.*

47.

ANNET AND NAVI were sitting together in the wheelhouse, tucked in at the table, drinking tea while the ship swung back and forth.

"Can I go through Kera's things?" I asked them.

They both pursed their lips at me over their cups with such similar, concerned expressions that I had to hold back a smile. They said nothing, just considered me. They were waiting for me to explain.

When I didn't, Navi touched a hand to her scarlet-gold scarf. "Do you think it would be healing for you, Hava?"

It would be healing for me to set fire to Kera's possessions while she watched, but that's probably not what Navi meant. "Yes," I said.

With a glance at each other, they bent down and dragged out two crates that were stacked under the wheelhouse table. Then Annet motioned for me to do what I liked. So I lifted them onto the table and began.

One, the bigger one, was full of clothing, smelling of sweat, stiff with salt. I felt into the corners of every pocket but found nothing.

The other, smaller crate contained a couple of books about sailing; Kera's references; one letter, very short, addressed to *Mama*, signed *Sera*, and written in a childish hand; a small tin box with a clasp lid; and a leather wallet.

"We found medicines in her things too," said Annet, "and a few syringes, but we passed those on to Coran."

"Of course," I said, opening the wallet. My eyebrows shot up; it was thick with Keepish banknotes. "That's a lot of money."

"Yes, and there's a promissory note," said Annet.

I found it, a small piece of paper tucked behind the bills. "Half on receipt and half on delivery," it said in Lingian, in black ink. Below that were scrawled a few indecipherable letters—someone's signature, designed to be unreadable. And that was all it said. No names, no dates, no amounts, no explications of what it was about, but I knew what it was about. Kera is smuggling the fox to someone, and when she completes the delivery, she gets the rest of her money.

I fingered the clasp of the tin box. It was big enough to hold my bird-girl.

When I flipped it open, I found no bird-girl inside. Instead, a little flannel mouse popped out, with an embroidered nose and button eyes. Under it, I found a pair of brown knit booties with worn leather soles. Under that, rattling around the bottom of the tin, was a grisly collection of small white teeth.

"Thank you," I said to Annet and Navi as I packed everything back up again, trying not to think about the teeth. I guess they're her daughter Sera's, like the mouse, the booties, and the letter? I guess not everyone has the same idea of what constitutes a non-creepy memento? I remember my baby teeth falling out. What happened to them afterward? Did my mother carry them around in her pocket, clacking like beads?

"Did that help, Hava?" said Navi.

"Oh, yes," I said. "I feel better."

It was a lie, of course, but I went out and gave Riz and Alzar a hand tightening the sails on the mizzenmast. After that, I did feel a little better.

48.

Turns out it's basically impossible to write anything, and especially to draw, when the waves are determined to throw you off your seat. So. I've lost my morning routine a bit. I try, just like Linta tried to work through altitude headaches, but my progress is probably as slow as her progress toward figuring out what the world is made of.

Water and wind, maybe?

"Linta Massera is cleaning her copper implements with a solution of vinegar and salt," I told my fox.

Vinegarsalt, she said.

"Precisely," I said, then caught her as the room tipped and sent her, half sliding and half scrambling, across my desk.

In addition to the storm behind us, there's a smaller one in front of us now. The sailors don't seem worried, so that's fine, whatever, but the wind's picked up so much that we've had to shorten some of the sails so they don't get ripped to shreds. And it's snowing harder. Annet's asked me to put aside my climbing practice for the time being.

While reconnoitering with my ear against our cabin wall, I overheard Coran and Barra, upset because Kera is our weather expert but we're not consulting her anymore.

I went to Annet, who was on the foredeck, studying the storm through her glass while snow blew into her face.

"This isn't the first storm like this I've sailed through, habpva," she said.

I can't seem to punch a hole in her calm confidence. "Is it the most northerly storm you've had to sail through?" I asked.

"Certainly," she said, smiling like this was a wonderful thing. "Would you like a quick lesson about the lines?"

DO YOU KNOW how many lines it takes to operate the rigging of this ship?

Fifty-nine.

It's my new favorite word.

Should I call you Fifty-Nine? I asked the fox.

No.

The lines raise the sails or drop them, spread them out evenly, fold them up when folding is necessary. They adjust the sails' tightness, looseness, and shape. They shift the angle of the yards and the booms. They're probably the ship's most important organ, like veins feeding blood to all the parts of a body. They can also flay your hands, in a wet wind. I still can't fathom all these sailors who wear no gloves.

"Some sailors wear gloves," Ozul told me while I helped her shorten sails on the mainmast.

"Like who?"

"The Mantiperans make a beautiful ship glove, out of kid-goat leather," she said, keeping her big back to the wind as she wound up the end of a line. Snow clung to her hat, and her brown face was flushed rose with cold. Or with joy? Ozul always seems as happy as Annet out here. "Mantiperan sailors wear them. They're light and thin, so you can still feel things through them, but they're warm and dry too."

"Why don't you wear those?"

"Mantiperans are rich. The gloves are expensive and they have to be replaced often. It's like the Lienid and their gold," she said, indicating Ollie nearby with a nudge of her chin, the studs in his ears glowing as he fed the animals. "I'm Keepish. If I have some money, I spend it on other things."

"Like what?"

"Scarves. Tea."

Across the deck, I saw my little fox dashing toward me through the snow. The wind pushed at her patchy hair as she moved, her eyes almost closed. When she reached me, she extended her nose up toward me, like a dog bringing a human a ball. So I crouched down and opened my hand.

Into it, she dropped Giddon's little star nail.

Where did you find that? I exclaimed.

Crack, she said. *In floor.*

Wow!

Vinegarsalt, she said.

Yes, vinegar salt. You remember our translation?

Sparkly, she said. *For you.*

The nail was too grimy from its time on deck to be sparkly, but I could pretend. *Thank you!* I said, twirling it between my fingers.

Pretty, she said. *Like my girl.*

49.

I found something out. And now I'm so furious, I could kick someone.

The wind is howling as I feed cheese and chocolate to the fox in the salon. Sometimes the wind rises slowly in pitch to a scream and I feel it rising inside my own throat. Snow is throwing itself against the skylight above and I know how it must be for the others, trying to pull ice down from the foremast shrouds. I hope Annet is out there getting soaked to the skin, because she's known us to be in danger for a very long time. Ever since that storm attached itself to our tail weeks ago, driving us north, she's known that the winds at sea are unusual this year, and she's known it was going to be hard to get us safely south again.

In fact, in Ledra, before we ever set out, she was warned. The Keepish—Navi herself—recommended she wait. Just as I heard my sister's advisers say through the wall. But I decided to trust Annet instead of them.

Every time we've talked about it, she has lied.

Here's how I found out:

Twice a day, Liel dishes a bowl of food for Kera and hands it to Ollie. I've seen this, and been curious about what happens next. So today, I hid on the afterdeck, pretending to be dock line, waiting for Kera's food delivery.

Turns out it's not Ollie who brings Kera the bowl. It's Annet. I wonder, does she take the bowl from Ollie and bring it to Kera herself because she doesn't want anyone else to hear Kera accusing her of deliberately sailing us into shipwreck?

Anyway. In consequence, I accidentally used my Grace on Annet, not that I care about that now. When Annet opened Kera's door, I heard their conversation.

Kera spoke first. "Congratulations, Captain. You've finally sailed us into the storm you've been looking for."

Annet said, "You conveniently forget that when I was deciding whether to set sail, you were strongly in favor."

Kera shouted a laugh. "Well, now you know I had other reasons for wanting to get out of Winterkeep. You were the fool for trusting me."

"I took the advice of many people, not just you."

"When did you know we were in trouble?"

"If you would talk like a sailor and an officer," said Annet, "instead of like a gloating child, I would speak to you about it. You know as well as I do what we're in for, and you know I could use your help."

"You want my help sailing us home, so you can have me imprisoned when we get there?"

"Would you rather we all end up together at the bottom of the sea?"

Annet's voice, as she said those words, was so calm, so casual. In my confusion, I risked movement, craning my neck to get a better look at them. Annet's shoulder was braced in Kera's doorway with her back to me, her pale hair, tied in a long, smooth tail, whipping in the wind. Inside the closet, Kera, whose movements had an angry force to them, sat on the floor, shoveling stew into her mouth with a spoon.

I decided that Annet was posturing. How else could she talk so offhandedly about something so scary?

Kera spoke again, in a different voice this time. A plain voice, and a grim one. She held her bowl and spoon in unmoving hands and focused on Annet. "How long have you known we were in trouble?"

Annet also spoke plainly. "Since that early storm that drove us north so fast. It moved us along less because it itself was moving, and more because it was growing, and making any west- or southward progress impossible. It was not a normal storm. It did not bode a normal winter."

"And now we're stuck up here?"

"We're between two storms," said Annet, "so I've chosen to battle the more southerly one. The northerly one will only wreck us on the ice fields."

"And what do you anticipate the southerly one wrecking us on?" said Kera dryly.

"The ship is sound," said Annet. "She will bring us, and our queen, through these storms."

"Your tone is very convincing," said Kera. "I'm sure you've got everyone fooled."

"I've kept everyone calm, yes," said Annet. "As I must."

"I hope you've at least told Navi? You really should. Maybe she'd let you into her bed at last, if she knew we were all running out of time."

Annet slammed the door on Kera. She stood there with her body braced against the wind and snow, holding on to the door handle as if her hand had frozen to it.

While she was fumbling with the key, I came up behind her. When she turned, I let her see me, just as I am. Tall, straight, ugly-eyed. Full of fury.

She started, for I'd surprised her. "Hava."

"Yes," I said.

We stood looking at each other for a moment. She didn't break my gaze. I saw she understood what I'd heard, though her face did not change.

Her voice did, though. When she spoke, it was gentler, and full of comfort in which I no longer believed.

"Would you help the others break ice off the shrouds, if you're free?" she said. "It makes them dangerous to climb, and it weighs us down. We're going to need to stay on top of every little thing as long as we can," she said, "if we're to survive this."

When I didn't move or respond, she added, "She is sound, habpva." Then she turned and went back to the wheelhouse.

I went to the galley to get snacks for my fox.

50.

WHEN THE EXPLOSION in Winterkeep that killed Linta Massera threw me into a cavern in the ground, my ankle got stuck. A ladder fell on it, breaking my bones. Then mountains of rubble fell onto the ladder. I was trapped, for a long time. A rib was broken too. Everything hurt. And all I could do was sit there, clutching Linta Massera's notebooks, knowing I was trapped inside the earth; believing there was no way for anyone to get to me; hurting with every breath; and increasingly, incredulously furious that there was nothing I could do to help myself.

Then Giddon climbed down a cliff face that opened to a cave, that led to me. Giddon, who it turns out is really strong, lifted the ladder just enough that I was able to drag my broken ankle free. It was excruciating. But it was also the best moment of my life.

If we must be trapped, let there be something we can do about it. Even if it hurts.

I'M NOTICING THAT lately, Jacky doesn't even care if we're assigned to work on something together. He steps in and helps if I need more muscle; if I'm blocking him on the shrouds, he climbs right around me, shielding me from the snow momentarily with his own body, not speaking a word of blame or shooting me a hurt expression or acting like he thinks any differently of me than he does of anybody else.

That's how serious things are, as the *Monsea* tacks through changing winds that shred our canvas.

I've been assigned to an official watch. One of the easiest watches, four hours in daytime, though sometimes I come out at night too if a knock sounds on our cabin door, which means I'm needed. I stumble up to the main deck, half-asleep, slipping and sliding while the ship tries to throw me down, and it's like I haven't woken at all. I'm having a nightmare of cold and ice and bone-cracking plunges of the prow into waves, and walls of water that rise up from the sea like the huge hand of a sea giant, then smack us.

Even in all of this difficulty, day in and day out, I can see how magnificently the ship is weathering it. I see how the fifty-nine lines are feeding power to the sails, I see how the sails are not just surviving the blasting winds, but harnessing them, riding them, carrying us across this storm. We will cross it to the other side. The *Monsea* is made for this; she keeps bobbing and weaving and fighting. Last night, for a moment, I laughed at the wind, then I shouted at it, a harsh, inarticulate, triumphant cry, because we are made for this. On the line beside mine, Linny saw me, shook his head like I was crazy, then a smile broke across his weary face. It transfigured him, turned him into beauty and light. His eyes were like the sun we never see anymore. For a moment, we laughed with each other, and I wanted so badly to be his friend. I never know what to say to him now when we're inside, eating our quick meals, or carrying wood to the furnace room together. (Yes, we use the lift.) It's when we're out here on deck, fighting with the storm, that it's easier.

Annet has sent a message to me through Ozul twice now, telling me to come to the wheelhouse. I don't go. I'll follow orders that keep the ship safe, but I'm not going to have a heart-to-heart with Annet. When we cross paths on deck or inside, I don't look at her. If she sits near me at meals, I turn my shoulder. Whenever I ignore Ozul's request, the others stare at me in a mute kind of shock, but I am not like them. I'm not a sailor. If my sister, the queen, can't force me to do things, certainly no one else on this ship can.

My sister is faring very badly. Even rauha can't make this tolerable. I don't think she's eaten in days.

51.

TODAY THE PIN that locks the anchor capstan—the one Kera showed me that time in the bow—popped out and the anchor dropped into the sea by accident.

The pull on the bow, when it happened, was incredible. The ship began to swing around on its tether, the aft trying to spin forward, the wind blasting the sails full on from the side.

Navi, who was in the wheelhouse fighting with the rudder, was screaming her head off. "Up anchor!" she screamed. "Up anchor!" Pretty quickly, this changed to "Cut the chain!"

Up in the tip of the bow, Noa and Jacky hacked at the anchor chain with axes while the ship bucked and swerved, and I swear, I thought one of them was going to go over. Linny struggled to them with a rope, wound it around each of them in some way I couldn't see, then secured it somehow to the rail. When all of this is over and we're back to calm seas, I'm going to get him or someone to teach me knots, so I can help in that kind of situation.

Once the anchor was cut loose, nothing stopped being terrifying, for it was hard work to bring the ship around. It was as if the wind, pleased to find us broadside and with our sails set all wrong for our position, saw its opportunity to capsize us, and blew even harder. It was impossible to hear the commands over the wind, and I'm so slow and clumsy compared to everyone else, but the people around me on the lines helped me, and we got her back on course.

"We could've lost the ship," Ozul told me. She looked dazed, like she wasn't sure where she was. Kera replaced that pin ages ago, and everyone agrees it wasn't her fault. She did a fine job. The ice just proved too much for it.

After it was over, Navi sent Noa and Jacky into the salon to sit for a few minutes with a hot drink. Then she saw me, gasping and dripping and pathetic, and sent me in there too, which was embarrassing, since I hadn't done anything heroic to justify my desperate state.

In the salon, Noa and Jacky stared grimly into their drinks. I don't know Noa well, but I'm used to her broad shoulders and radiant smile. It was alarming to see them both curled in on themselves, stony-faced.

"What is it?" I said.

Jacky shook his head. Then he looked straight at me. He seemed to see me for who I was, for the first time in a while.

"Princess Dardya," he said. "That anchor didn't drop far. This storm is blowing us into shallow waters."

"So, what?" I said, suddenly irate. "You've decided we're doomed? The ship is sound!"

"You're like the captain," Jacky said with a rueful chuckle. "Just angrier and more intimidating."

THAT NIGHT, AT bedtime, I went to our cabin, bursting through the door—not on purpose, but simply because it's impossible not to go where the ship throws you. I fumbled to my bed, where two fox lumps were curled up together. The foxes are weathering most of the storm under my covers.

I managed to sit somewhere other than on top of them, then

rested against the bucking wall, still thinking about what Jacky had said.

Across from me, Bitterblue was sitting up, melted against Giddon like a sodden pile of queen goo.

"You're alive?" I said.

"I'm fine," she croaked. "I want to help."

"You can't help," I said. "You need to stay here where you're safe."

"I know," she said. "I'm not going to risk falling in again, Hava. But it's so frustrating to be sick and useless when others are strong."

"Your spirit is strong," I said. "When you're on land, there's no one stronger."

"Listen to your sister," Giddon murmured into her ear.

"Listen to Giddon," I told my sister.

"Hava?" she said. "I want *you* to listen to Giddon."

"I will, if he has something to tell me," I said, suddenly wary.

Giddon was leaning his head against the wall with his eyes closed. The lamps that hung from our ceiling swung sharply, throwing light onto his bearded face and yanking it away again. It was nauseating. This storm touches even my stomach, now and then.

He opened his eyes and shot me a regretful look. "This'll probably make you angry," he said.

I didn't respond, just hardened myself.

"Annet, despite our frantic pace and her sleeplessness and the excellence with which she is captaining the ship—"

He stopped, checking the rising frustration in his voice. He spoke again, more evenly.

"—Annet has made more than one attempt to talk to you. She's our captain. We all have to follow her orders, for our safety. She's been patient enough. Hava! You need to go talk to her!"

He was right. I was fuming. Haven't we been through this already?

Giddon is not my boss and he doesn't tell me what to do. He wasn't even looking at me. He was sitting there with his eyes closed again, his mouth a hard, disgusted line.

"You don't order me around," I said to him. "Ever." Then I left, because I didn't want to be in a room with him.

Out in the passageway, I pounded the walls with my fists as I moved, as much to release my anger as to balance myself. Outside on deck, I shouted curses at the wind.

Then I went to the wheelhouse.

52.

When I entered, Annet glanced up, then pointed to a seat at the table and turned back to what she was doing, as if I weren't there.

I sat, furious at my own pricks of shame. Why should I feel shame?

I waited awhile. She kept running outside into the night, shouting things, helping people on the lines in the snow. I watched her. Her hair was a mess, her left cheek striped with a long rope burn, her big hands chapped and red. She looked intent, but not worried. Like a woman who could do anything. She looked marvelous, and suddenly I knew we would get through this storm. I just knew it.

"Hava," she said finally, coming to sit with me. "I would like to explain what you overheard."

"Okay," I said, swallowing sudden, confused tears.

"I never told you all I knew about how things stood," she said. "It's true. And it was a kind of deceit."

"Was it?" I said, no longer sure.

"Deceit is an injury," she said, "especially to a Monsean. Most especially, I suspect, to one who grew up in the king's court."

I began to cry. It is humiliating to be so clearly seen. *He was my father,* I didn't say. *Did you know that? He murdered my mother. He stole her from me with his lies.*

"Hava," said Annet, "can I explain to you what happened, and why I didn't tell you everything I knew?"

THROUGH MY TEARS and through my wanting to believe her, all that she said made good sense.

Yes, she'd received warnings from a few of the people she'd consulted, before she'd decided to set sail.

"But that's not unusual, Hava," she said. "It's the job of every harbormaster's office to tell any captain all the worst things that might be waiting for her at sea. As the captain of the queen's ship in particular, I consult any experienced person who'll talk to me. The Brumal Sea and the Winter Sea produce storms in December and January. I know. I've crossed those seas before, and the people I consulted know too. The consensus among the Keepish, Kamassarians, Dellians, and Pikkians I talked to was that the seas were perhaps a bit stormier than average for this time of year, but a northerly route would bring us around the most apparent observable weather system. They told me that ships have been crossing that way all season. They also advised me that if I waited, things would become worse. No one wants to cross the Brumal Sea in February or March, habpva. Nor did the queen wish to wait for the summer, though she would have, had I advised her it was necessary. I decided it wasn't necessary.

"Navi disagreed. If she were the captain of this ship, she would've advised the queen to wait. But she's not the captain. I am. And if I were in the harbormaster's office again, receiving the same information, I would make the same choice again. There are storms in summer too, you know. There's always the chance of danger at sea. And these crossings are new for all of us, every nation; we're still learning. We're crossing an ocean in a wooden boat," she said, shrugging one shoulder. "The ocean doesn't care that we have a queen on board. But ships are made to weather storms. This ship is sound."

It's been my own favorite refrain. "But when you talked to Kera,"

I said, "both of you sounded like you thought shipwreck was inevitable."

"Hava," Annet said forcefully. "Kera is a woman who's destroyed her own life. She might also be getting a little desperate in her closet. I don't speak to her the way I speak to other people. Certainly not the way I speak to a young woman who has an interest in sailing, no experience, and a lot of worries. Yes, it's true that when we encountered that storm early on, I began to suspect that things were worse than we'd thought. No one knew it would grow so big or force us so far north, but no one could have known. That's sailing. Now we have the challenge of pushing ourselves south, against the wind, through what may turn out to be a series of bad storms. When we reach Pikkia—yes," she said, noting the change in my expression, "I now think it's likely I'll decide to make land in Pikkia, rather than prolonging this—we'll be able to report this weather, and other ships will receive better advice. I never told you I anticipated danger because sailors always know danger is possible, and because morale suffers if the captain behaves as if every unexpected puff of wind spells disaster. Also, I couldn't be sure. I'm not going to make you more anxious than you already are when I don't, in fact, know what's going to happen. We're here now. The *Monsea* is sound. Kera may think shipwreck is inevitable, but I think we're doing all right, don't you? A little bumpy, maybe," she said as a swell practically threw her onto the table. A laugh pushed its way out of my throat. I couldn't help it. Her long-suffering expression was funny.

"I understand," I said.

"I'm glad to hear that."

"Often, in my work," I added, suddenly wanting her to know, "I need to keep things from people. Sometimes, even from the queen."

"There," she said. "Then you really do understand."

"I guess I don't like when it's done to me, though."

"That's a good thing," she said. "It'll make you careful not to abuse that power, because you know in your own heart how much it hurts others."

I'll need to think about that one.

"Go get some sleep, habpva," she said. "You have a watch in the morning, don't you?"

"Yes."

I studied her then, for she looked so tired. Her eyes were shot through with redness and she slumped in her seat.

Then she noticed me looking, and straightened her shoulders. She nodded.

"The ship is sound," she said. "Go get some sleep."

IN THE PASSAGEWAY outside my cabin, Giddon was leaning against the wall with his hands in his pockets, bracing his legs as the ship moved.

"What are you doing?" I said. "Did Bitterblue kick you out?"

"No," he said. "I just wanted to talk to you."

"What's wrong?" I said, suddenly alarmed because he looked anxious. "Is she okay?"

"Yes," he said, removing a hand from a pocket and patting the air in the universal "everything's fine" gesture. "It's not that. I'm worried because we can't have a conversation lately without fighting."

"You're fighting?" I said, becoming irate. "Because it sure doesn't seem like you're fighting."

"*You and I* are fighting," he said. "You know? Like what's happening this very minute?"

"Oh," I said, slightly deflated. "Right. It's because you keep criticizing my decisions."

"I know," he said, watching me with soft brown eyes. "I'm sorry, Hava. I've been worrying about you, and I keep wanting to help. I get you don't want my help," he said, raising a hand again in that same gesture. "I just want you to know where I'm coming from. I'm sorry I keep making you angry."

I put my arms out to brace myself as the floor tilted up and crashed down again. Giddon hardly moved. He's heavy, and steady. Sometimes I envy his big legs. Though not as much as I tire of these conversations he likes to have, where we talk about our feelings.

That's not really true. I don't hate that Giddon waited for me outside my cabin to apologize for pushing me into talking to Annet. I just don't know how to say what I mean. That I'm glad I talked to Annet. That I wouldn't have done it if he hadn't pushed me. That I still don't like people pushing me, especially him. But that Giddon has helped me a thousand times, and if he ever stopped wanting to help me, well, I would feel that, deeply, and it would not feel good.

"I'm sorry," I said.

His eyes widened slightly. "What was that? I don't think I heard you."

"You heard me," I said, biting back a smile.

"It was something that rhymed with 'starry,'" he said.

"Go away, bully."

He smiled a little too, then said, "Brat," the way he's supposed to. "See you."

"See you."

Then he pushed off the wall and walked to his cabin, not seeming to mind the ship that was tossing him around.

INSIDE OUR CABIN, Bitterblue was still sitting up, leaning against the wall.

"You all right?" she murmured.

"Yes," I said. "Are you all right?"

"Never been better."

Instead of staggering to my own bed, I staggered to hers and sat beside her. The wind howled. "When this journey is over," I said, "you'll recover quickly."

"Yes," she said, "and I'll never go to Winterkeep again."

I let out a small snort. "It hasn't been your best trip ever, has it?"

"How sad is it if I've had worse?" she said, and suddenly we were both laughing hysterically. Remember the impossible mountain pass, where the Monsean climber Grella wrote journals while he was freezing to death? Bitterblue has crossed that pass. She was only ten. Our father, the king, had chased her into the mountains; he chased her halfway across the world. She'd had no choice but to face Grella's Pass. She'd lived through the crossing only because Katsa, who's Graced with survival skills, had kept her alive. Now, in our ship in the middle of a horrible storm, it was the funniest thing that'd ever happened to either of us.

"Hava?" said Bitterblue, still giggling. "Do you need anything from me?"

"No," I said, for once feeling like it was the truth. "Do you need anything?"

"Nothing anyone could actually give me."

One of the foxes across the room shifted, a moving lump under the blankets. It was my sister's fox.

I've just realized something, he said.

We both quieted, looking at him. *Yes?* I said.

The fox is pregnant, he said.

"What?" I cried.

There are five baby foxes. At least five, he corrected. *I've just now become aware of five babies. There may be more.*

53.

In the morning, I woke to quiet.

I flipped around in bed, not understanding where I was, shocked to find myself in our cabin in the *Monsea*, with the ship rocking over gentle swells. Water sloshed lightly against our walls. I could hear no wind.

My fox was snuggled beside me, blinking up at me with glimmering gold eyes. She has a dark nose that curves down from her forehead, like a perfect little hill for sledding.

So, I said to her. *Babies?*

Babies? she said, blinking calmly.

It makes a lot more sense now, what Kera did—a depressing sort of sense. She didn't smuggle just one fox out of Winterkeep. She smuggled many. I suppose it should've occurred to us, given the size of the fox's belly.

Did you know about the babies? I asked her.

No? Yes?

I wasn't sure whether to keep asking her questions. It seemed like a dangerous topic to press her about, not knowing anything of her past. Or of sexual or romantic relationships between foxes, or of what fox smugglers might be in the habit of doing. Or of making foxes do.

Hm, I said, suddenly newly worried about her. *How many babies are there?*

Fifty-nine, she said.

Silly. That's the number of lines on the ship.

Not my name, she said.

Shall I call you Sled Nose?

No.

Mama Fox?

No.

Can you count the babies?

There was a pause. *Six,* she said.

Well, I said. *Congratulations.*

Congratulations.

Will they come soon? I said. *Is there anything you need?*

Chocolate, she said.

I'll bring you some, I said, *as soon as I find out what's going on outside.*

ALMOST IN A dream, I went upstairs. How strange it is when the ship is barely rocking. Apparently I'm clumsy, unable to remember how to walk on a floor that isn't trying to kill me. At no point on our journey have the seas been this calm.

Then, outside, the sun was shining. The sun! I almost couldn't bear it; I cringed, shading my eyes.

Ozul rushed past me.

"We sailed through the storm?" I asked.

She didn't answer, so I followed her up into the stern, noticing that almost all the sails were tied down. "Are we drifting?" I asked, confused, for in the water, jagged mountains of ice rose all around us, and we didn't seem to be moving in relation to them. But nor did the ship feel stationary.

Ozul joined Linny at the capstan for the stern anchor, ignoring me. Together, they grasped the handles and began to turn. The stern anchor dropped slowly, with a click-click-click of the links of its metal chain.

"Why are we anchoring?" I asked.

"Hava! Help me turn!" Ozul said.

I tore my eyes away from the mountains of ice and grabbed her handle. "Where are we? What's going on?"

"There's a tide," Ozul said. "Or a current, we don't know which. It's moving us, and all that ice too. And we're too close to shore."

"Shore?" I said stupidly, looking around again, seeing no shore.

"We need to stop moving," she said. "It's shallow and there are ice spars. I wish we had both anchors," she said grimly. "We're going to launch the boats and take some soundings."

"Oh!" I said. "That's interesting." Then the anchor chain went slack. "Does the slack chain mean the anchor hit bottom?"

"Already?" said Linny, raising startled eyes to Ozul's face.

The chain grew taut again as the ship drifted forward, dragging the anchor behind it. "Is that anchor going to hold us?" I asked in alarm.

"It's a very strong current," Ozul said. "And there's not enough wind for us to fight it with the sails. The anchor *has* to hold us, or we're in serious trouble."

"All right," I said. "Well, the ship is sound."

"It makes no difference if the ship is sound," Ozul said, exasperated, "if we can't stop her moving!"

I heard the faintest scraping in the water far below. I assumed it was the anchor on rock. Then the scraping grew in volume. It turned into sounds my ears couldn't understand, like snapping, cracking wood, as if a boulder the size of a castle were rolling through a forest of ancient trees. Then the ship jarred into stillness.

Why do our minds sometimes reject what's obviously happening?

Linny and Ozul were already scrambling down to the main deck. Annet, leaping from the wheelhouse and running forward, was screaming. "Ship aground!" she yelled. "Crew quarters may be breached! Everyone on deck! Launch the boats! Ozul, wake the queen and bring her to me! Ollie! Go wake the doctor, then Navi, then the other passengers, in that order. Send the doctor forward! Tell Navi to check the aft hold in case anything is salvageable! Ozul, do not leave the queen! Emergency supplies in the forecastle! Linny, to me, now!"

She was running to the front of the ship, reaching for the hatch to the crew's quarters, and I understood that the problem, whatever it was, was there. That she was frightened in case any of the crew, who slept at the front of the ship, were in their beds, in danger.

I staggered after her.

"Hava," she said, seeing me. "Go to the queen, will you? Stay with the queen, and bring her to me."

I could hear something like weeping in her voice. I couldn't understand it. The ship shuddered with another terrible series of scrapes and cracks and then I thought maybe we were moving again. Afloat. That was good, right? "What's happening?" I said in a strangled, high-pitched tone.

"That's what I'm going to find out," she said, calm as ever, starting down the ladder. "Send Ozul to me. I'm entrusting you with the queen."

Then she was gone.

THE PASSAGEWAY WAS full of useless, jabbering, hysterical advisers and there were so many people with the queen that I could barely fit in the cabin. Bitterblue was sitting up in bed, swarmed by them. The foxes ran past me and into the passageway.

I shouted over Ozul, Giddon, Ollie, and Coran. "Ozul! The captain asked me to send you to her. I'm to stay with the queen."

"She told me not to leave the queen," Ozul shouted back.

"She wants me to do it instead. She wants you, and Coran too."

"The queen is unwell!" cried the doctor.

"Coran!" said Bitterblue. "I command you to go to the captain! You're needed!"

"Yes, please," said Ollie, who was practically tugging on the doctor's arm.

"Giddon!" said Bitterblue. "Please, make him go."

Giddon gave Bitterblue a ragged look, then turned to me. "You swear to me you'll bring Bitterblue out on deck right away?"

"Yes."

Giddon put his arms around Coran and practically carried him out of the room. A moment later, they were all gone. My sister and I were alone.

"I know I'm very precious and important and everything," Bitterblue said, "but, honestly. How bad is it, Hava?"

"We don't know yet," I said numbly.

"What did Annet say?"

I stretched my mind back. "Crew quarters breached. Everyone on deck. Launch the boats. Don't leave—"

"That's enough," said Bitterblue, putting her hand to the wall, standing. "It means we're probably not coming back to this room. Help me think, Hava. What should we bring?"

I was staring at her stupidly. "What?"

Using the edge of her bed as a brace, she moved to the hooks on our wall, clothed herself in her coat, scarf, and hat, then began shuffling things into her pockets. Socks. Gloves. Candles. A gift Giddon gave her, this little golden thing shaped like a spyglass that shows you stars when you look into it.

When she saw I wasn't moving, she stood straight, her eyes flashing. She flared at me with anger and passion, transforming into the woman I'm used to, the woman I know.

"Hava!" she said. "When we're cast upon the shores of Pikkia, or wherever we are! What things in this room will we most wish were not at the bottom of the sea!"

"The ship is sound," I said, with the most amazing, stubborn stupidity. Then the room shifted with a terrible noise of singing, splintering wood, throwing us both to the floor. The ship was crying the strangest cries, echoing like a hollow, wooden instrument, as if we lived inside a violin.

Scrambling up again, my sister found a canvas bag of mine and began to fill it. She put her tin of lemon juice lozenges into it, then added the rauha. "Where are the formulas?" she said. "And your translations?"

Numbly, I reached under her sheets and into the cavity at the foot of her mattress. I pulled out my bundle of figurines, then Linta Massera's formulas and translations. Her eyebrows rose, but she said nothing. I handed the sealskin pouch containing the papers to her, then watched her enclose it carefully in a second sealskin pouch. She added it to the canvas bag.

"We have to get upstairs right now or they'll all come down for me again," she said, then leaned over and vomited onto the floor, casually, as if it didn't matter. "Hava, sweetie. I know you're in shock, but please. Think whether you have any precious possessions you'll be sorry to lose."

"My bird-girl!" I cried.

"Get it."

"It's not here!"

"Then we have to go now. Any warm clothing you should bring? Anything else?"

"These," I said, shoving my bundle of figurines into the canvas bag she held out to me. "Where's my fox?"

"Adventure tells me they're both on deck. Now let's go."

———————

I THINK I woke up somewhere between our cabin and the deck. When we climbed out into the light, I understood what I saw: a crew abandoning its ship.

People were divided into groups. The lifeboat that hangs on a davit behind the stern was already in the water on the starboard side, manned by Linny, and some sailors were passing sacks and crates down into it. I noticed it had a mast, a boom, and a jib now, which it never did before, and understood that the lifeboats convert into sailboats.

Other sailors were loading more supplies into the two boats on the main deck. On the afterdeck, Navi stood on the ladder inside the hold of the hatch, passing things out, then disappearing, then popping up again and passing more things out. Giddon was grabbing them and running forward with them. When Annet saw the queen, she ran to us and helped Bitterblue into the first boat, then told me to go assist Giddon.

Watch the queen, I said to my sister's fox, even though I had no idea where he was. *Watch my fox too. Let me know if either of them needs me. Okay?*

I will, I promise, he said.

While I was on the afterdeck, Annet came back and unlocked Kera's door. Kera came out, squinting at the light. Annet spoke to her, then ran forward again, leaving her standing there, unguarded, free. In a disbelieving part of my mind, I understood that too. We couldn't leave her, but nor did we have extra hands to guard her. Kera came to help us and I decided to go help elsewhere. She smelled terrible, but that wasn't it. She felt terrible. I couldn't cope with all the feelings that rushed me as she drew near.

Almost immediately after I left, there was some sort of altercation back there. I didn't see it, but I heard a shuffle, then Navi shouting for Annet, then Annet shouting for the doctor.

Afraid for Giddon, I ran back, in time to see Giddon holding

Kera in an armlock while Coran stuck her in the shoulder with a syringe. Giddon had blood running down the side of his face.

"What happened?" I cried.

"She tried to steal my knife," Giddon said in a disgusted voice, then, when Kera went limp, hoisted her onto his shoulder.

"Put her in the next boat," Annet said flatly, which surprised me. Saving Kera is a priority even if she's attacking people? "Navi, Coran, Hava, come forward," said Annet. "It's almost time to go."

IT ALL SEEMED to happen so fast. Unbelievably fast.

I guess when a ship runs into something sharp, all there is to do is load everything and everyone into the boats. Once you've done that, there's nothing else but getting away. You have to push away from her, even though she's still beautiful and strong around you, just listing a bit and making funny noises. You have to leave behind all the things you're working on. The sails that need mending, the wood you're going to chop, all fifty-nine lines you're learning to understand, all the parts of the rigging you know best how to climb, because you know where it's slippery and where the ratlines are tight.

I kept trying to find people to help, things to do. I needed more time. Liel was crying, silently, resisting other people's efforts to help him into a boat, and I understood that Tulip was missing. I decided I would find the cat. Then the floor moved again, shifting sharply, tilting toward the bow. A hand grabbed my shoulder and I turned. Annet looked into my face. "Go, habpva," she said.

In her voice I heard something that scared me. "You're coming, aren't you?"

"Yes, of course."

"I don't want to go."

"I know," she said. "We must. Quickly now. I can't leave until you do."

I understood then that everyone else was in the boats. The boat containing the queen and a few other people was already some distance away, disappearing behind an ice mountain, Linny and Ozul rowing fiercely. I saw a pig in the bow and the foxes in the stern, their paws propped up on the edge, their gold eyes looking back at us. The second boat, which contained Giddon, an insensible Kera, the goat, a few chickens, and a lot of people, was close behind the first. I swarmed down the ladder into the third boat, because Annet couldn't be safe until I was.

As soon as her feet hit the boards behind me, we began moving. Stupid, foolish tears streamed down my face and I asked if I could row, for something to do.

"Yes, in a bit," Annet said, her voice very gentle. "Not now."

That left me with nothing to do but sit and try not to think about what was happening.

I live in a castle in the Monsean Court, a castle the size of a city, five stories high with glass ceilings and gold windowpanes. Still, I understand now that this ship is the most beautiful home I've ever had. I've lived all across my kingdom, and gone away to the other side of the world, and still, this is the first time I've ever felt like I was being torn from my home.

I'm sure that others in our boat were wondering where we were going. They were looking ahead, wondering how far we were from shore. I turned around, like Annet was doing. I faced our ship. As we moved away, I watched the ocean chew her up, sucking her down. Her bell was ringing, louder out here on this water, echoing against this ice, than it had ever rung when we were on board. She tilted again, her stern coming up out of the water. It looked so wrong. I wanted to reach out and help her right herself. She let out a great moan.

It all happened very fast after that. The foremast disappeared, then the mainmast, then the ocean swallowed her entire hull.

I kept watching until the tip of her mizzenmast sank into the sea.

PART TWO

54.

How is it possible to be shipwrecked under blue skies? How can this be real?

Our boats moved through a sunny silence broken only by the creak of our own oars.

We rowed through waters that swam with boulders of ice. The ice masses flowed across our path like we were on streets meeting at right angles. They appeared from our left and swept past us, disappearing to our right.

"Annet?" I said. "How much do we know about where we are?"

Everyone in the boat started at the sound of my voice, seeming to wake from a stupor. They looked around in amazement at the jagged ice our rowers, Alzar and Riz, were rowing us through. Or maybe I was projecting. Maybe I woke myself up.

Then everyone focused on Annet. So did everyone in the boat ahead of us too. Giddon, Navi, Sorit, Noa, Lisa, Jacky, Coran, even the goat, all turned back to look at us, because my voice carried so clearly across the silence. Ice bumped against ice sometimes, with a faint, musical ding. Ice snapped or cracked. A breeze puffed, making the people near me shiver. That was all.

Annet, who sat in the bow of our boat looking like a woman made of shock and stone, cleared her throat. "We're in the northern Winter Sea," she said in a strong voice. "We have two objectives. The first is to move ourselves west through these icebergs and find the shore, so that we have the option of leaving the boats. The next is to move ourselves south."

Other questions crowded into my throat. How far are we from shore? How far from Pikkia? Is it normal that this water is so calm? How much food do we have and how long will it last? When will we put up the sails? Do we have a way to make fire? Did you bring the sextant, the chronometers, the nautical tables, and a compass? Could Giddon or I be in the same boat as Bitterblue, who's stuck up there in the first boat, with her two most useless advisers, neither of her guards, and a pig?

As we crept west, I stared into the low sun. It blazed a path of fire across the water. I knew it would set early, and that once it did, it would stay down for a long time. What is it like to be shipwrecked in the dark?

"Is there anything I can do to help?" I said.

"You can take a turn rowing," Annet said. "Every able person in every boat will take half-hour turns rowing. It'll help keep us warm and prevent any one person from overwork."

"Will we put up the sails?" I asked.

"Not with this ice all around us, habpva," Annet said.

I let her use of that name comfort me. And rowing for half an hour also turned out to be good for me. I rowed and rowed, trying to pump my fear down into the oars, out into the sea.

55.

When I wasn't rowing, I kept my eyes on the other boats.

In the middle boat, Giddon sat next to Kera, who was still unconscious. His mouth was tight and the side of his face seeped blood. Coran, the doctor, had given him a cloth, which he remembered to hold to the wound occasionally.

I reached my mind out to the first boat, so I could talk to my sister's fox.

Tell Giddon to pay more attention to Kera, I told him. *She could wake up at any moment and attack him again.*

Stop it! the fox yelled at me. *You and Giddon are both using me to send messages! I can barely even hear the queen with all your chatter! I'm not your message fox! LET ME TAKE CARE OF THE QUEEN!*

Is there a way to get us all in the same boat? I said, ignoring him.

What would that serve? he cried. *What if something happened to that boat? You'd all be in trouble, all three of you!*

Nothing would happen to that boat. It'd be the safe boat.

Oh, really? What are you going to do, break off from the group and sail it triumphantly home? Who else gets to be in this boat? Let me guess: Annet, Navi, and the doctor?

Ugh. Not the doctor.

Hava, said the fox. *When your mind has returned to logic, feel free to contact me. Until then, leave me alone.*

What's that supposed to mean?

THERE'S NO SUCH THING AS A SAFE BOAT, he said.

56.

He's right, of course.

It helped that he said it. Delusions are dangerous in situations like these. Not that I've ever been in a situation quite like this before. But there's no such thing as a safe anything, really, right?

In the afternoon, Annet ordered me to nap. I lay on the floor, wound around other people's feet, trying to ignore how badly I needed to urinate. Then I gave up and told Annet.

When this happens, we go to the stern and hang off the back, awkwardly baring our bottoms, holding hard to the edge of the boat to keep from falling in. Everyone tactfully looks away. Thank goodness mine is the last boat. I've had to avert my eyes several times now while someone ahead of us does this.

When I was done, I worked my way back to the middle of the boat, intending to lie down again. But then Kera stirred in the boat ahead. She sat up, looking around blearily, her black hat crooked, her auburn hair escaping. Seeing me staring, she froze, locked in my gaze.

Then, of all things, she let out a shriek and threw herself on Giddon! Punching, scratching, kicking. What was she thinking? That she would get his knife again? Then what? Pirate a rowboat and escape? Escape to where?

Jacky and Navi tackled her and pulled her back, then held her down while Coran stabbed her with another syringe. She screamed the whole time, swearing, calling us names, telling us we were pathetic and stupid and doomed. The echoes were incredible, a chorus of insults thrown back at us from very far away. It made me feel like we were at the ends of the world, with nothing beyond us but space. It made her words feel true.

Two of the four chickens launched themselves overboard in the tussle, flapping and squawking, then sat in the water clucking and looking confused as their boat pulled away. By the time our boat reached them, they were pretty subdued. Chickens aren't made for cold water, I guess. We plucked them out of the sea and now they're in my lap and let me tell you, they're not good company. Their butts are wet, they won't keep still, and they keep shitting.

But one of them laid an egg. It fell into my lap like a little hot stone. I held it in my hands till it grew cooler. "Egg," I said to Annet, holding it up for her to see.

"Mix it into your oats when it's your turn, habpva," she said, for that's what we've been eating: cold oats. We have a bowl and spoon we take turns using. We mix the oats with water from the sea ice, because it turns out that when seawater freezes, it pushes the salt out. The small chunks of ice floating around us are freshwater supplies.

Annet divvies the oats from a crate that sits near her in the stern. She puts a few slices of dried fruit on top and one nutritional biscuit, then hands the bowl to whoever's turn it is to eat. The biscuit is a dry, tasteless block that turns into glue in your mouth. She passes us a lemon lozenge too, which is so tart, it makes me feel like it's burning holes into my head.

While I was still deciding what to do about the egg, a seal pulled itself onto a broad, flat iceberg nearby. I was so surprised that I made a squeaking noise, pointing. Everyone in the boat turned and stared. Ranin, near me, started chuckling. "Dinner," he said.

The seal gazed back at us through dark, curious eyes. Its body was a gray, silky blob.

Then a huge white form surged from the water behind it, shouldering itself onto the iceberg. With one massive paw, it pinned the seal down, then tore it apart with sharp teeth while it screamed.

57.

So. Yes. There are bears.

They're white like the snow, so sometimes we don't see them until we're upon them. They like to stand on the icebergs looking down at us. They have small heads that narrow to a pointy jaw that doesn't seem big enough to contain such massive teeth. They have gigantic shoulders and paws.

One bear, a big one, slid down from its iceberg and swam after our boat as we rowed by, its eyes and nose just above the water. Our rowers rowed harder and it followed behind us, speeding up when we sped up, slowing down when we slowed down, showing us that our speed was a matter of indifference. Looking at us through small, dark eyes that had nothing in them but boredom, and an empty kind of predation. I suppose they've never seen humans before. They must be wondering how edible we are.

Annet pulled a long knife from her boot and sat in the stern with it raised in her fist. She looked ready, and fearless. Then the bear sank away, which was not comforting. When they disappear underwater like that, we have no idea where they've gone, or when they might return.

An hour or so after that chicken laid the egg, I realized I was still holding it, delicately, in my hand. It's distracting, watching for bears.

It was Liel's turn to eat. When Annet passed me his bowl, I cracked the egg against the rim and mixed it in. Liel didn't even notice. He's been huddled and shivering, with tears dripping down his face, ever since we left the *Monsea*. He can't stop crying about Tulip.

I passed him the bowl and spoon. When he stared at them without comprehension, I told him to eat up, because Annet needed the bowl and spoon back. He ate numbly, like it was a duty, which I guess it was. I'm beginning to wonder if every step of every day, eating, sleeping, rowing, looking away when someone's doing their business, watching for bears, keeping my panic buried, will be a duty from now on. Will I be able to remain calm, if I focus on each duty as it comes?

At some point, the chickens in my lap dried out and warmed up. Beside me, Mart was shivering. When I passed him the chickens, he accepted them gravely. He's a big man in his twenties, with a pale blond beard the same shade as his skin. He's been keeping his eyes craned anxiously toward the first boat, Bitterblue's boat. He's a queen's guard; I guess he's as impatient with the boat assignments as I am. Regardless, I thought he was looking whiter than usual.

"Mart?" I said. "You'll tell us if you start to get too cold, right?"

When he looked at me and nodded, a tear fell out of his eye, onto his cheek. I noticed he has freckles dusting his cheeks and nose, like brown sugar.

Fox? I said, speaking to Bitterblue's fox. *Could you cycle through everyone's minds now and then, and make sure everyone seems lucid?*

The queen has already requested that, he said sniffily.

Oh. Good. Thank you. How is my fox?

She's fine. Aren't you talking to her?

I was, sort of, to whatever extent it was ever possible to talk to her. I kept asking her, *Are you okay?* She kept responding, *Okay.* Sometimes she would say, *My girl,* repeating it like a refrain, and

I would see her in the stern of the first boat, peeking back at me. I badly wished I could reach her, tuck her into my coat.

Careful, I said to her. *Stay back from the edge. There are bears.*

Bears? she said.

I couldn't remember if Winterkeep had bears. *Do you know what a bear is?*

Bears, she said.

Hm, I said. *Fox of the queen?*

I have a name, he snapped.

Could you please encourage my fox to stand back, away from potential bears?

Yes, he said. *But I'm not talking to you again unless you start calling me by my name.*

Is this really the time to get into a snit about your name?

You mean because we're in the middle of an ADVENTURE?

I started to laugh. *Yes, all right. Adventure.*

"Share the joke, Hava?" said Annet, half smiling. "I'm sure we could all use a laugh."

No one besides me, Bitterblue, and Giddon knows how freely blue foxes can communicate. I'm not supposed to be able to talk to Bitterblue's fox.

"I was talking with my fox," I lied, "in the first boat. We have a joke about chocolate. It's not much of a joke, really. I'll ask her a question, and she'll answer 'chocolate.'"

"Ah," said Annet.

All the faces in the boat had turned to me, waiting for the joke. Now they all looked disappointed.

"She doesn't know her own name," I said hastily. "I've been giving her lots of options. If anyone thinks of a nice name, will you tell me?"

"I'm sure we could do that," said Annet, with forced cheer.

Silence fell over our boat again. Quietly, I assessed my fellow travelers. In addition to me, Annet, Liel the cook, and Bitterblue's guards, this boat contains the two sailors I know least well: the married Kamassarians, Alzar and Riz. They're young, with dark, bright eyes and deep brown skin, and they've been mostly turned in toward each other, always touching each other. Alzar is tiny, smaller even than Bitterblue, with a little gap between her bottom front teeth that's charming somehow. Riz is average-sized for a man and has a smile quick as lightning. He's the only person I've seen smiling in earnest since the *Monsea* sank, and he only smiles at Alzar, in brief, hopeful flashes. Their conversation catches my ear because I'm interested in Kamassarian. He's been trying to lift her spirits. "If the water is shallow enough to sink the ship," I've heard him say more than once, "then we're near land, Alzy."

My sister's other guard, Ranin, seems solitary, self-contained, much like Mart. Ranin has a ruddy face and reddish-gold hair and takes a lot of big, steamy breaths, like a teakettle trying to release some of its pressure. His eyes, like Mart's, are usually trained on the queen's boat.

Is the queen all right? I asked the fox again, because Bitterblue's subdued, hunched form ahead has been pulling on my heart. Small boats are even harder on her stomach than big ships like the *Monsea*.

She's very worried, he said, *because she feels responsible for everyone's well-being. And she's nauseated. But she's strong.*

We need to get to land, I said.

He didn't respond.

Adventure?

Land isn't going to solve our problems, he said.

58.

BEFORE THE SUN dropped into the sea, Annet called for the boats to come together.

We reached our frozen fingers out, grabbed each other's wooden sides. For a moment, I was able to grasp a hand Giddon held out to me. I tried not to see Kera, who lay slumped beside him.

"Who's willing to take turns rowing through the night?" Annet said.

Every sailor, even Liel, raised a hand. So did Giddon and I, and so, to my surprise, did the three advisers, Coran, Froggatt, and Barra.

"Your Majesty," Annet called across the boat to Bitterblue, "how are you?"

"Humiliated, but fine," Bitterblue said cheerfully. "I'm sorry I can't row."

"No one unwell is expected to row, Lady Queen. What's your sense of the manpower in your boat?" asked Annet, which I suspect was her tactful way of asking whether the queen wanted to replace Froggatt or Barra with sailors or guards. Behind Bitterblue, Linny and Ozul sat at the oars of her boat. Ozul was watching the queen, but when I looked at Linny, he was watching me. I wondered what he saw in my face. Studying him, I saw a tight, exhausted mouth, and eyes too remote for me to read.

"I believe we're fine for the moment," said Bitterblue.

"Very well," said Annet. "Given that it's likely to be a clear night with a bright moon and given the importance of reaching land, I suggest we keep rowing for as long as we can."

"That seems wise," said Bitterblue. Then she gripped the side of her boat with an expression on her face that I keenly recognized: She was trying not to vomit.

A small, cold person is not going to survive so much vomiting. "Could the doctor move into the queen's boat?" I asked.

"I'm afraid Coran needs to be in Kera's boat," said Annet grimly.

"Will someone in Kera's boat trade with me?" the queen asked.

"I don't love the idea of *you* in Kera's boat, Lady Queen," said Annet.

"Nor do I, Lady Queen," said Mart, who was still shivering beside me, and still holding the chickens.

"I can stay between the queen and Kera at all times," said Giddon.

Or, I thought but didn't say, *we could tip Kera into the sea. Save everyone a lot of trouble.*

"I'll trade, Your Majesty," said Jacky, "if it would help."

And that was that. The first and second boats were made to float side by side. Giddon stood carefully, stepped into the first boat, then lifted my sister into his arms and carried her back with him. He did it gracefully, just as if he weren't climbing from rowboat to rowboat. I saw tears flood his eyes as he lifted her, so happy to reclaim the care of her. Adventure jumped in after her too, of course. Best of all, my fox jumped in, then crossed that boat and jumped again, into my arms.

I've been thinking I was probably this cold sometimes up in the rigging.

But then the *Monsea* was always waiting below. I could climb down and warm myself in her salon. She's gone now. This cold is permanent.

When the sun finally sank into the water, I huddled beside Liel on the floor while Annet and Ranin rowed. My fox slept inside my coat. She seemed plenty warm, but having her near me heightened my sense of responsibility for her. How are we ever going to keep fox babies alive in this cold?

I did sleep a little, fitfully, but it was not restful sleep. At one point I woke to the feeling of someone stepping and feeling around me, as if looking for something. We're all pretty used to this. Seven people and a massive store of supplies make for crowded quarters. I opened one eye. It was Annet.

"Can I help?" I asked, but she shushed me.

"Sleep, habpva," she said. So I pretended it was possible, for her sake.

The next time I opened my eyes, I could see, in the light of the moon, that she was in the bow, holding the sextant to the stars.

I sat up. At my movement, she glanced my way. In the moon's white light, I saw something shocked in her face that made fear slide like a sliver of ice down my back.

Trying not to step on anyone, I crawled to her. "What is it?"

She spoke quietly. "I would rather not tell you, habpva," she said. "But you've caught me, and I know how you feel about pretense."

"Are we someplace very bad?"

She searched my eyes before she spoke. I was searching hers too, because there's a flat honesty to moonlight. She wasn't flinching from my gaze, and I saw weariness there, and grief.

"Though we've been rowing day and night," she said, "we're a lot farther north than when we started. There's a current, Hava. It's dragging us north, along with all the icebergs."

"Oh," I said, stunned. "That's bad." Then I was angry. "I rowed really hard!"

"Yes," she said. "Everyone's been working really hard. We've got to get out of this current and make land. There aren't as many icebergs now as there were before, so I think it's time to raise the sails."

I felt very young, like a baby. I can't explain it. I felt incapable of forming any thoughts of my own. "Okay."

"Would you like to practice measuring our position by the north star, then learn how to sail a boat in the dark?"

IN THE GRAY of early morning, Annet released me from my sailing lesson and told me to nap. The thud of the jib and the crack of the sails helped me sleep more soundly.

When I woke, the light all around was rosy and the landscape had changed. Instead of yesterday's ice boulders, I saw . . . ice boulders again, but they were huge, like giant fortresses, plowing through the pink water with intention.

Annet was asleep, tucked into the bow, and Riz was in charge of the tiller. He steered us past the nose of an ice island that seemed to sweep by our stern very close.

"Moving targets?" I said to him, speaking Kamassarian as best I could.

"Yes," he said, his smile flicking once in surprise. "And some of them have bears."

"Is everyone all right?"

"Yes. Kera woke again and had to be drugged. I can't imagine why she keeps fighting, when there's nothing to be gained."

Maybe she thinks there's nothing to be lost, either, I thought but didn't say. *Maybe we should lose her.*

As morning broke, we brought the sails down and began rowing again, because the ice mountains became faster and harder to dodge. We saw one ice mountain—a tall one, with high, jagged peaks—close in on a smaller, lower ice mountain, crash into it and drive through it, tearing it apart. Annet says that the current must be stronger the

222 — KRISTIN CASHORE

farther below the surface you are, so that ice mountains with deeper bottoms get dragged more forcefully than ice mountains with shallower bottoms.

Rowing is so much slower than sailing. I keep thinking I see land in the distance, but as we crawl toward it, it moves. My eyes keep cobbling together groups of ice mountains and making them look like a broad, snowy shore.

Around midday, while the sun shone weakly at the base of the sky, Annet took another reading. I think she was ready for the bad news this time, for she kept her face steady and even. But when I caught her eye a minute later, she gave me a tight-lipped shake of the head.

The days are short, the sun rising only slightly, then dropping down again, as if a hand in the sky is pushing it back below the horizon. In midafternoon, as the world was turning orange and pink around us, snow began to fall. Surprised, for the horizon was clear, I looked up, and saw clouds knitted thickly above us.

"Annet?" I said.

"Yes, habpva?"

I wished there were a language only she and I spoke. A way to ask this without bringing it to the attention of the others.

"How will we dodge the ice mountains in the dark, if we don't have the moon or stars?"

"Ah," she said with a hearty smile. "The same way we dodged them in the *Monsea*. Every boat has a lamp in its supplies."

I knew that wasn't much of an answer. A lamp's light won't reach far if this snow grows heavy. At the most, we'll be able to see the ice mountain as it pummels us.

But her answer seemed to comfort the shivering people around us, Liel, Ranin, Mart. Which helped me, because it made me angry at them, for being stupid, delusional automatons. Anger feels better than fear. It's warmer.

The snow that landed in our boat melted onto our clothing, making us damp. As it thickened, I watched Annet pack the sextant box, the chronometer box, the nautical tables, and three compasses into a sealskin bag that she strapped onto her back. *Going somewhere?* I wanted to ask her, but didn't.

Fox? I said to the fox in my coat.

My girl.

Could I call you Hope?

Hope?

As your name, I mean.

Yes.

Really? I said, surprised. *You like that name?*

It is hopeful, she said.

Yes. I was embarrassed about that, because hope seems unintelligent in these circumstances. But if it's my fox's name, well, then, it's just a name. No risk in calling someone by their name.

59.

Mart is dead.

The rest of us from boat three are crowded into the other two boats, soaked to the skin, because our boat is gone. Liel is weeping again. Alzar is really, deeply frightened about Riz's feet, which I'm not thinking about. I've warmed my fox—Hope—as best I can, rubbing her vigorously with a scarf Ozul gave me. Whenever I ask her—Hope—if she's warm enough, she says, *Warm*. I don't believe her—Hope. No one on this ocean, not one of us in these overcrowded boats, is warm. But we're alive. And Mart is dead.

We lost him in the dark after an ice mountain reared up and smashed us. It came out of nowhere, a gigantic blade that sliced right through us. A heartbeat later, we were all in the water. Everyone fought and screamed, everyone grabbed for an oar or a piece of the boat, and someone even grabbed for me from below, pulling me under. I fought them, I was terrified, I kicked them away. Maybe it was Mart. Maybe he's dead because I wouldn't let him pull me under. But everyone knows you don't grab on to another person if you're drowning. I will not die of other people's stupidity!

The boats were tied together loosely when it happened, with lines between them, to keep us from losing each other in the dark. And so the other two boats were close, able to maneuver to us and start hauling people in. My fox—Hope—is resourceful. She squirmed out of my coat and swam to Bitterblue and Giddon's boat to be rescued and, according to Adventure, kept him apprised of where I was and how best to rescue me. Then, once I was dragged into one of the boats, she climbed across to me and tried to crawl back into my coat as if everything were normal now and we weren't soaked through and half-dead from hypothermia and there weren't others in the water who still needed rescue. I tried to explain to her, I tried to help, but I was shivering violently, I couldn't move, and I couldn't hear anything. Gradually I realized that this was because the pig was scrambling all over me, screaming in my ear. I have bruises now from her sharp hooves. But she's quieted down, and I'm nestled against her. If I'm being honest, the pig's not bad company. I can mutter bitter, pessimistic comments to her and not worry I'm destroying anyone's morale.

When everyone had been plucked from the water, even the chickens, we did a head count. That's when we realized Mart was gone. Of course we rowed in circles for a while, cast our lamps on the water, shouted his name. We picked up the oars of the lost boat and the fractured pieces of its hull, to use later. But no Mart. I think we all knew that if he was findable, we would've found him already.

I'm not in Bitterblue's boat now, but I know she's taking it hard. Annet's in my boat again and I can tell she feels responsible too. She's perched herself in the bow with a lamp and is peering into the night with a ferocity I think she intends to maintain until sunrise. If there's any way to prevent another disaster, she'll find it. I notice that the sealskin pack is still strapped to her back and I understand now. She knew our risk. And she knows we need our navigation equipment.

It comforts me—and amazes me too—that she thinks ahead like this. I'm worried about her, for she spent more time in the water than any of us, helping others out of it. It must be a captain thing, that you don't save yourself until everyone else is safe. Annet probably wouldn't have kicked someone away who grabbed at her.

Linny is near me in this boat and his face is frozen with grief. It brings memories washing over me, moments I've never considered before. Mart sat by Linny sometimes at meals. Linny sat quietly with Mart in the forecastle sometimes, repairing pieces of the rigging. Were they friends?

We eat watery oats and nutritional biscuits on this boat too. When it was Linny's turn, he passed his final spoonful to me. I stared at the bowl in my hands dumbly, confused.

"No," I said. "You eat it."

"You're still shivering," he said. "You're wet."

"But I don't want it. It's yours."

He was quiet for a moment. Then he said, "Where I'm from in the Dells, we show care of each other with food. It's a way of saying I'm looking out for you."

I wanted to ask him why he was looking out for me specifically, when I've been loathsome. I mean, I really wanted to know. But not with everyone hearing.

"He gives me food too, Princess Dardya," I heard Jacky's voice say, nearby. "You should just take it."

"But if you're giving everyone your food, you go without," I said.

"You can give me a spoonful of yours tomorrow," Linny said.

But what if I forget to keep track? I didn't say. *Or,* I thought with a burst of resentment, *what if I want mine tomorrow? Do I have to worry about you hurting yourself with your own kindness?* Then I fed the spoonful to Hope.

Alzar and Riz are in this boat too. Riz, despite whatever's happening with his feet, is still cheerful. "I like that you call Hava *brave* in Mantiperan," he said to Jacky, speaking Keepish. "It's appropriate."

"Wait, what?" Jacky said, also responding in Keepish, though his Keepish leaves a lot to be desired. "I don't call Hava *brave*."

"I thought you called her *dardya*," said Riz.

"Jacky thinks *dardya* is the Mantiperan word for *annoying*," I said. "He asked me what the Mantiperan word for *annoying* was and I knew he was going to use it against me, so instead, I told him the word for *brave*."

There was a moment of silence as Jacky worked through my Keepish response, his mouth hanging open in confused indignation. Then he started howling with laughter.

"You are too much, dardya," he said in Lingian. "You win. I surrender."

IT'S FUNNY, BECAUSE Ollie gives me bits of his food all the time, and I accept them gratefully.

He means them for Hope, of course, and I feed them to her immediately. Ollie sneaks snacks to all the animals. I guess he can't help himself. It's ridiculous the way the pig presses close to him, even trying to sit on the bench with him when he's rowing, looking up at him with adoring eyes. Unfortunately, we didn't rescue her from the *Monsea* for her own sake. I hope Ollie remembers that. He's named the pig Rosie, a proper Lienid name, for Lienid names always have at least a hint of color in them. Rosie. Olivan. Bitterblue. Ashen.

I haven't told anyone that Hope has a name now. I'm too embarrassed.

Here are the inhabitants of my new boat: Hope, Annet, Ozul, Liel, Alzar, Riz, Jacky, Linny, Ollie, Rosie the pig, and the advisers Froggatt and Barra. Annet and Liel, Alzar and Riz are wet and shivering like me. No one has spare coats to lend this time, or body heat to share. Barra, who is *not* wet and shivering, is driving me crazy. He doesn't row when it's his turn. He sits there in his excellent Keepish furs looking confused and we have to replace him with someone else. He doesn't move when he's in someone's way. He doesn't notice when it's his turn to pass the oats bowl to someone else; you have to poke him and explain. This morning, even after I'd poked him and told him to pass the bowl to Liel, he took it into his hands and started eating it himself! I lost my temper. I shouted, "Hey!" which made him jump in alarm. When I said, "Pass that to Liel," he mumbled something indistinct, passed it along shakily, then sank back into a stupor.

Later, I woke from my allotted nap to the sight of Linny giving Barra his last spoonful of food and it was all I could do not to scream. Is Linny trying to starve? When it was my turn to eat, I shoved my bowl at him and told him to eat two bites whether he wanted them or not.

He flashed his amber eyes at me, made a *hm* noise, and ate two very small bites. "Bigger," I said.

He took one more tiny bite and I snatched the bowl back and focused on forcing the gooey mess down my own throat, to stop myself from yelling at him further. I can't look at anybody today. I hate everybody, except Hope and Rosie. Because we're so crowded, we now have to nap sitting up, leaning against whoever's near, and I'm tired of Froggatt and Barra bumping and leaning against me. At one point, Linny and Jacky helped Barra to the side of the boat so he could relieve himself. When he came back beside me, I realized that I'd been smelling urine on him all morning. And then I understood his reality, and added myself to the list of people I hate. I have known so many traumatized people. I have cleaned my mother's urine. It's not Barra's fault that he can't cope with this.

There's nothing about this that I don't despise.

I kicked someone away, I told my fox, Hope. *When we all fell in the water. Someone grabbed me and I kicked them. What if it was Mart?*

I could feel the empty bubbles of her thoughts, straining to understand, then coming to her own kind of logic. *My girl,* she said. *You are my girl.* I don't know why, but it made me think of Linta Massera in her workshop, working on her theory. The explosion I caused killed Linta, not me. Do I deserve to be anyone's girl?

I tried Adventure next, for I could see him peering back at us from the other boat. I explained what I'd done.

What if it was Mart? I said.

It doesn't matter who it was, he said. *You had to do that. What do you imagine you should've done instead?*

I could have helped the person!

By consenting to drown?

I changed the subject. There's no point discussing it with someone determined not to understand. *How are the queen and Giddon?*

They're fine. The queen blames herself for Mart.

That's ridiculous, I snapped.

Oh, forgive me. I forgot that you're the only person allowed to take the blame for Mart.

I bit back on a number of retorts. *How is it, being in the boat with Kera?*

There's a certain poetic justice in watching Coran drug her with the same drug she used on your fox all those weeks, he said.

I don't think I'd quite registered that Coran was using the same drug. I touched my hand to my stomach, where Hope was sleeping inside my coat. I guess I could feel the justice of it. For some reason, it didn't fill me with the righteousness you might expect.

Your fox has told me your name for her, said Adventure.

I didn't want to hear what he thought of the name. *Excuse me,* I said, *I have to do something now,* which was ridiculous, because what could I possibly have to do?

But as I turned away, Annet handed me a glass.

"Look," she said, pointing in the direction we were heading.

I squared the glass over my eye and looked where she was pointing. At first, all I could see was a bear perched on an upcoming ice mountain.

"The bear?" I said.

"Beyond the bear," she said.

Beyond the bear were more ice mountains. Ice mountains stretching to left and right; ice mountains that perched upon gray rock.

Rock!

Land.

60.

I read or heard once that distances at sea are greater than they seem to the naked eye.

Well, it's true. We've been rowing all night, but we don't seem much closer to land yet. The sky's cleared, making it easier to avoid the moving ice, but the boats are heavier now, low in the water, harder to row. And we're so tired of rowing. I have a blister on my thumb. I don't understand how such a tiny thing can make every movement agonizing.

In the bow, under the stars, I watched for ice and bears with Annet. We held our shoulders hard against a southerly wind.

"How are you holding up, habpva?" she asked me. "Are you dry yet?"

I doubt that any of us who fell into the sea are dry. Some of the edges of my clothing, like my trouser cuffs and the outer layer of my scarf, have frozen solid. But if my furs take longer to dry, they'll also be warmer than the wool coats I see Linny wearing, and Jacky, and Liel, Alzar and Riz, and even Annet. I'm still carefully not considering Riz's feet. I'm not thinking about the things I know about coldness, from Grella's journals.

"Almost dry," I said. "You?"

"Almost."

As we crouched in the bow, I had so many questions for Annet, but I couldn't decide if any of them were worth pressing on her.

Anyway, I could figure out most of the answers for myself. What's it going to be like when we reach land? Cold and difficult, just like this. What will we do with the boats? We'll have to carry them, in case the land turns out to be an island.

I don't know the answers to all the questions, though. Why does Kera get to live, if Mart has to die? And what'll we do with her if she continues to refuse to behave? Punish her? If so, can I be the one to do it?

Hope is worrying me. Earlier, as night fell, she started exploring every nook and cranny of the boat. She climbed over people, squeezed into the spaces between them, tried to get into the supply boxes, for all the world as if she was looking for something. When I asked her what she was doing, she answered, *My girl*. When I asked her, *Did you lose something?* she answered, *Finding something*.

I watched now as she wedged herself under the knees of Ollie and Linny, who were trying to doze. Waking, Ollie looked under his legs in confusion. I saw the starlight catch the gold in one of his ears.

"You can move her," I said to him. "I don't know what's gotten into her."

"It reminds me of what dogs do when they're about to give birth," Ollie said blearily. "They like to find a dark, enclosed space."

"Oh," I said, my heart sinking. "Have I mentioned she's pregnant?"

"What?" said Ollie, his eyes popping open.

"Bear," said Annet quietly beside me.

I turned to look where she was looking. On the peak of a nearby ice mountain stood a bear, staring down at us with eyes that glinted with moonlight. I took a careful breath, hoping this was one of the bears who found us boring.

But this one was a curious bear. It picked its way down the icy slope to the water's edge, then slipped in.

"Bear," I said, scrambling around, patting people's shoulders, trying not to step on anyone, human, fox, or pig. Keeping low, so the boat's rocking wouldn't pitch me overboard. "Bear," I said louder, so the other boat would hear. This is our routine, anytime someone spots a curious bear. Everyone remains alert until the danger is passed.

Hope? I thought. *Stay down and low. Do you understand?*

Down and low, she said.

"There it is," Linny said, speaking Dellian in his sleepiness, pointing to a nub on the surface of the water. Yes. I saw its eyes and its small black nose; I watched it draw closer, pushing itself along with its powerful legs and big paws. Though we were moving as fast as Jacky and Ozul could row, the bear circled our boat, swimming lazily, peering at us with an expression of calculated apathy. I've come to hate that expression. These bears look at us, consider their own survival, and decide if we're worth the trouble.

The bear sank into the black water and disappeared. We stayed alert, our knives, if we had them, clutched in hands that were numb with cold. After a few minutes, we began to relax.

"Ow! Rosie!" said Ollie as the pig climbed over him. "Ow! Rosie!"

Ignoring his protests, the pig continued past him to the starboard side and perched her feet on the edge. Rosie keeps doing this. She's thirsty, but she doesn't understand that the seawater won't quench her thirst. The other boat has the same problem with the goat. They balance on the edge and try to lower their tongues to the water. The goat, a better climber, more often succeeds, and she kicks sometimes when anyone tries to stop her. During daylight today, I watched the goat kick Kera on the cheekbone. Then I watched Coran waste our bandages and medicines stopping the blood and binding the wound, while Kera lay pale and insensible.

As Rosie climbed onto the boat's edge, the bear surged from the water, closed its teeth on Rosie's throat, and hauled her into the sea.

61.

I'VE BEEN RANKING ways of dying from best to worst.

Please, if I must die, let me die of hypothermia, I've been saying to myself, inside my own mind. *Not bears. Let me fall asleep and freeze.*

Who are you talking to? Adventure finally yelled at me. *Do you think I have the power to arrange your ideal demise?*

I was talking to myself! I replied, indignant. *What are you doing, spying on my every thought?*

You yelled it at me! he said. *You're ALL yelling things! Humans are such children! No mental strength! You're not going to die! I won't let you!*

Oh? Now who's in denial? How is a fox the size of a shoe going to keep us all alive?

I'm not going to keep you ALL alive, he said in a chilly voice. *I'm going to keep those of you alive whose deaths would destroy the queen. You and Giddon. Annet, Navi, and Ozul. Coran, Froggatt, and Barra. Noa, Sorit, Lisa—*

So, everyone? I said, interrupting.

Of course not! I cannot keep everyone alive all by myself! he yelled. *Why are you being obstreperous, when I've expressed my wish that you stay alive?*

I sighed, raising my eyes to the horizon again to measure our distance to land. *I think our tempers are wearing thin.*

Yes, he said, chastened. *These are trying times.*

Grella's journals pushed into my mind then unbidden, because he used those words once, in the journal about his final expedition.

"Trying times." That's what he called it when a small, numb spot at the end of one finger began to blister and turn dark, which was only the beginning of what eventually happened to his hands.

I wondered if Bitterblue remembered her mother reading that part aloud. I hoped she didn't. I pushed it away.

We have the same goal, I said to Adventure. *How is she?*

We need to get to a place where she can disembark and start to keep her food down, he said.

IT SEEMS THAT everything out here is as difficult as it possibly can be.

As we near the rocky shelf of land, the sea ice is thickening, forming barriers around us. With every pull on the oars, the ice bends and shifts, parts and bumps, then locks us in. The rowers pummel at the ice with their oars. In the first boat, Giddon and Ranin have begun taking turns balancing in the bow and breaking a path with an ax.

"Surely it's thick enough to walk on?" I said at one point, but the answer was a definitive no.

"Could it be thick enough for small people?" I said, persisting. "Like Alzar or Sorit, or the queen?"

"We can hardly send the queen out to test it for us," said Ozul, who's from northern Winterkeep and knows about ice.

Our progress is slow, maybe a handspan with every strike of the ax. The ice that closes behind us brings a kind of panic into my throat, for I do not like being trapped.

Slowly, we're creeping our way to the rocks.

ALZAR AND SORIT, our two smallest sailors, are my new heroes.

For hours now, they've been walking across the ice sheets with ropes over their shoulders, pulling the first boat behind them, breaking its path through the ice with the strength of their own bodies.

I caught Alzar's eye once and she gave me a gap-toothed grin. Sorit is all focus, her hat pulled low over her short hair, Noa watching her proudly from inside the boat she's pulling.

Once, a seam began to open under Alzar. Instantly she dropped to her stomach, calling to Sorit to do the same, changing her weight distribution so quickly that the ice held fast. Briefly, the two of them slithered and crawled while the people in the first boat used the ax and oars again. Then Sorit and Alzar reached ice firm enough that they could stand again.

Now Ozul has allowed Lisa, who's the next smallest, out of the boats, to help.

"Ollie?" said Ozul. "How much do you weigh?"

When Ollie answered in Lingian units of measure, the queen's voice came softly from the first boat, converting it into Keepish measurements for Ozul. Bitterblue has a quick brain for math.

"Thank you, Lady Queen," said Ozul. "Ollie, you'll be next."

As the ice gets thicker and more firmly pressed together at its seams, our progress slows, because it becomes more difficult to break a path for the boats.

"When can we drag the boats up onto the ice?" I asked.

"Not yet," said Ozul.

Ozul's an ice engineer, I thought to Adventure. *Annet's smart to defer to her knowledge.*

Yes, he said. *And Alzar, Sorit, and Lisa are excellent at jobs that require smallness, lightness, and strength.*

Are you keeping a catalog of who's good at what?

Yes.

So am I. Ollie has a good attitude. He mourned Rosie the pig for about five minutes, then said, "Bears have to eat too."

The Keepish in my boat have admirable spirits, said Adventure.

Navi, Sorit, Noa, and Lisa are determined to survive. Alzar is too, but mostly she's worried about Riz's feet. We all are. The doctor is having grim thoughts.

Does anyone have a strong mind against you, Adventure?

The bears have strong, closed minds.

Great, I said. *Super.*

I can't feel them until they're near, he said. *It's interesting, and unfortunate. Ah well. I think I'll run ahead and see if I can report on what's in store for us.*

I watched a small, dark shape bolt out of the forward boat and streak across the ice, passing Alzar, Sorit, and Lisa, shooting on ahead.

Don't forget that the bears have strong minds! I cried after him, but got no response.

In our boat, Hope slid out of the space she was occupying between Linny and Liel. She propped herself up on our prow, looking out at Adventure as he raced away. Her belly was heavy and distended, her back arced from its weight, and I tensed, fearing what would happen if she decided to jump out after him.

Careful, I said. *Stay, Hope. It's not safe.*

Not safe, she said, her front paws trembling on the boat's edge, as if she were waiting for the right moment to spring.

But then she dropped down into the boat again and worked her way back to the space between Linny and Liel. A moment later, she climbed under Linny's bent legs.

A moment after that, Linny wrinkled his nose. Then he peeked under there.

"Oh," he said, in Dellian. "Hava? You said she's pregnant?"

"Yes," I said.

"Well, the babies are coming."

62.

CORAN HAS CROSSED into our boat to help with the birthing foxes.

Of course he made himself tiresome first, complaining and resisting, because he didn't want to leave the queen. Finally, her voice became sharp.

"You will go," she said, "and you'll give them as much care as you would give me."

"At least let me drug Kera again, Lady Queen," Coran begged, his skin papery white inside his fur hood, his lips almost as pale as his skin.

"Very well," said Bitterblue. "Do it quickly."

While he stuck Kera in the shoulder with his syringe, the rest of us pulled the boats together. Then he crossed grumpily and crouched at Linny's feet.

"I have no training with the delivery of foxes," he said. "We'll make sure their airways are clear, keep them warm, and encourage them to nurse. Beyond that, they'll have to fend for themselves."

"She's skin and bones," I said, crowding next to him. "She may not have any milk."

"We must hope she does," said Coran, "or this endeavor will come to a speedy end."

"We have the goat," I said hotly, which made Coran humph.

It was hard to tell how aware Hope was of what was happening.

She lay there on the boat's hard, cold floor, her eyes closed, her forward paws scrambling for purchase. The nose and paws of the first tiny baby poked out of her body, then didn't move beyond that.

"Is it stuck?" I said.

"Trust nature to perform its process," said Coran, which didn't impress me much.

Hope? I thought. *Are you okay?*

Heavy, she said. *Sleepy. Hurts.*

Maybe push? I said, remembering hiding in the castle infirmary as a child, watching what women did to bring babies into the world. But Hope must have misunderstood me, for she pushed on the boat's rough wood with her paws.

"Her name is Hope," I whispered to Linny. "Don't tell anyone. But help me encourage her." I think I was stuck in another place. I've seen women die, in the infirmary, from not being able to get the baby out. That's "nature in its process." I hate words like that, that mean nothing, that are designed to obscure meaning. Like "labor." Like "delivery." Here's my idea of a delivery of foxes: A guy shows up wearing a jaunty hat, carrying a box of foxes. He hands them to you. There you have it: a delivery of foxes. Does he have to pass that box through a small orifice in his body while he tears and bleeds? No. He does not.

Ahead of the boats, our smallest sailors continued to strain on the ropes, and the ice broke in an uneven rhythm. After a while, though, I noticed that the boats weren't moving anymore.

"We need to get the boats up onto the ice now," Ozul said. "It's gotten too thick to break. That means everyone has to get out." She began shouting, organizing the remaining people. "We'll walk in a single line," she said, "but no one is to stand close to anyone else! Lady Queen, I know you're dizzy. Can you walk?"

"I'll crawl, if need be," Bitterblue said.

"Crawling is a good idea," Ozul said. "Our biggest people will crawl: Ranin, Jacky, Giddon, Liel. I myself will crawl. Until I shout that it's safe, you must keep crawling, do you understand? And behind everyone else, our smallest people will pull the boats up onto the ice and drag them. Kera will remain in the first boat, since she's unconscious. Coran will remain in the second boat because he's helping the fox mother. Does everyone understand?"

I understood that I wouldn't be allowed to stay with Hope. "Maybe Coran could teach me what to do?" I said. "Then I could stay here, and Coran could be out there on the ice in case anyone needs him?"

"The fox needs a doctor," Ozul said flatly. "And right now I need you to obey orders, Hava."

I closed my mouth tight around a mutinous retort. Ahead of me, Bitterblue climbed out of her boat and began walking toward shore with small, unsteady steps. Noa stepped out behind her, then Navi, then Ranin, who dropped to his stomach and crawl-slid.

The tiny baby poking from Hope's body popped out, landing on the scarf Coran held extended to catch it. Still grumbling, Coran wiped gently at the baby's pointy face, then tied off its umbilical cord with a string he produced from nowhere. He put its little body to his ear.

"Alive," he pronounced. "Male. We must keep him warm."

Then he opened the throat of his jacket and tucked the little kit inside with a care, a tenderness, I wasn't expecting. The scarf he was using, I realized, was his own scarf. His hood was down and his neck was bare. As he bent over Hope again, he shivered, but touched her gently.

"Hava?" said Ozul. "It's your turn."

63.

I SUPPOSE WE MADE a strange procession, sliding, some of us crawling, in a long, stretched-out line toward the shore.

I hardly paid attention to my own progress. When, far ahead, Bitterblue fell, then behind me, Giddon jumped up in alarm, I snapped at him to get down again. As he dropped back onto his stomach, a web of cracks formed all around him, popping and hissing.

"Idiot," I shot at him, but I don't think he heard me. He was focused on Bitterblue, who was completely fine and not in need of rescue from the biggest, stompiest person in our entourage.

I wanted to be in the boat far behind us, with Hope. I slid along, impatient with the slow pace, craning my neck back, trying to read the expressions on Coran's pale face.

After an eon, I reached a pebbled beach slick with ice where the others were gathering, trying not to fall. Shivering but smiling, even laughing together. Idiots. Land is not a reprieve.

Above us, a rocky overhang loomed. A shelf of snow hung over its edge, looking like an avalanche about to drop on us. When Navi called out that she'd found a path up onto higher ground, everyone began to shuffle in her direction, but I stayed behind, waiting for Lisa and Ollie, who were pulling Hope's boat.

Giddon reached the beach, stood, and went to Bitterblue, who was waiting for him. Wrapping her in his arms, he helped her to the path. Ozul and Noa supported Riz, whose feet were apparently unreliable. Ranin stood grimly, watching the approach of the boat containing Kera. When Alzar and Sorit dragged it onto the pebbles, he bent down, then hauled Kera's body up onto his shoulder. As he joined the line climbing the path to higher ground, Noa came back, her smile incandescent, and wrapped her arms around Sorit. They climbed the path together, attached to each other.

"Hava?" said Linny beside me.

"I'm waiting for Hope," I said to him.

"Okay," he said. "I'll wait too."

"You don't have to."

"I want to."

"Okay, thanks," I said, obscurely relieved that someone besides me was remembering Hope, instead of rushing ahead.

When Lisa and Ollie dragged Coran's boat onto the beach, I climbed right in with him.

"How many?" I said. "Is everyone okay?"

"Three so far," said Coran, unsmiling. "All alive."

"I can hold them and warm them," I said.

Coran shot me a skeptical glance, humphed, then loosened his coat and began passing me tiny, damp little bodies. I pulled off my gloves, opened my own coat, and slipped them in gently.

"Are you dry from your own dunking?" said Coran.

"I'm dry inside my coat."

"And what about you?" said Coran, directing a pinched expression at Linny, who was hovering outside the boat, watching us. "Are you going to help, or just block the light?"

Linny climbed into the boat immediately, pulling off his own gloves. While I focused on warming the kits, he took over the job of wiping each new baby's nasal passages clear, then holding it to his ear, his face so intense with concentration as he listened for their heartbeats that it made me trust him, very suddenly, as nothing else had before. *Linny and Coran,* I thought, *are careful with Hope's babies.*

Linny held one to my ear once. Its heartbeat was a tiny, steady thwap against the side of my face.

"Do you think Hope looks okay?" I asked him.

"I'm not sure how she's supposed to look," said Linny. "But she doesn't look *not* okay."

Hope? I said, scratching her behind the ears. *How are you?*

She flashed her gold eyes at me, still scrabbling with her feet, like she was trying to escape. *Babies,* she said. *Tired. Hurts.*

I had an image suddenly of her dividing into her essential parts. All the little foxes she's made of.

You're doing a wonderful job, I said. *You're such a brave fox.*

Don't want these babies, she said.

I think I gasped a little.

"What?" said Linny.

"Nothing," I said, hunching my shoulders.

"Hava?" said Linny. "You look really cold." He took my hands, began rubbing them between his, and that's when I realized how hard I was shivering.

"I'm fine," I said.

"We should join the others soon," he said. "See if anyone's building a fire."

"I'm fine," I insisted, feeling the calluses on his palms, which were hot against my fingers. "Linny. Why are you helping us?"

"What?" he said. "Why wouldn't I help you?"

"Why *would* you?" I said, then stopped, conscious of Coran, who could hear us, no matter how hard he was ignoring us.

Suddenly, Jacky and Ranin appeared at our bow, grabbed on to the boat's edge, and yanked the entire thing, pulling all of us toward the path that led above.

"What are you two doing?" Jacky demanded, staring in at us.

"Fox babies," Linny said.

"And that requires holding hands?"

"Maybe you remember about how we're all freezing?" Linny said to him dryly, then let my hands go as another baby popped out of Hope's body and Coran passed it to him. "This is number six. Does that mean it's the last one?"

"We'll know in a moment," Coran said crisply.

"Here," Linny said, holding the sixth tiny fox out to me, then reaching for me, helping me as I fumbled to open my coat again.

"Maybe you should take one or two," I admitted, not wanting to give any of them up. "It's getting crowded in here."

"Okay," Linny said, unbuttoning his own coat, flashing the smallest grin at the little fox. Tucking it inside gently, murmuring to it. I could feel Jacky still watching us, and I didn't like the flavor of his gaze. I recognized it: jealous schoolboy, though I'm not sure which one of us he was jealous of, me, Linny, or the fox kit inside Linny's coat. I didn't care. Ignoring him, I examined the kits in my own coat, one at a time, finding the biggest, strongest-looking one to pass to Linny.

I studied each closely, noting the differences in ear shape and size, in the blueness of their fur. One had big, floppy paws and another had a squat little head with a long crease of a mouth. All of their eyes were shut tight.

I am going to keep these babies alive.

64.

ABOVE THE SEA, on a snowy plain that glows with the orange of sunset, we've built a fire with the salvaged pieces of wood from the lost boat.

It took a long time to get those waterlogged boards burning. Then, when they caught, the tar that seals them was almost explosive. Navi and Ozul are a stubborn team, first fighting for the smallest lick of flame, then fighting for a conflagration that wouldn't hurt anyone. A colorful team too, with their bright Keepish scarves.

Now we're all trying to warm ourselves and dry our wet things. It's turning out to be a mucky mess, because the fire is built on snow and ice that melts and then runs with water. We have to bail out our fire as it sinks farther and farther into a hole of its own making. We've draped our drying scarves and blankets over the boats and brought them as close to the flames as seems safe, but our own butts on the ground are melting the snow and getting soaked.

Nonetheless, this difficult fire is the most beautiful thing any of us have experienced in a long time. The warmth is a kind of ecstasy. And my sister's soft voice chattering nearby is a balm to my soul, because it means she's feeling better. Now we just have to fill her up with food.

Hope and the kits are nestled together in a blanket in my lap. Hope seems to have milk for them, but she also seems impatient with nursing. She keeps trying to get up and leave, then falling back in frustration when she finds six little mouths latched to her, trapping her on her side.

It's the babies, Hope, I keep telling her. *You're nursing the babies.*

Don't want babies. Someone else nurse babies, she says. *Hate babies,* she said once with a burst of fury, and I had to stop myself from chastising her. It's not her fault. She's woken up from a nightmare the extent of which I can't ever know, and here we all are, in a desperate place. She doesn't have to like what's happening to her. But I was afraid that even on their first day of life, the kits might feel the thrust of such feelings, being telepathic. I couldn't bear them knowing they were unwanted. *I love the babies,* I insisted, not sure I meant it, because they were only little blobs. It was just words. But I hoped it counterbalanced something.

As my bottom sank into the ground and became wetter and wetter, I decided to start a new ritual. One at a time, I took each kit into my hands and nestled it against my chest, stroking its fur and telling it I love it. Sort of like what I used to do with my figurines, but for the babies' sake more than mine.

As THE STARS began to prick the sky, Bitterblue came to sit with me. "How are you, sweetie?" she said.

"Okay," I said. "You?"

"Better."

"May I have the little bundle I gave you the day we left the *Monsea*?" I said. "Wrapped in a scarf?"

"Of course," she said, then reached into the canvas bag she keeps near. I remembered then that my translations are in that bag too. Is it silly if I'm relieved that Linta Massera didn't sink with the *Monsea*?

Bitterblue pulled the bundle out, squinting at it as she handed it to me. "That scarf is familiar to me."

"Oh," I said, suddenly hot with embarrassment. "I stole it from your mother when I was six." I didn't want to think about it now, that moment when I'd pulled one of Ashen's scarves to myself, wanting to know how it felt, how it smelled. The memory was too far away now.

She surprised me by shouting a laugh. It made everyone in the camp stop what they were doing and look over at us, firelight in their eyes. Some of them smiled, hopefully, wanting to hear something funny.

"The queen just realized I stole this scarf from her when I was six," I explained, taking some liberties with the story. Reminders of Bitterblue's murdered mother aren't going to cheer anyone up.

"What's your punishment?" asked Giddon, grinning at us from across the fire.

"I leave it to my captain to dispense this punishment," said Bitterblue with pretend gravity.

"Our habpva is pardoned for all crimes committed as a child," Annet intoned from the fire, where she was taking her turn bailing water. I thought she might speak differently, if she knew more about my childhood, but anyway.

Then Linny appeared, carrying a steaming bowl and spoon, both of which he placed in my hands. "The first bite is yours," he said.

"Oh, my," I said, too overwhelmed by its warmth and scent, my relief, my happiness about the kits in my lap, to surge into my usual doubt. "It smells amazing. Maybe I won't give it back."

"Maybe you're not appreciating my feat of heroism in carrying that bowl all the way from the fire without eating any."

"The fire's half a step away," I said, laughing.

"If you don't eat it within ten seconds, your bite is forfeit."

"You can't make up arbitrary rules!" I said, heaping the spoon as high as I could and closing my mouth around it. It was the single most delicious thing I've ever eaten in my life, a stew made of dried beef, dried peas, beans, carrots, and presumably snow. It exploded inside my throat, tracing a warm and wonderful path down to my stomach, and I wouldn't release the bowl when Linny tried to pry it from me.

"I understand it's yours," I said. "I just can't seem to let go."

With a snort, he took the spoon from my hand, crouched beside me, and began to eat his dinner while I continued to hold the bowl against my chest. Then he seemed to realize that the Queen of Monsea was sitting beside us, quietly watching us behave like animals.

"Oh," he said, stopping mid-spoon, then straightening, switching into Lingian. "Forgive me, Lady Queen. I should've offered the bowl to you."

"Certainly not," my sister said. "Liel is making me a special dinner of the things I digest most easily. I'm still a bit sick, you know."

"Oh. All right," said Linny, who seemed ever so slightly flustered. I let him have his bowl back so he could escape.

"I like people who look after you," said Bitterblue, watching him go.

"He always shares his food, with everyone," I said. "I don't know why he shares it with me."

Hope, struggling to stand again, discovered that the babies were still attached to her body. Sending me a blip of irritation, she flopped back down.

"Poor Hope," I said, stroking a line from her ears to her tail.

"I like her name," Bitterblue said.

It turns out the emergency supplies contain a few wonders beyond the oats and the chalky nutritional biscuits. A stove and oil. A variety of other foods. Two longbows. Blankets. And two canvas tents, oiled and water-resistant, which give us walls and roofs to stop the wind that's picked up since we reached land.

I let Grella into my mind briefly, when I saw the stove and the oil. Grella didn't have anything like that, when he died in the pass that bears his name.

Then I pushed him out again, remembering that he had far more food per person than we do.

We lost the third tent when we lost the third boat. It's cramped, ten people in each tent, all pressed against one another on a freezing canvas floor, but Annet says we conserve body heat that way. I know how to sleep in tiny spaces, but it's different when your walls are living people. I don't sleep well with other people. I lie on my side with my sister behind me and Ozul in front of me and I wish I could be on the end, touching only one person.

Annet says that in the morning, there'll be a series of announcements about our new responsibilities and routines. I can't turn off my brain. I keep wondering if it's possible to build skis for the boats to help us slide them across the snow. And I wonder if people like Riz, Barra, and Liel, with their fragile feet and minds, are going to slow us down.

Three of the fox babies are curled up inside my coat, each wrapped in rags so they don't pee and poop all over me. I don't know what else to do, because Hope won't stay with them. I don't know where she is right now. She crawled out of my coat a while ago and isn't responding when I call, and Adventure is asleep. Should I get up and try to find her? I keep repeating her name. It's become a sleep incantation, making me drowsy. *Hope. Hope. Hope.* Then I remember what I'm saying and my worry snaps me back awake.

The other three babies are inside Linny's coat, against Linny's chest. Linny is sleeping three people behind me. It goes me, Bitterblue, Giddon, then Linny. Then Jacky, who's on one of the ends.

Hope? Hope? Hope!

With so much snow, we should have enough water. But when will we reach a place with trees, so we can have more fires? Is there game to hunt here? What is our position? Are there bears?

Hope. Hope. Hope.

What is that noise? Is it the snuffling of a bear? No. It's the chickens, in the next tent. I will not keep my strength up if I can't fall asleep because I think every sound is a bear.

Hope? Hope?

What about Kera? She woke again this evening, started another fight, and was drugged again. I wonder if she's doing it on purpose, to escape all this. It's not fair. It's one thing for Riz or Barra to hold us back, and another entirely for Kera. I won't be held back by her. I'll take care of it, by myself, alone, if I have to. I still have a knife in my boot.

I fell asleep, finally, to a sense of the world turning under me.

65.

I woke to Hope climbing back into my furs.

Where have you been? I asked her grouchily.

Running. Eating.

Eating what?

Chocolate, she said, with her usual bubble of humor, but it was hard to be amused.

Do your babies have names? I asked her.

Not my babies, she said, as the babies, feeling her, squirmed toward her and latched themselves on.

Until they tell us their names, may I name them?

Don't care, she said, then fell asleep.

66.

THIS MORNING, WHEN the sun stretched across the water and touched my face, I was standing on land. My own continent! I'm not sure I believe it yet.

Annet took a navigational reading, then gave us a speech that was short and to the point. She stood before us, squinting against the brightness of snow and sky. Her face was ruddy, her gold hair flapping, hands pink and ungloved. Beside her stood Navi, dark curls escaping from her hat, chin high. She and Annet were shoulder to shoulder, their expressions equally fierce.

First Annet held up a map and pointed to the icy, mountainous coastline far north of Pikkia.

"On the one hand," she said, speaking plainly, "we're somewhere around here. On the other hand, this map, like all maps of this part of the world, was drawn by people who've never been here. It's based on rumors, speculation, and theory. Its usefulness is limited."

She rolled the map and handed it to Navi. "What matters more is that according to my navigational readings, we are, to my best estimation, about twenty walking-days from the inhabited mountains of northern Pikkia. A walking-day assumes steady progress over a range of terrains that may be difficult but aren't impassable. It also assumes dry weather, and the health of our party. Furthermore, it assumes that we aren't carrying two large boats.

"In other words," Annet said, "it assumes a number of conditions that don't apply to us, or that we can't know yet. In our emergency supplies, we have twenty days of food for everyone if we ration carefully, which we'll certainly do. We also have four chickens and a goat. At the moment, we have ample snow from which to make water. And we have two longbows, twenty-four arrows, and two highly skilled archers. Unfortunately, one of them is Kera. Linny," she said, directing her steady gaze at Linny, who stood beside me. "We can't afford to put a bow in the hands of someone who'll lose arrows. So there's going to be an undue hunting burden on you."

"That's fine, Captain," Linny said.

Well, that was interesting. I used my Grace to glance at Linny. Most Dellians learn to shoot because of the need to protect themselves from Dellian monsters, but that doesn't make them all highly skilled. And Giddon's a skilled archer. If he's not good enough, Linny must be very good indeed. This'll be part of Linny's other life, I guess. The one where he's the illegitimate son of a lord who taught him chemistry.

Then Navi brought Linny an unstrung longbow, and when Linny grasped it and tested its grip, then propped it against the ground and put his muscle into measuring its bend, something shifted in my memory. I saw Linny with that same calm, serious look on his face. I saw him nocking an arrow to a bow and hauling the string back, squinting his amber eyes at the sky. I remembered the smooth *whoosh* of the arrow as he released it, and the scream of a raptor above. A lifetime ago, when the *Monsea* first left the Dells for Winterkeep, a sailor I hadn't met yet was our guard against the Dellian raptor monsters that prey on the crews of departing ships. Every ship in the Dells has such a guard.

Linny had been ours. I realized that now, but he'd been a stranger to me then. A quiet, slender person I'd studied for a moment, trying to decide if he was a boy or a girl; and then I'd left him to his shooting, impressed that anyone could hit a moving target while standing on a bucking floor, but more impressed by the ship. Enthralled by the wind filling the sails, propelling us away from land. It was the first time I'd ever set out across an ocean before.

"Now," said Annet. "Daily jobs and responsibilities. Navi, Ozul, and I will make a list of the jobs that need to be done every day. Every morning, we'll decide who'll be assigned to which job. I expect obedience. This will be easy for some of you, harder for others. I'm generally open to questions about why I've asked you to do something, but there will be times—often—when I need obedience in the moment, and your questions or doubts will have to wait for later. This is not because I don't value your thoughts. It's because we're in a dangerous situation. It's my responsibility to see that we all survive. I absolutely require that you repay my dedication to your survival with obedience. Understood?"

I raised my hand. Then I realized, when Annet gently said, "Yes, Hava?" that her speech had probably been meant for me. I'm the one who's always asking questions, wanting the plan to change, or needing to understand why I should do something before I do it. And here I was doing it again.

"What'll happen with Kera?" I asked, persisting. "Are we going to carry her to Pikkia?"

Annet nodded, seeming to acknowledge the justice of this question. "We're not going to survive the journey to Pikkia unless every member of the group furthers the group by working as a team," she said. "When Kera wakes up again, our expectations of her behavior will be explained to her."

It wasn't really an answer. "Okay," I said. "And when she doesn't behave?"

Annet's eyes found Bitterblue. "Lady Queen?" she said.

"If Kera decides not to rise to our expectations," said Bitterblue, "she'll be left behind."

67.

WELL. NOW I have something to look forward to: Kera waking up, starting another fight, and being left behind.

Annet has assigned me the job of making an inventory of our stores of food with Coran, Froggatt, and Barra. I can now report that the advisers are useless, especially Froggatt and Barra. They're so cold and frightened, so convinced that the queen isn't going to survive this and neither are they, that it's all they talk about, and then Bitterblue has to come over and use up her own reserves of patience to comfort them. It makes me want to break their necks. How can they think it raises her chances of survival for them to state out loud, in her hearing, that she might die?

Over a box of carrots, I finally lost my temper. "The queen has survived Grella's Pass," I said, loudly. "Why shouldn't she survive this?"

"The queen had the protection of Lady Katsa in Grella's Pass," said Froggatt, then indicated himself, Barra, and Coran, all bundled in the world's finest coats and mittens, all slender and muscleless, shivering and distressed, like spoiled princes. "We're not Lady Katsa!"

"Too true," I said as a passage from Grella's journals pushed itself into my mind. He wrote many journals, not just the ones he buried under the rocks in Grella's Pass before he died. Once, when he was almost as young as Ollie, Grella joined an ill-fated party that tried to cross the eastern mountains into what we now know is the Dells. They didn't make it across, of course, and a third of them died. One of them, knowing that his necrotic feet were slowing the group, crawled off into a blizzard one night, to remove himself from their list of problems. It was a kind of courage I doubt these men could fathom.

I gave Froggatt my best copper-red glare. "If you want to help the queen," I shot at him, "stop speculating about how she's going to die, then giving her the job of soothing your feelings. A truly loyal assistant would sooner leave camp and die alone on the ice than drag his sovereign down—"

"Hava," said Bitterblue quietly. "That type of talk isn't necessary."

"People have done such things," I insisted.

"Yes," she said. "I didn't know you were so familiar with Grella's journals."

She didn't know I'd become familiar with them the same time she had, hiding in her rooms, poaching the coziness and comfort she shared with her mother.

"This is a different situation, Hava," she continued. "It asks a great deal of men who were trained to work in an office. It's frightening, and I'm their queen. Please, stop yelling at them. It's my *job* to comfort them."

Throwing a handful of carrots back into the box, I glared at Froggatt, then Barra, then Coran. "See?" I said. "See who's helping whom?"

Of course, they all looked entirely ashamed of themselves, which made me ashamed of myself. Pushing myself up, I went for a walk.

Ozul, Navi, and Giddon were kneeling in a patch of trampled snow, taking one of the boats apart. I think they were using its wood to build some sort of sledge for the other boat.

"Hava?" said Navi, looking up from her task. Even though she was wearing a hood now over her hat, I could see her scarlet-gold scarf peeking out. Why was that comforting? "Aren't you supposed to be inventorying the food?"

"I lost my temper," I said.

"What about?" said Ozul, not pausing in her hammering. Could she possibly be warm enough in that coat?

"I yelled at Froggatt and Barra to stop giving the queen the job of comforting them about how she's likely to die in the wilderness," I said.

"Sounds fair," said Giddon, grinning around a row of nails in his mouth.

"Technically," I said, "I may have implied they should lie down in the snow and die."

Ozul snorted, but Navi stood up and considered me seriously. "This ordeal is going to make all of us irritable," she said.

"Yes," I said irritably.

"Each of us has a responsibility to keep from lashing out," she said.

I turned a shoulder to her.

As I did, one of the kits squirmed inside my furs. I knew which one it was: the kit with the big floppy paws. I've been calling her Moth because she flaps her paws around, slapping my belly with soft little whacks, like a moth trying to find its way out of a room. In Monsea, we have beautiful moths that visit the flowers in the court-yards at night, soft blue, with thin black veins running through their wings. I saw a man trying to kill one once, clapping it against a marble pilaster with his handkerchief. I cried out. When he looked up in surprise, I turned into a sculpture. When he left, I went to the moth and found it alive, but its wings broken. So I killed it with my own hands and fed it to the fish in the pools, because a moth can't live without wings.

This Moth inside my furs will live.

Nearby, where Jacky, Ranin, and Annet were taking down the tents, a flash of movement caught my eye. Kera, waking, shot to her feet. She was wild, her auburn hair matted and messy, her face dirty.

Then Annet said something sharp and quick and Jacky and Ranin grabbed Kera and hauled her around the half-standing tent, out of my sight. I heard Kera's shouting voice and the sound of a blow. I heard Annet's voice, clipped and grim.

"Hava?" said Navi, reclaiming my attention. I turned back to her familiar, soft eyes and scarlet-gold scarf. In the morning light, I could see the dark freckles scattered across her brown face, and pieces of her loose hair pushed by the wind. But it was hard to focus on her.

"Yes?"

"You may always come talk to me whenever you're feeling irritable," she said.

I was ashamed. "I'll manage it better."

"Good," she said. "Now, go back to your inventory and apologize to your crewmates for abandoning them."

68.

I f L i n t a M a s s e r a were here, I would tell her what the world is made of: cold. Snow. And light.

She's not here. Nothing familiar is here.

We're moving now, at a crawl. We take turns pulling the heavy sledge. The advisers are the slowest. They trudge at the end of the line, struggling along the path the rest of us break.

I hate snow. It's possible there's nothing on this earth I hate more than snow. Sometimes it comes to our knees and sometimes to our thighs, and even in the back of the line when I'm walking through snow others have trampled down for me, every step twists my sore ankle, every step lands at a different depth than the last, every step requires lifting my feet ridiculously high, every step involves shifting wet, heavy snow. What if I get frostbite in my feet like that climber in the eastern mountains did and I can't walk? What if we all do? I seem to have lost my ability not to think about it. Riz rides in the boat some of the time, because his feet are so painful. His smile still flashes, especially when Alzar is around, but Coran's face gets very grim whenever he examines Riz's feet.

Also, the wind whips the snow into tiny, icy shards that sting our faces. And it's blinding, because we're always walking into a low sun that turns our path into blazing fire. Annet shouts at us to close our eyes whenever we're resting, to make brims of our hats and scarfs so our eyes will be in shade. I want to be contemptuous of this order, because I happen to know it comes from Kera, who's walking among us now on her own two feet like a free person, looking peaky and ill. I hope she is ill. I hope when it's her turn to eat, she chokes and dies. She pulls the sledge like everyone else, has a turn leading the goat like everyone else. I can feel the ghost of her hands on the lead or the sledge ropes when I take hold of them later.

Anyway, I heard her tell Annet this morning that we need to guard against snow blindness. I'm angry with her that she's right, and that she thought of it before I did. Grella wrote about snow so bright it can damage the eyes, even make you blind.

When I had a chance to walk alongside Giddon, I asked him how his eyes were feeling.

He gave me a keen glance, then shook his head. "When I'm one of the people at the front breaking the path in the snow and there's nothing but white stretching out before me, I can barely look at it, it's so painful."

I wished I hadn't asked. "Maybe we should move at night," I said. "The snow wouldn't blind us and the surface would be more frozen. Easier to walk on, easier to pull the sledge across."

"That's worth mentioning to Annet."

"How's Bitterblue?"

"Still dizzy. She says the world is still moving. But she's eating better. How are you, Hava?"

"I'm fine. You're giving her half your food at every meal, aren't you?"

"Everyone tries to give her half their food," he said, flashing his tired smile at me. Giddon has a wound on the left side of his face, red and angry-looking, from where Kera sliced him with his own knife. It stretches and moves when he smiles.

"Is that cut healing all right?" I said. "It still looks fresh."

"Well," said Giddon, "it's only been three days."

Then Annet called out that it was time for everyone to switch jobs, as she does every hour. Giddon moved away to take his turn pulling the sledge, leaving me goggling in astonishment. Three days? Impossible. As I took the goat's lead from Ollie, I ran my mind back. Two nights sleeping in the rowboats. Then last night sleeping on land.

He's right: The *Monsea* sank only three days ago.

"I can't believe it," I told the goat.

She didn't care; she just balked and pulled, with a gleam in her eye like she was plotting a mutiny. It's possible the goat hates snow even more than I do, and also possible that over time, I could come to hate the goat more than I hate the snow. When the goat is your responsibility, it means that for the next hour, not only must you struggle through the snow yourself, but you must persuade the goat to struggle too, and let me tell you, the expression should be "stubborn as a goat," not "stubborn as a mule." The goat, quite reasonably, doesn't understand why the snow to the south is always more preferable than the snow we're already standing in. And apparently she doesn't do things she doesn't understand.

Is this what I'm like to other people? I wondered. Then I gave such an angry wrench on her lead that the tie of my coat must've loosened, because one of the fox kits popped out. It broke through the surface of the snow and vanished.

Behind me, Froggatt saw it happen. He dove with a squeal of alarm, surprisingly fast, throwing snow aside with his hands, extricating the kit and holding it close to his chest, while I readjusted my clothing and anxiously checked that the three others in my possession were still there. Linny is carrying two, but these four are my responsibility.

They were all present and accounted for. I had no idea they could fall out like that. I could be strewing them along behind me, a trail of frozen kits, all my fault.

Froggatt was staring down at the kit in amazement. "My wife is about to have a baby," he said. "Will I know how to hold it? How does one know these things? Will I just have an instinct?"

When I stuck my hand out for the kit, he looked at me with an expression that was a mix of wonder and reluctance. I could tell he didn't want to give her back. When he did, I brought her to my face and kissed the place where her ears met her head. She was one of the smaller kits and had long, soft white hair tufting out of comically large ears. I'd taken to calling her Cornsilk. *I'm sorry I dropped you, Cornsilk,* I said.

Then, trying to hide the war I was having with myself, I held her out to Froggatt again. "Would you like the care of her?" I said.

He gaped at me. Then at the kit, as if I were offering him a creature from the moon. I didn't know why I was doing it. I hoped he would say no.

Instead, he took her quickly against his chest. "How do I keep her safe?"

"Just tuck her into an inside pocket, or somewhere else warm, while we're walking. If she's restless, let me know, because she might need to nurse," I said, though I wasn't sure what to do when that happened. Adventure and Hope keep running ahead together. Whenever I suggest Hope stay near her kits, she ignores me. "Keep her bottom half wrapped in that cloth, unless you want her relieving herself in your pockets. She's called Cornsilk."

"Because of her ears?"

"Yes."

He opened his beautiful furs and fiddled with his inside pockets, trying to find the best place for her. He had such a look of wonder and responsibility on his face that I probably should've been feeling good about my kind deed, but I don't like to give one of my kits away. I don't need anyone's help with them; I can care for them better than anyone. And if he forgets about her, or drops her, or lets her come to harm in any way, I am going to twist his head off his body. But something made me do it.

"I don't know about this," he said, suddenly doubtful. "Maybe she should be with someone stronger."

"Were you on the king's staff, Froggatt?" I asked. "Before he died?"

Froggatt stared at me with a new expression, one that scared me, for he seemed muted and blank suddenly, very far away. My words had pulled him into a bad place inside himself. I shouldn't have asked.

"Yes," he said quietly.

I swallowed, remembering how I'd yelled at him before.

I forget sometimes that there are different kinds of resilience.

"Then you're a survivor," I said. "You've survived things far worse than a long walk, or a little bit of cold."

69.

SOMETIME LATER, LINNY moved away from the group and pushed off to the right, his bow and a quiver slung over his back. He looked strong and sure, like the snow he was breaking through was no more trouble than the rigging of the *Monsea* had been.

The whole world is so white that it was hard to see the horizon he walked toward, but I could make out Adventure trotting beside him, balanced on the surface of the snow.

Hope? I cried out anxiously. Usually when I check on her, she's with Adventure, but I couldn't see her now.

My girl, she said.

Where are you?

On this boy, she said.

What boy?

Linny-Boy!

Squinting, I saw her, bouncing around inside of the hood of Linny's coat.

But, where you going?

We are hunters! she said proudly.

For a while after that, I put one foot in front of the other, having a little fight with the jealousy that squirmed inside me.

Adventure? I called out. *I need to talk to you.*

I can't talk now. I'm helping Linny hunt, he responded importantly.

Are the kits safe? He has two of them, right?

Yes, they're in his pockets, each of them inside one of his gloves.

Are you telling me Linny isn't wearing gloves?

Gloves impede archery.

Losing fingers also impedes archery, but I kept that retort to myself. *And Hope is safe?*

Yes. Hunting seems mainly to involve walking around, standing still, doing nothing, and waiting for Linny to dig himself out whenever he sinks into the snow.

Hang on, I said, realizing something. *How are you helping him hunt, if he thinks you're only able to communicate with the queen?*

I told him.

What? You told him!

It's a new world, he said.

With the sunset, a bank of clouds rolled in, cloaking us in darkness. So much for my idea to travel at night.

As soon as we stopped, I retrieved the kits from Froggatt and Linny and collected them in a blanket in my lap with Hope, so they could nurse. I think they were ravenous. They mewled with cries that stopped when they started nursing. My butt grew wet and cold, because the rock I'd thought I was sitting on turned out to be ice. But I waited until they were done.

Babies eat too much, Hope told me with a blip of irritation.

"I wonder how one milks a goat," I said aloud.

"I'll ask Ollie," said the voice of Froggatt. I turned in surprise. He was nearby, kneeling on the trampled snow, slicing carrots and transferring them into a pot. "I predict he knows." Then he carried the pot to Liel, who was working over the tiny stove.

Later, after I'd passed Cornsilk back to Froggatt, I saw Ollie giving

Froggatt a milking lesson. I was surprised by how much milk they were getting out of that creature, then remembered that it's only been three days. Next I saw Froggatt experimenting with the curled end of a handkerchief, dipping it into a tin of milk, then holding it to the dark little mouth that poked out of the top of his coat.

Jealousy twisted inside me again.

"Hava?" said Annet. "Would you help raise the tents?"

OUR TENTS HAVE frames of flexible wood with pins and pegs that snap neatly together and oiled canvas sides that fit tightly around every corner. They remind me of sails and rigging, not least because the wind picked up as we raised them.

I battened down the canvas, Jacky and Linny at my side. Once, when Jacky tripped on part of the frame and fell sideways into the snow, he shouted with laughter. I've noticed this about Jacky. When something happens out here, he laughs. In the meantime, I grabbed for the frame anxiously, checking to see if he'd broken it, because it's thin and light and we need it; we cannot afford to lose it.

"How's hunting?" I asked Linny.

"Cold," he said shortly, trying to fix a stake in the snow. "Lonely. I caught nothing and lost two arrows."

"How is it lonely if all the foxes want to be with you all the time?" I said, hating myself for the meanness in my voice.

He stilled his hands and looked at me hard. He started to speak, then seemed to change his mind, deliberately ignoring me, fighting with the stake instead. Every time he drove it into the snow, it popped back out again. I noticed he was wearing gloves.

I tried to make my voice more reasonable. "Are your hands warm enough while you're hunting?" I said, which was what I'd meant to ask originally.

"I keep them inside my sleeves," he said, still not looking at me.

Not reassuring. What about the air that rises up into his sleeves? "And is Hope any help out there?"

He snorted. "Not particularly."

"Does she talk to you?" I asked, already knowing the answer, already feeling the surge of resentment.

"She talks *about* you," he said. "At least, I assume it's you. Her girl, her hero, her rescuer. She says those words over and over. Then she complains about your babies, because she seems to think they're yours."

Tears flooded my eyes. I wasn't prepared for them; trying to hide them, I flashed into a sculpture of myself. Linny's breath hitched.

"Sorry," I said miserably, fighting to return to myself. "It's harder to control when I'm tired."

"It's okay," he said. "It doesn't bother me. It just startles me." He'd given up on his tent stake and was kneeling in a puddle, just watching me now. His face was drawn with weariness, his body swaying in a kind of exhausted surrender, and he no longer seemed annoyed. "I guess I'm not used to it yet."

"Yet?"

"Don't you think it's something I could get used to?"

In the falling light, I knelt in my own puddle, studying this person who keeps offering me friendship I'm pretty sure I don't deserve. His eyes were quiet, his mouth soft while he waited for my answer. It's a mystery to me where his sweet temper comes from.

"Why are you kind to me," I said, "over and over, when I'm mean and jealous?"

He pursed his lips in thought. Then he shrugged. "Maybe to see what happens."

A bubble of surprised laughter rose into my throat. "Like an experiment?"

"Sure," he said, "science," which made me snort.

Shuffling over to him, I took the stake from his hands. "Here, I'll hold it while you hammer it."

"Thanks."

We worked together for a minute, huddled close. With gentle taps, he eased the stake into the snow, and finally it began to hold. Then I thought of what he'd said about Hope and the babies and, to my humiliation, flashed into a sculpture again.

He froze.

"Sorry!"

"It's okay."

"I gave one of the kits into Froggatt's keeping," I explained, wiping a rogue tear with my sleeve. "The one with the white, silky hair in her ears. Cornsilk."

"I see," he said. "Do you want one of the two I carry, to make up for her?"

Yet again, I flashed into a sculpture. Maybe this is why it's taken me so long to trust Linny. He makes me feel transparent as glass.

This time, I didn't apologize, and he didn't jump. "Well, yes," I said, "I do, but that's ridiculous. You need them too. You said hunting is lonely."

"True," he said. "Okay. But maybe every night, once the tents are up, you should collect all six of them together, with Hope. Go in out of the wind and spend some time with them, give everyone a good inspection. Make sure they're all healthy and have what they need."

70.

I PROBABLY DON'T HAVE to tell you what has become my favorite time of day.

Annet thinks it's sensible that Hope, the kits, and I join each other at the end of every day's march, so that I can give each fox focused attention and determine if anyone has unique needs. For that brief stretch of time, we come together as a whole in the tent, then afterward, I crawl out, find Linny and Froggatt, and divide us back into our essential parts.

I've lost hold of Linta's theory of indivisible particles. I know it's about minuscule building blocks of nature, not some fox kits who are fundamental to me, and I'm sure that when I apply it haphazardly to everything in life, she would tell me I'm misusing it. But she made it a metaphor too. Silbercows chasing their tailfins; foxes bumping chocolate along.

I wonder if she'd be fun to argue with about it?

"Are any of the kits bonded to you, Hava?" Annet asked me as we made camp after our second day of walking.

"I don't think so," I said, intentionally vague. I'm going to have to talk to Adventure about that soon. When do kits start communicating and reading minds? How do they learn that they're supposed to pretend they can only communicate with one human, the one they're "bonded" to? Are they born with that knowledge, or do other foxes teach them? Is Adventure going to teach them? Or is he going to throw all the secrets of foxkind to the wind and let them start babbling at everybody?

Luckily, I don't think Annet's much interested. When she asked, her attention was on the careful removal of the boat from the sledge, because already, two walking days in, the sledge needs repairs.

I wanted to ask her, if we've walked for two days, does that mean it's only eighteen more days to Pikkia? But I didn't, because I know as well as anyone that Annet hasn't been able to take a reading since we started walking. It's been snowing since last night.

IN THE MORNING, it was still snowing, sharp, wet flakes stabbing our faces, driven by a relentless and painful wind.

The snow hasn't let up as we move, and Riz can't cope with it. For most of the day, we've had to pull him in the sledge, the chickens nestled around him.

In late morning, Barra also stopped walking. He just stood there, hunched, mute, and pale, refusing to pick up his feet. I made a joke about putting him on a lead like the goat, but the wind was shrieking too hard for anyone but Giddon to hear. He gave me a disgusted look, then helped Barra onto the sledge beside Riz and the chickens.

The sledge is a horror. When it's my turn to help pull it, it takes all my strength to budge it at all, with a rope that burns my shoulder and cuts into my hands. Then, once it starts moving, it keeps jumping, crashing, plunging into holes. The curved stays that make its runners bend and break, and our boat, our one remaining boat, gets wrenched and bashed, and I begin to wonder why we're even bothering. If we reach water again and the boat's too damaged to sail, won't we have gone through all this effort for nothing? Anyway, it's not like all of us can fit into one boat.

In the afternoon, Annet began distributing some of the supplies we keep in the boat, to make it lighter. Now, most of the time, except when we're responsible for the sledge or the goat, we carry something heavy on our backs.

There is a balloon of hunger inside me, filling the space that stretches from my throat to my gut. I'm starting to notice that it never goes away, not even when I eat my allotted rations. In fact, it expands, like a hole eating up my insides. When it's my job to carry food, it's hard to think about anything besides the food on my back.

Grella wrote about people hiding food from their companions, stealing it for themselves. I'm not going to do that. But I understand now, better than I did before.

IT'S NIGHTFALL, AND the snow has stopped.

We've camped on a black, rocky plain with a southerly wind so fierce that it's swept all the snow away and scoured a large bowl into the rock. We've pitched the tents inside the bowl. It wasn't easy. The rock is shiny on the surface, with clumps of loose, dark stone. When we first placed the stakes, the ground around them broke apart, dissolving into pebbles and ice.

Nonetheless, Annet is happy. She says we're walking well every day, better than she thought we would be. "And stars keep peeking out behind the clouds tonight," she added. "We might have clear skies tomorrow." Then she went off to look at Riz's and Barra's frostbite. How she can be cheerful when Barra's toes are turning purple is a mystery to me.

"Everyone go to Coran before the evening is out," she called, "for your hand and foot inspection!"

I brought my foxes into the first tent we managed to prop upright, then sat with them on the floor in the dark, holding them all together in my lap. Immediately, my butt and legs began to melt a puddle under the canvas. This happens now when we sleep. The capacity of our tents (and even my furs) to keep water out has become severely stretched; everything smells and nothing is dry. I'm so tired of it, so tired of being wet and cold.

But I visited with each fox individually while their siblings nursed, happy at my ability to keep *them* warm and dry.

Afterward, outside the tent, I joined the groups of people standing, sitting, perching on crates or on the edges of the sledge. Our firewood is precious, so we haven't had a fire since that first night. I saw Liel nearby struggling with his stove, which keeps sinking into ponds of its own making.

Searching through the darkness, I found Linny. He stood at the camp's far edge, swinging the ax at a low wall of ice, breaking chunks of it for our meltwater. I had no doubt that like all the ice around here, it was full of pebbles. If we can't melt enough water, someone'll have to hike out to a place with standing snow.

Anyway, Linny hunts all day. He shouldn't be chopping ice at night.

"Linny?" I said, approaching him, the bundle of seven foxes in my arms. "Why don't you let me take over?"

He squinted at me. Then his smile reached me across the dim light, and in it, I saw his exhaustion laid bare. "Looks like you have your hands full."

"We can trade."

"It's all right," he said, glancing beyond me. "Here comes Jacky."

As Jacky approached, Linny took a couple more swings with the ax, reaching up high, bearing down hard on the ice, smooth and easy. I couldn't find the tiredness in his arms and shoulders that I saw in his face; and I remembered suddenly the time I'd approached him on the foredeck of the *Monsea* while he was chopping wood, then tried to boss him into helping me decode Linta's chemistry.

"Let's find a place to sit," he said to me, passing the ax to Jacky, exchanging a few words with him. Turning back to me. "Hava? You okay?"

I was ashamed and confused. I wanted to give him something, to make up for that time.

"I'm worried you're about to drop," he said, "all eight of you." He took my elbow. "Come on."

A moment later, we were perched on the runners of the sledge, Linny slumped with his eyes closed, me cradling the foxes carefully. It was less windy, tucked against the sledge with him.

"When you're chopping wood, or hunting, or whatever," I said, "you never look as tired as you probably are."

He grinned, his eyes flashing open. "Maybe I have the power to look like something I'm not, just like you."

"But you are tired, right?"

"I'm exhausted," he admitted. "What about you? Are you how you look?"

I didn't understand the question. "How do I look?"

"Don't you decide how you look?"

"Well, not all the time," I said, with mild indignation. "I'm not using my Grace right now."

"All right," he said diplomatically. "Well, you look like you sprang from a fairy tale about righteous heroes who screw the heads off of tyrants, which is usual. And also like you're trying to keep your expression blank so that I can't tell what you're thinking or feeling about anything. Which is also usual."

I did use my Grace then, just for a moment, to do exactly the thing he was accusing me of: hide my confusion. Because what was he even talking about? A fairy tale about righteous heroes? Who was I, the person hiding in the corner, pretending to be something else?

New topic. "Do you remember the chemistry I refused to tell you about?"

He made a small, surprised noise. "Sure, I remember. It was, hm. How shall I put it?"

"Not my best moment?"

"Okay, we can put it like that."

"You've seen a lot of my not-best moments, I guess."

Linny turned to study my face. When he spoke, his voice was gentle. "What's going on, Hava?"

"I just," I started, then stopped, feeling suddenly that it was silly, that it didn't matter, and that he would think me foolish for bringing it up now, on this sledge in this cold while we're hungry and tired and fighting our way south. "I wanted to explain that I *couldn't* tell you about that chemistry. Not because I didn't trust you, but because it's other people's secrets. It's also dangerous, and upsetting. I shouldn't have tried to push you into helping me with it."

He was still studying me, which made it impossible for me to look into his face. I knew that the touch of his eyes would turn me into a sculpture.

"I see," he said. "I appreciate you saying so. I did guess it was stuff you couldn't tell me."

"There's a part of it I could have told you, actually," I said, wanting to give him at least that. "It's not a secret, not really. It's about . . ." I paused, trying to do my best with it in Dellian. "The theory of tiny objects that can't be divided."

"Ahsoken?"

"What?" I said, not understanding.

"Tiny, tiny particles, too small to see," he said. "Indivisible and indestructible. Our bodies are made of them. This ice is made of them. Even the air is made of them. I don't know what they're called in Lingian, but in Dellian, we call them 'ahsoken.'"

AH-sok-en. He pronounced it like a sigh, then like the word *soak*, then the *en* appendage that usually makes things plural in Dellian. "One particle is an ahsok?"

"Yes, and there are different kinds, with different properties and purposes. A fox is different from a rock because of what kinds of ahsoken it's made of, and how they combine." Linny was squinting at me. "Right? That's what you mean?"

"Yes," I said, repeating the word in my mind again, *ahsoken*. It was like a breath, and a hiccup. It was a gift. I'd wanted to give Linny something, but instead, he'd given me a gift of this word. "I don't know what they're called in Lingian."

"It's funny to talk about it out here," he said, his smile coming into his voice. "Don't you think?"

Chemistry, said Hope in my lap, apparently opening the thought to both of us, because Linny responded.

"Yes," he said. "Chemistry. A perfectly normal topic while awaiting one's tiny dinner in the cold."

What we are made of, said Hope.

I was looking around our camp at all the distinct, moving people, each indivisible, each with their own properties and their own particular purposes. Annet, our captain, was one kind of ahsok. Liel, our cook, was another. Bitterblue was our best ahsok, Kera our worst. Which one was I?

Then I snorted, because again I was persisting in misusing Linta's work. I can't help it. I have my kind of mind, not hers. Our brain ahsoken must've combined differently.

And then I was suddenly grim, because of Mart. People aren't indestructible. They aren't even indivisible. Hope has lost all of her memories. Kera's thrown her freedom away. My mother lost part of her mind whenever she was with the king. And I will not think about Barra's or Riz's feet.

"Hava?" said Linny. "Are you okay?"

"I'm fine," I said, trying to shake myself back to the present. "Just thinking about—parts and wholes."

"Okay. Do you still want my help?"

"With—the kits?"

"With the chemistry, Hava."

"Oh, no. It just—interests me. The scientist whose work I was translating, it interested her. And I wanted to tell you, since I wouldn't before."

"I see. Thanks."

Linny seemed easy, unperturbed. But I had the sense that I was bumbling around inside a misguided attempt at something, I wasn't sure what. "Have you had your turn with Coran?" I asked, wanting to change the subject again.

"Yes."

"He examined your hands? He knows you don't wear gloves when you hunt?"

"He knows," said Linny. "My hands are fine. Have you?"

"I will."

"You promise?"

The concern in his voice did more than anything else to knock me out of whatever rumination I was stuck in. "I promise," I said firmly, sitting straighter. "Want a kit or two?"

"Yes, please."

I gave him the one I call Blueberry because of his round, dark blue nose, and Cornsilk. I chose those two for selfish reasons: Cornsilk because she's Froggatt's charge and I'd have to give her up soon anyway, as soon as Froggatt came looking for me with hopeful eyes and outstretched hands. Blueberry because I didn't want to give up Moth slapping her floppy paws against my stomach. Or Ladybug, the one with a dark spot on each shoulder blade. Or any of them, really, including Blueberry.

I love you, Blueberry. I love you, Cornsilk, I thought as I dug them out. *I love you, Moth, I love you, Ladybug,* I added. *I love you, copper-eyed kit with no name,* for the kits have started opening their eyes lately, brief flashes of gold, and one of them has eyes that contain a surprise burst of copper, like my own copper eye. *I love you, tiny, wide-necked kit with no name.*

I remembered then that my mother also had a litany. Of course, she often failed to take care of me in the day-to-day way of mothers and children. It wasn't her fault. The king would summon her. While she was with him, the effort of remembering not to admit my existence took every piece of strength she had. Then she would come back from him, numb and mute and confused. She would look at me like she couldn't remember who I was and I would put her chisel in her hand and lead her to whatever sculpture she was working on. She would sculpt as the sun rose, until she started to nod off and I helped her into bed. Sculpting would bring her mind back, and her memories.

Maybe after sleeping, she would wake to a clear head. She would feed me, bathe me, talk to me, ask me about my day. Read me stories, gave me hugs and kisses the way I saw Bitterblue's mother do. But often the king came for her again, before she ever got through the sculpting and on to a whole, clearheaded place.

Still, she had a litany she would repeat, when I was around. I'm not sure she even knew what the words meant or why she was saying them. But she would say, "I love you. I love you. I love you." Even when she came stumbling back from the king, confused and crying, she would start to say it as soon as I appeared. Even when I set food beside her working hands, she might not look at me or understand I was there, but she would say it. I was left confused, wondering what love was, if this mindlessness and obsession and confusion and tears were all part of love. But I believed her.

I love you, Hope, I said.

My girl.

71.

IN THE NIGHT, I woke to a deep, scraping moan beneath the ground.

I was having a dream of climbing the rigging of the *Monsea* while moths flitted around me. As I woke, the world darkened and tilted. Behind me, my sister quietly snored. I reached instinctively for the foxes inside my coat and realized Hope was missing.

Hope?

No response, as usual. I tried to go back to sleep, but my bladder was pushing for release. I didn't trust its message. I'm not peeing much lately. But I couldn't relax.

Tying the belt of my coat tightly so the kits would be safe, I wriggled out of my blanket, found my boots, and slipped outside.

The stars were extraordinary, low and thick. While I was trying to pee, I tilted my face up to them and let them sink into the back of my skull.

Then a band of green light stretched across the sky, undulating like a sheet in the wind, and I was so startled that I almost lost my balance and peed on myself. It disappeared. I stood carefully, pulling my pants back up, checking on my kits, telling myself I'd imagined it.

On a ridge nearby, I saw the silhouette of a person kneeling, looking up at the southern sky. It was Kera.

Hope! Hope! I cried out, convinced that Kera had come out here to hurt Hope. I stumbled toward her.

"Kera!" I shouted. "What are you doing?"

When she turned, I saw that she had the sextant raised in one hand.

"Stealing the navigational equipment?" I cried, stopping near her, but not too close. One hand was protecting the lump of fox kits in my coat and the other was reaching for the knife at my ankle.

She let out a small, tired laugh. "How exactly would I steal the navigational equipment, Hava? Maybe you think I have a fence for it around the next ridge?"

"You took it from Annet," I said, gripping my knife hard now, a little wild and confused. I knew she had to be doing something bad.

"I took it from the corner of my tent, where it's stored," she said. "So I could measure our position."

"So you can escape!"

A lamp sat at her knees. One of the navigational charts rested on a sealskin square on the ground. In the light of her lamp I saw her dirty, bruised, bandaged face, thin and tired, laughing at me, laughing outright. "Escape?" she said, her merriment exploding around the word. "Oh, Hava. No, wait, what do people call you? Habpva? You think it's possible for any of us to escape this?"

"Well then, what are you doing? Why should I believe you're doing anything good?"

"I'm measuring our position," she repeated, "so that in the morning I can tell Annet that we're even farther north than when we started walking."

"What?" I cried. "That's impossible. We've been walking south for three days."

"Please," she said, shrugging. "Check my work, if you like. You know how to use the equipment, don't you? You're the captain's pet."

She held the sextant out to me, but she wasn't going to distract me that easily. "Where's my fox?" I said.

"Lost her, did you? You're not much of a mother to her. And she's not much of one either," she said, smirking at the lump in my coat, "if she keeps leaving you with her kits."

"You're one to talk," I said, instantly on fire with outrage that she should insult Hope. "You'll spend the rest of your life rotting in the queen's prison. Your daughter won't even remember you exist."

"My daughter knows who I am," she said with sudden viciousness. "She's not going to forget me."

"Well, you're never going to see her again."

"If that's true, then it's your fault, not mine."

"Oh, sure, right. For refusing to let you murder me?"

Again, she jabbed the sextant toward me, then stopped when she saw my blade, bright with starlight, steady in the air between us.

She sighed with impatience. "You should check my work, Hava. My calculations tell me we're a good distance north of where we made land. Because this *isn't* land. It's an enormous, floating plain of ice. It's why the ground is always melting under us and why more sensitive people like the queen haven't gotten their land legs yet. We've been walking south, but the currents are dragging this ice plain north faster than we can walk. In the morning, I'll tell Annet to turn us west. That's my best guess as to where to find land."

"You're wrong," I said. "You're trying to sabotage us. You want us all to die."

"I hope I'm wrong," she said. "Maybe you'll find I am, when you check my work."

She was still holding the sextant out to me. When I continued to refuse it, she shrugged, then placed it on the sealskin beside the navigational charts and the lamp. Then she turned and went back to her tent.

Frantically, I knelt where she'd been kneeling. Ice water soaked my knees, but I hardly felt it. I raised the sextant to the sky and measured the position of the north star, as Annet had taught me. I ran my fingers down the navigational tables, just to confirm. I did it again, and again.

Kera was right. We were much farther north than when we made land.

I think I would have started sobbing right then, even screaming, about how much I hated every part of this. I hadn't been prepared; Grella never wrote about anything like this. I hated Grella for not warning me. I hated the snow and my cold feet and my squishy boots. I hated my smelly fur coat and the way the fox kits peed and pooped inside my clothes. I hated being wet. I hated cold grains. I hated my hunger and my burning pee. I hated the sledge. I hated the goat. I hated carrying things on my back, raising the tent, and sleeping with other people. I wanted to *kill* the wind, and I knew we were never going to get home.

But Hope appeared over a ridge of snow nearby. She stopped there, her silhouette small and quiet against the backdrop of stars. And that reminded me of the kits in my coat, and my responsibility. I must not despair inside any fox's mind.

I took a breath. I did what I've always done: made myself and my feelings small, smaller, invisible. I closed them in a wardrobe and forbade them from making a sound.

Hope? I said.

My girl?

She padded to me on tentative feet, then climbed inside my hood.

As I returned the sextant carefully to its case, that green sheet appeared in the sky again, bending and flapping, eerie and frightening, whipping the stars.

72.

THIS MORNING WHEN I stepped out of the tent into a bright, cold wind, people stood scattered around the camp with frozen bodies and shocked faces. It was like entering a forest of dead trees. I guess they'd just had the news.

Nearby, Alzar and Riz were crying in each other's arms, as if they were saying goodbye. It made me furious. No one is saying goodbye. Ozul and Lisa, Sorit and Noa were taking down one of the tents, and Sorit had tears running down her face. Ozul's expression as she gave orders to the others was anguished. Then Noa gave Sorit a hug and I guess Ozul finally decided to stop being the second mate for the time being, because she joined their hug too, pulling Lisa in with her.

Annet and Navi stood together near the sledge, shoulder to shoulder, heads bent, talking quietly, looking serious and certain. Farther away, on a ridge against the morning sky, Bitterblue and Giddon stood with their arms around each other. Giddon is so big and my sister so little that it looked like he'd taken her inside himself, like she was the bear and he was the cave. I couldn't see her face, but he was calm and grim, staring out into the middle distance. I don't think I've ever seen him looking more determined.

Nearer to me, Jacky stirred himself. I heard him let out a breath. Then he took a bowl from Liel and carried it to Kera, who was standing beside the tents. Jacky's face was flushed, twisted with mulishness, and he walked with a swagger. As Kera reached out to take the bowl, he dropped it into the snow, pulled his arm back, and punched her.

Immediately there was an uproar. Ollie ran to join them and, to my astonishment, started hitting Kera too, then, when she fell to the ground, kicking her. Kera scrambled up and surged toward me, screaming, frightened and angry, and before I knew what I was doing, my hand was in my boot and my knife was between us again. I was ready to sink my knife into her abdomen, under her rib cage and up. I know how to do it. I was ready to end her life.

Then someone grabbed Kera—Annet, Navi, both of them shouting. Someone grabbed Jacky and Ollie—Ranin, Ozul, Linny. As they pulled Kera back from me, I dropped my knife. It clattered onto the icy pebbles at my feet.

With sharp, certain words, Annet swept the group of them, fighters and helpers, to the other end of the camp. I heard shouts, curses, and Annet's voice saying, "Enough!" I saw Bitterblue and Giddon come down from their ridge to join them.

I hugged the shapes of foxes inside my coat.

"Are you all right, Hava?" a voice called to me.

Distractedly, I turned. It was Froggatt. He and Coran were gathered around Barra, who was sitting in the boat atop the sledge.

Returning my knife to its holster, I walked to the advisers. Froggatt and Coran were standing side by side in front of Barra like a wall, to protect him from the worst of the wind. I joined them, making the wind barrier wider.

"Tempers are high," said Froggatt, his eyebrows wrinkled in concern. I think of these three men as interchangeable, because they all have the same papery skin, the same nondescript build, the same coats, and the same aggravating effect on my patience. But Froggatt is the one whose expression is perpetually concerned. Coran is the busybody, and Barra is the gloomy one.

"Yes," I said automatically.

"It looked to me as if that attack was unprovoked."

"I see," I said, feeling weirdly detached from my own temper. I watched Barra, who was holding Froggatt's kit, Cornsilk, in his mittened hands, dipping a cloth into the tin Froggatt held out to him, feeding her drops of goat milk. Every time Barra pulled the cloth away, Cornsilk slapped at the air with one paw, as if trying to grab it back. Her eyes were open, flashing gold. "Barra?" I said.

He looked up, squinting at the light. "Yes?"

Now that I'd gotten his attention, I didn't know what I wanted to say. "How are you?"

"I'm all right," he said, with matter-of-fact unhappiness. "Coran is going to operate on my toes this evening."

"Oh!" I said, then immediately tried to tamp down the horror that rose with the memory of too many passages in Grella's journals. "Oh dear. I'm sorry."

"Who needs toes anyway?" he said, shrugging.

Froggatt and Coran chuckled, so I knew it was a joke. "How's Cornsilk doing?" I asked.

"She's getting along excellently," said Froggatt. "She is now potty-trained."

"What?" I cried. "How?"

"She relieves herself only when I've removed her from my coats and placed her on the ground," Froggatt said proudly.

"But how did that happen?"

"I sent her some thoughts about it," Froggatt said. "Some wishes. Some pictures of her waiting until it was time."

"You *taught* her?"

"Yes, I suppose I did."

"And she understood you?"

"Yes," he said. "Maybe we're bonded?"

There was something about the way Barra was holding Cornsilk, his shoulders curled around her protectively. There was a touch of a smile on his pale, cracked lips, as if caring for her was a distraction from his own pain. I did a little thinking, the kind of thinking where your heart is twisting and shouting "No!" while your mind tries to stab it in place with a pin. I was thinking about how fat some of the kits are getting, while others lag behind. And how it's easy to give them warmth and tell them I love them, but harder to keep them fed throughout the day.

Reaching into my coat, I found the unnamed wide-necked kit, the tiniest kit. When he blinked at me, I kissed him carefully behind the ears. *I love you,* I said.

"I'm worried about this one," I said, holding him out to Barra. "He's smaller than the others, and the easiest lost. I'm always pulling the sledge or dealing with the goat or something, and I can't always tell if he has room, or gets enough sleep. I think he could use extra milk."

"Do you want us to take charge of him?" asked Froggatt.

"Yes," I said, deliberately holding him out to Barra, no one else. Barra blinked at the kit, then at me. He tried to say something, but no words came out. Carefully, he passed Cornsilk back to Froggatt, then pulled a little notebook and a piece of graphite out of an inside pocket and cleared his throat.

"What is his schedule?" he asked me.

"Um, well, I guess that's up to you," I said. "His entire life is nothing but eating, sleeping, pooping, and peeing. In the evenings, I'll need him for his daily inspection. Beyond that, you can decide."

Barra nodded. Clearing his throat again, he jotted something down, then tucked his notebook away. He held his hands out, his face full of light. "He looks like a little owl," he said.

"Owlet," I said, suddenly noticing the way the kit's wide neck, his squat head and pointy ears, suggested his name. "That's what we should call him."

73.

We've set out southwest.

It feels a little pointless, because we don't know if we'll find land, *real* land, to the southwest. But we know we won't find it to the north or the east. It's hard not to think about the currents beneath us, dragging us relentlessly north. It's hard not to worry about the fact that we have only one boat. As we walk, I'm finding it best to choose a small focus, then concentrate hard on that tiny thing. It makes me think of my mother, whenever she came back from the king. Often she zoned in on a small corner of a sculpture—a wing, a tooth, a claw—and worked on it for hours. Maybe she was trying to fill all the space in her mind with that little thing, so that everything else, all the awful, swirling truth, got pushed away.

Potty training, I thought as I trudged. *That's something I can focus on.* I had Moth and unnamed copper-eyed kit in my coat, and I could focus on teaching them to pee in the snow.

Also, my toes. I could appreciate how much I loved my toes, and how easy they make it to walk, and how lucky I am that every night, when Coran inspects them, he tells me that they're some of the best he's seen.

"Why do you suppose that is?" I asked him last night.

"You probably have good circulation," he said. "But it's also because you have boots that were paid for by a queen, and expensive Keepish furs keeping you warm."

I'd forgotten about my boots. It's not just my coat; my boots are superior. Linny, Ozul, Jacky, Ollie—the majority of our group don't have boots paid for by a queen.

But that was too broad and awful a focus, so I pushed it away. Kits and toes. Kits and toes.

Behind me, Jacky and Ollie pulled the sledge, as they'd done all morning, even after the first couple of hourly announcements that it was time to switch jobs. Being punished, apparently.

Behind them, Kera walked near the end of the line. The skin around her left eye was purpling and she trudged with clenched teeth, sometimes bracing her hand to her side. But whenever Coran approached her, as he tried to do several times, she waved him away with a snarl.

Ahead of me, Linny broke off to the left with his bow. Adventure and Hope trotted along beside him, and I knew he had Blueberry and Ladybug in his pockets.

Adventure? I called. *I need to talk to you.*

Right now?

It's about the kits, I said. *Froggatt has potty-trained Cornsilk, which means they might be starting to communicate. Froggatt's even wondering if he and Cornsilk are bonded. Are kits born knowing they're supposed to pretend they can only bond to one person?*

No, he said. *Adult blue foxes teach kits the secrets of foxkind.*

Well? I said. *Are you going to teach them?*

Certainly not, he said.

But, Adventure—this group is full of Keepish people! If they all start realizing that blue foxes can enter anyone's minds, then the secrets of foxkind will be revealed. Someday they'll go back to Winterkeep and tell everyone. All your fox brethren will be exposed!

We can tell them that when the kits were born on a different shore, he said, *they were born with a different kind of mind.*

Just like that? I said indignantly.

Just like that.

And I suppose it altered your mind, and Hope's too? I said. *Hope's talking to any old person she likes, besides me.*

Just Linny, he said, offended. *Linny isn't any old person. I have to go now. I'm helping.*

Yes, I know you're very busy and important, I said, with a flash of sarcasm. *I think you're being pretty cavalier about this.*

I think you're the one being cavalier, he said. *You don't know what it's like to be bonded to a terrible human and feel trapped, unable to warn other humans of the bad things she's planning to do. I know what that's like. I don't want that for these kits. They should be allowed to choose honest lives. They should be allowed to have honest relationships with as many humans as they like. Blue foxes are different on the Royal Continent,* he said. *That's what we'll say, and people will believe us.*

KITS AND TOES. Kits and toes.

I took step after step, sending messages to the kits in my coat about bladder control, nursing my irritation toward Adventure.

For a stretch of the afternoon, Bitterblue and Giddon walked near me in line.

"Do you still have all that rauha?" I asked my sister.

She was plodding along resolutely, her hands in small fists. She raised a dirty, gray-eyed face to me, then pinched her lips thoughtfully. "We must," she said. "I haven't thought of it since the *Monsea,* but I remember putting it into the canvas bag. Giddon, didn't we tuck that canvas bag back into the boat?"

The canvas bag with Linta Massera's papers. I touched my hand to my own pants pocket, where I've been carrying my mother's figurines. I should keep closer watch on Linta's papers too.

"I think so, yes," said Giddon.

"Okay, good."

"Why?" said Bitterblue.

"Barra," I said. "We should make sure Coran knows we have it, to distract Barra later from his toes."

74.

WELL, I JUST assisted with an amputation. That's a new one for me.

Grella wrote of witnesses fainting and vomiting, so I was a little apprehensive, but it was fine. Annet and Navi assisted too. Actually, a lot of people assisted, but Annet, Navi, and I were the ones who held Barra's feet, so we were the ones who saw everything, and whose stomachs are supposed to be turned now. My stomach isn't turned. I'm just hungry, as usual.

Coran told us we had to keep pressing Barra's feet down, no matter what. The toes—nine of them—were so black and dead that they looked like ashy stumps on a log that's been in the fire for a while. They sliced off easily too. Hardly any blood. There was a smell; that was the only difficult part. Coran's worried about the smell. He cut into some of the living flesh once the toes were off, to clear away the gangrene, because he says that's where the smell comes from. Then there was blood, and Barra did struggle, fiercely, but he was singing and laughing too, because he was high as a kite on rauha. I can't think what it was like inside his body, his feet clearly sensing disaster but his mind full of happiness and song. Keepish medicines scare me a little. Anything that takes your mind away and replaces it with lies scares me a little, and I went to Bitterblue afterward and sat with her, wondering about her, not asking her what I wanted to know. Why is she so comfortable with rauha? Doesn't it remind her of the Grace of the king? He used to hurt people too, while telling them they liked it, making them believe they liked it.

After my time in the tent inspecting the foxes—later than usual, because we did the surgery first—Linny sat with me. The middle of this ice plain is different from its edges. There are boulders here, riding on top of the ice barge. We love them passionately, because we can sit on them or lean against them without getting wet. When I first saw them, I asked Ozul why there would be boulders on top of a mound of floating ice. She said that before this ice became an iceberg, it was a glacier, flowing across land and then breaking off into the sea. She said that flowing ice collects everything in its path, then releases it as it melts. "You never know what you'll find as icebergs fall apart," she said. "Trees? The skeleton of some beast from the Pikkian mountains?"

Anyway. After the surgery, it helped to sit with Linny, at first. It was easy, and I could let my preoccupations go. He shot a bird today, a tern. Liel's adding it to tonight's stew, along with one of the chickens that's stopped laying eggs. I can't imagine the birds are going to make much of an impact, divided among twenty people. But I kept that to myself.

"Hope helped me shoot the tern," Linny told me.

"Did she?"

"Her litany of *my girl, my hero* suddenly changed to *Linny hunt stupid bird.* So I looked up and there it was."

I raised Hope from my lap to my face, sticking my nose into her fur and giving her a kiss.

"I've been wondering if we should offer the care of a kit to Liel," said Linny. "Maybe Ladybug? Cooking for all of us with too little food on that tiny stove must be hard. And he's been limping. And he did lose his cat."

"A blue fox isn't like a cat," I said tightly. "Anyway, maybe Hope doesn't like us spreading her children all around the camp."

Don't care, said Hope. *Not my babies.*

Hope! I cried at her.

Linny was touching both of us with his careful amber eyes. "Of course we don't have to," he said. "You can keep the rest of them, Hava."

I needed a minute to control my face. I tried to use my Grace, but I think I only managed to flash into my bird-girl sculpture. I'm so tired, and every stupid little thing feels like a tragedy. Every blow cracks me apart. Is there something wrong with me, if I wish I could hide them away as my own? Like my mother did with me. Like Kera did with Hope?

"The kits should have the opportunity to form relationships with anyone they like," I forced myself to say. "And Liel would spoil Ladybug. I mean that as a good thing. It'd be good for one of them to be cared for by the person in charge of the food."

"Okay," said Linny cautiously.

"If we gave him Ladybug," I said, "we'd have three left between us, besides Hope. Moth, Blueberry, and the copper-eyed one we still haven't named. We could keep things even. Maybe whoever has Hope carries one kit and whoever doesn't carries two."

"That's fair."

"Could I—" I started, then stopped, because I didn't want to express a preference.

"Keep Moth with you?" he said, with a half grin.

I was too tired to care that he'd figured me out again. "Yes."

"Of course."

I love you, Blueberry. I love you, Ladybug. I love you, copper-eyed kit with no name. "I don't like to think thoughts like that, because I don't want the kits to feel my preference."

"Do you know how to guard your mind?" he said. "Like we do with Dellian monsters?"

"Of course I know how to guard my mind," I said with sudden ferocity.

"I'm sorry," he said, confused.

"No," I said quickly, ashamed, "I'm sorry. I grew up in the court of the Monsean king. We had to guard our minds all the time."

"Oh. You mean King Leck?"

He was my father. The queen is my sister. Hardly anyone knows. "Yes."

"I see. I'm sorry, Hava. I don't know anything about what it must've been like to live in his court. I mean, I know a little about his Grace. And his crimes. But not what it would mean about your childhood."

I brought Hope to my face again, pressed my nose to her fur. Linny was watching me, seeming like he wanted to say something else, like he was perched on the edge of a question. I needed Linny not to ask any questions just now. Digging the unnamed copper-eyed kit out of my coat, I pressed my nose to him too. Then he began crying to nurse.

Stupid babies, said Hope in annoyance.

"What about Bir as a name for that kit?" said Linny.

Bir is the Dellian word for *fire.* It rhymes with *dear,* and it's also the name of a famous Dellian hero, a woman with scarlet, pink, and coppery hair who's half human, half monster. She has the mind-controlling abilities of a Dellian monster, but the conscience of a human. A kind human. I saw her once, years ago. She's terrifying and beautiful, and very, very old.

"Bir?" I said.

"I like the fire in his eyes," said Linny.

Now I was silent for a new reason, because this is the kit with eyes like my own copper eye. Something about the way Linny said the words, something in his intonation, felt like he was paying me a sideways compliment. For one of the ugliest things about me.

"One of them should probably have a Dellian name," I managed to say, "since you're one of their caretakers. I mean, language doesn't really matter to foxes, but it's still a nice idea. I'm fine with Bir."

"Good. See you later, Hava."

Then he took himself off, which was an enormous relief. Inside my coat, Moth was patting my stomach. I curled around her, trying to focus on keeping her warm.

That night I dreamed about the *Monsea* again. I was up on one of the yards, watching a tattered section of the course flap in the wind. My footrope bounced. I looked up to see that someone had joined me, but I couldn't tell who it was.

Suddenly the ship was sinking; the water was almost lapping at our boots.

"It's okay," Linny told me, for the person was suddenly Linny. "She'll show us the way home."

I didn't understand what he meant, until he pointed to a moth hovering above my shoulder. Its wings were canvas sails.

75.

AFTER TWO DAYS' trudge, we've reached the southwest edge of our ice barge and we're sure we see land this time. That's because we're watching the sun set behind a glacier. Glaciers are rivers of ice that flow, slower than molasses, across *land*.

People around me are celebrating, don't ask me why. Between us and that stark, treeless land is open water, then a river of moving, crowding ice floes, then a stretch of ice that I can't look at without remembering that long day of Alzar and Sorit pulling the boats. And our one remaining boat is a wreck. There's a crack in her starboard hull that Alzar, Noa, and Navi are trying to patch with the wood from the sledge.

There are seals on the ice out there too—and long streaks of blood, which means there are bears. Linny has been standing with his bow and quiver on his back, straight against the wind, staring across the water through a glass. The slashes of red are shocking, after so much white and gray.

We'll camp here tonight, then try the crossing in the morning.

"How's your potty training going, Hava?" Froggatt asked me, coming to stand beside me while I watched Linny watching the seals.

"Moth is doing well," I said to him. "Blueberry, not so well."

He nodded. "Cornsilk and Owlet are progressing, and I spoke to Linny earlier. He said Bir pooped in the snow today. He said it was the best thing he'd ever seen. And Liel reports that Ladybug is a genius."

The feeling of my face stretching into a smile was unfamiliar. "Liel thought Tulip was a genius too."

"I do think he's a bit biased," Froggatt admitted confidentially. "Ladybug is progressing no faster than Cornsilk."

Nearby, Barra sat in the sledge, taking notes against his chest in his little notebook and chatting to Owlet, who was perched in his lap. Like Bitterblue, Barra is only allowed to have rauha every few days to prevent addiction, so he's in a lot of pain. You can see its strain in his face if you spy on him when he doesn't know you're looking. But he also seems awake in a way he never did before. Aware. Engaged in his surroundings.

He noticed me watching him and held his graphite pencil to his temple for a moment, a strange little salute. Then he pointed at Owlet and mimicked writing and I understood that he wanted me to know that he was keeping close track of Owlet's schedule. I nodded back, that strange stretch of smile pulling at my face again.

That evening, I dug through the canvas bag and laid my eyes on Linta's papers, just to make sure they were still there.

Then I found a boulder from which I could see the land. I sat behind it by myself, hidden from everyone else. With a deep breath and shaking fingers, I took my scarf bundle from my pants pocket and carefully unwrapped my mother's figurines.

I had the sense I hadn't looked at them in years, or maybe even that they were from someone else's life. Someone who has enough food and is warm and dry enough, who doesn't need to be frightened of bears. I can remember that girl. It seems dangerous to remember her, because remembering makes me wish for her life.

I visited with each of them in order. My mountain lion–girl, protecting me. My bear-girl, so different from the bears of this wilderness, because she's ferocious in my defense. My porpoise-girl, who could dive beneath this ice and escape. No bird-girl. My bird-girl lives at the bottom of the Winter Sea, with the *Monsea*. Amazing that even out here, facing all this difficulty, the loss of my bird-girl still hurts. I guess I'd started to think of her—of myself—as a habpva, a seasparrow.

I reached into one of my front coat pockets and was surprised, then surprised at my delight, when I touched Giddon's star nail. I couldn't believe it was still in there, after falling out of the boat, after my fights with the sledge, after everything. I twirled it around in my fingers, then held it up to the starry sky.

Something keeps sparking inside me. A little flame that keeps finding enough air to breathe, every time I turn my head and look across the water at that black silhouette of land. I try snuffing it out with my litany of kits and toes. I try cycling through my *I love you*s to the kits. But I can feel that unnatural smile on my face again.

Land. Land!

76.

THE PLAN WAS to complete the crossing in three shifts.

I was in the first shift. I wanted to be in the last shift, because at Bitterblue's insistence, she was in the last shift. The queen has to put her people first and blah blah.

But when I opened my mouth this morning to object, Annet gave me such a look. It was a *Remember what I said about obedience* look, but also an *I expected better of you in this moment* look.

And so I was angry while I was crossing the wind-whipped, freezing strait in our leaky, crowded rowboat with its tattered sail, everyone in a panic using bowls, cups, and their own frozen hands to bail out the water. Which was fine. Anger makes for good bailing.

When our boat bumped up against ice that wouldn't break, we crawled out, plopped onto our bellies, and slid. Annet stayed in the boat, watching us squirm across the ice. I passed a group of foul-smelling seals that bumbled against one another trying to back away from me, emitting earsplitting screams. The sound made my teeth ache. And my coat is now stained with a slime that I'm pretty sure came out of their butts.

Wriggling, slithering, creeping for a long, uncomfortable time, we finally reached a beach of rocks. Spreadeagled beside me, Ollie began to laugh, then sob with dry, hacking gasps that weren't much better than the clamor of the seals. I heaved myself up, helped him to his feet, and submitted to his hug, but my attention was on Annet, who was sailing the leaky boat back across the strait on her own. Fighting the wind, fighting the current, with no one to help her bail. Of every visceral moment from our crossing, this is the one that keeps bursting to the front of my mind: Annet in that boat. Her steady shoulders and her flapping hair, her determined gray eyes behind her glasses, as, five separate times, she navigated that wreck of a boat across a windbitten strait.

She hasn't talked much since we made it safely across. All of us, even the goat and chickens, even that wreck of a boat, which she dragged across the ice by herself when everyone else had gone on.

I don't know what to say to her, because I don't know how to tell someone how marvelous they are.

77.

LAND.

And not just any land: the far north of my own continent. For real this time.

All we have to do now is get ourselves south. Right?

We're on a low, snowy shelf, walking south, with the sea to our left. Land has variety, solidity, rock and dirt, different from ice. I'm surprised it took us so long to realize we weren't on land before.

I wouldn't say it's better walking, exactly, because the snow is as deep as ever and now we encounter hills. But uphills are followed by downhills, which are always welcome, especially if it's your turn to drag the sledge. As we trek south along the coast, we catch glimpses sometimes of mountains far to the west. At sunset today, the sun dropped below the thick roll of clouds and we got to see sunset over those mountains. I hid my tears behind my Grace, scared of my own feelings, because it made me feel close to home.

When the clouds clear, Annet will take a reading and determine how far we have to go.

WHEN WE CAMPED for the night, dinner had the air of celebration, because Linny shot us two seals.

He told me they're so easy to kill that he feels bad about it. He can walk right up to them and they stare at him in bewilderment while he draws his bow. "I have to look away," he told me. "They have trusting eyes."

Seal meat is oily, greasy, and delicious in your first few ravenous bites. Then it becomes strong-tasting, tough, and honestly kind of disgusting, but I kept eating it anyway, until Coran told me that if I didn't stop, I'd make myself vomit.

I guess I've taken to trusting Coran, because I stopped when he told me to.

"What about you?" I asked him, since he was eating sparely. "Shouldn't you build up your own strength?"

"I have a digestive ailment," he said. "If my body copes well with the seal meat overnight, I'll eat more in the morning."

We all have a digestive ailment. Mine, like most people's, is constipation, followed by diarrhea, followed by constipation. Coran's must be pretty bad if he isn't gorging himself, and briefly I considered offering him the care of a fox kit. My solution for everything. But then I realized that someone else to take care of is probably the last thing Coran needs.

I watched him move around the camp, cautioning others not to overindulge. Some of the sailors were having a belching competition that would've made me feel superior once, in a different life, but there's not a lot we can do about our bodies out here. A seal belch is a disgusting, fishy, fatty eruption, and it's better to let it out than hold it in.

My girl? said Hope once in consternation. She and Moth were inside my coat, where it must've seemed like a series of earthquakes.

Sorry, I told her. *Seal burps.*

Seal burps, she repeated, then said it again, knowingly, every time I belched. Grella never wrote about seal burps. When he and his companions suffered for food, they were never anywhere near an ocean.

I'm starting to think that one of us should be keeping a journal, of all the things Grella left out, or got wrong.

Coran spent a long time with Barra, who still rides in the sledge and still wears a mask of pain most of the time. Then he visited Riz, whose feet seem to be improving.

Next, Coran approached Annet, who waved him away, but he returned when Navi called him back. I watched Navi force Annet to take off her glove and show Coran her hand, and suddenly I was on my feet. If something was wrong with Annet's hand, I needed a better view.

Across the camp, Navi's eyes rose to mine. In the low light, I couldn't see her expression, but I saw clearly enough when she patted Annet on the shoulder and began to walk toward me.

"How are you, Hava?" she said, motioning to my low, flat rock. "May I sit?"

"What is it?" I said. "Does she have an infection?"

Navi took my arm and sat, pulling me down beside her. "She has a scratch, habpva. She's fine. I just wanted Coran to fuss over her a bit, because she's always making sure everyone else is having hand and foot inspections, but sometimes she doesn't sit still long enough for an inspection of her own."

"Is that true?" I said. "Are you lying to me?" I heard my voice, shrill and young, but I didn't care. Annet has learned to stop lying to me, but that doesn't mean Navi never would.

"Habpva," said Navi. "If I had any true concern for Annet's well-being, I wouldn't be sitting here calmly talking to you while the doctor visits her. You know that, right? You're observant enough to know what Annet and I mean to each other?"

It was such a frank thing to say. And she spoke in such an easy, almost musical tone—a tone, I realized, reserved for joy, of all things—that I was embarrassed, suddenly, of my panic.

"Yes," I said. "I see. I'm sorry."

"Don't be sorry for being a caring person," she said, which confused me further. Am I a caring person if my care for Annet is really about myself? About her keeping me safe?

Across the camp, I watched Annet with Coran. They weren't even looking at her hand anymore; they were just talking, about the weather for all I knew. I used my Grace to glance sideways at Navi and reassure myself of her steady face, her scarlet scarf, threaded through with iridescent gold. I thought about how Annet and Navi are the first and second in charge, so back when we were in the boats, they were always separated. Now they walk near the head and foot of the line every day and sleep in separate tents. I wondered, is it hard for them to be so much apart?

After a while, Navi got up and went back to Annet, who raised a shining smile to her as she approached. It was a private smile I felt I shouldn't be looking at, so I looked away. Then wondered if I'd ever once done that before.

Coran went to Kera next. He sat with her for a long time.

THAT NIGHT I woke to the sound of rustling behind me. Bitterblue, coming in from outside.

"Giddon?" she whispered. "Giddon."

After a moment, the deep rumble of his voice became audible. "Mm? What?"

"My bleeding came."

"Oh, thank goodness."

"I told you the Keepish teas prevent pregnancy," she said. "Giddon! Are you crying?"

"I was so scared," he said. "I never told you how scared I was. It would've been so dangerous out here. I couldn't have forgiven myself."

"We didn't know the ship would sink, silly."

"We're responsible for each other."

"Yes. I know. But I was never going to be pregnant, Giddon. Giddon! Come here. We're safe now."

I lay, still as a sculpture, while they comforted each other. I lay unmoving until they fell asleep.

Then, suddenly, my seal meat needed out of my body. I wasn't even sure in which direction, but it was lurching its way out.

Digging the foxes from my coat, I tucked them under the blanket. I bumbled outside, crashing through darkness. I found a boulder and heaved behind it a few times, but nothing came up. I'm not a person who gets sick a lot. Injured in the course of my work, sure, but not sick. I don't like it much. I sat on the boulder and took slow breaths through the waves of queasiness, trying to relax.

Above me, that green light was drawing shapes across the sky again. It danced and waved in streaks and arches and I watched it with rising nausea, hating it, because we're on land now, we're heading home. Doesn't that mean the sky above me should be familiar? Is it too much to ask for the sky of my home?

"It's the aurora borealis," a voice said, breaking into the wind, making me jump.

"What?" I said, then recognized Kera standing near me.

"It happens in the far north," she said. "It's normal, though no one knows why it happens."

You're not normal, I wanted to say. *Why are you always creeping around in the dark?*

But when she clutched her stomach and staggered off, I had my answer. In fact, my own stomach cramped in sympathy.

Traitor, I told it viciously. *I hope she vomits her brains out of her body. I hope we find her dead in the morning.*

I watched the green wands cross the sky, annoyed at Kera for knowing what they were. I don't like people who know more about my life than I do.

I was thinking of Bitterblue, taking turns with the sledge like everyone else, because a queen must do her part.

How long has Giddon been letting her do that, while thinking she might be pregnant? And how much sex did they have on the *Monsea* anyway? Was it when she was sick? When she was high? I'd forgotten, here in the north. I'd forgotten their lies. Idiots. They deserved whatever they got for indulging their secret relationship.

For a while longer, I sat there, trying to separate my stomach from my heart. I had this feeling that had no edges, like the streamers of light swelling above me. It filled all the space inside me. I mean, even Navi, who hardly knows me, is willing to tell me what she and Annet mean to each other. And Bitterblue is my *sister*. I feel everything she feels. We had the same father. He murdered both our mothers. We're united in the same grief. And for months now, she's had a secret happiness.

Why hasn't she shared it with me?

78.

THIS MORNING, WHILE we packed up the tents, Annet took a navigational reading.

"Twenty-three walking days to the inhabited parts of Pikkia," she announced.

I calculated. We started with twenty walking days and twenty days of food, and we were on the ice plain for five days.

"If you're trying to do the math," Annet said, "we have fifteen days of food left out of our original supply. If we ration further, we can stretch that to seventeen or eighteen days, and in the meantime, game has become plentiful."

She nodded at Ozul, who was now wearing the other bow and quiver on her back, her braids hidden under her hat and hood, her cheeks flushed, and her dark eyes determined.

"There's less risk of losing arrows here," said Annet. "So Ozul will join Linny on the hunt. We'll eat off the land to preserve our supplies. The land here is generous."

She was looking at each of us, catching every eye. A smile grew on her face, as bright as the snow. A smile!

"Let's get moving," she said. "From this moment, every step brings us closer to home."

79.

CLOSER TO HOME.

That's my litany now, with each step: *Closer to home. Closer to home.*

Home? Hope said to me once as I marched, riding in my hood, peeking her golden eyes out at the endless plain of snow before us, the endless sea stretching to our left. The endless mountains to our right. White and gray, white and gray. Linta Massera, the world is made of white and gray.

Do you remember your home, Hope? I asked her.

She sent me a bubble of uncertainty, then an image of the deck of the *Monsea.* It was from the perspective of one of the lifeboats, where she used to huddle with Adventure. It was a view of the sky, the rigging; of me, climbing the mast.

It fell from my chest to my stomach, heavy and painful: grief. The *Monsea* is lost. She'll never be my home again.

Your original home isn't the Monsea, *Hope,* I said, guarding my sadness from her. *Do you remember Winterkeep?*

Monsea? she said. *Winterkeep?*

Then she was quiet for a while.

Closer to home, I chanted. Inside my coat, Moth stirred. *Closer to home,* I told her. *I'll bring you home, little Moth.*

Winterkeep, Hope said suddenly, in my hood.

Yes? I said. *Hope?*

Barn, she said. *Sea.*

A sharp surprise struck me. I know a barn above the sea in Winterkeep. It's at the north edge of the city of Ledra, part of a farm owned by the prestigious Winterkeep Academy. *You're remembering?* I said. *Did you live at the Academy?*

I could feel her blip of confusion. Then her indifference; it was gone.

I thought of another barn by the sea, this one in Winterkeep's north. Linta Massera's workshop used to be in a storehouse that sat beside a barn, in a forest, on a cliff above the sea. Until I blew it up, that is.

Suddenly, trudging through the snow, the memory filled my mind, a great flash of light, and a blast so loud, it was beyond sound. I stumbled, almost losing my footing, then righted myself.

Where have my defenses gone against the worst moments of my life?

Inside my coat, Moth stirred, then cried out for milk.

Stupid babies, said Hope crossly.

WE ARE DRAGGING ourselves across this world, day after long, cold day.

I think we've grown accustomed to silence. We plod without talking, pushing through pain, counting the steps to home. The silence helps me hide how tired I feel, whenever my sister or Giddon come to walk with me and I can't find it in me to be nice to them. They lied to me.

You know who else I'm starting to think lied to me? Well, not lied, exactly. But misrepresented something.

Here's the thing: Grella writes as if he and his companions are heroes. As if their suffering is noble; as if they're sacrificing themselves for a higher cause. *What* cause? Is there some reason why they needed to identify the world's most dangerous and impassable places, then go there? Was there some reason they couldn't stay home, doing some work that *helped* someone? We didn't choose this. Grella chose it! What did he *think* was going to happen? How arrogant does someone have to be to appoint themselves the official conqueror of snow and ice?

A RIVER HAS burst into view.

It's rushing toward us from the southwest, pouring across the rock and snow, emptying into the sea.

The wind is so high and the surf so strong that we were practically upon it before we heard it. A river! A steady supply of fresh, melted water, and more than that: Its banks are littered with driftwood. Driftwood! That means fires.

Also, not just the driftwood of dead trees or fallen branches. While we ran around the edges of the river collecting kindling, Bitterblue suddenly held something above her head and shouted, "Rusty nail! Rusty nail!" And everyone crowded around her, laughing and crying at a slat of wood impaled with a rusty nail, because a nail means that this river is a path to a place with people.

Well, everyone but Kera. Kera stood apart from the rest of us, looking pale, sick, and grim.

"What is it?" I heard Annet say to her, breaking off from the group, pushing through the snow to stand beside her.

"I know what you're about to suggest we do," Kera said.

"Go on," said Annet, with a touch of impatience.

"You want to change course and follow the river inland, because you think this nail is proof that the river leads to civilization."

"And?"

"It's a nail in a curved piece of wood," Kera said. "Like from the hull of a boat."

Annet's voice was growing sharp. "Get to the point, Kera."

"What if it's a boat that belonged to shipwrecked people like us?" said Kera. "In that case, its journey down the river indicates that maybe they didn't fare so well on that particular route. Maybe we should stay along the coast. At least here, we know there are seals."

Annet stood for a while with her hands on her hips and her lips pursed, thinking. I noticed that I was using my Grace almost without meaning to, to distract their attention from me. I turned back to the group, making myself stop.

A few minutes later, despite Kera's advice, we set out southwest along the river.

THAT NIGHT, WHILE the foxes nursed in my lap beside a fire—a fire!—Linny brought me my dinner.

It was a bowl of seal stew—seal soup? It was a bowl of rubbery, smelly, floating seal chunks, which I forced myself to chew and swallow. I'm not going to starve out of distaste for my dinner.

Linny sat with me while I ate. "Somewhere to the southwest," he said, "I'm sure people fish on this river."

He spoke in the same hopeful tone everyone else has been using, so I tried to keep my worries to myself. "Fish will be a nice change," I said. "Did your father teach you to fish too?"

"My father?" he said, surprised.

I remembered then that Linny has never actually told me about his father.

"You said your mother was a servant on the estate of a lord who taught you chemistry," I said. "I assumed he took an interest in you because he was your father. I assumed he taught you archery too."

He considered me for a moment, through even amber eyes. "He did teach me archery," he said. "And he taught me to fish. But he's not my father, Hava."

"I shouldn't have assumed," I said. "In Monsea, at least, it's the usual reason for a nobleman to take so much trouble."

"It wasn't his reason," Linny said, with a twist in his voice that suddenly opened a new story to me.

It wasn't a nice story. It was about Linny, who must've been sweet when he was little, with his delicate face, his quiet eyes and sweet, quiet lips. His mother, who'd been a servant, with little power. And a lord who'd liked to teach Linny things.

"Oh," I said, wishing I'd never brought it up. "What—" I started, then stopped. Thought about what I wanted to ask, and made my voice casual. "How old were you when you left home?"

"Twelve," he said.

"How old are you now?"

"Twenty-one."

I nodded. "I'm also twenty-one."

"Oh?" he said, sitting back a little, seeming to relax. "Have you always known the queen?"

I've always spied on the queen, I didn't say. *She's my sister.* "I've always—" I started, then amended myself. "She's always been an important part of my life. Most Monseans would say so."

"Is it true she's survived an ordeal like this before?" he said. "She crossed Grella's Pass?"

She was being chased by King Leck. Our father. "Yes. She was ten. Lady Katsa carried her across. You've heard of Lady Katsa?"

"Of course," he said. "And you? Have you always worked for the queen?"

"That's more recent," I said. "I worked for myself for most of my life."

"But you grew up in the castle?"

"My mother worked for the king. She was a sculptor."

"Oh," he said, alarm flashing in his face at the mention of the king. "Does she still sculpt?"

He'd given me part of his story, maybe more than he'd meant to. I didn't want to give him nothing in return. But I felt that if I started speaking about my mother, my control would unravel. The cold, the wet, the stomachaches have worn down my defenses too much; I would unravel, and fall apart.

I studied his face, really studied it. Linny has gotten thinner out here. His cheekbones are sharper, his cheeks gaunt, his brown skin covered with a film of grime. The fineness of the bones of his face used to make him look like a girl to me. I don't see it that way anymore. He just looks like Linny. A Linny who I wish had more food.

If I couldn't give him my mother, maybe I could give him something else.

"She doesn't," I said. "But I used to sneak around the castle while she was working. I used to use my Grace to hide. It's how I learned a lot of the things I know; I used to sneak in on the lessons of other children."

"Really?" he said. "What kinds of lessons do children have in the castle?"

"Well," I said, thinking of the children who'd been employed by the castle, and the children whose parents were nobility. "I know how to make butter and candles and paper. I know a little physics, and I've heard a lot of poetry. I can read music, and I could probably teach you how to play the harp—except that I've never touched one."

"Really!" he said, with laughter in his voice. "You never had music lessons of your own?"

I never had lessons of my own. "No."

"Is that how you learned chemistry? Sneaking into other people's lessons?"

"A little, I guess. Most of what I know, though, like about the theory of ahsoken, is from listening in on the conversations of the queen's friends. Regular listening, with them knowing I'm there."

Chemistry, said Hope in my lap. I stroked her behind the ears.

"I see," said Linny. "And is there fishing in the castle?"

"No, but I taught myself how to fish."

Fish? said Hope.

Yes, Hope, I said. *Do you know fish?*

Silbercows, said Hope.

Yes! Silbercows. Are you remembering?

Chocolate!

I snorted. *Good one, Hope.*

Linny was watching us, a smile at the edge of his mouth. "It's hard to piece together all the parts of your life, Hava," he said. "It seems like you've done an awful lot of different things."

I wanted to tell him all the parts of the story I wasn't saying. That I was nine when I taught myself to fish, and before that, I stole what others caught, all along the river that runs west and south from my sister's city. I wanted to tell him that you can hide and steal food, but you can't always steal warmth. Not if you're in a stretch of forest where no one lives; so I taught myself to read the forest floor for signs of human paths, because those led to human shelters where I could hide; but mostly I learned to stick to towns. I can't survive by myself, but I can survive where there are people to hide from, people to sustain me.

It all sounded so desperate and grim in my mind. And selfish. I didn't want him to think I was a parasite.

"I'll tell you more sometime," I said, wanting to mean it. Wanting that badly, but not sure if I did.

80.

THERE ARE NO fish in this river.

We drag lines while we walk; we sit with lines whenever we stop. We bait them with the bits of seal we kept for this very purpose, but our lines come out untouched.

There are bears. We find their footprints in the snow all around us, big as plates. What are they living on, if not fish? There are no seals here. There's nothing; we've had to eat two more of the chickens. During the day, we collect all the driftwood we can find, then at night, we build a fire and hope it's enough to keep the bears away.

Once, we saw one, standing atop a long, high hill. It was a good distance in low light, but Linny fired at it anyway. The arrow landed right between the bear's front feet and it stared at the vibrating shaft with an intense kind of boredom, then stared, for a very long time, at us. Linny and Annet were debating whether he should risk another shot when it closed its mouth around the arrow, turned, and carried it away. Casually, as if this was what it had been out hunting for. I was relieved to see it go. I'm hungry, but one of those cold-eyed beasts lumbering toward us does not strike me as the solution to any problem.

We've stopped dragging the boat, because it's too bashed up to salvage. From its parts, we've built two smaller sledges to drag our supplies; Barra; and now, for parts of most days, Liel, who's been keeping a leg wound secret from Coran. He'd probably still be keeping it secret if Coran hadn't overheard Kera demanding to know the reason for his limp. I'm sick to death of Kera being right about things. It's never anything good.

Coran is furious. Apparently it happened some time ago, while Liel was pulling the sledge. The sledge slammed down into a rut and bashed into his leg and Coran says that because Liel never told him, now it's infected and all of Coran's options are dangerous. He didn't elaborate on what he meant by dangerous, but I know what he meant. He needs to remove Liel's leg, or else Liel might die of infection. But if he does remove Liel's leg, Liel could still die of infection, or of blood loss, of shock.

Coran told all of us, in a shrill and exasperated voice, that from now on, we must come to him with any injuries immediately. Now Liel lies on the sledge, feeding goat milk to Ladybug, weeping. I can't blame him. But he's my least favorite person to pull through the snow, because he's big.

The snow here pretends to be a hard shell, then you crash through to your thighs. We walk with our lightest people in front, including Bitterblue, so that their lesser weight creates a hardened imprint that the rest of us can then tread on without breaking through. It probably works for every four steps out of five. That fifth step, when I plunge, then get trapped, then need help emerging to a spot where the snow will hold my weight, is evidence of how tired I am, because I don't care. Nothing is more hateful than anything else.

We found some lichen along the riverbank, and ate it. We ate some mushrooms we found one night too, which turned out to be a mistake. Everyone from the Royal Continent suffered terrible stomach pains and vomiting, and everyone from the Torlan continent experienced hallucinations. Riz kept screaming at us to stop burning his feet. All night, he woke up screaming about the torches we were holding to his feet, until Alzar, who was also hallucinating, decided she believed him, then stood over him, shielding him from our supposed torture. In the meantime, Ozul kept trying to jump in the river, because she insisted she was being chased by a kind of bear that melts in water. Those of us who were vomiting but in our right minds had to stay up all night, keeping the others safe.

The next morning, the Keepish and Kamassarian sailors kept sheepishly apologizing for their behavior. Once Riz reached out and touched my wrist. "I owe you an apology too, Hava," he said, speaking Kamassarian. "That day our boat capsized, I grabbed on to you in the water. Pulled you under. I was panicked, I wasn't thinking. I'm sorry."

I stared at him blankly, trying to remember how much I'd cared about that once. I knew that I had, but the caring was gone, along with the reason for caring. "It's okay," I said. "No harm done. How are your feet?"

"Still on my body," he said. "Coran says we'll find we never needed to get married so soon."

"That's great," I said, with absolutely no idea what he was talking about. What did getting married have to do with anything?

I must've looked confused, because he explained. "Alzar and I got married because we knew it was likely to be a rough winter at sea," he said. "In Kamassar, marrying bestows benefits on a widowed spouse."

"I see," I said, understanding that he was educating me about cultural differences. Trying to sound intelligent. Then maybe he said something else? I'm not sure. I keep losing parts of conversations. Soon after that, we loaded up and started walking.

My mind opens and closes in flashes. I'll have moments when I notice suddenly that the small people in front—Sorit, Lisa, Alzar, Ollie, my own sister—have eyes constantly streaming from the brightness of the snow. Moments when I'll remember the existence of the kits and Hope, then panic until I've confirmed where each of them is. Moments when I'll be talking easily to Giddon, worrying about how thin he's become, and then I'll remember I'm angry at him.

I have moments too where I think of Grella, who died of infection after trying to perform surgery on his own fingers. Or maybe the cold took him, or an animal; we'll never really know. He buried his journals before his physical limitations could make it impossible to do so.

These moments flash at me, then my mind goes dark again, like a cloth over a birdcage. All there is is walking.

81.

I WOULD RATHER NOT think too much about how it was to help with Liel's surgery.

The surgery itself was a little rough, but fine. Coran doesn't have all the instruments here that he would have at the royal court, so everything is slower, less precise, but he seemed comfortable tying the tourniquet, applying the knife. When it was too much to watch, I closed my eyes and reached out to each fox in turn. Hope, Moth, Bir, Blueberry, and Liel's kit, Ladybug, were with Linny. Cornsilk was with Froggatt, and Owlet with Barra. *I love you, Hope. I love you, Moth. I love you, Bir.* And so on.

The unbearable part was Liel's pain. Not just his pain, his sorrow. Coran has some powerful drugs for pain, and Liel drank rauha as well, but he could feel our hands on him and hear the sound of sawing and he knew what was happening. He's so heartbroken. Liel didn't want to lose his leg. Also, Coran says his pain later, when the drugs wear off, will be terrible, and Coran's drugs aren't limitless.

Bitterblue's with Liel now while he sleeps. She's staying near him to hold his hand and wipe his forehead when he wakes up. He's her cook and she brought him here. She feels responsible. So she'll keep her face quiet and her voice soft and say all the kind, queenly things that give people comfort. I suppose later she'll go to Giddon and curl up in his arms and shake and cry inside his furs. Bitterblue reached any normal person's limit for the pain of others long ago, but the Queen of Monsea doesn't get breaks from things like that.

Sometimes I'm glad for the part of my brain that turns off. After Coran removed Liel's leg, he gave me the job of disposing of it. "Throw it into the river," he told me quietly.

I went off on my own, sliding down the snowy bank. There, with the water at my toes, I spun Liel's leg into the river, careful not to think.

As I turned back, I saw the broken shell of a small boat pressed against the bank, half-hidden by snow. I was so surprised that for a moment I just stared. Then something frantic took over me and I began digging at it, crying out when a nail pierced my glove and tore a gash in my palm.

I uncovered what remained of a small prow: curved boards breaking apart from each other, with a few rusty nails exposed. The whole thing was stuck behind rocks that held it back from the steep plunge into the river, but I could certainly see how pieces of it might fall in and ride the water to the river's mouth, where we found that board.

Then, still burrowing into the snow, I uncovered a flash of scarlet-and-gold fabric.

I think my body understood before my mind did, because I stopped digging. I knelt there, clutching the fabric. There's a thickness to Keepish silk, and a distinctive style to the way the Keepish weave gold thread into variegated stretches of bright colors like scarlet, creating that iridescent effect. If I hadn't known Navi was back at camp with a scarf like this around her neck, I might've thought to myself, *How did her scarf get here?*

My hands started digging again. When I found a long, white bone, I left it there, stood, and climbed numbly up the bank to get Annet.

82.

ANNET AND NAVI came back down to the riverbank with me.

Grimly, they knelt beside the boat, the scarf, and the bone, then began shifting more snow with their hands. I stood above them, trying to shake the feeling that I was asleep.

"There are nails," I said. "Don't cut yourself."

"Did you hurt yourself, habpva?" said Annet, glancing up at the torn palm of my glove.

"Yes."

"You'll show it to Coran immediately," she said.

"Yes," I said automatically, expecting her to send me away that moment. But they let me stay while they dug through the snow, unearthing the rest of the scarf, finding a few other, smaller bones, talking to each other quietly in a mix of Lingian and Keepish. *That must be how they talk*, I thought, *when they're alone. Weaving their languages together like a blanket.*

"Do you understand what this means, habpva?" Annet asked me at one point.

"The rusty nail we found at the mouth of the river was from other shipwrecked people from Winterkeep," I said. "Not from Pikkians who live on the river. Just like Kera said."

Annet lifted tired eyebrows. "Is Kera's interpretation generally known?"

"I don't think so. I overheard you talking."

"I see," said Annet, sighing over the little pile of bones at her knees. From their size, I thought they must be fingers.

Then she raised her gray eyes to my face again. "This is an example of knowledge that would damage the group more than it helped," she said.

I vaguely remembered a time when I would've cared about this. Now I was too exhausted. "Whom will you tell?"

She took a breath, thinking, then glanced inquiringly at Navi. "Ozul and the queen?"

"Yes," said Navi. "No one else."

"The queen will tell Giddon," I said.

"Then maybe Giddon is the person we should ask to come and dig further," Navi said. "You and I'll be missed if we stay here too long, Annet."

"Must we dig further?" I asked.

"We should make whatever effort we can to identify this poor soul," Annet said.

"I could dig," I forced myself to say.

"You've done enough, habpva," Annet said, pushing herself to her feet with knees that made cracking noises in protest. "Have you inspected your foxes yet?"

"No."

"You go do that," said Annet. "It's a better use of your time."

Back at camp, I collected the foxes and crawled into my tent. I curled myself around their warm little bodies, and slept.

I WOKE WITH my usual foxes beside me, Hope and Moth. The rest were gone.

It was dark. Behind me, Ozul slept fitfully. I was wearing my boots, which I don't normally sleep in, and I couldn't remember ever having had dinner. My hunger was both painful and nauseating.

I tucked Hope and Moth inside my coat and stumbled outside.

Coran, Bitterblue, and Giddon were sitting on rocks around a low fire. Stars pricked the sky and a stripe of orange painted the horizon in the direction I thought was east, but I was so groggy and confused that I couldn't be sure.

"What time is it?" I said as I joined them.

"Almost morning," said Bitterblue. "Did you eat last night, Hava?"

"No," I said. "Where are my foxes?"

"You were fast asleep," Bitterblue said. "Linny took them from you and redistributed them. Coran, where are the food supplies? Hava needs her dinner."

Coran pushed himself up and wandered into the darkness.

"Why are you awake?" I asked, dropping onto a rock by the fire and burying my face in my hands.

"Liel had a bad night," Bitterblue said. "He's asleep now, but we've been with him."

I remembered Liel's leg spinning through the air into the river. Then finding the boat in the snow. The bones. "Did you dig, Giddon?" I asked. "Did you find anything?"

"Very little," he said. "More bones. A few rings," he said, touching his breast pocket. "Are you all right, Hava?"

His question reminded me that I was angry with the two of them about something. I grunted, fully intending to leave, but I didn't have the strength to push up from my seat. Liel's leg was still spinning through the air in my mind.

"Here you are, Hava," said Coran from somewhere nearby.

At the sound of his voice, my palm suddenly began aching. "Oh," I said. "I have a wound."

"What?" said Bitterblue, alarmed.

"Where?" said Giddon.

"Let me see it," said Coran sternly.

I held out my gloved hand.

With a puzzled glance into my face, Coran removed my glove and inspected the gash on my palm in the firelight. "How did you do this?"

"I cut it," I said.

"Hm," he said. "Give me a minute."

With another particular, concerned look at my face, Coran handed me a nutritional biscuit and three dried cherries, then walked away again. It was like eating caked dust and three tiny pieces of leather, but I forced it down, wishing I could tell Linta Massera. Look, Linta. Our food is so small. Is it sufficiently indivisible yet?

When Coran came back, he sat beside me and fussed for a while. "You were right to show me," he said, applying a salve that felt like a line of icy fire along my palm. "I'll take a better look at it later in the daylight, but I'm not too worried."

"Great," I said.

"Are you all right, Hava?" he asked, with the same puzzled tone Giddon had used.

"Why do people keep asking me that?"

"I'm going to recommend you have a day off from the sledges," Coran said.

"I'm stronger than most people. I have a better coat, and better boots."

"I insist upon it," said Coran, "for your hand."

Fine. Whatever. I asked, *Is anyone keeping a journal? What about Barra's little notebook?*

I asked, *When should we bury our journal?* When no one answered, I realized I was only speaking inside my own head.

The sun rose, the light pouring straight into my aching skull like I had no skin or bones to shield me from the attack.

"Eighteen walking days to go," Annet shouted cheerfully.

I walked.

83.

LIEL HAS BEEN high on rauha for three days straight.

When I asked Coran about it, he shook his head. "His risk for addiction is high," he said grimly. "But his pain is too great to bear without it, and his cries and screams decimate the morale of the group. I don't have enough of my other pain medicines. The rauha is the least bad of several bad options."

"What about the medicine Kera used on Hope?"

Coran made his lips very thin and shook his head again.

"You used it on Kera," I said.

"I hated to do that," he said. "Depending on one's constitution, it can create—" He hesitated. "A sort of dimming of the soul."

After he said that, I pushed myself forward to Linny, because Linny had Hope. I had to walk past Kera to get to him. It was all I could do not to knock her down into the snow.

Then I took Hope from Linny and carried her for a while, holding her tightly. Trying to share with her all my love and fury for the dimmed parts of her soul.

IN HIS FEVERISH rauha state, Liel is having hallucinations. They're horrible visions, like watching the *Monsea* sink into an icy ocean while Tulip climbs the mizzenmast yowling, but the rauha makes them funny to him. Sometimes he giggles. We trudge along, pulling him on his sledge at the end of the line while his leg seeps fresh blood into its bandages and he sings out one gleeful hallucination after another.

And so, when he sang about a bear, we didn't believe him, until he screamed. The scream spun us around. A gigantic bear watched us with empty eyes, its head low and its mouth bloody, from biting Liel's wound.

I had my knife in my hand and was running before I knew it. Kera was pulling Liel's sledge, so she was closest. As I ran, she did something unbelievable: She lunged at the bear and punched it in the face.

Her fist bounced off its nose like a rubber ball. The bear swung away from Liel's leg, raising its eyes to see who'd tapped him. Then it reared up with a roar, swiped with one paw, and Kera went spinning into the snow, blood splattering around her.

Pushing herself up, Kera lunged at the bear with her fists again. I saw Linny running toward us with his bow, drawing an arrow, then freezing, yelling. I understood that he couldn't shoot the bear, because Kera was in the way.

I tackled Kera, knocked her down into the snow. Behind me I heard Liel crying and the thwack of an arrow. People shouted. The bear roared. Blades scraped across the back of my skull and Kera was yelling, grabbing my knife from me, reaching past my shoulders to stab up at the bear. I heard another thwack. Then the bear fell like a tree in the snow beside us.

For a moment, there was silence. I stared down at the woman under me. Blood was running into her auburn hair. I thought it might be dripping from my head.

I punched Kera in the face. I punched her again, then again; when her nose ran with blood, I kept punching her. "You hurt Hope," I cried. "You hurt Hope."

Strong hands pulled me back and the world turned to stars.

84.

When I came to, it was to the sense that I was cuddling with someone who was jabbing daggers into the back of my head.

"How are you, Hava?" came the voice of Barra, too close to my ear.

I understood then that I was pressed against Barra on his sledge. We weren't cuddling and he wasn't stabbing me; we were being pulled across a rough patch of snow. My skull bounced against the wooden boards with every yank.

Tentatively, I reached my hand to the back of my head. There I found sticky, matted hair and an awkward strip of bandage. And pain.

"Awful," I murmured.

"You've been scratched by a bear," Barra said. "Coran says you'll live."

The bones of my hands felt like they'd been stomped on by giants. I tried to open my eyes to inspect them, but the light seared my brain and I cried out, turning my face away.

Before I fell asleep again, I got a glimpse of Owlet on Barra's chest, staring back at me with a solemn gold gaze.

The next time I woke, I felt well enough to prop myself up on one elbow.

It's strange, watching the progression of the group from such a low angle. Everyone seems so tall and looming—and slow. Ozul and Jacky were pulling our sledge. Craning my neck back, I saw Ollie and Sorit pulling Liel's sledge, which meant Liel must be alive. Right?

"Is Liel alive?" I said, suddenly panicking.

"Everyone's alive," said Barra, "except for the bear." He patted his hand on something next to him and I blinked, startled, as the whiteness beside him differentiated itself from the snow and became the mounded carcass of a bear.

No wonder it's so cozy on this sledge.

"We must be a heavy load," I said. "Ozul and Jacky must be tired. I can walk."

Then I fell asleep again.

When I woke, the sledge wasn't moving and Barra was gone.

Inside my coat, Moth flapped against my stomach. I pushed myself up and looked around, groaning.

On a plain of snow, a fire spit orange sparks at a black sky and people were raising the tents, milking the goat, butchering the bear. Bear for dinner. I touched my skull gingerly. I earned my meal tonight. Didn't I?

Well. Except that I myself didn't hurt the bear. I only hurt Kera.

I saw her with the group raising the tents. Ozul was working with her, side by side, just like they'd done on the *Monsea* before she'd tried to kill me. I saw them share a laugh about something.

Is she a hero now, because she tried to beat up a bear? It was an idiotic thing to do. Linny's arrows killed the bear, not Kera's fists.

"Hava," said Bitterblue, coming from the fire to join me. There was a rush of pleased affection in her voice. "You're awake."

"Yes," I said shortly.

"I've been worried," she said. "Coran says it's not too bad, your head. Superficial wounds."

"Great."

"He's anxious about Liel," she said, "because of the chance of infection from the mouth of that bear. But he's keeping a close eye on it."

Inside my coat, Moth slapped against my stomach again. I took a moment to pat the lump that was her and the lump that was Blueberry. "Are all the kits okay?" I said. "And Hope?"

"Linny checked. They're all accounted for."

"Good."

"Kera's pretty bashed up," Bitterblue added, in a different voice. A not-thrilled sort of voice.

"She looks fine," I said.

"She reminds me of Katsa," Bitterblue said. "Pops right back up as if a drubbing is nothing."

Then she stopped, seeming to notice the quiet shock in the air between us, that she would compare Kera with *Katsa*, the hero of the Seven Nations, the founder of Giddon's revolutionary Council, and the champion who carried Bitterblue through Grella's Pass. Katsa killed our father and put an end to that nightmare. Katsa kills monstrosities, while Kera tried to kill *me*.

"Maybe you'd like to have Kera on your royal team," I said.

"I think you know that's not what I meant," said Bitterblue quietly.

"She hurt Hope and she threw me into the sea."

"I haven't forgotten, sweetie," said Bitterblue. "But Hava, you've put me in an awkward place here. I need to ask you not to beat her senseless again the way you did today. If you do, I'm going to have to punish you."

"What?" I cried. "Punish *me*?"

"When Jacky and Ollie attacked her, they were punished. Your conflict with Kera is more personal, so we can let it pass, once. But if you do it again, I need you to know that as the queen and the leader of this expedition, I'll have to punish you. I have no choice, Hava."

I was practically spitting. "I'd like to see you try."

"Hava, she's my prisoner! It's my responsibility to protect her. Can't you see the position I'm in?"

"The position *you're* in," I said. "How hypocritical is that? When we get to court, you'll put her behind bars to rot in the dark for the rest of her life, or maybe you'll even execute her. But out here, it's your responsibility to protect her? In the meantime, she hurt me. *Me*, not you! She's no more your prisoner than mine!"

"She broke the law," Bitterblue said flatly. "I'm the law, whether we like it or not. And no one's allowed to break the law openly. Including you. How does it look for everyone to be punished but you?"

"Everyone but you, you mean," I said. "You're allowed to do what you like, right? You can make up the rules as you go along. You can even have illegitimate babies with your big, stupid, secret boyfriend in the wilderness if you want to, and then when we get back, decide they're legitimate after all. Right? You're the *queen*. You can change the rules anytime and you never owe anyone anything. Especially me, right?"

My voice had risen enough that the camp had gone still. Faces turned to us, then turned aside again quickly, trying not to pry. And now Bitterblue was staring at me with a light dawning in her eyes, like she was finally realizing something she should've realized eons ago. From across the camp, Giddon moved away from the bear operation and came to stand behind her shoulder like a guard, or like a tree for her to lean against. Who can I lean against? Why does it have to be out here, in this desperate place, when my head feels so awful, that I realize I can't lean against my own sister? Because she's the *queen*. Caring for my murderer is her precious responsibility. And I can't lean on Giddon, either, because he belongs to Bitterblue too.

The mild, sympathetic expression he was resting on my face right now made me want to scream.

"Hava?" said Bitterblue. "Is that what this is about? Giddon?"

"You endangered her," I said to Giddon, jabbing my finger at him. "What kind of love is that, making her pregnant in this wasteland?"

"I'm not pregnant," said Bitterblue. "Hava! I'm not pregnant!"

"You could have been," I said. "It was selfish and careless and—"

"Hey! Stop talking to Giddon like that!" said Bitterblue.

"I'll talk how I like," I shot back. "I can't trust either of you to remember *me*. You care more about Kera's rights than about *telling* me what's going on in your own *lives*."

"Hava!" said Bitterblue. "That's not true!"

"It is true!"

I sounded like a child, a brat. I could hear it in my voice, and the water flying from my eyes made me furious. There was no way out of this. Everyone was watching.

Then Annet came forward from the tents, interrupting. "Hava," she said crisply. "Have you inspected the foxes yet?"

I couldn't look her in the face. "No."

"Do that immediately," she said, "then go to Coran to have your wounds looked at. Everyone, return to your duties," she said, raising her voice to be heard. "Giddon, get back to the bear. Lady Queen, I need your thoughts about the plan for tomorrow."

85.

LINNY BROUGHT ME the kits.

There was a tension to his shoulders and face as he handed them into my arms.

"Are you okay, Hava?" he asked me. "I've been worried."

I was shy of his quiet, light eyes. I was embarrassed by my outburst. "I'm fine," I said, "as you can see."

"My first arrow hit the bear in the shoulder and enraged her," he said. "That's when she swiped at your head. I feel responsible."

Well, that was ridiculous. "That wasn't your doing. I threw myself into that situation."

"Fearlessly."

"Recklessly!"

"You gave me a clear shot."

"And you shot well," I said, "and killed the bear. And now it's over and everyone's fine."

I thought he would loosen his shoulders at that, soften his mouth and grin at me. Instead he stood there rigid and unhappy, and I understood that I'd ruined things. Maybe by attacking Kera the way I'd done. Maybe by yelling the queen's secrets for everyone to hear, like a child. I suppose Linny has witnessed a lot of my tantrums by now.

"Ladybug, Bir, Owlet, Cornsilk," I said, focusing on the kits crowded in my arms. "Where's Blueberry?"

"Don't you have Moth and Blueberry?" he said. "I felt them in your coat, after the bear."

"Oh, right."

"Here comes Hope," he said. He watched as the little fox padded to me across the camp, but he looked like he wanted to be elsewhere.

"Thanks," I said, in a voice that was a dismissal.

At my feet, Hope, slope-nosed and sweet-faced, gazed up at me. *Babies?* she said.

Hope, I said. *Do you love me even though I'm a brat?*

My girl, she said, then stood on her hind legs and propped a paw on my shin, trying to see into my arms. *Babies?*

With a sense that everything I cared about was off-kilter, I carried the foxes into our tent.

86.

THE NEXT PART was clean, swift, and awful, like Coran slicing off a toe.

As I collected the kits together and began to inspect them one by one, Hope was acting strange. She climbed into my lap among the babies and kept touching each one with her paws, which was unusual, since normally she interacts with me, but pretends they're not there. When they squirmed around her and latched themselves to her body, she didn't complain, only stretched a paw out to my stomach and said anxiously, *Babies?*

Yes, I said, reaching into my coat. *I have Moth and Blueberry here.* I pulled Blueberry out and tucked him, sleeping, against the others. I was reaching for Moth, who was wriggling against me, when Hope began to keen in my mind, a haunting, tearing cry.

I pulled Moth out and held her close to my chest while I stared at Hope, who was pushing a paw against Blueberry, over and over, almost shoving him. He wouldn't wake up.

As I reached for him, Hope began to howl. When I lifted him, I saw why. His neck was broken.

87.

I LOVE YOU, BLUEBERRY. I love you, Blueberry.

It's too late for that now.

He was the most extraneous kit, the one Linny and I passed back and forth depending on who was carrying Hope. Moth was mine, and Bir, unofficially, was Linny's. Cornsilk was Froggatt's. Owlet was Barra's. Ladybug was Liel's.

Blueberry was nobody's—but not because I didn't love him. I did. He was one of the first I named, practically the moment I saw his round blue nose. We simply hadn't found his place yet. Now we never will.

I must've carried him dead for hours. It had to have been when I threw myself on Kera and tackled her to the ground. It's the only time I can think of when his body could've been crushed like that, unless it was when I was punching Kera. Could it have been then? Could I have killed him in my temper? It doesn't seem likely, but that's not much comfort. Whenever it happened, it was because I'd forgotten to be careful of him.

"I should've checked more closely," Linny said when he came into the tent and found me sobbing. "We were in a rush. I felt him in your coat. I thought he was asleep. I should've made sure," he said, swiping at the tears that were dripping down his own face.

"It doesn't matter," I said. "It wouldn't have mattered. He was already dead."

"You know it's not your fault, right?"

"Of course it's my fault," I said roughly, gasping through tears.

"You were saving people's lives."

Saving people's lives. Whatever.

Alone, consulting only Linny, I gave him a funeral in the river. I was afraid of what would happen if I asked hungry people what I should do. Linny stayed with the other foxes while I went.

Standing on the bank, I tossed him into the middle of the current. He sank straight to the bottom, which felt wrong somehow; I imagined the force of the water knocking him against rocks on the river floor.

I turned away and stopped thinking.

HOPE IS INCONSOLABLE. She's always, always crying in my mind. She won't walk with Adventure or hunt with Linny; she wants to be where the kits are, but the kits are spread out. I've taken to carrying her in my arms a lot, trying to soothe her. She cycles through their names, counting them. It's such a reversal from how she was before.

I'm so ashamed, I can barely speak to her. Over and over I tell her I'm sorry, but it doesn't help. She doesn't understand it, because she doesn't blame me.

I'm worried she blames herself. What if Blueberry's death woke her to the fact that they're her babies and now she blames herself for not caring for them better? I can't bear the thought of her regretting behavior that she couldn't have helped.

I'M WALKING AGAIN.

It isn't easy. My head flashes with pain and sometimes my vision blurs into blackness. I have to pound my feet hard on the ground to keep myself focused and alert, which hurts my head more.

I think Giddon notices. I think he's walking near me on purpose.

Once, when I stumbled, his hand materialized, catching my arm and helping me stay on my feet.

"Thank you," I said.

"I'm sorry, Hava," he said.

"I'm sorry too, Hava," said Bitterblue, appearing out of nowhere, the surprise of it sending pain bursting through my skull.

"Me too," I said, "probably. But my head hurts way too much right now to have this conversation."

Around midday on the day after Blueberry died, our river bent sharply to the right, the west. It was at a place where the water ran fast and deep, pouring down from steep white hills that I, for one, did not think this group could climb. Even the strongest among us are so tired. Our lips are cracked, our feet blistered and starting to rot; we have cramps, and every breath burns.

"Do we even want to turn west?" I said aloud, then regretted it as my head increased its pounding.

Navi had pushed herself onto a boulder and was surveying the land that lay straight ahead to the south. Her face was expressionless. I could see her freckles, standing out on cheekbones that were sharper than they used to be.

"There's a glacier to the south," she said, "flowing toward the ocean."

"You mean, flowing west to east across our path?" said Giddon. "Cutting us off?"

She didn't respond, just caught Annet's eyes and held them with such grim solemnity that I knew the answer was yes.

"There's a channel here in the ground," Ozul said, "leading to the glacier, do you see it?"

I saw what she meant, barely—a dip in the snowy landscape ahead that stretched forward, drawing a long line toward the south.

"I bet it's a riverbed in the summer," she said. "Meltwater flows from the glacier and joins the river here."

"Does that signify something to you about our route, Ozul?" said Annet.

"I'd like to take a look at this glacier," said Ozul, starting forward. "If there's a river that flows under the glacier in summer, it could mean that in winter, when everything freezes up again, it leaves a tunnel behind."

Half an hour later, we entered an opening at the base of Ozul's glacier and stepped into a pale blue tunnel of ice.

88.

Linta Massera, I need your help. Didn't you say something about change once? That we learn what things are made of by watching them change? So? How can I figure out what the world is made of if what I think I see keeps changing?

When we entered the tunnel, the only reason Ozul agreed to do so was because light was visible ahead. The end of the tunnel.

But then as we neared it, the light changed. It turned out to be a flowing cascade of reflections from cracks in the ice ceiling above us, cracks that have made Ozul so tense with anxiety that she's begun to drive us at a pace we can barely maintain.

"This has become a very bad idea," I heard her say to Annet, low-voiced.

"What should we do instead?" Annet responded, which silenced Ozul for a little while, because our other three options are untenable. We can't turn west and climb those hills, which most likely lead to the mountains we saw. Even if we had the strength, west is the wrong direction. Turning east would lead us to the sea, which would be a fine route around the glacier for a party with a boat, but we're beyond boats now. And we can't walk south across the top of the glacier, because Ozul has categorically refused to sanction that plan. The ice atop a glacier is far too unsteady, she said. Someone would definitely fall into a crevasse and die.

And so we're utilizing a tunnel carved by a torrent of summer water through the base of the glacier—meaning that the unstable ice is above us, which seems little better to me. It also means that we've chosen a path with no certainty about where it'll take us. So far, our compasses tell us we're moving south, but why shouldn't this tunnel veer west, or east? Why shouldn't it dead-end?

At night, we made camp in a cavern with a high, rounded, translucent ceiling. Ozul's face was drawn and tight and she spoke sharply when Ollie started to build a fire. Ollie's our cook now, while Liel shivers and weeps, sings and giggles on his sledge.

"We still have a few potatoes," Ollie told her. "They'll make the bear meat less tough."

"We can't risk the heat of a fire when our roof is made of ice, Ollie," she said. "No potatoes tonight."

I sat by myself at the edge of the cavern, chewing on my small portion of cold, roasted bear meat. I could see the moon, blurry through the ice above. As the ceiling sent echoes of sharp cracks and glassy tinkles down to me, I remembered my last experience of being in a cave. Stuck under a ladder, holding Linta Massera's stolen notebooks. Linta was dead, from the bomb she herself had created. Well. She created it, I activated it. I didn't care about her then.

Now I wonder what her heart was made of, and why she chose the things she did.

LINNY FOUND ME in my corner. He sat with me, saying nothing, chewing on his own leathery meat. His closeness made me think of Blueberry.

Hope jumped out of my lap, where she was nursing Moth, and climbed up Linny's body into his hood, where he was carrying Bir. It was almost funny to watch his hood bob and change shape, or anyway, it would've been funny in different circumstances.

His silence was setting me on edge, because of the strain and unhappiness in his face.

"I have something to tell you," he finally said.

"Okay," I said, surprised.

He reached into a pocket, pulled out a small bundle, unwrapped it, and handed me my bird-girl.

My habpva, my seasparrow. I stared at it, flabbergasted. "Where did you find it? Who had it?"

"I did," he said.

"You!"

"I took it," he said.

"*You* took it! What do you mean?"

"It was falling out of a hole in your mattress," he said. "I grabbed it before it fell. We were filling your tub, remember?"

"I remember."

"You left. I noticed it. I grabbed it, but then," he said with a sigh, "when I saw what it was, I didn't want Jacky or Ollie to see it."

"What do you mean?" I said again, confused, because none of this explained why he still had it.

He flapped a hand helplessly. "It was *you*," he said. "I recognized you immediately. It was this extraordinary, tiny sculpture of you, and you were turning into a bird, and the expression on your face was so agonized, and it felt private. I didn't want them to see it."

"You're right," I said. "I wouldn't have wanted them to see it either."

His eyes dropped to his lap. He was clenching his teeth; for someone who'd innocently rescued my bird-girl from falling, he looked awfully ashamed about it. Things were starting to shift in my understanding. A small sickness was twisting inside me. I wondered if he was going to volunteer the part he was leaving out, or wait for me to accuse him.

"Also," he said, "once I had it, I realized I wanted it."

Well, there it was. Just like Jacky's cheap move with the rauha, Linny was a thief. "It was mine," I said. "You even saw how upset I was about it. You should've given it back right away."

"I was terrified of how upset you were," he said.

"You mean you were a coward?" I said coldly. "Why are you giving it back now?"

He raised his eyes to mine and held my gaze, which seemed to take some effort. He was still working his mouth. Behind him, his hood bobbed as Hope shifted position again. "Because my wish to be a person you can trust is bigger than my fear of your temper," he said.

"Oh, my temper?" I shot back. "Why should you care if I trust you? It doesn't sound like you trust *me*."

"I *don't* trust your temper," he said. "You're scary when you're mad."

I sat up straighter, choked with anger.

"But I trust your heart," he continued. "You're brave, and righteous. You saved Hope, even in a moment when someone was trying to kill you. You ran right at that bear. I think you would *fling* yourself at a bear, to save the kits. And—I *like* you, Hava. I like talking to you. I want you to be able to trust me."

"But how could I trust you?" I said. "You lied to me!"

"I'm trying to fix that," he said.

"You stole from me!"

He nodded, seeming suddenly confused. "Yeah," he said. "That was a strange moment for me. I'd never stolen anything in my life before that."

I peered at him sharply. "Is that true?"

"Yes," he said. "Something came over me, Hava. It's so beautiful, and—" He raised those amber eyes to mine again. "It's *you*."

"You keep saying that."

"I liked you then," he said, "as I like you now. I didn't see us becoming friends then. I wanted something that was a part of you. It's not an excuse." He began to shake his head in frustration. "The more I explain, the creepier it sounds. Did your mother make it? I should've guessed how much it meant to you."

He was saying so many astonishing things that I couldn't figure out which ones to aim at. I settled on the ones that were less about me. "You've really never stolen anything before this?"

"Is it so shocking?" he said. "Do I seem like someone who steals a lot?"

"Well," I said. "I've stolen more things than I could count."

"I guess that doesn't surprise me," he said, with no hesitation, and no criticism in his tone. I gave him another hard, searching look. Embarrassment still flickered in his face, and worry. He'd said, *I want you to be able to trust me.* He'd said, *I trust your heart.* But he'd said, *I don't trust your temper,* and he wasn't surprised that I stole.

I wondered if he was afraid of my temper right now, in this moment. I wasn't sure what I thought about Linny being afraid of me. I didn't think I liked it.

But shouldn't he be afraid of me, if he betrays my trust?

But does it shift something, if he comes to me and tells me about it afterward?

"I'm not sure about you right now," I said.

"Okay," he said. He started to get up.

"Where are you going?"

"I guessed that maybe you wanted me to go away," he said.

The thought of him leaving right now, with things so unsettled, tugged at my throat. I didn't want him to go. I measured the risks of telling him the truth about that.

"Would you sit with me a little longer," I said, "while I think things through?"

89.

HE DID STAY a little longer. We talked about ahsoken. Whenever there are thoughts I want to explain to Linny but I feel like I can't, apparently I start talking about chemistry.

"The chemist whose work I was translating," I told him. "She wasn't supposed to be studying ahsoken. She was supposed to be doing something else, she was *paid* to do something else, but she kept using that money for her own work, the work she loved."

"So she was a thief?" said Linny, then shot me a small smile. "Like me?"

I snorted. "You stole one thing, once. If anything, she was a thief like me."

"Well, I guess I don't know for sure what she was being paid to do, but I've gathered it was something bad. Maybe it's good that she did her own beloved work instead."

"I would like," I said, "whenever I break the rules I'm given, for it to be for something good."

Then I was so surprised by the words I'd just said aloud that I let him talk for a bit while I listened, trying to gather myself in. With Hope peeking out of his hood, he told me about the ahsoken believed to compose water. He told me about how water expands as it freezes, becoming less dense than its liquid form, which is a good thing, because it means ice rises and floats. If ice sank, the rivers and lakes and maybe even the oceans would turn to blocks of ice in winter.

I'd never considered that. It was a new way to think about icebergs. When he got up to go, I felt less strange about everything.

I thanked him for returning my bird-girl to me.

"You're welcome," he said. "I'm sorry I didn't return it right away."

I couldn't quite get my mouth to say, "It's all right," but I managed, "You didn't know how important it was to me." I was a little ashamed about that as he walked away. As the distance increased between us, Hope popped her head out of his hood again, then sprang down and scampered back.

Ice, she said. *Expansion.*

Yes, I said, *expansion.*

Linny-Boy knows chemistry.

Yes, he does, Hope.

Big brains.

I was chuckling and hugging her, her fur warm against my face, when suddenly Bitterblue sat beside me. Her arrival was so abrupt that I wondered if she'd been watching me, waiting for Linny to leave.

"What's that?" she said, indicating the bird-girl in my lap, nestled beside Moth.

I tucked it into a pocket and didn't answer. She watched me for a moment.

"Hava," she said quietly. "I owe you an apology. We planned to tell you. And then, at a certain point, we felt like it was so obvious, there was no need. I see now that there was a need."

"I did know," I said hotly. "I've known from the beginning."

"I expect that I took advantage of your perceptiveness," she said, then dipped her gaze to the hands in her lap. "Also, I was a little shy. It felt very new at first, and fragile. If I'm being honest, it still does."

"Giddon's been hopelessly in love with you for more than three years," I said.

"Yes," she said. "It took me longer to realize my feelings."

"Well," I said, my words still rushing out in small, indignant bursts. "You have daddy issues."

Bitterblue snorted. Then all at once, she was gasping with laughter, holding her stomach and swaying, practically collapsing onto her side. I tried to maintain my offended silence, but her howling made it impossible. A spluttery laugh forced its way out of my throat.

"I'm still upset," I insisted.

"I know," she said, still laughing. "I'm sorry. I should've sat you down and said something. But you know, it's hard to talk to you sometimes. Whenever I bring up feelings, you get this look on your face like you'd rather I stuck a fork in your eye. Can you at least acknowledge that?"

"I'll acknowledge it as long as you're not using it as an excuse," I said.

"No excuses," she said. "I promise. Oh, Hava. I'm sorry. I've been avoiding certain sticky topics out here. A lot of topics, actually. Mostly I've been focused on Estill, and my mines, and the zilfium weapon."

"What?" I said, incredulous. "Here?"

"Well, it's not like us getting shipwrecked in the north is doing anything good for Monsea's relationship with her neighbors!" she said. "Monsea's sitting on all this zilfium, and by now the whole world will know that someone in Winterkeep made an explosive weapon out of it. Estill's been looking for excuses to antagonize Monsea for years—Estill's already tried to buy the weapon!—and here we are stuck in the north with no one knowing where we are. My court could be dealing with any number of threats to Monsea's sovereignty. I'm half-afraid we'll get home to the news that I've been declared dead and Estill has allied with Sunder and laid siege to our zilfium mines."

"I can't believe you can think about all that out here."

"You have no idea how compulsively I check your formulas and translations every day to make sure they haven't gotten wet," she said.

Yes, and I check them too sometimes. But for a different reason. I'm not checking on the plans for building a weapon; I'm checking on Linta.

"I haven't thought about Estill or Sunder once since the *Monsea* sank," I said. "I mean, not like that, anyway. I can barely see beyond my own feet."

She took a small breath. "I need to think about it," she said. "Remembering how much Monsea needs me is the only thing that keeps me from becoming paralyzed with fear."

"Ah," I said, stroking the backs of Hope and Moth, who were curled together in my lap. I could understand that. And then I dropped my head, remembering Blueberry.

"I'm sorry about the kit you lost," said Bitterblue.

"Thanks."

"You know it was an accident, right? You were getting Kera out of the way so Linny could shoot."

"Sure," I said, "if it happened then."

"It was an accident whenever it happened."

"Sure," I repeated, unconvinced.

"Hava?" she said. "There is one more thing I wanted to say to you about Kera."

This again. I took a breath and steeled myself, not responding.

"I know I'm the queen," she said. "I know it can make things complicated, and sometimes you feel like I'm not on your side. But Hava, there are ways in which I'm always on your side, and you on mine. There are things we understand, you and I, that no one else can understand."

"Okay," I said. "What does that have to do with Kera?"

"I watched the way you were hitting her."

"Yes?" I said with clenched teeth.

"It's just this: Not everyone who hurts us is our father."

For a moment, the world was too bright. I was somewhere else, watching something else.

Have I explained that I saw my father kill my mother?

There was no blood. He broke her neck. He did it with one small, neat twist of her head, in a room at the back of his hospital of horrors. He seemed very pleased with himself for doing it so well. Then he became bored and upset again, as he always did, and stormed away looking for me, not understanding that I was right there, hiding, staring at my mother's body slumped on the ground. He never understood the nature of my Grace, that I could hide in plain sight. She managed to keep that from him, even though every one of her sculptures, every girl or woman transforming into something else, was a clue. That's why he never found me. He was looking for a small girl with red and copper eyes and lank hair the color of dirty water, a girl he could see. He should have been looking for a subtle change in the air around him. An invisible blade of anguish and fury.

"That's a hard one for me," I said.

"I know," she said quietly. "Me too, sometimes."

"She tried to kill me," I said in a voice that squeaked.

"I know," Bitterblue said. "When the time comes to sentence her, Hava, I promise you, I'm not going to forget that."

A strange chill touched me with those firm, certain words. It's one thing to punch someone in the face. It's another to make a considered announcement about her fate. As angry as I am at Kera, I would never want to be the Queen of Monsea. I'm not sure what I would choose.

Bitterblue touched a hand to my shoulder. "Are we going to be okay, Hava?"

I searched myself for all the indignation that had swelled me up before. It was gone. I was empty.

"Yes," I said. "I'm sorry I yelled your secret to the entire group."

"Oh, it was time someone did," she said, standing. "Who's LV?"

"What?" I said, startled to find my defenses rising.

"I've read your translation. *Ask LV for the quantity here. If the sulfur is added too quickly, the zilfium dust clumps, et cetera. Refer to LV for the procedure.*'"

"Right," I said, unsure why I wanted to hide Linta's secrets from Bitterblue, the way Linta had hidden them from her employer. The way my mother hid me from the king. "I don't know who LV is," I said. "Linta Massera's colleague, I guess."

Bitterblue sighed. "Well, hopefully the ceiling won't come down on us while we're sleeping, and someday soon we'll have the opportunity to find out. Annet says we have thirteen walking days," she said, her voice suddenly hard with determination. Then, to my great surprise, she bent down and kissed a spot on my filthy forehead.

After she left, I lifted Hope and Moth in my arms.

LV, said Hope. *With Linta.*

Yes, I said. *That's right, Hope.*

Then I bent my face to her, touching Bitterblue's kiss to her fur.

90.

THE CEILING HELD while we slept.

Now Ozul is pushing us along our path with an urgency that seems to have spread to Annet and Navi. The tunnel, which yesterday shimmered with light straining down from cracks above, has become dark, silent, and damply cold. When we breathe, it's like inhaling a cloud.

We've lit the lamps to find our way through the caverns of ice. Even those tiny sparks of heat make Ozul anxious, so afraid is she of melting the walls around us. In the meantime, the compasses tell us that our path is veering to the west.

"We need some sky," I heard Kera say harshly once. "We need to orient ourselves." Her face in the lamplight is garish, broken and bruised. Her nose is crooked and swollen. That's my doing. I should be pleased, but it turns my stomach. It draws my eyes too; I can't stop looking. It reminds me of a ruined face I saw once, peering through bars in my sister's prison, which is built into the rock under her castle. Her prison is made of low-ceilinged, dark passageways like this tunnel, and humans are trapped there. I don't want to die like those people, in a trap.

"Admiring your work?" Kera finally asked me, when we were near enough to speak.

"Do you admire your work when you see Hope?" I shot back. "You destroyed her mind. She can barely string a sentence together."

Kera let out a small, annoyed breath. "I'm not a fox doctor," she said. "I couldn't have known that would happen."

"Why do it, if you don't know what's going to happen?"

"Why do you think?"

I remembered the wad of cash among her belongings. "Money," I said scornfully.

"You say that with such contempt," she said, "you who grew up surrounded by every luxury. You're the companion of a queen. How would you know what it's like to lack money?"

I noticed that both Giddon and Linny were now walking beside me, which hadn't been the case a few minutes ago. Giddon's expression was calm and amiable, as it often is the moment before he springs into action. When I gave him a narrow-eyed look, he smiled back at me pleasantly.

Linny's expression was more closed, cautious. His hood hung heavily on his back, Hope inside.

"Did you do it for your daughter?" Linny asked Kera in Lingian, surprising me.

"What would you know about my daughter?" said Kera hotly.

"I know she was taken away from you," said Linny. "I could imagine doing some pretty extreme things to get your daughter back."

Any astonishment I might've had at this line of conversation was interrupted by Kera raising her fists and surging toward Linny. Giddon was between them at once, grabbing Kera by the scruff of her coat and shoving her back where she'd come from.

"Isn't your lot bad enough already, without making it worse?" he said to her.

"You're another one," she said to him, spitting. "Born to luxury and gentility. I did what I was paid to do. I was told to drug her, so I drugged her. If I hadn't, someone else would've, yet you blame me, not the rich people who hired me."

"You threw Hava into the ocean," Giddon said flatly. "That was your own clever—"

"Wait," I said, interrupting. "Your employer told you to drug her like that?"

"I'm done with this conversation," said Kera.

"Who's your employer?"

"My lot is bad enough without making it worse," she said, with a sneer at Giddon. Then she turned her shoulder and pushed on ahead, almost knocking poor Froggatt over as she passed him.

"Always nice to chat with Kera," said Giddon.

I snorted. "Bully."

Giddon looked straight at me, his eyes bright. "Hava," he said, "you're not a brat. You've never been a brat. I think I'm going to stop calling you one."

"Oh, *ugh*!" I said. "What are you trying to do to me, Giddon!"

For a minute he watched me with an expression on his face like he was going to cry, or worse, hug me, but he pulled himself together. Then, his eyes still suspiciously bright, he kissed his own index finger. Then he tapped his index finger to my head!

"Maybe I'll go check in on Liel," he said.

"That's a really good idea," I said.

He turned and walked to the back of the group. "Is he seriously not going to call me a brat anymore?" I said, speaking to the air.

"Would that be a bad thing?" said Linny, still walking beside me, speaking Dellian.

"It's tradition."

"Got it," he said, good-humoredly enough. "If the queen married him, would he be king?"

"Him? No. He'd be the prince consort."

"Do you all live in the castle?"

"Sort of," I said, "though technically, Giddon doesn't live anywhere.

He used to be a lord in the Middluns but his king accused him of treason, banished him, and burned his estate to the ground. Because he helped depose the King of Nander," I said, waving a vague hand. "And so on."

I expected him to ask me about the "so on." Instead, he said, "But you still live in the castle?"

"I guess so," I said. "It's never felt like home."

"Why not?"

Because I grew up inside closets and wardrobes, I didn't say. "It's claustrophobic. Like being in a city with ceilings. It doesn't suit me."

"Like a birdcage?" he said, surprising me. I touched the pocket that held my sculptures, including my bird-girl. If I'm a bird, then the castle is definitely a birdcage.

"Yes," I said. "Where do you live?"

He shrugged. "At sea."

"That's home?"

He gave me that smile, the one I haven't seen in a while that transfigures his face. It was like warmth, and food, and dry feet. "No roofs or ceilings at sea," he said.

I needed a minute to recover from that smile. I walked silently for a stretch. Then I said, "What did you mean about someone taking Kera's child away?"

"She got drunk once," he said, "and yelled at Jacky and Ozul about it. Jacky was teasing her and she snapped. She survived shipwreck before, somewhere near the Royal Continent, I'm not sure where. Afterward, she was ill and unable to find work for a long time. Then, I don't know the details, but she tried to take her daughter along on a sailing job and her husband's family showed up and made a scene and took the girl away. There was some law they claimed to be upholding, something about her being unfit to care for her child."

91.

OUR TUNNEL HAS started branching.

We always take the left branch, because we want to go more south than west through the glacier. But of course we don't know what we're choosing.

The branches are narrower than our original passage, darker and more closed-feeling, with staler air and muffled sound, and when I watch Ozul in the light of our lanterns I see a woman trudging with a stony, defeated face. As dangerous as it would have been, I think she wishes she'd advised Annet to go over the glacier. I think she fears we're walking into a dead end. Or maybe that's just me.

I'm finding it hard to keep track of the days, and I seem to be in a constant state of low, humming panic. I spent my childhood in wardrobes and closets. This feels too much like that. If we're walking toward something terrible, could I at least have open sky above me?

I've noticed that when I look at Kera in the darkness, it's not just Kera I see.

If, in my childhood, there had been a law that an unfit mother couldn't care for her child, my mother would've been taken away from me. I know what "unfit" means when applied to mothers. Or anyway, I know what it would've meant applied to mine. Yes, an outsider would have seen her "neglecting" me. But would that outsider have understood the abuse she was suffering? Would they have understood that despite what she was contending with, she still saved my life?

Of course, she wouldn't really have been taken away from me, because in my childhood, no one knew I existed. Until the king found out about me, and then he did take my mother away from me.

What if she'd been allowed to live, and keep me as hers? After Katsa killed the king, could she have healed? Would we have had a chance for a different kind of life together?

At night, I dream of my sister's prison. I feel the heavy ceiling above me, cutting me off from a world of things I want to know.

92.

JACKY KNOCKED KERA over again, shoved her because she bumped against him by accident.

Bitterblue's right; she just picked herself up and kept walking. She even laughed. It was nothing like a noise my mother would've made, but her persistence makes me think of my mother, doggedly working her chisel against the same corner of rock for hours on end. Numbly repeating "I love you, I love you" whenever I came near.

Annet has commanded Jacky to pull Liel's sledge and keep pulling it, until she's convinced he's learned to stop taking his feelings of powerlessness out on Kera.

IT'S BEEN TWO days and Jacky's still pulling Liel's sledge. I guess Annet isn't convinced yet.

Liel is more awake now, less delusional. His pain is bad. Coran's trying to wean him off the rauha, and Liel's demands for the tea can get loud and vicious. Since losing Blueberry, I've been carrying Ladybug a lot. Sometimes when Liel gets angry, I walk near him with Ladybug in my arms. He stops asking for rauha and asks for Ladybug instead.

I was scared to hand the kit over at first, worried Liel would crush him in a fit of fury. But when Liel has Ladybug, he quiets down and nestles the kit against his chest, seeming to remember gentleness.

Still, I stay near.

Two hopeful things, though hope is terrifying in these tunnels:

This morning, Barra walked across the camp.

Well, he shuffled and stumped while leaning hard on Froggatt and Coran, but it counts. Coran's smile was so big that it threw the strain and thinness of his lined face into sharp relief. I wondered suddenly who's been looking after Coran while Coran looks after the rest of us. The answer is no one, of course.

I watched Coran eat his breakfast, such as it was. We got to the end of our bear reserves a few days ago and now we break the nutritional biscuits in half. Along with that delectable feast, we chop ice from the walls and melt it over an infinitesimal fire that Ozul guards as if it's an explosive weapon liable to bring the ceiling down.

Coran ate his half biscuit without hesitation. We have eight walking days, supposedly, though who knows what that means in these ice caves. We have five days of food left, if one nutritional biscuit per person per day along with assorted indivisible particles of dried fruit, a few raw potatoes, lemon lozenges, and one emaciated goat is your idea of food. Of course there's no hunting in the tunnels. The last chicken is long gone.

But I was listing our two hopeful things.

The second thing is that the tunnels have widened, drastically. There's light again, pouring through cracks, revealing great caverns far above us with smooth, luminescent ceilings of pale blue. Somewhere, the sun is shining. Somewhere out there is the world we're trying to get to.

Can you see why hope is terrifying? What if this light narrows into darkness again?

TODAY JACKY COLLAPSED while he was pulling Liel's sledge.

Annet knelt on the ground beside him, feeding him a trickle of water and talking to him quietly.

"Well, Jacky?" she said.

He was weeping. I could hear the rough noise of his tears. "I won't hurt Kera," he said.

"If you do," Annet said, "you understand that you'll pull this sledge again?"

"I understand."

"Can you get up?"

He did, with the help of Linny, who gave him a shoulder until he could walk on his own. I tried not to look. His face was a mask of pain and humiliation, slimed with tears, snot, and dirt.

When we stopped next, Coran spent some time over Jacky's hands and feet. When Coran pulled off Jacky's gloves, Jacky cried out. His palms were raw and bright with blood.

He saw me looking.

"Lucky you're a fancy person, Princess Dardya," he said. "I only knocked her over. Imagine if I'd beaten her daylights out the way you did."

It rankled. "She tried to kill me," I said. "What did she ever do to you?"

"She tried to kill you," he said, his face lighting up as he grinned at his own joke. I couldn't help it, I laughed. I think Jacky is a little bit of a bully, a real one. But his happy face is contagious, and its unexpectedness too surprising.

As evening came and we stopped to make camp, I found a place by myself, behind ice stalagmites. I sat, pulling my sculpture bundle from my pocket and visiting each figurine in order. Mountain lion–girl, bear-girl, porpoise-girl. Bird-girl last. I held her up to the cavern's dying light, trying to examine her face as if it were my first time looking.

Is that winged, clawed girl so obviously me? How? Because her nose is thin and her mouth a downturned line, her hair lank and shapeless? Her face is all pain, fear, and ferocious determination. It's confusing to think of Linny recognizing that as me. Stealing it, then carrying it around close to his body. It makes me feel strange.

Somewhere along the line, I think I've forgiven him for stealing my bird-girl.

And somewhere along the line, I've gotten confused about Kera too. Not confused about what I think of her; she's malicious and low, as bad as a murderer. But confused about my wish for her to feel pain.

We all feel so much pain out here. Even those of us who haven't been punched or scratched or bitten, or lost parts of our bodies to the cold. We're so hungry and scared. We only keep walking because we know perfectly well what's following two steps behind.

Punching Kera felt good, for a moment. But thinking about it afterward, the way her bones crunched and her blood flew, makes me feel sick. And it hurt my hands. And it didn't quell my outrage about what she did. It didn't *help*.

I don't really want to punch her anymore. Why? Is something wrong with me? What part of myself have I lost?

I've been thinking about something my mother did. It's one of the stories she told me, over and over: She took another woman's dead baby.

It was right when I was born. Another woman in the castle gave birth to a stillborn baby that same night, a woman who worked in the laundry and who had no direct connection with the king. My mother brought that dead baby to show to the king, so that he would believe his own child was dead, and never look for me. Then she went back to her rooms and took me out of the drawer where she'd stuffed me. My strange, secret childhood began.

I asked my mother once what she did with the dead baby after she was done with it and she said she couldn't remember. She thought maybe the king had taken it away.

I asked her if that baby's mother had given her baby's body willingly. She said she couldn't remember anything about the mother. She'd heard about the baby, gone into the room where it lay, and taken it. That part of the story always seemed irrelevant to her. The story was about saving me.

I think of that other mother sometimes, the one who lost her child. I think of my mother, and wonder if people are ruthless in matters concerning their own children. Is that the wrong word, "ruthless"?

In my secluded spot behind an ice pillar, something moved. It flashed across my vision like an arrow, then chirped; in the dusk, I recognized the shape of a small, grayish bird. Before I could move or shout or decide whether or how to catch it for dinner, it took flight and zipped up to the cracks in the ceiling, perching somewhere far above my head.

A thousand thoughts flew across my mind. Was it a sparrow? If it was a sparrow, did that mean we were close to home?

Also, what if I could fly? If I could fly, I could escape this place, rush south and find people, get help. I could fly back and forth with food, carrying it piecemeal to my companions, the way a mother bird swallows worms, then regurgitates them for her young, except less disgusting. I could feed Giddon and Linny, Bitterblue, Coran, Liel. Everyone. Everyone! I could get us out alive.

Also, if I could fly, what would my questions look like from up there? If I could be a spy-bird, what would I be able to see about Kera's crimes? About her daughter? About whether I could have avenged my mother's death? About the pieces of my own life?

The bird took wing again, zooming into the darkness above.

Suddenly I realized that what I'd taken for reflected light on glacial ice was actually the sky. There was a large opening, far, far above me, exposing a long swath of stars, pale against a blanket of violet.

"Annet!" I cried, then stood, bumbling my way around my stalagmite. "Annet!"

She called back to me from our camp. "Hava? Are you all right?"

"Stars!" I cried, pointing at the ceiling.

She came quickly. Everyone came who could walk; everyone wanted to see the stars.

"Can we take a reading?" I asked.

"Not through that crack," said Annet, "not without a clearer sense of the horizon."

"Oh right, of course not," I said, instantly disappointed.

"But it makes me hopeful," said Annet, her glasses glinting with the sky's light and a smile on her face. "Doesn't it make you hopeful?"

There's no reason for a patch of stars to make us hopeful. Sky above us doesn't mean we're safe.

But Annet is right. I feel it. I don't want to, but I do.

So I guess hope isn't about being safe?

I wonder if my mother kept hoping, even to the last moment. I wonder if she died still hoping for my sake.

Is that what love is? Hope for other people?

93.

IT'S HARD TO explain what this next part was like. When I think of it, it's not in words. Instead, every cell in my body turns into light.

I'm not even sure if it was two days later, or three. I maintain it was two, because we most particularly had two days of food left when it happened, and that would add up in my head. But Bitterblue insists it was three and that I got the food count wrong at some point.

I'll be content to argue with her about it for the rest of our long, warm, well-fed lives.

Either two or three days after the night with the stars, we stumbled out of the tunnels into a land of open sky.

Before us, almost too bright to look at in the searing sun, was this: a village of small, wooden houses, clinging to the shores of a snow-covered lake.

PART THREE

94.

I'VE BEEN TOLD the Pikkians are unfriendly people, war-loving and dangerous. But you'd have thought their own long-lost children had stumbled out of the tunnels, the way they received us with wonder and joy.

I can share flashes. The disbelieving cry of a woman with a voice loud enough to summon the entire village. A smile that cracked an old man's face into a beacon of delight. More faces, pink and healthy, well-fed. Then more voices, speaking rapidly in a language I couldn't figure out, because every time I decided it was one I didn't speak, a phrase would open its meaning to me.

"Is it Dellian?" I asked Linny in confusion.

"Sometimes?" he said with a shrug, throwing his head back and laughing, as we all were doing. We were delirious. Not just in that moment; it was a bigger delirium than that. It felt permanent. I wondered, is this why Grella climbed impossible mountains? Because of how it feels afterward, when you realize you've survived?

They brought us food. Stew, thick with meat and carrots, potatoes and turnips, gravy, hot, savory, filling, the most delicious meal I'll ever eat. They brought us bread, soft as a mattress. I don't know if I ate it or fell asleep inside it because they brought us ale and I drank its golden sharpness deeply and then I slept for a year.

I dreamed of moths fluttering around the deck of the *Monsea*. I dreamed of moths glowing in the tunnels under the glacier. I woke to Moth flapping urgently against my stomach because she was hungry and thirsty and irritable, which was a good thing. She can be my tether to reality.

We stayed in that town only two days, because now that we were back among people, Bitterblue was in a rush. She needed to send messages; she needed to get to a place with fast riders; she had to get back to her court, her throne, which is her home.

But I needed none of these things. In fact, now that we were safe, a kind of languor swept over me. I wanted to stay here and watch these people, who had such sympathy in the lines of their faces. They had lovely, sensitive mouths and mild, thoughtful eyes and I found them so astonishingly beautiful that I began to wonder if something had broken in my own sense of things. Surely no one's *that* beautiful?

They insisted on bringing us back into the caves under their glacier before we left. In their language that Linny was the best at unraveling, they explained that rich people from the Pikkian cities travel north to their town every winter to look at their caves, which change in shape and color depending on the flow of the glacier melt every summer.

"But why would anyone do that?" I asked Linny. I was standing as close to the cave exit as I could; I was keeping one eye on the world outside. I didn't want to look up at the hanging ice pillars our guides urged us to admire.

"People find the caves beautiful," he said, which made me stare at him in astonishment.

He laughed at my expression. "I'm guessing it makes more sense if you haven't almost died in them."

I tried then to look at the caves differently. I pretended to be a wealthy traveler in pursuit of beautiful things. I stood with my feet planted and gazed up at the carved ceilings of ice, streaked with blue and green, bright in places where the ice was translucent and sunlight poured through.

I'm not sure what I saw. The glass ceilings of my sister's castle, pressing down? Waters closing above me as I drowned? I didn't see beauty.

I did understand, though, why I loved the faces of the northern Pikkians. I saw it when Linny laughed. The people here are pale like me, whereas Linny is brown. But their eyes crinkle like his and their mouths have the shape of his. We're in Pikkia, with the Dells to our south; we're in his part of the world now. When these people smile, I see Linny's smile.

95.

As before, we're walking, but it's different.

For one thing, none of us can walk as far as we used to be able to in a day. We're well-fed every day now, so you might expect us to be capable of more than when we were starving. But I guess there's nothing as motivating as death trying to catch you from behind.

We feel every ache so acutely, and we're so, so tired. The distance between towns is great and these people don't have horses for us; they are sharing all they have. So we walk. We have to keep encouraging each other. "One more hour to a town." "The town will have food." "The people will give us beds." "The healers will give us medicines."

Ozul, of all people, steady, determined Ozul, sat down on the ground and began to sob one morning, when our path to the next town grew steep.

"I'm sorry," she said, racked with cries that sent a panicked bird shooting out of a crack in a ledge of rock nearby. Sorit, Noa, and Lisa knelt and took her into their arms together, holding her until she calmed down. Annet and Navi stood quietly, waiting. Then Ozul got up again, and we climbed.

We're walking through trees now. Brown, gray, tall, and leafless, branches clacking together in the wind. I touched the first one I saw, expecting my hand to pass through it like a mirage. It was solid, and cold. Linta Massera, what kinds of ahsoken make a tree? Why don't ahsoken come together to make any trees in the north?

Trees? said Hope, looking around at them.

Yes, I said. *You remember trees? And a barn? And the sea?*

Remember forest, she said.

Winterkeep is full of forests. Trees crowded near Ledra, the capital city. Unbonded foxes live in the forests of the Keepish north. *Good remembering, Hope!*

Father of the babies, she said, which startled me deeply.

What?

In forest, she said.

You remember the father of the babies?

But her voice and her mind went quiet again. I was left with an uneasiness that she didn't seem to share.

The people we meet tell us it's mid-February. "Not the best time to take a tour of Pikkia," one of our beautiful hosts joked, moving Liel for us, picking him right up and carrying him inside his winding, wood-hewn home to a place near a crackling fire. They build passageways from house to barn here, sometimes even from house to house, for ease when it snows. Sometimes the snow piles itself as high as a house, they tell us. Sometimes there's no light for months. We're lucky it's a dry, sunny winter, they tell us.

Our reactions to comments like this depend entirely on what's happening in the moment the words are said. If we're walking on sore legs and blistered feet, we know we're not lucky. If we're sitting before a fire with a bowl of something warm and meaty in our hands, we're certain we're the luckiest humans alive.

A few days after Ozul's brief collapse, we saw a raptor monster, which means we're making good progress south toward the Dells. It streaked orange-gold across the sky like a shooting sunset and my hands flew to the lump in my coat, where Hope and Moth were sleeping together.

Adventure? I cried.

I'm in the queen's hood, he said. *I'm safe. All the kits are safe.*

After that, Linny and Ozul started carrying the bows again. The monsters are dangerous. They ensorcell you with their beautiful colors and the power of their minds and while you stand there awestruck, they attack. There's evidence they're more drawn to Gracelings than they are to regular people, actually, so I should especially be on guard. But I don't have the vigilance I once had. Something's fractured in my mind. I forget things; I sink into a cold, white blankness. If Hope didn't talk to me and Moth didn't flap at me sometimes, I would forget who we are and what we're doing here.

As we make our way south through thicker forests, the buildings grow bigger. The people here live in brightly colored houses—green, blue, yellow, the paint peeling to reveal soft browns beneath. The houses have fires, baths, and beds. And food, always food. The people know to expect us now. Each town sends messengers ahead to the next town. When we arrive, people come out of their houses and shout in that language that's almost Dellian, "Survivors of the *Monsea*!" Is that what we are? Because the *Monsea* herself wasn't allowed to survive. When they shout it that way, I remember our ship, and feel like I've abandoned her.

Sometimes we climb to towns nestled in the rocky foothills of mountains. From there, to the east, we have a vast view of the sea. Pikkians are avid shipbuilders, sailors. The water is dotted with ships, like white seabirds unfurling their wings.

We saw a ship once with scarlet, pink, and gold sails, heading north.

"That one's Dellian," Linny said, with a wonderment I'd never heard in his voice before. Dellian ships often have sails like the bright hair of their hero, Lady Fire, Lady Bir. He handed me his glass. I looked at the vivid, proud sails and tried to feel something about the ship being beautiful, colorful, Dellian, but all I could see was the *Monsea* sinking. My dreams never change: the *Monsea*, the rowboats, the walking, the tunnels, moths. I've forgotten what the rest of the world is made of. When my eyes sweep a town of colorful houses, all I ever really understand are the blues, whites, and grays, as if I'm looking everywhere for the places we've left behind.

96.

ONE DAY, AFTER days of walking, three things changed in quick succession.

The first was that in a town in southern Pikkia, I watched a bird carry a message away in a little leather pouch attached to its leg.

I'd never seen anything like it. In a tall stone tower, we met a woman with skin brown like the forests we're moving through. On the top floor of her tower was a cage almost as big as the room it was in, full of soft tawny birds, medium-sized, bigger than sparrows. The woman gave Bitterblue a tiny sheet of paper and told her to write whatever note she liked to King Nash of the Dells.

When Bitterblue was done, the woman rolled the note into a skinny rod and slid it into a small cylindrical pouch. Then she opened the cage and held her hand out to the nearest bird, which jumped onto her fist and stood there clucking, fat and drab and thoroughly pleased with itself.

Next the woman attached the pouch to the bird's leg by means of a series of infinitesimal buckles. Then she went to the window and hurled the bird out of it!

"Remarkable," said Bitterblue. "King Nash has told me of his homing doves, but I've never seen one before." Then Bitterblue went on to say something about training and meals and rewards, but I'd gone to the window and leaned out. I was trying to find the dove. Far in the distance, I saw gulls swinging themselves across a cold, gray sea, but the homing dove was gone.

"Do they want to live in a cage and carry human messages?" I asked the woman, interrupting my sister.

The woman glanced between us, plainly surprised at my manners in the presence of the Monsean queen.

"They want to fly and be in out of the weather at nights," she said cautiously. "They want the food we give them as rewards."

When I looked hard-mouthed and perplexed, she added, with a touch of defensiveness, "There's nothing to stop them from refusing to fly where we ask. They're never punished for failures or mistakes. They choose to come back to the cage, as you call it."

I was thrown into sudden confusion about Moth, whom I'm always tucking inside my coat. She was there this very moment.

Moth? You know you're allowed out anytime, right?

"Weren't you a little rude to the ambassador, Hava?" Bitterblue said as we left the building.

"The ambassador?"

"Hava?" said Bitterblue, scrunching her face at me. "You're aware we just visited the Dellian ambassador to Pikkia?"

"Yes, of course," I said, remembering. Bitterblue has a thousand messages she wants to send to everyone. Since the moment we made contact with humans, she's been paying whoever she can find to travel ahead with news that we're alive, but this visit to the ambassador is her first opportunity to communicate with King Nash of the Dells directly. Once he knows, he'll start spreading the news all across the continent.

"I think we'll reach the Dells today," Bitterblue said. "Isn't it exciting?"

———

THAT WAS THE second thing that changed: We crossed a wooden bridge that spanned a narrow, icy river. When we stepped off the bridge, we were in the Dells.

The other side of the river was exactly like the original side of the river: rocky and gray, with small, stubborn trees that grew sideways from the pressure of a relentless wind. But everyone in our party acted like something momentous had happened.

Then we spotted a swarm of raptor monsters flying toward us from the south and something momentous *did* happen: Annet untied Kera's wrists, took the longbow Ozul was carrying, and handed it to Kera. Kera!

"Where monsters are concerned," Annet said, seeing my face, "we need our crack shots."

"You mean our killers?" I cried, louder than I'd meant to. Kera heard me. She shook her head and breathed a laugh.

"I'm sorry, Hava," Annet said. "I understand. Ranin is always near Kera. She's guarded. We'll hire monster guards soon."

I found myself moving as far from Kera as I could get, keeping a lot of other people between us. Hope was in my hood; I felt for her weight against my back with every step. I was remembering that at the beginning of all this, Kera was paid to kidnap Hope. Kera is a fox smuggler. I wondered: If I were in Kera's situation now, what would I do? Someone on the other end of that promissory note is waiting for Kera to deliver Hope. If I were Kera, would I try to grab Hope—and the babies too—and run for it?

But Kera didn't seem to be thinking about Hope. She walked with her bow and quiver swung comfortably on her back and her eyes sweeping the sky. Her black knit hat was ragged, but we're all ragged. She walked like Linny was walking—like someone meaning to guard the group from monsters.

While I was trying to organize my jumbled thoughts, the third thing happened: We reached a Dellian settlement that had horses waiting for us.

MANY OF THE sailors have never been on a horse before.

Of course Linny has. That worrisome lord of his again, I suppose, who seems to have taught him all the things a devoted parent would teach a child. Linny gave Jacky, Ollie, and Noa some quick riding lessons that had all of them howling with laughter. Jacky and Linny, and most of the men, have started shaving again. Their thin, clean faces are shocking, especially when they laugh.

At the edge of the group, I sat on my own horse with my coat half-open, trying to imbue Moth with a sense of freedom.

It's not a prison, I told her. *I love you, Moth.*

She tucked herself down lower, shivering. Then Hope climbed out of my hood and crawled in with her.

Moth cold, she chided me. *Stop making Moth cold.*

I want her to know my coat isn't a prison.

Moth thinks coat is WARM, Hope said, more sternly than she's ever said anything.

I closed my coat.

Then the horses started to move and I was almost dizzy with trying to comprehend where we were, what it meant. These horses were taking us straight to King's City. Two weeks, tops, I heard the people in that settlement say. From King's City, depending on one's mounts, it's the ride of a week or two more across the Dells to the tunnels, then another week to my sister's court. In good weather on fast riders, the mail can make it from King's City in ten days.

I have an uncle at court. My mother's brother. He's Graced with physical strength. Can you believe I haven't mentioned him? It's because I haven't thought of him in months. We've only known each other well some six-ish years. He's ill, unpredictable. He spent too many years working as a guard for King Leck, too long committing atrocities because he had the king's lies in his head. He's not easy to be around. He doesn't feel like my family. Or maybe I should say he feels exactly like I might expect my family to feel.

As we rode an ever-widening path toward King's City, the trees grew taller and grander around us, wintery and stark. In a place where the world was still and silent, we saw a stag monster, standing like a statue in a glade of leafless trees. Its hide was a breathtakingly iridescent blue-green that shifted to silver in its face. Its antlers sparkled gold.

When Kera reached for her bow, Linny raised a hand.

"A stag won't hurt us," he said, "as long as we leave it alone." He glanced around at us. His amber eyes touched mine. "Is everyone remembering to keep their minds closed?"

My mind, I realized, was wide-open. The stag was inside it, spreading out into all my empty spaces. Where was my strength? Where were my defenses? I couldn't go home like this. It's not safe to be so open at King Leck's court.

My sister's laugh broke into my thoughts.

"Adventure just told me he thinks the stag is the silliest animal he's ever seen," she said. "He called it 'clownish.' I guess that means monster power doesn't work on blue foxes."

"That's useful information," said Annet. "Maybe each of your foxes will be able to help you remain mentally alert."

Hope? I asked her as we continued on. *Will you help me remain mentally alert?*

My girl, she said from inside my coat, in that same stern tone as before. *My girl is sleeping.*

Was I? Because I was trying to wake up. I was trying to remember that it's Bitterblue's court we're riding toward, not my father's.

But I'm also starting to realize that after all this time, all this wishing for safe, familiar places, now I feel like I'm attached to a line that's dragging me home too fast.

97.

As we neared King's City, happy people began to line the road and throw flowers on us.

It was so confusing—where were they even finding flowers in February?—and I was so tired of being confused that the ambush stripped my nerves raw. I wanted to be in my little workroom in the bow of the *Monsea*, with no one but Hope, focused on thoughts that lived inside someone else's head.

But then Hope and Moth both climbed to the neck of my coat and poked their heads out to watch. Their fuzzy fur and silky ears helped. Linny, who was riding next to me, helped too. When people cried out greetings, he simply smiled, thanking them in Dellian. He had a serene look on his face, like their regard was our due. His shoulders were straight, and made me realize I was hunching. The people, recognizing him as the only Dellian among us, showered him with flowers especially.

It was soothing, how it transformed him to happiness. I started to search the faces around us. I saw kind, curious eyes. I saw delighted smiles in open faces. I also saw, to my surprise, monster fur around people's necks; monster feathers in people's hair.

And in every visage, an aspect of wonder at the sight of us, as if we were extraordinary. I didn't feel extraordinary, so it was jarring.

Maybe that's the sort of thing you need to see reflected in the expressions of other people, in order to realize it might be true?

"Survivors of the *Monsea!*" they shouted at us. "Survivors of the north!"

98.

Lady Bir herself was waiting for us at the city walls. Or maybe I should say she was waiting for Liel.

Lady Bir is a monster in human form, but as I've said before, she has a conscience. She can read and control minds, but she uses that power only with permission, and mostly for healing. There's a story that fifty-some years ago, she kept the injured King Nash alive on a battlefield with the power of her mind. She's very old, but that's not what you notice when you look at her. What you see is her utter beauty, and you need to make yourself breathe.

She was waiting in a long, open carriage. As we arrived, she climbed down and walked among our horses, giving us her greetings. Her hair, scarlet and pink and silver, was hidden behind a pale gray scarf, but her green eyes shone like moss beaded with water. Her face was brown. I'd never been so close to her before. I wondered, would my Grace work on her?

Then she looked straight into my Graceling eyes and somehow I knew it wouldn't. I slammed my thoughts shut and the most unexpected smile touched her mouth, like she was grateful for the door I'd closed. It left me feeling more exposed, not less.

She went directly to Liel, who lay exhausted in a sledge behind Navi's horse. Her attendants unrolled a stretcher and moved Liel to her carriage so smoothly that I almost missed the other thing that was happening: Annet got down from her horse, went to Kera, and took her bow. Then Dellians in uniform ordered Kera from her horse, bound her hands, and hustled her away to a different carriage, a closed one.

Lady Bir's carriage led our horses through the city gates. Kera's carriage followed behind.

THE BUILDINGS OF King's City are tall and vividly colored. The king's palace is a luminous black stone that shines with the reflected colors around it. By the time we reached the castle gatehouse, the colors had become an assault. I couldn't find my whites and grays anywhere. Linta? Why does the Dells have to be so colorful, and why is it hurting my soul?

Then we passed into a courtyard of dazzling quartz and suddenly there was too much white. Attendants approached us. A kind of wonder glowed in their faces too as they gazed up at us, but it was the wonder of alarm, which made me realize how thin and ragged we must look, our hair in our eyes, our skin burnt with cold. I considered the state of my coat. We've all had the opportunity to bathe since our ordeal, but my once-beautiful Keepish furs feel like a part of my body now. I hardly notice that they're stained with my own blood and smell like seal feces.

Grooms took our horses. On my feet again, I positioned myself where I could watch Kera being removed from her carriage. The uniformed guards put hands on her shoulders, then guided her across the courtyard and through an archway. To where? A cage? I had the strangest feeling as I watched her disappear, like it wasn't right for her to be taken away by people we don't know. How will they know who she is and what she needs?

I've been assigned a room as big as twenty tents, with ceilings as high as an ice cave. It has a bed that ten of us could sleep in back to back. It has walls of shelves containing books bound in brown leather, more than any one person could read. It has a roaring fire. It has a bathing room with a gray marble tub that runs with warm water pouring from silver faucets shaped like doves. It has windows that look down onto a garden of bare trees. My last true bedroom was with Bitterblue on the *Monsea*; every corner of space was accounted for. The bathtub hung from the ceiling and we had storage compartments under the floor. Why is this room so wasteful?

I went to the windows. Birds, gray and brown with flashes of blue, were squabbling in the trees, the branches of which hung heavy with feeders. Other birds, big and black, dined on the seeds scattered in the snow below, stabbing and shrieking at each other. Why were they fighting, when there was so much food?

The attendant who'd showed me to my room had closed the door behind her when she'd left. I turned back from the window to find myself alone, truly alone, for the first time since . . . I couldn't remember. It was such a strange and bewildering feeling that I stood there for a while, trying to remember how to be alone. What did one do? Take a bath? Read something? Think? Grella? What did you do when you got back from a journey that no one could understand?

Grella probably sat down and started planning his next daft adventure.

A thwack against my stomach reminded me that I wasn't truly alone. I gave the seat of a fat-looking armchair a suspicious poke. It was too soft; my finger sank right in. So, opening my coat, I sat myself down in the middle of the marble floor.

Blinking their golden eyes curiously, Moth and Hope climbed out. I noticed that Moth's legs, if possible, had grown even longer in proportion to her tiny, round body. She looked like a pincushion propped on long, bendy pins.

Hope went to a bookshelf and poked her nose at the lowest books. Meanwhile, Moth set her sights on the bed, lowering her nose to her paws like the stealthiest of hunters, then barreling toward it and throwing herself into a running leap.

Her momentum carried her all the way across the bed, then hurtling off the other side with flailing legs and a squawk. I laughed so hard, I fell onto my back, fighting off sudden tears.

I stayed there for a while, lying on my side, my arm bent and my head propped on my hand, watching them explore.

99.

THE NEXT DAY, Bitterblue had meetings with important Dellians. When Bitterblue has meetings, I prepare myself to be bored.

"Why don't you go to the harbor with Annet?" she said to me.

"You're sure you don't need me?" I asked, relieved, but also a little surprised.

"I'll need you when we get home," she said. "Here, it's liable to be me and the king alone in a room all day, and I haven't decided what to tell him about the formulas yet."

The formulas. "Where are they?" I asked, trying not to sound like I cared.

"I have them. I keep them close."

"I should probably start translating them again."

"Will that be comfortable while we're still traveling?" she said.

"No more uncomfortable than that teeny room in the bow of the *Monsea*."

"Okay," she said doubtfully. "We can figure it out, though I can't imagine how you could work on them secretly if we're camping in a group. Do you *want* to join my meetings?"

I left before she could get any more ideas about that, Moth tucked inside my coat. Hope stayed behind to visit Cornsilk and Owlet.

King's City sits on a river, right at the point where its water flies off a cliff and plummets into the sea. Bridges cross the river, linking the north city with the south. A canal of locks connects the river to the harbor far below.

A steep road of hairpin turns leads pedestrians like me and Annet down to Cellar Harbor. It was strange to walk with Annet alone; when's the last time we've been alone? But the views distracted from the strangeness. Everywhere in the harbor, the falls create a mist of water and a constant pouring percussion of sound. It is, in my opinion, the most beautiful and exciting place you can stand while looking out at a cluster of massive ships with their sails full of wind.

"You like the harbor, don't you, Hava?" said Annet.

"Who wouldn't like this?" I said, laughing at a man nearby who sparkled from head to foot with tiny beads of ice, frozen from the mist of the falls.

"But you have a particular taste for it, I think."

"Maybe," I said, glancing at Annet curiously. She was quiet today; we'd barely talked since leaving the castle. "What do you need to do in the harbor, anyway?"

"The queen didn't tell you?"

"No. Wait. You're not leaving, are you?"

"No, not yet," she said. "As the queen's captain, I'm contracted to accompany her all the way back to court. We're here to order the building of a new royal ship."

"Oh!" I said, understanding. Monsean ships that travel to the Torlan continent must be built and housed in the Dells, because there's no known water route from Monsea to Torla. But I was startled by my own—what? Shock? Sense of disloyalty? "Does the queen want another barquentine?"

"She's left that up to me," said Annet. "I'll talk to the builders, see what new designs have come into being since the last time we ordered a ship."

386 — KRISTIN CASHORE

"They won't . . ." I stopped myself. "They won't paint her hull teal again, will they?"

"No," said Annet. "I'll request another color."

"I'm being foolish," I said, ashamed of myself.

"Oh, habpva," said Annet, a sad smile making its way across her face. "It's not foolish. The *Monsea* was a beautiful ship. No ship will ever replace her."

WELL, NOW I know what a ship is made of.

Wood; mostly wood. Iron, brass, copper, glass, canvas, hemp. Empty space.

Also: tension. Proportion. Balance. I know that the diameter and height of a mast are proportional to the ship's length. I know that a round stern lifts the hull clear of the water, but a sharp stern makes for faster sailing. I know that Keepish airship design has influenced the way Royal Continent shipbuilders think about lines and sails. I also know that a three-masted ship the size of the *Monsea* costs more in gold than I ever quite appreciated my sister had at her easy disposal. Should I be so surprised that a ship is such a grand thing?

I know a bit more about what sailors are made of too. As bad as the seas were while we thrashed around near the northern ice fields, Annet—and it seems most sailors—has been through worse. There are times when a storm is so rough that every sail is furled except for one or two. There are times when you ride out the storm with no sails at all, "lying to under bare poles," hauling on the rudder and hoping for it to end. The way Annet and the shipbuilders were talking, it seems like this stuff is normal.

I had to step outside the shop several times during the meeting to stop myself from interrupting with questions. I like when my brain is stretched out and stuffed full of ship things, like a ship itself, every corner filled with hidden storage. I'd choose that any day over the blankness my mind is beset with lately.

As Annet and I walked back across the harbor toward the road, we saw some familiar faces at a tavern window. Jacky, Ozul, Alzar, at a table with others I couldn't see.

"They're saying their goodbyes," said Annet, noticing me looking.

"What?" I cried. "What goodbyes?"

"A few of our sailors will be staying here when we continue on tomorrow," Annet said. "Alzar, Riz, Noa, Sorit, Lisa. They'll be looking for work on ships going back to Winterkeep."

"So soon?" I said. "We just got here! They're still skinny and underfed! Riz's feet are still weak!"

"Well, I don't think they're in a rush to leave right away," said Annet. "But they aren't joining us on the journey across the Dells to Monsea. They're sailors and Torlans, Hava. Wherever they go next, it'll be by ship."

"We have ships in Monsea too!"

"Sure. But Alzar and Riz miss Kamassar. And as much as Noa, Sorit, and Lisa would like to see Monsea, their families are waiting for them in Winterkeep. Anyway, they wouldn't have the same rights there. You know?"

"The queen is fair-minded," I said indignantly. "She wouldn't take away their rights just because they're not Monsean."

"Could Noa and Sorit marry?"

There was something just a little bit barbed in Annet's tone. "Oh," I said, stung. "Right." Noa and Sorit could marry in Winterkeep and most of the Torlan continent; they could marry here in the Dells. They could marry in Pikkia. But the laws are different once you've passed through the tunnels into the seven western nations.

In fact, Bitterblue has a marriage bill she's never finished drafting, to open marriage in Monsea to couples like Noa and Sorit. I mean, she has a thousand bills she's never finished drafting, but that's one of them. Is it a secret? Am I allowed to tell Annet about it? I was angry now about all the times Bitterblue's permitted herself to become distracted from it; and suddenly I hated the way everything was changing back to how it was before. Meetings with kings about game-changing weapons. Grandiose orders for replacement ships. Unkind, unfair laws about who's allowed to attach themselves to whom. Politics. There are politics on a ship, but it's not like this. There were politics in the north, but survival was our higher cause.

"This means I'll probably never see them again," I said dismally.

"Oh, I wouldn't go that far, habpva," Annet said. "We're all connected to the Monsean court now. Our paths may cross on a ship again someday."

When? How? Also, what's wrong with me anyway? What've I've been imagining? That the entire group will live together forever in Bitterblue's castle?

I just didn't imagine us dividing so soon.

"Liel is staying here in the Dells too," said Annet gently.

"Liel?" I repeated miserably.

"He hopes to return to Monsea one day," Annet said. "But the hospitals here are among the world's finest, and Lady Bir can help him with his pain in ways others can't."

"But what does that mean about Ladybug?" I said. "Will he stay here with Liel? Will Hope be okay with that? How will we know if Hope understands?"

"Hm," said Annet. "Good questions. It seems like it should be Hope's decision. Can you talk to her about it?"

"I'm not sure," I said, doubly unhappy at the notion of Hope having to say goodbye to Ladybug.

"Maybe you'd like to join them?" Annet said, indicating the group in the tavern window.

"No."

"We might be rushed tomorrow," said Annet. "This is a chance to say goodbye."

"Who's coming with us tomorrow?"

"The queen has offered an open invitation to anyone who'd like to visit her court," Annet said. "Jacky is Monsean and Ollie's Lienid, so they're coming. Navi's coming. Ozul's coming. Linny's coming at least as far as the western Dells, because his mother lives there. I don't think he's decided beyond that."

I swallowed.

"Go get a drink, Hava," said Annet.

"I don't want to leave you to walk back up to the palace alone," I said.

Annet raised an incredulous eyebrow at me.

Then Navi emerged from the tavern and headed toward us, smiling. She was wearing new, clean trousers—we'd all been given new clothing at the Dellian court—but her brown coat and her red-gold scarf were familiar, and comforting now that everything was changing. So was the warmth of her smile.

What would she and Annet do, once they'd delivered the queen to her throne? Turn around and retrace their steps to the Dells or Winterkeep, where the laws were kinder?

"Are you going to continue captaining Monsean ships?" I asked Annet.

She was watching Navi's approach with a faraway expression. "I haven't decided," she said. "Some things become intolerable, after you've had your life taken away, then handed back to you. You know?"

I remembered, then, Annet sailing across that frozen strait in the leaky boat. Five times, her face wind-chapped and her hair whipping behind her, so that every person and every animal in her charge would survive. And I knew that no one had handed Annet's life back to her. Annet had fought for her life, and for ours, every day. I think I understood then what decision she would make.

"I'll walk back to the castle with you," Navi called out to us.

"See, Hava?" said Annet. "No need to worry I'll be lonely."

"Go join them, habpva," Navi said to me as she reached us. "They're asking for you."

In the window, Jacky was holding a finger up at me in a rude gesture and Ollie was crossing his eyes with his nose and mouth pressed against the glass, which was probably covered with decades of grime and germs. He was going to fall sick and die of an infection, after surviving the north.

Then Linny stepped out of the tavern and crossed to us. "Want a drink?" he said, with a look on his face like he might give me that smile of his if I said yes.

100.

I'VE BEEN IN plenty of taverns, but I've always used my Grace to hide. I'm there to spy. I'm not there *with* someone, unless it's Giddon and we have an agenda. Giddon is big and noble and takes up all the space, detracting attention from me while I do my job.

This time, my job was to squeeze into Navi's old place at the table and act like I wasn't about to have some sort of tantrum because of the way things were ending.

No one seemed to need me to speak, which was a relief. Jacky and Ollie were talking enough for everyone and most of the attention was on Ozul, who was crying, tears slowly trickling down her face into a black-and-silver scarf as she drank her ale, talked, laughed. I gathered that Ozul was eager to travel farther and see Monsea, hopeful for a good position on another Monsean ship, but heartbroken to be leaving Noa, Sorit, and Lisa, who were staying behind.

Her unselfconscious crying was remarkable. It made me less ashamed of my own disheveled feelings. When Moth began flapping inside my coat, I released her, settling her into my lap. Bir, who was on Linny's knee, flashed his copper eyes my way, then climbed across to my lap and nestled in beside his sister. I sat quietly, feeling their light, warm weight on my thighs, letting myself be sad.

Moth reached out and pressed her big paw against my chest. She looked up into my face, her golden eyes paler than her brother's, but just as luminous.

Hava? she said.

101.

I'M NOT GOING to be able to bear it if we keep having to say goodbye to people, over and over.

Lady Bir and her husband came into the wing where our group was staying this morning. Lady Bir was wheeling Liel in a chair. Ladybug was in Liel's lap.

When Lady Bir's husband—Prince Brigan—caught my eye, he gave me a small, secretive nod. It's because I had a moment yesterday, after the tavern, and he knows something I did, or wanted to do. In the end, he did it for me.

It's because I got it into my head that if we're leaving Alzar, Riz, Noa, Sorit, Lisa, and Liel behind, then they should have warmer coats, fur coats like mine. Just in case.

But I don't know how to tell what size coats people need, and I don't know where to go in King's City to find the best coats, and while I could reconnoiter where to go, I'd need money from Bitterblue to buy that many coats. Unless I stole them, which didn't seem entirely right, not to mention challenging—steal six coats all at once?—and then how could I give the sailors the coats without them knowing they were from me? And making a big fuss out of it. And then I would have to explain myself.

I just wanted them to have coats and it not be a thing.

So I went to Bitterblue.

She herself was as hard to locate as six fur coats, until I overheard someone alluding to her having a rest in Lady Bir's own residence. Lady Bir lives in a tiny, dark green wooden house that sits in one of the palace gardens, nestled among trees and vines. Somehow, even in winter, the house looks both completely out of place on the grounds of a palace, and also like it grew there naturally. Maybe because it's the color of a pine forest.

Anyway, some stiff guards in gray let me into the house when I approached, so I guess someone had described Bitterblue's ugly-eyed spy to them.

Inside, I found Bitterblue sitting before a fire, in a room that seemed full of soft chairs, blankets, and books. A small table piled with pastries stood at her elbow.

"Are we alone?" I said, barging in.

"Yes," she said, a spray of crumbs flying out of her mouth as she spoke, which was lovely. "Sorry."

"Two things," I said. "One, you need to complete that marriage bill."

"What! Why is that important now?"

"It's not, if you're okay with losing Annet and Navi the moment we reach Monsea."

"Okay," she said dryly, swallowing. "Point taken. The other thing?"

"I think you should give the sailors we're leaving behind warmer coats, as a parting gift."

"That's a very nice idea," she said. "They'll be from you, of course."

"I don't want to be involved."

"I'm not going to take credit for your idea."

"Then don't do it," I said, my voice rising. "I don't want to be involved. I just want them to have the coats."

"But only if they don't know you care about them, Hava?" she said, sounding tired. Looking tired; her face was drawn and thin. She popped another pastry into her mouth. It was shaped like a tiny ship, with sugar-sculpture sails. Watching it disappear into her mouth with a crunch was somehow alarming.

"How can you eat that? You look like a cannibal!" I said, and that's when someone in the doorway behind me cleared his throat.

I spun around to find a white-haired old man looking back at me, through gray eyes lit like the sky over the northern sea. He was brown-skinned, straight-backed, slight, like Linny. He had a nice face.

"I don't suppose you'd allow the Dellian crown to give gifts of fine fur coats to every member of your party?" he said.

Now I was annoyed at Bitterblue, who'd said we were alone. "Some of us already have good coats," I said. "Who are you?"

"Hava!" said Bitterblue. "Manners!"

"I'm Brigan," said the man, with a smile twitching at his lips that should've made me angry, but didn't, because he was speaking Lingian with an accent just like Linny's. Also, he had a giant brown dog at his side and his hand was resting gently on the dog's head. A dog isn't a blue fox. Dogs are morons. Still, my own hand went to the Moth-lump in my coat, in a kind of sympathy.

"*Prince* Brigan," said Bitterblue austerely. "Brigandell, retired commander of the King's Army, father of the current commander, husband of Lady Fire, and brother of King Nash. Prince Brigan, that's an extremely generous offer."

"Yes, it is," I said, more than ready to excuse myself from the conversation, now that someone rich had taken over the problem. "Thank you very much. I myself have no need of a new coat."

"Hava, your coat is a mess," said Bitterblue, wrinkling her nose at me. "Mine is too. If you decide to push a coat on me, Prince Brigan, I won't refuse."

"Each member of your party shall have one of our warmest winter coats," said Prince Brigan. "It'll be a small gesture to welcome you back to the world. You'll have to accept one, Hava," he added mildly, "if no one's to suspect it was your idea."

I wanted to say to him that the north is part of the world. That suggesting it isn't hurts somehow, like when people seem to forget about the loss of the *Monsea*. I've been to the north. So he's not allowed to erase it from the world.

But that didn't seem like a normal thing to say. Nor did it seem like an effective means of removing myself from the interaction, so I could return to my enormous bedroom, where I could be alone with my foxes.

"Yes. Thank you, Prince Brigan," I said.

Then I left.

ANYWAY. WHEN PRINCE Brigan came into our wing with Lady Bir and Liel, I kept to the back of the group as Annet and Navi, Giddon and Bitterblue stepped forward to thank them for everyone's beautiful new coats. Liel, sitting quietly in his chair, seemed melancholy, but calm. His shaved face made him look thin and vulnerable and tugged at my heart. I was obscurely comforted that his hair was still long and unruly. All of our hair is still long and unruly. Mine is basically a stringy mop.

Smoothing the fur behind Ladybug's ears with an intent focus, he told us that he was relieved not to have to go anywhere for a while. "Lady Bir keeps insisting I'll walk again someday with a prosthetic leg," he said. "I don't believe it, but I like her telling me."

Then Liel thanked us for the care we'd given him, Coran especially. While Coran's eyes filled with tears and the two of them clasped hands, I was ashamed of my earlier wish to sneak away without saying goodbye.

Hope nursed Ladybug one final time. Last night we talked about leaving him, and since then she's said repeatedly, *Ladybug stay with Liel*, as if she thinks it's right. I hope I've understood her correctly. While she nursed him one last time, I reminded her that Ladybug was staying behind. But she wasn't really acting like she heard me.

I held Ladybug close and gave him a thousand kisses. The dark spots on his shoulders have turned a deep blue while the rest of his baby fur fades to gray. I hope he keeps those spots. I hope I'll know someday if he does.

"Don't stop talking to him," I said to Liel. "Moth has started talking to me."

A light broke through the grief in Liel's eyes. "Does that mean we could bond?"

"Adventure says that foxes are different on the Royal Continent," I said casually. "They can talk to as many people as they like and they don't bond, exactly. But I think you'll always be his most special person."

WHEN ANNET LISTED the sailors going with us, she left one out: Kera.

We departed around midday on horses. Kera's hands were bound and she was flanked by two Dellian guards with longbows, one woman and one man. I understood that they were our monster guards, but also our Kera guards. We had Ranin too, of course, who seemed always to position himself between Kera and the queen.

Like everyone in our party but me, Kera was wearing a beautiful new coat. Every time she crossed my line of sight, indignation rose within me. I'm not saying that if they'd asked me "Should Kera get a coat too?" I would've necessarily said no. But she's my would-be murderer. Couldn't they have run it by me?

Hope was restless as we rode.

Ladybug? she said.

Ladybug will be safe, I said. *Remember? Liel will take care of him.*

Dissatisfied, she turned around inside my hood and flopped back and forth for a while. Then she scrabbled up onto my shoulder and I understood that she wanted to be inside my coat with Moth.

Smelly coat, she said disdainfully as she disappeared inside it, which was funny, because the attendants in Nash's castle took my coat away last night to help them size the new coat I'm never going to wear, then brought it back glossy clean, brushed smooth, and only slightly damp. My coat smells like *soap.*

Ladybug? she said.

I took a breath through clenched teeth, beginning to be certain I'd made the wrong decision. Searching for the patience I would need to answer this question repeatedly all day long. Then another voice rose.

Ladybug with Liel, it said, tiny, scratchy, and inflating my heart like a balloon.

Is that you, Moth? I said.

Moth, she said. *Hava. Hope-Mother.*

Ladybug? said Hope, as if we were singing a naming song together.

Ladybug with Liel, Hope-Mother, Moth said.

Ladybug with Liel?

Liel take care of Ladybug.

They continued like that, chattering quietly. Hope kept asking the same question, but Moth never seemed to tire of explaining where Ladybug was in her small, unpracticed voice. Their conversation receded into the background of my mind. It made itself a soft bed of pine needles there.

I rode on, letting myself rest.

102.

I want to ask Linny his plans for after he visits his mother, but I never do. When we ride together, I can't get the words past my throat. Linta? Why can't I ask him? Am I such a coward?

Why am I asking Linta Massera a question like that?

Instead, I ask him things like how Bir's doing.

"He's fat and cheerful," said Linny. "But no, he's not talking yet," he added before I could inquire, shooting me a little grin. "Moth seems to be the genius of the litter."

"They're all geniuses," I said.

The Dellian forest is made of cold, and quiet, and hidden living things. Rabbits and squirrels burst from the snow as we pass and our nights are saturated with the low, haunting hoots of owls. Jacky and Ollie have started an owl-imitation competition. They fill our bedtimes with silly birdsongs that wouldn't fool a mouse, but make us smile. The trees, white-barked and leafless, are heavy with birds. I've started to see sparrows in the snow.

Some of our companions aren't normal animals. A rabbit monster watched us from a fallen tree trunk once as we passed, its fur the mottled fuchsia of crushed raspberries.

Moth was peeking out of my coat. *What color?* she asked.

Pink, I said.

Then, one evening as the light fell, a wolf monster, scarlet-gold like

Navi's scarf, slunk onto the path ahead of us, staring at us through golden eyes.

Our archers moved so fast that the monster was dead before I even understood what was happening. I gaped at Linny, who slid down from his horse, the string of his bow still quivering. He and the guards collected the wolf and tied it onto one of their mounts, for our dinner later.

"You didn't waste any time," I said when he came back to his horse.

"The wolves can be vicious," he said. "Better not to give them a chance to start preening."

"What other vicious monsters should we be watching for?"

"Oh, mountain lions, raptors. Leopards."

"Bears?" I asked, shuddering with memory.

"Bear monsters are rare," he said, "and the regular bears are hibernating." Then, noticing my face, his tone changed. "Dellian bears aren't like the northern bears, Hava. And monsters are incapable of camouflage. You don't need to worry. We've got two armed Dellians, plus me. We'll spot any threats in time."

WHEN WE CAMPED that night, Linny helped me break through the ice of a nearby pond to collect our water.

"Just a warning," he said as he submerged one of our flasks. He had the funniest, faraway look on his face, and the grin of an eight-year-old, as he knelt there with his hair in his eyes and his hand in the water. His new coat is the deep brown of his hair, and sleek, clean. Too clean. All of my companions are weirdly clean in their new coats.

"A warning?" I said.

"There are little monster fish in the pond," he said. "They're sucking on my hand."

"What!"

"They won't bite you."

"How reassuring," I said, submerging another flask beside him. We knelt among thick, icy rushes at the pond's edge, reaching awkwardly into the water, and it was uncomfortable enough without the feeling of little suckers all across my hand. The touch was light, but insistent. "It tickles!"

"I kind of like it."

"Of course you do. This is a strange place you're from."

"What can I say? It's home."

"I thought the sea was your home."

"That's my chosen home," he said. "But the forests of the Dells are in my blood."

"Did you grow up near here?"

"Very near."

Are you leaving us soon?

I couldn't ask it, though I wanted to know, more than anything.

Then his hand touched my arm, his eyes catching mine. He cocked his face to one side like he was listening. I went still, catching my breath, because I heard it too: a long, low, sonorous snore.

It stopped, then started up again after an extended pause. It was impossibly deep and slow.

"What is it?" I whispered, staring at Linny in amazement, knowing it couldn't be human.

He was smiling. "I told you the bears are hibernating."

"That's a *bear*?"

"Dellian bears are much cuter than northern bears. They're brown and fat and huge."

"And that's *cute*?"

"Just imagine it curled up in its den with its nose tucked into its paws, all sleepy," he said. "Snoring like that for three whole months. Anyway, they hardly ever attack humans."

I snorted. "Maybe you should get yourself a bear. You can carry it inside your coat with Bir."

"Let's just listen to it for another minute before we go back, okay?"

So I waited with him, listening to that slow, gravelly drone and wishing it could tell me what I was doing here. I craned my face to the sky, where a low, heavy moon lighted our errand. There were no wavering colors up there, no aurora borealis. I saw only familiar stars. But this didn't feel like my sky.

"I don't like that people keep leaving the group," I said. "I'm still only just getting used to having food every day, and being warm."

"That's funny," Linny said. "Jacky keeps saying the same thing."

"But not you?" I said. "Aren't you still back there? When I wake up every morning, I see the glaciers. When the trees get thick above our heads, I see the tunnels."

"It might be different for me because this is where I grew up," he said. "Here, everything's familiar to me, so my body can relax. Maybe when you get to your court, we'll change places. You'll see what's really around you and I'll remember the ice."

"You're coming to the Monsean court?"

"Jacky's talked me into it," he said. "As long as my mother doesn't need me to stay, I'll come. Our route brings us near her in a few days. I'll visit her and see what she prefers."

"Hope wouldn't like to have to say goodbye to Bir," I said.

Something about that made him grin again. "I hope I won't have to say goodbye to you."

"Oh," I said, the word a puff of air.

"Should we go," he said, "and leave the bear to her dreams?"

103.

A COUPLE DAYS AFTER that, Linny veered off to the north by himself.

"I'll find your camp in the morning," he told us, "or catch up to you. Don't wait for me."

He seemed awfully lackadaisical, both about venturing into the monster-infested forest alone and about finding us again. I kept my eyes on my horse, making a point of not watching him go. Relieved he has a warm coat.

Bir? Hope asked as we continued west.

Bir is with Linny, Hope-Mother. Bir will be back tomorrow, Moth explained.

I WOKE THE next morning to a small rustle and a grunt, followed by the sound of someone moving around our camp. A saddlebag shifting, water sloshing in a flask. Footsteps.

I don't know what it was about those footsteps that made me sit up. Even when I saw the silhouette of shoulders receding into the forest and recognized them as Kera's, I'm not sure why, bleary and slow, I tucked Hope and Moth into my blankets and pulled on my boots. We all go into the forest to relieve ourselves, even Kera. What else would she be doing, without a horse and with her hands bound?

It was early, the gray of sunrise doing little to illuminate our camp.

One of the Dellian guards was sitting near the almost-dead fire, leaning back against the pile of saddlebags we stack there for the purpose of our nightly watch-person. I thought it was the male guard, but it was too dark to tell. He was only a shadow. He didn't look worried. When I whispered "Be right back" in Dellian, he grunted.

I'm made for sneaking and following. With my Grace, I can turn myself into the trees and shrubs around me and I know where to step, I know how not to breathe. A forest has its challenges when it comes to being quiet, but a forest also has its own noises. The best way for a human to disappear in a forest is to stop walking on two feet. Get low and scramble, like the other animals are doing.

She was heading north through soft snow. The snow was a welcome noise buffer; I followed close behind. I could tell from the way she moved that her hands were still bound. She turned her head once, hearing my boot crunch on an edge of ice. But all she saw was a broken stump of tree, maybe vaguely girl-shaped in the dimness of morning.

I was wishing now that I hadn't come alone, because it was plain that this wasn't a pee break. Kera was moving swiftly and with intention. She was going somewhere. Then she dropped to her knees on the path ahead and I knew what she was doing: trying to free her hands.

I burst upon her. Before she could rise or even react, I had my knife at her throat and my other arm tight around her torso. "Drop it!" I yelled, seeing a flash of steel in her bound hands. "Drop it or I'll cut your throat!"

I guess she believed me, because she dropped it, a long, thin blade like the ones the Dellian guards carry. I pushed my mind back to that guard by the fire, wondering suddenly if something had been odd about the way he'd been leaning back, the way he'd grunted. About his decision not to follow Kera.

"What did you do to the guard?" I asked, still holding her tight with the knife at her throat.

"I'm not answering your questions while you have a knife to my neck," she said in a voice of frustrated gasps. I suddenly realized she was sobbing. Hot tears were spilling onto the hand that held my knife.

"Where are you even going?" I said. "You have no food! There are monsters in this forest! What kind of escape is it if you just run off?"

"Why should you care how I die? It's not like anything that happens to me out here would be worse than what's likely to happen to me in Monsea!"

"Well, for one thing, the queen isn't going to feed you to monsters!" I said, incredulous.

"My daughter will not have a mother who died in a Monsean prison!" she said, almost shouting. "My daughter will have a mother who did everything she could do to try to get to her!"

She began to struggle, which was terrifying, because her movement sank my blade into her throat, deep enough that she cried out with a choking noise that made me frightened I'd hurt her badly. I dropped my blade and shoved her down into the snow. I rolled her over, climbed on top of her, and yanked the collar of her new coat down, relieved almost to the point of dizziness to find only a thin trickle of blood there.

"This is a familiar position," she shot at me. "I guess this is the moment you start pounding my face in?"

"You idiot," I said. "I'm not going to hurt you."

"Then let me go."

"I won't," I said. "You're coming back to camp."

"Oh? How are you going to make me do that without hurting me?"

I started changing, first into a sculpture of myself, then a monster wolf. A gigantic, fuchsia rabbit, then an owl. For fun, I changed into a version of Kera, then realized it wasn't fun. I've changed into versions of other people before to get into places where I don't belong, but I've never shown someone a version of themselves. Her face flashed with such a particular kind of horror that I felt like I'd violated something. "Stop!" she cried.

I found the knife she'd dropped and slipped it into my ankle holster. I found my own knife and held it where she could see it. "I'll stop if you stand up and start walking back to camp," I said, turning into a tree and then waving my hand-branches in front of her face for extra effect.

"You're a freak," she said, a word that stung, and made me less sorry about showing her herself. I turned into a white bear with a small head and enormous teeth. She gasped, scrabbling to get away from me.

A horse stepped into the clearing.

By the time I'd turned back into myself, Linny was on the ground with his bow in one hand and an arrow in the other. "What's going on here?" he said.

"She tried to escape," I said. "I'm bringing her back to camp."

His eyes on Kera were grim. "Want help?"

"Sure."

With a tiny, musical ping, Linny notched his arrow.

Her face hard and furious, Kera pushed herself up to her feet. "I'm sure you'd love to shoot me between the shoulders as I ran," she said sourly, then turned and started trudging back to camp. I took the bridle of Linny's horse and let him go first.

"Where were you headed, Kera?" Linny asked her as we walked.

"Why should I answer your questions?" she snarled.

"Maybe because we could help you get word to your daughter," Linny said.

Kera's shoulders went stiffer. "Why would I want any of you near my daughter?"

"What do you think we're going to do to her?" said Linny. "We don't have anything against her. Where were you headed? To the Cave Road?"

"I don't know what you're talking about," said Kera.

"What's the Cave Road?" I asked.

"There's a road just north of here," Linny said. "It's the road I was on when I heard you both shouting. Kera would've intercepted it soon if you hadn't stopped her."

"Where does it lead?"

"If you turn right, it takes you through a tunnel and on to a town, then to the estate where my mother lives," said Linny. "Eventually, it leads all the way back to King's City. If you turn left, it takes you to the tunnels into Estill."

Estill, I thought. *Monsea's enemy.*

Does Kera have reason to run to Estill?

104.

THAT'S IT: I'VE now decided Kera was trying to get to Estill.

I pester her about it whenever I'm near her. "Are you really Estillan?" I asked her later that day as we rode. "Not Monsean at all? I know you're not from Hawkery."

"How could you possibly know that?" she responded scornfully.

"What are the names of the people who live there? How are the houses arranged relative to the road? What grows like a weed along the waterways in summer? What's the best path down to the mine?"

"You're making things up," said Kera.

"When Estillans pretend to be Monseans," I said, "we at the Monsean court find it pretty interesting. Why were you trying to get to Estill, Kera?"

"You're right," she said. "You've figured it out: I'm an Estillan spy. So I followed the queen to Winterkeep, stole a fox like any spy would do, sank my own ship, and arranged to be attacked by bears. Imagine the secrets I have to share with the Estillan government now. The Monsean queen gets diarrhea when she eats seal meat, just like other people."

Ahead of us in line, I heard Bitterblue's giggles ring out like bells. So I stopped asking Kera questions, because I didn't need a delighted audience.

That evening, when we camped, I found a low, smooth seat in the nook of a tree. It was far from the fire and chilly, the tree's cold bulk seeping through my coat. But I liked its solidness, and I wanted to be alone.

When I saw Bitterblue making her way through the trees to me, I considered using my Grace to hide. But that never works on her.

"Hava," she said quietly, stopping before me. "Do you really think Kera has Estillan political connections?"

Estillan political connections. Despite the accusations I've been throwing at Kera, I've truly not been thinking about the politics of Monsea's war-hungry neighbor. Their attempts to purchase the weapon; their interest in the zilfium in Monsea's mines. Her question, which was sincere, left me awash in a flood of my own foolishness.

"No, not really," I admitted. "I do think she could be Estillan, but I don't see her as anything more than a common smuggler trying to get home."

"Ah," said Bitterblue. "I couldn't tell if you were trying to get at something real, or if it was just—you know."

"Just what?"

She flapped a tired hand, then considered my face, smiling a little. "How shall I put it?" she said. "A talent for antagonism?"

I bristled. "She attempted an escape," I said, "after trying to kill me."

"I know, Hava," said Bitterblue. "I'm sorry. I shouldn't have teased. Though I do think she regrets all of that now."

"Sure she does," I said indignantly. "Because it didn't play out how she planned."

"I meant that she has shame, Hava," said Bitterblue, suddenly, briefly losing her patience, and with it her temper. "You know shame? That emotion that causes people to be antagonistic and defensive?"

Then she spun on her heel and stomped back to camp. I saw

Giddon watching her approach, tall and grave and worried. I heard his gentle, inquiring voice say "Bitterblue?" and knew that she would let off her steam talking to him, he would comfort and reassure her, while I sat here alone with my cold tree trunk, fulminating. Or maybe just startled. For all I snap at Bitterblue, she rarely snaps at me.

I did make myself invisible then, so I could lean out of my tree and watch the activity of the camp. Jacky and Ollie were building a fire while laughing over some joke together. Navi was snorting at them, saying something that lit their faces with humor, and Annet was smiling nearby. Coran was attending to the guard Kera concussed this morning, doing that test where he moves his finger back and forth in front of the man's eyes. Froggatt and Barra sat near them, their fox kits in their laps. Behind a tree but perfectly visible, Giddon hugged Bitterblue. *Ugh*. Kera sat on a rock by herself, her hands and now also her feet bound. I couldn't see her face.

Are we a group still, if we're no longer in any terrible danger? If people keep spinning off, joining other groups, somewhere else? If our very goal is to get to a place where the group is going to fracture even more? Journey's end?

Linta?

Linny is continuing on with us to Monsea. I haven't talked to him since he helped me with Kera this morning. He came back from his visit to his mother quieter. More somber, with fewer smiles. Also, he's not wearing his new coat anymore. He's been in his old wool coat since he returned. It comforts me. He looks more like himself.

Now I watched him collecting firewood on the edges of the camp by himself. I thought of the lord who taught him to ride, shoot, and do chemistry. I wondered, when he visits his mother, does he have to see that man? Is that why even though he loves the Dellian forest, his chosen home is on the sea?

105.

WE'VE ENTERED THE tunnels.

I never cared one way or another about the tunnels between the Dells and Monsea before. But now I have to remind myself to breathe. I put my hand on the figurines wrapped in my pocket—remember my figurines?—and fantasize about turning into a bird. *Every step brings us closer,* I tell myself with each dip of the saddle.

But closer to what?

Moth distracts me with questions, and Moth and Hope together keep a soothing patter going. I notice sometimes that Moth, who's still a baby, is surpassing Hope in vocabulary and comprehension. She's already speaking in grammatical sentences. I try not to dwell on that too much either. It makes me too sad.

What is spelunking? she asked me one day, overhearing a conversation in Lingian between Ranin and the Dellian guards.

Cave exploration, I said.

What is a stalactite?

A stalactite is a long, skinny deposit of minerals in a cave, I said, *though I'm not sure if it's the one that hangs down from the ceiling like an icicle, or the one that rises up from the floor like a pillar.*

I interrupted Ranin and the guards. "I can never remember the difference between a stalactite and a stalagmite," I said, "and Moth is asking. Do any of you know?"

"There's a trick to that," said Ranin, flashing a smile at me. "Stalactite has a *C* in it because it hangs from the ceiling. Stalagmite has a *G* because it rises from the ground."

"Oh! That's good," I said, pleased. Then suddenly, out of nowhere, I was blinking back giant, stupid tears, because I remembered, like a flash from another person's life, how much I'd once loved words like that. I'd loved playing with them like they were games; I'd gone out looking for them, and when I'd found them, I'd pulled them around me like a blanket.

How do you forget something like that about yourself? Where did it go? Did I leave that girl in the north? Linta? Can a person's most fundamental parts change?

THE TUNNELS ARE easier when Linny rides near me.

"I've never had a problem with tunnels before this," I told him.

"It seems natural you might have one now, after what we've been through," he said.

"Do you have a problem with tunnels now?"

"This tunnel's okay. I think it's because it smells different, you know? The glacier smelled like cold, and rock, and trapped air. This tunnel smells like moss and water. Like it's the cellar of the earth and we'll come to a door in the ceiling soon, and light will pour through."

I thought about that. When he explained it, I could almost feel it, almost feel comforted by it. "The sound is the same," I said. "I think that's my problem. I don't actually think I mind the close walls, and I don't really notice the smell. It's the way the sound is muffled and echoes back at us. Our voices are the same as they were in the glacier. It's a trapped sort of sound."

"Right," he said, with a glance at the walls pressing in around us. "I can hear that."

He's softer now than when he first came back from his visit. He's smiling again, his eyes gentle on my face, and he doesn't seem to mind riding, or darkness, or cold. He doesn't seem to mind much, really. He's just himself.

I asked him what happened to his new coat.

"I gave it to my mother," he said simply.

I made a mental note to see if my new Dellian coat fits Linny. After all, weren't we sailor twins once? "Is your mother well?"

"She is, thanks," he said. "She wants me to write her letters describing the queen's court."

"Did you have a nice visit?"

"I did," he said, then paused. "It's always hard to go home. Then, once I'm there, it's hard to leave again."

I wanted, so badly, to ask him what he meant by that. I wanted to be able to picture his home, imagine his time with his mother. See how often he smiled when he was there, see if his mother had his radiant smile too. But I didn't know how to ask without intruding on the parts he might not want to share.

"Are there—people at court you're looking forward to seeing?" he asked, so carefully that I wondered, as I've wondered before, if Linny's guessed some things about my life, just as I've guessed some things about his.

I decided to answer the question he wasn't asking. "My mother is dead."

"Oh," he said, "Hava. I'm sorry."

"It's all right."

"Oh!" he added, with sudden chagrin. "And I stole the figurine she made for you."

"It's all right, really, Linny. You didn't know."

"I'm the worst friend on the Royal Continent!" he said, in a tragic voice, both silly and sincere, that made me sniffle and laugh at the same time.

"It's not the only figurine she made me," I said. "Relax."

"I'll try, but it puts the thing in a different perspective. When did you lose her?"

Lose her? I guess I did lose her, like I lost my figurine. I forever misplaced her. "I was eight."

"I'm so sorry, Hava," he said.

The king killed her. Because of me. I saw it happen.

"Are any of her sculptures at court?" he said.

I needed a moment, to collect and hide all the things I wasn't saying. "A great many."

"Will I be able to see them?"

I needed another moment. "I used to love spending time with them," I said. "I used to practically live in the sculpture gallery. I'm— not sure how I'm going to feel when we get there. But maybe I can show them to you."

"Okay," he said, not seeming to mind my response, which sounded strange and inadequate to my ears. Because everything sounds wrong in a tunnel? I glanced back at Kera, who was riding a few people behind us. I keep glancing at Kera, but her face shows me nothing. She bobs up and down rhythmically with the movement of her horse, looking irritable and bored. I keep thinking of the other place I've been where the ceiling is low, the walls close, the sound muffled, and voices echo against stone. My sister's prison, which is what Kera is riding toward.

106.

I wasn't prepared for our reception when we exited the tunnels into Monsea, though I should've been.

I guess I'd forgotten Dellian homing doves, Dellian efficiency. And I'd forgotten how much has happened since we left Monsea, how many people would be yearning for Bitterblue's return. Months ago—it feels like years ago—the people we left behind were told that Bitterblue was lost at sea. Then they were told she'd been found. Then they lost her again while all of us were lost in the north. Of course no one was going to let us arrive quietly.

In the forest outside the tunnels, a unit of Monsean guards awaited us. They had tents and fires, stoves, card tables, even a line of washing, as if they'd been living there for a long time in anticipation.

The moment they spotted us, two of them leaped onto horses, peeled away, and galloped south toward the city. The rest swarmed our mounts with hoots and cheers, some of them with tears streaming down their cheeks at the sight of Bitterblue. When she gave them a few quiet words about her relief to be home and her gratitude for their welcome, you'd have thought, from the shining faces they turned up to her, that she'd delivered an address to inspire the ages. These are the hearts that would've been crushed had she never come home. And she was glowing. She looked like the weight of a sledge had been lifted from her back.

Anyway. It's a ride of several hours from the tunnels to court. Remembering our arrival in King's City, I guessed then what we were in for.

First it was just a couple of greeters, galloping toward us from the south, swift, but alone. But they weren't just any greeters. They were Bitterblue's Lienid cousin, Prince Po, and of course Lady Katsa, both of them crying their Graceling eyes out and hugging Bitterblue so passionately that they kept pulling her right up out of her saddle. Hugging Giddon. Shaking Annet's hand, then Navi's. Laughing with joy. They hugged me too, and Jacky and Ollie watched this with their eyes bugging out of their faces. Katsa and Po are awfully famous in the Seven Nations. Ollie couldn't stop goggling at Po, who has his same coloring, the same gold in his ears and on his fingers like all Lienid do, but brighter, finer, the gold of a prince. Ollie probably grew up to bedtime stories about Prince Po.

Next, a large, flashy, loud Lienid man came galloping from the south with what seemed to be an entire Lienid battalion on his tail. This was Bitterblue's uncle and Po's father, King Ror of Lienid, who'd apparently crossed the world to wait for his niece to come home. I truly thought Ollie was going to fall off his horse.

And that was only the beginning. No one seemed to want to watch for us calmly in the city. Everyone who heard the news came out to meet us partway; I saw royal advisers and royal clerks on horses whom I've never even seen outside the castle before, their faces incandescent with happiness. The world was made of noise, and the sharp, curious eyes of people. Everyone's jubilation was as overwhelming and exhausting as any grief. And I began to plan my escape, because I couldn't do this. I couldn't be here. When we got to court, I would collect what I needed, then go.

Linny drew his horse closer to mine. The sailors around us were shouting, laughing. Moth, propped in the neck of my coat, kept asking me questions, but even though she was speaking clearly, I couldn't really understand her.

Finally, I took her gently from my coat and handed her across to Linny. "Would you keep her safe?" I said. "I'm no use right now."

"Of course," he said, tucking her into the neck of his coat beside Bir. "But what's going on, Hava?"

Suddenly I was fighting, hard, not to turn into a sculpture. I almost saw stars with the effort of it. "I don't know," I said. "I hate this. I don't feel what I'm supposed to feel. Everyone's so happy."

"You've told me yourself that the court doesn't feel like your home," Linny said. "You don't have to be happy."

"You're right," I said, my voice rising to a squeak. "And I hate all this attention. I'm afraid I'm going to turn into something and shock everyone. Everyone'll start screaming."

"Want to turn into saddlebags?"

"What?"

"Lean down over your horse and rest," he said, pointing toward my horse's neck. "Then I'll take your reins and you can turn into saddlebags. Everyone'll think I'm some kind of Dellian steward in charge of the luggage. They'll ignore us."

"You wouldn't—mind that?" I said. "It wouldn't—make you uncomfortable for me to be a creepy pile of saddlebags?"

"It won't bother me in the slightest."

So that's how I rode into Bitterblue City, then all the way into the castle, bombarded by noise, but alone, safe inside myself, where I could be invisible. Guarded by Linny, and then also by Ollie and Jacky, who didn't understand, but who did what Linny asked and brought their horses close. Such a relief.

Lying across my horse's neck, pretending to be saddlebags, I found a rhythm of conversation with Hope, who was in my coat.

I love you, Hope.

My girl.
Are you all right?
Chocolate.
That one never gets old, Hope.
Chocolate!
I love you!
My girl.

107.

My sister's castle is and isn't how I remember it.

It's as big as a small city; it's made of marble and glass with tall, sunny courtyards and fountains and gargoyles and staircase after staircase leading to the queen's offices in the highest tower. I remember all that. But now the low, curving ceilings of the vestibules feel like tunnels. A shrubbery sculpture of a bear in the great courtyard made a cold sweat prickle on my back.

The guest apartments where the sailors are staying are in the upper west castle, a few minutes' winding walk removed from my own rooms, which are isolated, near the art gallery, where no one else lives. I went with them and saw them settled in first. They have views over the castle roofs and the city. Annet and Navi are staying in adjoining rooms, with tall, wide windows that look over the west city, all the way to the mountains beyond.

"And the river," said Navi contentedly. "I'm happier when I can see some water."

"Good," I said. Then I took a circuitous path to my own rooms, to avoid one of my mother's sculptures that stands in a corridor. I never used to do that. Why am I doing it now? I can feel a map of this castle opening around me in my mind. The map includes blank spaces I intend to avoid. The art gallery, where my mother's sculptures fill an entire room. The courtyards and some of the uppermost passages, where glass ceilings feel like ice pressing down. The maze King Leck constructed outside his own rooms, dark and stifling. A courtyard with climbing vines and a pink marble floor that makes me think of water running with blood, which I could see from the windows of the rooms my mother and I occupied over thirteen years ago.

I will pick and choose my routes, as if this castle is a body with isolated, bright, sharp wounds that can't be touched.

And soon I'll leave. Maybe I'll follow the river to those mountains. I'll go somewhere with no memories, where nothing hurts.

MY ROOMS ARE just that, no more: rooms. Walls and ceilings with windows and doors. The most basic configuration of room ahsoken.

I suppose I'm using it wrong as usual, Linta?

I have a sitting room, a bedroom, and a bathing room. I have two small rectangles of glass in the canted ceiling above my tub that I remember used to make me feel exposed to the sky when I bathed.

Now, when I look around these rooms, the main thing I notice is that they're stark. I have bookshelves with nothing on them, whitewashed walls with no decoration. I have a desk with dim lamps, a small fireplace, a plain brown sofa, a table I eat at sometimes alone, a plant in the bathing room with big, waxy leaves. Helda, Bitterblue's elderly spymaster and domestic fusspot, came to my rooms once looking for me. She peered around, wrinkled her nose, and sniffed. Next time, she brought me that plant.

"You need some life in here," she said, as if I weren't alive.

Well, I had some life in here now. Hope was poking her nose into the corners of my wardrobe and Moth was careening around the carpet. Eventually they settled themselves on the sofa together, blinking soft golden eyes at me and sending me a joint sense of contentment I couldn't understand. I was embarrassed by how little of beauty or interest my rooms had to offer them. They deserved more.

I went to my hearth, considering the empty mantel. This was the sort of place where people kept mementos. What did I have that I could bear to look at?

I reached into the front pocket of my coat and pulled out my star nail. After Giddon had given it to me, I'd wanted to attach it to the top of the *Monsea's* mast. Later, Hope had found it in a crack in the floor of the deck. It felt like a piece of our ship. I placed it on the mantel, right in the middle.

There. My rooms are totally decorated now, I said to the foxes, but they didn't seem to get the joke. I touched the nail's greenish side. *I wonder how to shine it up?*

Vinegarsalt, said Hope.

I turned to her. *What? Vinegar salt?*

Cleans copper, said Hope, blinking at me calmly from the sofa.

Right, I said, with a vague sense that this conversation was familiar. That it related to something I'd translated in Linta's notes, a million years ago. It was startling, that Hope remembered something I couldn't. It made me wish I could see inside her brain. What kind of landscape does she have in there? Is it like the Dellian forest, gray and brown with the occasional vivid flash of a monster? Is it a glacier, crawling through a valley at the pace of a snail, then occasionally dropping an iceberg into the sea?

Good remembering, Hope, I said.

Get vinegarsalt, she said, with more force than usual.

All right, I said, knowing no reason why the metal under this tarnish should be copper, but deciding it probably wouldn't hurt. *I will.*

I built a fire. Then, when the flames began to push the chill away, I removed my coat and laid it on the sofa, wondering when I'd be putting it on again. I touched my hands to my arms, feeling skinless.

Linny owns my new coat now. It fits him well, though he's packed it away and continues to wear his old coat. "But I'll be glad for it someday," he said.

Studying the room again, I decided that the desk against the wall would be as good a place as any to get back to work on my translations. I have a hiding place in the floor under one corner of my rug. I built it myself, prying the nails out of a short floorboard and gluing nail heads where the nails had been, so it looks like a regular floorboard, not the opening to a cavity below. I could keep the translations there. Hiding places like that are better than safes, better than trusting the lock on a door, because safes can be broken and locks can be picked. I know; I do those things myself.

I took a bath. For a long time, I lay in the water, staring at the sky. I was thinking about the tub on the *Monsea*, and the lake in Hawkery with the mint on its banks. The frozen pond in the Dellian forest, where monster fish tickled my hand. The sky was a pale winter blue. As I lay there, idle-minded and weightless, I had the sense that I was trying to find something up there in that sky, but that my windows were too small for me to see it.

After my bath, I slipped through corridors and downstairs to the castle kitchens, where I stole a small jug of vinegar and a packet of salt. Then I went back to the guest apartments, drawn to Linny again, Jacky, Ollie, Ozul, Navi, Annet. But I guess they were already out in the city, exploring. No one was home.

108.

I THINK THAT IF it weren't for Hope and Moth, I wouldn't sleep at all. The bed is too big; its bigness confuses me. Sleep creeps over me like spreading cold and I wake with a start, then pile an unreasonable amount of wood on the fire. I think of Blueberry, at the bottom of a river. I think of Kera. Where is she now? I know the answer: in the prison, many floors beneath my rooms.

I go back to bed, needing the foxes' warm, snoozing bodies near mine.

109.

IN THE MORNING, while the foxes were still sleeping, I dressed quickly, then brought the little bowl on my mantel to the window, checking on my star nail, which had spent the night bathing in a pool of vinegar and salt.

In the rising light, the star nail sparkled copper.

My heart swelled with pride. *Smart fox,* I thought gently, not wanting to wake her up.

Under my door, I found an envelope. Tearing it open, I recognized a ciphered message in Bitterblue's hand. Our informal key is the day of the week two days ago, but I had no earthly idea what day of the week it was. When have I last needed to know the day of the week? So I went through the lengthy, mind-numbing process of trying each day of the week. You can probably imagine how irritable I was by the time I figured out that the key was "Saturday."

"Please come to my office as soon as you get this," the first line said. Impatient, I began skipping ahead. I saw something about "meetings," then something about "zilfium mines," then a list of foreign nobles who've evidently already descended upon Bitterblue's court asking nosy questions. When I saw the name of an Estillan lord I particularly dislike, Joff, I stopped deciphering. Joff wants to marry Bitterblue. He's aggressive about it. I threw the note onto the fire, grabbed my coat, and snuck out, leaving my door propped open so the foxes wouldn't find themselves trapped.

I was rounding a corner toward one of the more remote staircases, meaning to keep to the castle's edges and work my way to the exit, when a squirrelly clerk of Bitterblue's skittered into my path.

"Oh, good," he said, in a tone of triumph, eyeing my coat. "Her Majesty needs you right away, Hava."

Ugh.

ALL MORNING, I sat in on meetings where I wasn't allowed to voice opinions.

While Bitterblue talks to every foreign visitor who's arrived in the wake of the news that Monsea has zilfium and zilfium can be used to make weapons, I'm supposed to watch. And listen, and die of boredom apparently. Then, when the foreigners leave, tell her if I trust them.

Of course I don't trust them. Who would? They're mostly noblemen from Estill and from the kingdom on our western border, Sunder. Sunder has a power-grasping king with a big, hungry army and a history of allying with Estill. And Estill, which is supposedly a young republic, seems to have grown into even more of a military autocracy while we were gone. The reason Linta Massera was building a zilfium weapon in the first place was because someone in Estill wanted to buy it, remember? The Estillan government's own envoy to Winterkeep, a pink pimple called Lord Cobal, was the person in Winterkeep brokering the deal.

"How about I follow these visitors to wherever they're staying," I said to Bitterblue, "sneak into their rooms, and read their correspondence? Then we'll know whom to trust." We were in her tower office, where the windows all around touched us with the pale sunlight of March. March! I couldn't remember what March was like in Monsea and I wanted to be outside, alone.

"We don't need to take those risks," she said, sitting down at her gigantic desk and reaching for a pen.

"Why do you need me for this at all, while you have a telepathic fox?"

She pursed her lips. "We haven't decided Adventure's role yet."

"All right then, while Po is at court?" I said, because Prince Po is a Graceling, Graced with hand-fighting, except that that's a screaming lie. In secret, he's actually Graced with a kind of mind-reading and object-sensing. He's blind, but he can sense the way objects and people are situated around him, and he can also sense any feelings or intentions people have toward him. When people lie to Po or try to hide things from him, he knows right away.

"The Queen of Monsea can't have a known Council leader sitting in on meetings with foreign nobles," said Bitterblue, not even looking up from the papers on which she was scribbling. "Anyway, he's busy."

"I'm also busy," I said under my breath.

"Hava?" said Bitterblue, watching my face now with clear, even eyes. "We've been back for less than a day. I don't want to start fighting. Will you tell me what you'd rather be doing?"

"I want the translations back," I said. "I was only maybe three-quarters through when I stopped. I should continue."

"Okay," she said. "But do you think it's better suited for someone with a chemistry background? Didn't you say so before?"

"I could do the general translating for that person, though. Save them some time."

"Hm. That's true." She put her pen down, thinking. Then she said, "The truth is, I haven't decided whom at my own court I trust with it anyway. I want to keep it myself, on my person, because it's just too important not to, Hava. But I can give you small sections you haven't translated yet." She reached into her own voluminous pockets and shuffled something around in her lap.

"If you're keeping the formulas in your pocket," I said, watching her with misgiving, "I hope you have a sufficient guard presence."

"They follow me so close, I feel crowded," she said. "If I'm inside a room alone, they pile themselves outside my door. If you're to take some of these pages, I'll have to put guards in your corridor too."

Great. "Basically advertising that we have something important we're trying to keep safe."

"Good point. I'll have to increase the guard presence everywhere, to avert suspicion. Maybe start a rumor that I'm feeling vulnerable ever since our ordeal." She held about five pages out to me; I could see Linta's writing. "After you translate these and give them back," she said, "I'll give you more. How does that sound?"

It sounded like I was never to have Linta all to myself again. And what would happen to the parts of Linta's notes that weren't about the zilfium weapon? Was Bitterblue going to discard the theory of indivisible particles, because it wasn't relevant?

"I might need to refer back to work I've done in order to progress," I said.

"Anytime you need to do that, come to me," she said. "You can work on it as much as you like here in this office."

I took the five pages, before she decided I should work on them here too. Then I tried to think of something to say to her that would sting, because she was keeping Linta's work from me.

"Well?" I said. "Have you changed your outdated marriage laws yet?"

The question seemed to leave her a little winded. "Hava," she said. "It's my first morning. Would you prefer I never eat or sleep?"

I saw then how thin she was, dressed in a pale blue gown that had fit her once but hung on her now like a sack. I saw the dark smudges under her eyes, and the mountains of paper on her desk. I stared back at her, stricken. "Sorry," I said.

428 — KRISTIN CASHORE

"Are *you* eating and sleeping?" she said. "You look tired. Shall we make a pact that we'll both eat and sleep?"

"Yes," I said. "All right." Then, confused about whether I was annoyed or ashamed, I turned and left.

DOWNSTAIRS, IN BITTERBLUE'S lower offices, Barra sat at his desk writing, while Cornsilk and Owlet, perched beside his papers, took turns batting at his pen.

"Hava!" he said, smiling up at me as I approached. "I've observed that on occasion, they're positively catlike. Tell me, does Moth like cheese? Owlet has developed a passion for cheese."

"Moth likes all the foods," I said.

"Hava!" came another voice. I turned to find Froggatt walking toward me holding a baby, of all incongruous things. A baby! A human one, I mean, bald, with fat arms that kept flailing sideways and crusty mucus sticking out of its nose. A woman with blond hair piled atop her head stood at Froggatt's elbow, smiling, holding a large book.

"Hava!" Froggatt said again, a brightness to his entire thin, pale being that made him almost unrecognizable. "Do you want to meet my daughter? And have you met my wife?"

Of course I had to pretend then that I wanted to meet Froggatt's daughter and wife. So I rolled up Linta's papers, shoved them into my pocket, and stood there trying to look pleasant.

"Her name is Brittabo," Froggatt said, beaming at the baby. "It was the closest we could get to Bitterblue without stealing the name entirely."

It was a lot of name, for someone that small. I looked into Brittabo's face. Her lashes were long and dark. One eye of green and one of gray stared back at me.

"Oh," I said, startled.

"Yes," said Froggatt proudly. "That too. Of course, we don't know her Grace yet."

"I hope it'll be something that brings her joy," I said.

"How kindly put, Hava," said Froggatt. "Have you met my wife, Fralla?"

"No. Hello," I said.

"Froggatt says only glowing things about you, Hava," said Fralla.

I found this so unlikely that I was momentarily unable to think of the appropriate platitude to say in response.

"Show Hava your book, Fralla," said Froggatt.

"Oh, she won't want to see it," said Fralla with flustered embarrassment.

"You want to see it, don't you, Hava?"

"Of course," I said obediently, reaching for the big book Fralla was holding. It filled my arms, hefty and solid. "Very nice," I said, turning the pages, pretending I knew what I was looking at. It seemed to be a lot of line and watercolor drawings of a baby with green and gray eyes.

"It's a book to honor all the firsts in Brittabo's life. Her first bath, her first snowstorm," Fralla said shyly, standing at my shoulder, helping me turn the pages.

"You're an artist," I said, understanding that Fralla had done these drawings. Realizing, as we progressed from page to page, that the drawings were beautiful. Understanding too, with rising disbelief, that these people were fawningly obsessed with their baby. Why would Brittabo's first lullaby deserve a painting? Why memorialize anyone's first smile?

"She met the queen for the first time just today," said Fralla, "but of course I haven't painted it yet."

"You're very talented," I said, because it was true, but also because it was all I could manage. I was thinking of Kera's tin of ratty baby memorabilia, lined at the bottom with tiny, clattering teeth. I was trying to imagine my mother, clearheaded enough to notice that I'd smiled or rolled over or hiccuped, not just the first time, but ever. And I was jealous. I recognized the hot, sick feeling in my throat. I was jealous of their attentions to Brittabo, and my resentment of a baby felt like such an aberration that I shoved the book at Fralla and took a step backward.

"I'm sorry," I said. "My hands are dirty. I don't want to smudge it."

"Of course," said Fralla. "How kind you are. It's all right, it's not a precious artifact."

"Certainly it is," said Froggatt.

"I—ah—excuse me," I said, noticing a man who'd just entered the offices and was conversing with a couple members of the royal guard. It was that Estillan lord, Joff. Before we ever left for Winterkeep, Joff was always showing up here to propose marriage to Bitterblue. He and his powerful Estillan friends believe it would be advantageous for him to marry her. He's tall and slick, with graying hair and cold, pale eyes, and I don't like his persistence. He's a southern lord with a holding near our borders, one of several Estillan lords who in the wake of the overthrow of their king amassed gigantic "private guards" that they use to police their own lands and people.

I was staring at him. I turned back to Froggatt and Fralla, who were watching Barra feed Owlet and Cornsilk pieces of cheese.

Then I noticed that Joff was also observing the advisers, their baby and foxes, their soft indulgences, with outright mockery on his face.

The funny thing is that from what I can remember of myself, I would've mocked them once too. But not now. I'm never going to laugh at my sister's advisers again. They're men who brought one another safely out of the north.

Joff walked to us. "And where did all these foxes come from?"

I was glad Hope and Moth had stayed in my rooms, where his oiliness couldn't touch them. "Winterkeep," I said flatly.

"Are they babies?" he said. "They seem small."

"Yes."

"Where did you acquire baby blue foxes?"

"Winterkeep," I said again, unhelpfully.

"What a relief everyone in your party made it back safely," he said.

I remembered Mart, quiet and shivering, sitting beside me in our boat with the chickens in his lap. I remembered Blueberry, the arc of his little body as I threw him into the river. I wasn't going to tell Joff about Mart or Blueberry. I wasn't going to open them to his indifference.

Setting my chin, I gave him my best red-and-copper glare. When he met my gaze, he had glaciers in his eyes.

110.

NEXT, FINALLY, MY escape.

First, I went back to my rooms briefly to check on Hope and Moth, which turned out to be an error. The instant Moth saw me in the coat I was still wearing, she wanted an adventure.

Where you going? she cried. *Are you going somewhere?*

I'm just taking a walk, I said, imagining her bolting away from me and getting lost in the city, or trampled by a horse. *It'll be boring, Moth.*

I want to come!

All right, but only if you stay inside my coat or my hood.

I want to be free!

You can come with me while staying inside my coat or my hood, I said firmly, *or you can stay here in my rooms, or you can leave my rooms and explore the castle.*

Explore the castle! Moth said. *That way, if I want to, I can sneak out of the castle and come find you!*

Wait, what? I said in alarm. *The city is big, Moth. You'll never find me. You could get lost!*

Foxes don't get lost, Moth said scornfully. *And no changing your mind,* she added, which of course was what I was in the process of doing. *You gave me those options.*

I was flabbergasted. *But you're deliberately misunderstanding the options I gave you!*

Why do you get to give me options anyway? said Moth. *You're not my mother or my queen. Foxes don't have a queen!*

She was standing in the middle of my sofa as she said this, her legs braced straight and her head and tail erect, as if her defiance filled her entire body. I expect it did. Her eyes glimmered at me with a softness that didn't obscure her tiny, sharp outrage.

Hope? I said in annoyance, appealing to the older fox, who sat with her nose to the crack of the door, waiting for it to open. She is Moth's mother, after all.

Pretty castle? she said, which wasn't helpful.

You can't control me! Moth practically screamed, which left me no choice. I'm not going to be the queen in the story of her life.

All right, all right, I said, bumbling to the door and opening it. Moth shot out past Hope, sped down the corridor, then disappeared around a corner. I had the sudden, breathtaking sense that I might never see her again.

Will you come back to me, Hope? I asked my remaining fox helplessly.

My girl, Hope said, then primly went on her way.

I TUCKED LINTA's pages under my secret floorboard, then kept to the castle's most obscure corridors on my way out. There are hidden passageways inside some of the walls, but they're no good to me just now. They require facing too many of my mother's sculptures.

I made it to the exit without being stopped. I had no certain destination. When my feet hit the ground outside the castle I veered left toward the east city, because there's always something happening there. It turned out to be another mistake. The east city is where all the people are, not to mention the extravagant bridges King Leck built across the river. He built them where no bridges need to be, because there's nothing but boggy, unusable land on the opposite shore. He built them to be broad and magnificent so that his city would feel as beautiful and important as King's City in the Dells, but the bridges in King's City have a function. They connect one half of the city to the other. Leck's bridges connected him with one thing only: a hidden cave across the river where he took people to torture them. He called it his "hospital." It's where he killed my mother.

I moved swiftly, using my Grace to detract attention, pulling my scarf off as I walked, growing far too warm in my fur coat. Apparently I've lost all sense of how to dress for March in Bitterblue City. Honestly, I'm a little startled to realize it's possible to be both outside and warm. Surely I knew this once?

I pushed myself along the docks and past all three bridges to a place where I could put their long expanses behind me and focus on the water instead. The river is full of ships. Monsean ships, with hulls and sails that have the familiar, tall, narrow grace of the *Monsea*. Ships bringing silver north from the silver mines, to store in Bitterblue's treasury. Ships bringing fish from the southern coast to sell in the city markets. And ships carrying goods and people away from Bitterblue City, south to the wide-open sea.

111.

I wasn't gone long.

When I stepped into the great courtyard upon my return, Moth came careening across the tile floor.

She made an ambitious leap at me, I think with the intention of landing gracefully atop my shoulders. Instead, she crashed against my thighs, scrambled wildly, then dragged herself up my coat by her claws as if she were the sailor and I were the rigging.

The entire time, she was chattering joyfully at me, as if we'd never had a fight. *Hi, Hava! Welcome back, Hava! I visited Coran where he works in the infirmary! I went to the kitchens and a nice lady gave me an apple tart! Then someone spilled an entire sack of sugar! Have you ever eaten pure sugar? I counted all the courtyards, there are seven! I visited Cornsilk and Ladybug in the tower! I played with Bir!*

My breath was trying to find an easy rhythm, so I wouldn't start leaking tears in the middle of the great courtyard. I'm used to deflecting attention, but it's hard to do that while a fox is moving so much across my body, and while I'm emotional because of being relieved at my reception.

Wow, Moth, I said. *I'm glad you had such a nice day. Where did you play with Bir?*

In the library, she said, *but there's a scary cat!*

The library does have a mean old cat who belongs to the royal librarian. *That's Lovejoy,* I said. *Was Linny in the library?*

Yes!

Is he still there? I asked hopefully.

No! He went out with Ollie and Ozul and Jacky and Bir! They looked for you! I told them you stormed off on your own! Also, Adventure keeps asking me if you're back yet. The queen wants to invite you to dinner. Adventure's been annoyed about it all afternoon. Oh. Here comes a guy!

The "guy" was another of Bitterblue's little clerks who walk around like they've got poles shoved up their asses all the way to their brains. He approached me warily while I glared. Moth, on my shoulder, also glared. I knew this because she was yelling, *I'm glaring! I'm glaring!*

"Good day, Hava," he said, with a nervous clearing of his throat. "The queen asked me to deliver this note."

"Thank you," I said, then took the note he extended toward me, which seemed to relieve him. As he scurried off, I opened it. "Dinner tonight?" it said in Bitterblue's hand, unciphered.

I considered the library, which is visible through the north vestibule. Its tall shelves, full of books touched by soft light from high windows, made me think of a forest of secrets. The library is one of the places in this castle that doesn't feel like a trap. You can find corners in there where no one knows to look for you, especially if you have a Grace like mine. It's a good place to hide from clerks and queens.

Except that there's a sculpture in there that guts me. It's a very young Bitterblue, maybe five or six years old. Her arm is extended into the air, her eyes staring with interest up at her forearm, which is transforming into a stone tower. Each of her fingers has turned into a tiny guard, protecting the fortress her body is becoming. I remembered my mother sculpting it.

Maybe if Linny were in there too, I'd feel different. But he wasn't. And I didn't have it in me to face my mother's sculptures yet.

I'm going back to my rooms, Moth, I said. *Want to come?*

I'm going to the kitchens again! she yelled, leaping off my shoulder and racing away. *They were making caramels earlier!*

I found Hope sitting quietly outside my door, waiting to be let in.

Moth's teeth are probably going to rot out, I informed her.

My girl, she said.

Want to help me translate some of Linta Massera's formulas?

Chemistry. Help my girl.

Yes, you're good at chemistry, aren't you? My star nail is shiny again, did you notice?

Inside, I brought the star nail down from the mantel for her to see.

Hope does chemistry, she said proudly.

Yes.

We did a little translating before dinner. But it was all about the weapon, not the ahsoken that make the world.

112.

Dinner.

When Bitterblue, Giddon, Katsa, Po, and Helda are together, no one ever stops talking. And then there's King Ror, who's the biggest, loudest person I've ever known.

I found myself eating quickly, then going to the sofa nearby, lying on my back and making myself insignificant. Staring at the gold and scarlet stars stenciled on the midnight-blue ceiling; pretending I was elsewhere, alone. They're like a family that's been reunited. I'm on the periphery.

"Everyone wants to know how much I know about the formulas for the explosives," Bitterblue said, decimating a slice of chocolate cake as she talked. I'd brought cake with me to the sofa; my plate lay balanced on my stomach. Hope, tucked beside me, asked for a forkful from time to time. Moth scampered and leaped around the room with no apparent focus or pattern, while Adventure sat at attention on Bitterblue's crown stand, right smack in the middle of the Monsean crown, peering out of it as if he were a fortress and it were his pointy wall. I kept imagining him perched like that atop Bitterblue's head while she wore it.

"The trouble is that I can't decide my strategy," said Bitterblue. "Maybe I want Estill and Sunder to know I have the formulas. Or maybe I want them to think no one has them. Or that several of us do—I, the Dellians, and you, Uncle, for example."

"Do the Dellians know you have the formulas?" Ror asked gruffly.

"Yes."

"You told them, just like that?" said Ror, with a touch of censure. "Wasn't that hasty?"

"I also told *you* just like that."

"I'm your uncle!"

"But that's not why I told you. I told you because I trust you, as I trust King Nash."

"And also this so-called Council, apparently," said Ror, waving his hand grouchily at the rest of the table. "Which hasn't exactly demonstrated a respect for law or for monarchy."

"We wouldn't have the formulas if it weren't for the Council," Bitterblue said, which nettled me, because I'm not in the Council, so she must've meant "if it weren't for Giddon." And yes, after I stole Linta's formulas and accidentally blew everything up, it was Giddon who rescued me and the formulas from that cavern. But I'm the one who stole them, even suffering broken bones. I'm the one who copied them symbol for symbol, then staged a fire that burned the originals so everyone else would think they were gone. I'm the one who's been translating them. Nobody cares about them more than me.

"That was all Hava," said Giddon.

"Thank you," I said in a peeved voice from the sofa.

"Nonetheless," said Bitterblue, "Giddon is a Council leader, Uncle, and I don't keep secrets from him. He will always know everything Monsea knows."

Ror, who isn't aware of the extent of their relationship—Bitterblue and Giddon seem to be keeping that news close—spoke sharply, his voice rising. "And what do you mean me to understand from that rather specific announcement?"

"Only that the Council will always know my business," said Bitterblue innocently, "and I'll always value their advice."

"And have you considered how your close alliance with this renegade group affects how nations like Estill and Sunder will deal with you?" Ror shouted. "How *any* of the nations will deal with you?"

"I gather that Lienid will yell at me," said Bitterblue, then put her chin in her hand, jammed some cake into her mouth, and seemed to enjoy it thoroughly.

As the din of Ror's indignation continued, Ror's son, Po, rose from his seat and came to sit on the end of my sofa. He shot me a rueful grin and showed me his eyes, one silver and one gold, glowing like a fox. I thought of my Hope, my Moth; I thought of those, like Prince Po, whose magic makes them beautiful. Years ago, Po sought me out before my sister ever knew I existed. On the day that lord I worked for, Danzhol, tried to kidnap Bitterblue, Po discovered me, because my Grace doesn't work on him. He trusted me with the secret of his mind-reading, a secret even his own father still doesn't know. I still struggle to understand this sometimes, that of all people to trust, he chose me, a stranger, a girl behaving foolishly, a sneak. Even being able to see into my mind, which he must've been able to tell was not a kind place, he chose me.

"Hava?" said Po quietly. "You *are* kind."

That's what happens, if you think about him in his presence. He knows what you're thinking. "I don't expect many people would say so," I said.

"I know what it's like to inhabit a difficult Grace," he said. "I believe you have reasons for everything you do."

Now he was the one being kind, far too kind. Time to change the subject. "I'm impressed at Bitterblue's fortitude in the face of your father's yelling," I said. "Aren't you?"

Po twitched another grin. "Mainly he's angry at me. Bitterblue merely provides an outlet."

"Really?"

"Look at the way he's turned his body since I got up," he said.

I saw what he meant. Ror was still yelling at Bitterblue, but he was yelling sideways now, shifted slightly toward Po.

"Did you—" *Tell him the secret of your Grace?* I asked, without speaking it aloud. You can talk into Po's mind just like with a fox, though he can't talk back that way.

"No," he said. "But I'm in the lawless Council he hates so much, and I'm his own son."

"But you've been in the Council for years. You deposed your first king ages ago!"

"Mm-hm. He's been yelling for years."

Across the room, still battered by Ror's fulminations, Bitterblue raised a hand. When Ror spluttered, then seemed about to start up again, she said, "That's enough, Uncle, and I don't just mean for tonight."

"Then what *do* you mean?" shouted Ror.

"I mean that I'm in a unique position," said Bitterblue, her voice crisp and clear. "Don't you see it? I'm in a position to decide the shape of the entire world. What I do or don't do with these formulas, what I do or don't do with this zilfium—*my* formulas, Uncle; *my* zilfium—has the potential to change everything. I get to build *the entire world*," she said again, her voice growing quieter, her face flat, uncompromising. "Do you realize that that includes your part in it, Uncle? That *I* get to shape that? And let me be plain: I want the help of Nash and I want the help of the Council. Nothing you yell at me in a fit of ire is going to change that. And I *want* to want *your* help. I'm not indifferent to the needs of Lienid. I'd prefer to include you. But I'm not going to, if you can't stop yourself telling me what to do. I'm not yours to bully. I'm not a child, I'm not your tool, I won't be yelled at, and I don't think your opinions are inherently superior to mine. I'm the Queen of Monsea. Are you hearing me, Uncle? You have two choices. Stop telling me what to do, or forfeit your place in this conversation and go home."

At the end of my sofa, Po's mouth was hanging open. The room was silent; I realized my own jaw was slack.

As I closed my mouth, Ror stood stiffly. He glared at each of us in turn, breathing hard, his face almost purple.

Then he spun around and swept out of the room.

At the sound of the outer doors closing, Po said, "Ooo-kay then. At least he's not mad at me anymore."

"You're welcome," said Bitterblue, but her face was still hard, her humor grim. "I need a minute," she said, standing. "I'm going to my bedroom. Please, eat the cake, everyone."

"Maybe you should bring the cake with you," said Giddon.

"Good idea," said Bitterblue, picking up the entire cake and gliding out of the room.

"Well," said Helda briskly, after she'd gone. "Hopefully this won't come back to bite us in the behinds."

"It won't," said Po. "Ror loves Bitterblue, almost as much as he loves himself. He wouldn't do anything to hurt Monsea."

"He loves Po too," said Katsa. "He wouldn't hurt the Council either."

Po made a small humphing noise. "He's overwhelmed by all of it, as we all are, and he's not sure what Bitterblue should do. When he gets scared, he yells at people."

Katsa got up from the table and came to Po, who was looking tired, and also rather young. His eyes are so bright that it can be hard to tell, but I thought he might be blinking back tears.

Katsa leaned down, wrapped her arms around his shoulders, and kissed his neck. He kissed her dark hair, which she wears short. She flashed her Graceling eyes at me, blue and green, gorgeous, and I don't know why, but I thought of my sailors. Linny, Jacky, Ollie, Ozul; Navi and Annet. Liel, Alzar, Riz, Sorit, Lisa, Noa, Ranin, Mart. We'll never be all together again.

"You did amazingly well," said Katsa, still clinging to Po, "getting those formulas the way you did."

"Oh," I said, startled to realize she was talking to me. "Thank you."

She nodded. "If Bitterblue's in a position to 'build the entire world,' or whatever she wants to call it, it's because of you. Not Giddon," she added, shooting Giddon a wry expression across the room.

"Mm-hm," said Giddon, who was reaching his fork around the table, scraping up everyone's leftover cake. When he approached Helda's plate, she slapped his hand. "But *I* get to know all the queen's secrets," he said. "Did you hear?"

"Indeed," said Helda, narrowing keen eyes on him. "Is there a particular secret you and the queen have been meaning to share with us, Giddon?"

"There is," said Giddon, then pushed a hand through his shaggy hair. "We're getting matching haircuts. But she wanted to surprise you. Act surprised, okay?"

Katsa snorted into Po's neck. Then Giddon gave me one quick, sideways grin, and I had the sudden sense of the familiar. I looked up at the stars stenciled on the ceiling and remembered that I've always retreated to this sofa during Bitterblue's dinners. My body has always taken me to the conversation's edge, wanting to be alone; that's not new.

I thought of my sister, who'll build the entire world. For Bitterblue, the world is made of political boundaries; natural resources like zilfium—*her* zilfium; the shifting needs of people—*her* people; and a shifting balance of power between allies and enemies. Those building blocks are as fundamental to her as Linta Massera's ahsoken. I don't understand everything about Linta's ahsoken. But I think I prefer her way of seeing things to Bitterblue's. Linta is trying to fathom the world and Bitterblue is trying to design it. Control it. And not the way my mother used to sculpt, letting the contours of a piece of stone guide her tools to help some form escape from within. Bitterblue will force the world into a shape she chooses. That is her job.

Then I noticed a small book, open on the mantel above the fireplace. I recognized its size, its vermilion cover, the gold gilt lettering. It was one of Grella's journals.

Why is Bitterblue reading Grella's journals? What is she looking for in there? A memory? Of what? Her mother? Her own desperate crossing through Grella's Pass? Or is she looking for the cold and the ice too, just like I keep doing?

"I saw your uncle today, Hava," said Giddon, startling me, my mind was so far away. "He seems well."

Something inside me drew tight. "Did you?"

"Yes, in the smithy. Have you seen him yet?"

"No."

"He asked after you."

I didn't respond, then ignored Giddon's curious look.

Inside myself, I began to armor my heart for the work of visiting Holt.

113.

I WENT TO THE guest apartments first, again. Moth and Hope came too.

I think I had some vague idea of asking Linny or someone to visit Holt with me. My uncle is less unpredictable when we're not alone. But no one answered my knocks. They were still out, having fun all together in the city somewhere, not thinking about me. It was so strange, to see none of them for the length of an entire day, after weeks of being with them every minute. Am I the only one of us who finds that strange?

Bir? asked Hope, who was standing with Moth at my feet.

Bir isn't in, Moth told her. *We'll have to see him another time.*

When?

Another time, Hope-Mother. Maybe tomorrow.

We slipped back through the corridors, wending our way to the ground-floor barracks in the castle's southwest corner, where my uncle lives. My body knew where to go, and what routes to avoid. And yet, my eyes kept catching on unfamiliar sights. From a vantage point several stories up, I circled a courtyard with the foxes, staring down at the checkered marble floor below, feeling like I was looking at a picture in a book about a foreign court. Had that floor always been composed of black and white squares?

Then I heard a series of metallic dings. They touched my memory and brought me a name: *artisan courtyard*. This was the artisan court-yard. Someone down there was working late, making a pot, or a barrel, or a drum. And then I remembered faces, people that went with those activities. I saw the insides of their shops in my mind and recalled the checkered floor outside their doors.

I also noticed birds now, sparrows, flitting from the floor to the small trees in the gardens below. They make their nests in the tree branches, or in nooks in the courtyard walls. Sometimes the artisans sprinkle seeds to feed them.

Pretty, said Hope.

Is it? I said doubtfully, looking down at the floor of squares, the lanterns on lampposts spotting the courtyard with golden light. The birds.

Castle pretty, said Hope.

I had nothing to say to that. We continued on, my muscle memory finding the stairs that led down to the barracks. In a stark, white corridor lit by bright lanterns, I knocked on Holt's door.

There was no answer. I took a breath and forced myself to knock again, but there was still no answer. He wasn't home.

And now that I didn't have to visit him, I could wish for his sake that wherever he was, he was having a lovely time. I care about my uncle, but when he looks at me, he sees his dead sister. We might begin with joy at being together, and sometimes we can hold on to that joy, but other times, something cracks open in his mind, and his grief and shame come flooding out. It becomes my job to comfort him for his sister's loss, to forgive him for never having been able to protect her or me, to do whatever needs to be done to soothe him, before he works himself into a state of anguish so dire that he flies into one of his berserker fits. My uncle is Graced with strength. His berserker fits are scary. I watched him try to bash a hole into his own stone wall with his wardrobe once, shards of wood flying everywhere, before the others in the barracks rushed in to stop him. He was dismissed from the royal guard some time ago, but thankfully, the guard lets him keep living here among his friends. Many of them are Graced with various kinds of physical prowess too, so they can stop him.

Anyway. He's always so happy to see me. But it's hard to relax.

While I was thinking about this, my body led us away from his door and brought us to a place I hadn't realized I wanted to go. Near the barracks are the long steps that lead down to the prison.

Numbly, I sat at the top of the steps. It was quiet here, far from the lives of other people. It was cold, and reminded me of the cavernous entry to the *Monsea*'s hold.

For a moment, I don't know why, I used my Grace to blend myself into the steps. It wasn't for anyone's eyes. My Grace doesn't work on foxes. It was just for me, to see how it felt.

It felt depressing, to be part of the staircase leading down to a prison.

Pretty, said Hope, who was sitting pressed against my hip, gazing down.

What? I said, startled. *You think this is pretty?*

Pretty steps, she said.

I looked at the long, curving steps of gray stone. *Are you sure you know what* pretty *means, Hope?*

Girl pretty, she said.

I snorted. *Maybe that explains it.*

Linny-Boy pretty, she said.

Okay, well, Linny actually is pretty.

Steps pretty.

Below us, the curving stripes of stone flickered in the lanterns' glow, making a dance between shadows and light. Moth, touched by whatever inspiration turns her legs into springs, bounded down the stairs and back up again, her eyes flashing gold in her fuzzy, dark face.

I suppose I can see how the steps might be pretty, if Moth is prancing on them and you don't know they lead to a labyrinth where people live in cages.

Moth, I said, speaking only to her because I didn't want to push this question onto Hope. *Do you feel the people in the prison?*

She didn't pause in her bouncing. *Yes. Lots of people!*

I swallowed, trying to understand why I was here. *Can you find Kera?*

Yes! The feeling of her is big!

Does she . . . I stopped. *Is she . . .*

She's angry, said Moth. *She's thinking about a little girl with auburn hair. She's cold!*

This was more information than I'd wanted. I stood quickly. *All right,* I said. *Let's go.*

Go to pretty courtyard? said Hope.

Yes, we can walk by the pretty courtyard on our way back to our rooms.

At the artisan courtyard, the noises had stopped. On our balcony walkway, Hope gazed down happily at the checkered floor while Moth flew back and forth, racing her own shadow.

I had that incongruous feeling again, like I'd never been here before, while at the same time I'd been trapped here forever. I thought of sparrows who live in courtyards with glass ceilings. It isn't the kind of bird I would ever want to be. I touched my pocket, where I carry my figurines, thinking of habpvas streaking north above the sea.

114.

AFTER MOTH FELL asleep, I did a little translating. Hope sat in my lap, "helping."

It was mostly about the weapon, so I muddled through as best I could. *I was not made to be a chemist,* I told Hope. Because it wasn't just that I've never learned how to understand chemical equations; the more I work with them, the more I realize I'm not all that interested in learning. I think it's great that scientists are striving to know what we're made of at the most fundamental level. I too want to understand the things we can't see. But not the properties of ahsoken. I want to understand the properties of *people.* Of *me.* I want to know what I'm supposed to do. Where I'm supposed to go.

Hope chemist, said Hope.

Yes, you are a chemist, Hope.

Moth made a snorting noise, then started awake, blinking sleepy eyes at us from the sofa.

Hava? she said. *What are you doing?*

Translating someone's journal from Keepish into Lingian, I said, trying not to make it sound interesting. Moth isn't my first choice for confiding state secrets.

Do you need help? she said.

I may, I said gravely, *sometime soon. But you can go back to sleep for now.*

When she did, I bumbled along, recopying one of those diagrams with bulbous apparatuses that make me think of gourds. Then I got to this: "I think we're being watched."

Watched! I said to Hope.

Watched! she repeated.

Linta wrote: "The guards caught sight of a stranger at the property's edge and gave chase through the forest. A young man, small and quick, likely Royal Continent by his coloring. He got away. It seems highly unlikely it could be unrelated to the weapon, which my employer intends to sell to Estill. I've asked LV to go around to our neighbors for a bit of casual surveillance, in case any happen to have Royal Continent guests."

Well! I said to Hope. *What do you think of that, Hope?*

LV spying.

Indeed, I said, wondering if the Estillan envoy, Cobal, had been sending Estillans out to snoop on Linta's workshop. I remembered enough about this incident from my first time through the formulas to be pretty sure that LV never found any clues while spying on the neighbors.

I had less of a memory of the next thing Linta wrote: "I asked LV for a ratio yesterday and the subsequent experiment failed. It was the third time that's happened recently, always with some part of the weapon's explosive mechanism. It seems odd that LV's ratios should be consistently unreliable on just one part of the mechanism— doesn't it?

"LV has never liked the weapons work."

Well, I said. *What are we supposed to think about that, Hope?*

Hope chemist, she said.

Yes, that's right, I said, gently stroking the fur around her ears. But my mind was far away, in Winterkeep, with Linta. Trying to remember, from my last time through the formulas, whether Linta ever came to any conclusions about LV's mysterious ratio errors. Something about it made me sad. Because Linta's friend—her only friend, from all I can tell—may have been lying to her?

Maybe. But it was also that I don't like these reminders that Linta wasn't merely trying to fathom the world. She was shaping it too, forcibly, just like Bitterblue. The weapon she invented has changed its shape forever.

115.

IN THE MORNING, I woke with the same need to go out into the city.

Again, I snuck into my clothing and coat as the foxes slept. Again I found an envelope, probably containing a ciphered note, in my entrance, but this time I made the strategic decision to put it on the fire without opening it. I left the door cracked open for the foxes.

Fox door, I thought, remembering the tiny square flaps set into the base of many Keepish doors. *I need a fox door;* then decided I don't need a fox door just for the sake of being able to close and lock my door, because anyone who wants to get into my rooms will find a way, and anyway, I'm not going to be staying in Bitterblue City long enough for it to be worth all the trouble.

A couple of guards stood in my corridor. I used my Grace so they'd think I was coatless, then wound my way down toward the exit at the gatehouse. On the castle's lower level, I stopped in an archway that led to the main courtyard, interested to see Lord Joff crossing the marble floor, wearing a light jacket. He was headed for the gatehouse too, on his way out for the morning.

After brief consideration, I changed my plans.

RECONNOITER. I THINK that's one of the words I used to like?

My new plan was to reconnoiter Joff's rooms in the castle.

I had an idea of where he was staying, because I knew where he'd stayed before: in the apartments, and probably the bed, of a lady who's the widow of a Monsean lord from near the southern silver mines. The lady moved to Bitterblue's court when her husband died, preferring the city to the foothills of the southern mountains.

She's Estillan. I sat in on their dinner once when Joff was visiting, hiding in the sitting room next door, pretending to be part of the curtains. It wasn't a particularly thrilling bit of reconnoitering. I had to sneak into her rooms early while they were away, then hide in there all day, then wait until they went to bed to sneak out again. And they talked of nothing political. Not the new government of Estill, not Joff's private army, not his intentions to ally Estill and Monsea by marrying the Monsean queen. They talked of the food, her dress, her social plans for tomorrow. I don't think she has political loyalties. I think she's loyal to the tall, hard man with the cold, pale eyes.

And he's loyal to himself and to his cronies in Estill. So today I would go through his things. Maybe he had papers somewhere, letters or instructions, that could tell me how Estill's planning to respond when Bitterblue refuses to marry him.

The lady's rooms are fairly central, on the castle's third floor, with windows and balconies overlooking that same pink-floored, vine-covered courtyard I've been making a point of avoiding. The courtyard my mother's own rooms abutted when I was a child. I took a route to her door that avoided the courtyard, hoping I wouldn't have to spend a lot of time hiding in her curtains with that view to my back. Of course, it was going to be difficult to get in, not knowing yet if she or anyone was home. But I would play that part of the plan by ear, like I always do.

Then, when I turned the corner into her corridor, I came face-to-face with Po, planted with his arms crossed, blocking my way. When

I opened my mouth to say something sharp, he gave me the slightest shake of his head.

Leaning to look around him, I stopped as if slapped. A blond woman I recognized stood at the corridor's far end, right before the door of Joff's Estillan lady. Her eyes were closed, her arms raised as if she were feeling the air with her fingers. It was Trina, the Graceling Giddon and I met in Winterkeep who has the Grace of finding things with her mind. The one I sent eight cautionary letters home about; the one who escaped from Estill to Monsea with Giddon's help, then betrayed Bitterblue by telling the Keepish all about the zilfium in Monsea's mountains. The one who then did an unlikely about-face and announced she wanted to work for the Council.

And now I could only assume Bitterblue had sent her here with Po. To do the kind of work that's supposed to be *my* job.

Po, standing before me like a beautiful barricade, almost certainly knew the gist of my thoughts, since they involved him. He took an incremental step toward me and I understood it as aggression. He was trying to bully me back around the corner.

Then he shot me an exasperated look and I understood that actually, he was just asking me to go away before Trina saw me. To protect me, because he knew mine was a rogue operation and I wasn't supposed to be here? Maybe. Or maybe to protect himself, because Trina probably thought he was merely her bodyguard. Not a person who could sense approaching individuals and intercept them before they even entered the corridor.

I turned and left without a word. There was nothing for me to do here, and anyway, I was no longer in a mood to help Bitterblue with her problems.

I wondered what they were looking for. I didn't think there were many objects Trina could find that Po wouldn't be able to sense with his own Grace. He can't tell what color things are and he can't figure out flat things, like drawings, or writing on a page. When he lost his sight, he lost his ability to read. But aside from that, Po should be able to stand outside those rooms and identify every object inside them.

On the other hand, Trina can only find something if she's looking for that thing specifically: She needs to know some particulars of what she's looking for. A pocket watch from Wester made of gold and crystal. A seam of zilfium in rock. A scarf knitted by a particular artisan. The more information she has about the thing she seeks, the more likely she is to be able to locate it. She can't reach out with her Grace, riffle through the correspondence on Joff's desk, and figure out who's written him letters.

But I wondered if she could reach out and determine whether there was a letter there from some distinct individual. Joff's mother? The Sunderan king? Lord Cobal, the Estillan envoy to Winterkeep?

I guessed that Trina was looking for some specific written thing.

As I worked my way back down to the gatehouse again, one of my sister's clerks spotted me. He came racing after me, squeaking my name.

"Hava? Hava! The queen wishes to see you!"

With one very long, very patient breath, I removed my coat.

Then I turned around again and made my way to Bitterblue's offices.

116.

Outside the entrance to Bitterblue's offices, a young man with a toolbelt and rolled-up sleeves crouched at the base of the doors, measuring something.

Beside him, Hope sat on her rump, watching him with quiet golden eyes.

Hope? I said.

My girl! she said, turning her steady gaze up to me. *Carpenter man. Fox door!*

"Pardon me," the man said, glancing up into my face, then flushing pink, as people do sometimes when they recognize my eyes.

"You're building a fox door?" I said.

"Yes, at Her Majesty's request," he said, standing, moving aside.

Carpenter man! said Hope. *Told him about my girl!*

What! What did you tell him?

Takes care of Hope, she said. *Takes care of babies.*

Hm.

HAVA! screamed Moth, suddenly appearing around a corner and streaking down the corridor toward us. *Hava, where did you go? Hava, why don't you wake me up in the mornings? What if I want to go with you!*

I didn't go anywhere, I said. *You didn't miss anything.*

HAVA!

Moth, stop screaming! You're hurting my brain. Here, come inside so this man can get back to his work, all right?

Inside the offices, Bitterblue stood at Barra's desk, her eyebrows furrowed over something Barra was writing. When she saw us, she pointed to a room at the back of the offices, her face betraying no expression. I trudged to it reluctantly, feeling like a child being isolated for bad behavior. The foxes clambered around my feet.

Inside the room, Adventure was standing at attention in the middle of a table.

Moth! he said, jumping down to the floor. *Come with me if you want to see a place in the great courtyard—*

I don't, said Moth. *I was just in the great courtyard.*

—where you can climb all the way up the rain pipes—

I already know how to climb up the rain pipes.

—and visit a hive where bees are making honey.

Now Moth halted, her fluffy tail twitching. She peered at Adventure with suspicion. *What are bees?*

Tiny flying beans with swords on their noses, said Adventure.

Um, I began, then silenced myself when Adventure did the mental equivalent of shooting me a quelling expression.

On second thought, he said to Moth, *maybe you're not old enough for flying sword beans.*

You can't stop me! cried Moth. *You already told me where they are!* Then she shot out of the room.

Kits, said Adventure with a heavy sigh, following her. As he left, Bitterblue pushed in.

"What was that about?" I asked.

She was blinking tired eyes, her mind clearly elsewhere. "What was what about?"

"Adventure and the bees?"

"Oh, right," she said, rubbing at her braids the way she does when her neck hurts. "This morning, Cornsilk asked a Sunderan lord why he styles his hair to look like a drowned cat. Then later, Froggatt confessed he'd been wondering the same thing. The kits are telling people our thoughts. And of course they know some of our secrets, even if they don't entirely understand them. Wasn't Moth present last night when I yelled at Ror? Adventure's going to talk to them about their responsibilities as part of my court. And until they've learned discretion, we've decided they shouldn't be in the offices."

"Doesn't Froggatt know to guard his mind?"

"I think Froggatt is too happy and underslept to guard his mind," said Bitterblue wearily. "He has a baby now," she reminded me, when I looked confused.

"Oh, right. And Hope?"

Bitterblue glanced at Hope, who was pressed against my feet. "Adventure doesn't think Hope poses a threat."

Because her comprehension is shattered, she didn't say, but the implication hit me like a sharp stone. "Who are we meeting?" I asked, annoyed.

She shut the door. "No one."

"What?" I said. "What is this? A lecture? A scolding?"

"A scolding for what, Hava?" she said, impatience crying out through her voice. "Did you do something I should scold you for?"

"No!"

"Then sit down!" she said. "I want to ask you about the formula translation!"

IT WAS BETTER than being yelled at, but a lot more boring.

She had about twenty questions per page, and we went through every page. It was plain her eyes were stinging and her head pounding—my own head began to ache just watching her—but she asked me to identify the parts I understood, versus those I'd merely copied. She wanted to know whether we needed the help of a Keepish scientist specifically. Would chemists from the Seven Nations be able to sit with the words I'd translated, and understand the rest on their own?

"I really don't know," I said. "You'd have to ask them. Are you sleeping any better, Bitterblue?"

"Don't you start too," she said. "I'm fine."

"You don't look fine."

"Well, of course I'm not fine!" she suddenly exclaimed. "I have a resource that everyone wants, both to make powerful engines that pollute the environment and to make *bombs*! And here," she said, slapping her hand to the formulas, "I have the means to blow up the world, Hava! To my north and west, I have neighbors with motivations that could put me in the position of needing these weapons! How could I possibly be happy about the prospect of a war like that? And it's not like Estill and Sunder are the only nations capable of aggression! The Middluns has armies and a greedy king. Wester may be far away, but they've allied with Sunder in my lifetime. And there are rumors now that Wester may have coastal zilfium! What if *any* of them ally, and force my hand?"

"That would be suicidal on their parts," I said.

"No," she said vehemently. "*I* would be the one killing their soldiers, Hava. They would not be killing themselves. And besides, let's not pretend that a weapon we can build here in Monsea can't be built in Estill or Sunder or Wester or anywhere. They have chemists too. If I build them, everyone else is going to scramble to figure out how to build them. And then what?"

"All right, but you're jumping ahead to the worst possible outcome."

"As I must! What's gotten into you? Since when are you an optimist?"

"I'm just being contrary," I said, "as usual."

She breathed a tiny laugh, then rubbed her temples. The pain and worry in her face pulled at my breath. *I don't really care what any of the other nations do. I just wish Bitterblue didn't always have to carry so much on her small shoulders. Maybe I'm mad at Linta for that.*

Hope, who was sitting in my lap, popped her head up and rested her chin on the table, also settling her golden eyes on Bitterblue. *Bombs,* she said. *Bad.*

Are you talking to both of us, Hope? I said.

Just my girl.

"The two of you are glowing at me like fireflies," said Bitterblue. "You suit each other. She's gotten awfully fluffy and soft, hasn't she?"

Now I studied Hope, surprised, realizing that Bitterblue was right. When had her fur filled out and grown so silky? How had I missed it?

I love you, Hope, I said, raising her to my face, kissing her fuzzy neck, then glaring my crimson and copper eyes at my sister just in case she had any intention of teasing me about my behavior.

She'd already turned back to the translations. "What about these 'LV' sections?" she said. "'Ask LV for the ratio of zilfium dust to sulfur. It must be mixed in a vacuum in precise increments. If the sulfur is added too quickly, the zilfium dust clumps and becomes useless. Refer to LV for the exact procedure.' Would one of our chemists be able to figure this stuff out? Or do we need to try to locate this LV?"

"I really don't know," I said.

"I hope Raffin and Bann will agree to come," said Bitterblue, almost to herself. Prince Raffin is Katsa's cousin and the heir to the throne of the Middluns, and Bann is his companion. They're Council leaders, but more to the point, as I've said before, they're chemists, and people Bitterblue trusts. Raffin's father, King Randa, is often ill, though. We haven't learned yet if Raffin can travel.

"If LV is a person with intimate knowledge of the formulas," she continued, "I suppose we need to locate them regardless. They could be selling their knowledge to anyone."

"I'm not sure what they'd be doing," I said. "I got to an interesting section last night in the new pages you gave me. Linta Massera seemed to think maybe LV was misremembering ratios on purpose, so that the weapon wouldn't explode."

"Wouldn't explode!" said Bitterblue, staring at me. "As in, LV was sabotaging the weapon? Does that mean LV wanted exclusive use of the weapon? Or does it mean LV didn't want the weapon to work at all?"

"I suspect the latter," I said. "It sounds like LV didn't like the weapon. But either way, you should give me more pages."

"Bring back those five and I will."

"Just give them to me, Bitterblue," I said. "Do you think *I* want exclusive use of the weapon? I don't think we should be wasting any time."

Grumbling, Bitterblue shuffled to the back of the pile of papers and found the place where my translation ended. She counted five more pages and held them out to me. "Please return the others as soon as you can," she said. "It makes me nervous to have them spread out all over creation. Well, now I'm even more convinced we need to locate this LV. Maybe they're on our side. Or if not, maybe they can be bought."

"What would locating them involve?" I said. "Sending more spies to Winterkeep?"

"Maybe," she muttered, running her fingers along another line of translation. "Trina, possibly? But I've been thinking of asking Trina to go to Wester, to find out if the rumors of zilfium there are substantiated. It's the opposite direction."

"Trina?" I said, not quite managing to keep the barbs out of my voice. "Is she your spy now?"

"She's working with the Council, and the Council's helping me out." Bitterblue glanced into my face, then spoke again in a more sympathetic tone. "Po's spending a lot of time with her, Hava. We'll know right away if there's any reason not to trust her."

"Super," I said. "Great. What are they doing together?"

"Going to the rooms and hotels of my foreign visitors."

"As I offered to do," I said sharply.

"I haven't wanted to overburden you, Hava. We just got back."

"What's she looking for?"

"Letters they've written to each other," said Bitterblue, "to figure out who's allied with whom. She's also looking for more chemical formulas."

"You mean for making explosives?"

"Yes. I need to know who knows what."

"But if your enemies have their own formulas, they might not travel with them."

"I know. It's a start."

I subsided into silence, focusing on Hope for a moment. Petting her soft fur, and trying to get ahold of my temper. "Have they found anything yet?"

"Nothing helpful."

"Not even in Lord Joff's rooms?"

"Not even there. Are you interested in him particularly?"

"Does Trina know the truth about Po's Grace?"

"Absolutely not," said Bitterblue. "She thinks he's her muscle."

I was a little embarrassed at how much this mollified me. And I remembered having this jealous, out-of-sorts feeling before; I think a lot of my visits to Bitterblue's offices leave me prickly and defensive, while she sits there looking clearheaded and sure of herself.

But also weary. "Bitterblue?" I said. "Are you really okay?"

She changed then, very suddenly. She shrank into someone unhappy and uncertain, and I was frightened. "Let me tell you how I think it's all going to play out," she said.

"Okay," I said, pretty sure I didn't want to know.

"I think I'm going to offer my zilfium for trade," she said, "since that's what everyone wants. The trade will be contingent upon the purchasing nation signing a treaty swearing not to use it to produce any objects with a violent, explosive, or military purpose. I don't know if I'll be able to make environmental demands too. We'll see. The purchasing nations will then have to prove what they're using the zilfium for; they'll have to agree to Monsean oversight. I'll sign the treaty too, and I'll promise the other signers that I don't have the formulas.

"Then," she said, "I think I'll break the treaty and build the weapons secretly, so I can have them stockpiled, just in case. Because I have to," she said in a hard, unhappy voice. "That's the world I'll be building: one that rests atop my deceit."

117.

AFTER I LEFT Bitterblue's office, I made my way downstairs to the great courtyard, Hope trotting at my feet.

When we passed through a doorway, I found myself thinking wistfully, *Hatch*. When we climbed down some stairs, I thought, *Ladder*. *Everything is unnecessarily big*, I said to Hope. *I've been in houses smaller than this foyer. It's an inefficient use of space. Don't you think?*

Pretty castle, she said.

The great courtyard isn't my favorite place, but it's the only way to exit the castle, unless you want to climb out a window and scale a heavily guarded wall. The shrubberies, another of Leck's Dells-obsessed designs, are cut in the shapes of bears, mountain lions, gigantic birds. Since they're green and flowering year-round, they're meant to look like Dellian monsters.

I stood among them, staring up at the rain pipes that feed the fountains on rainy days, looking for bees, and little foxes climbing like sailors.

Hope? Where's Moth?

Library, she said.

I shifted my attention to the north vestibule, where I could see the doors to the library, broad and open, the space beyond glowing with yellow light.

Moth's in there?

Moth, Bir, Cornsilk, Owlet, Adventure, Linny.

Really? All in the library? I asked, because sometimes she gets caught up inside lists. But before she could even answer, the four kits raced out of the library and into the courtyard, moving in a changing formation that had the shape of a sheet flapping in the wind.

Hava and Hope-Mother! they shouted, running around us, between us, careening back toward the library, leaving me dizzy. As they disappeared within, they almost tripped a man who was coming out. Teddy, a friend of Bitterblue's who's part of her Ministry of Education.

"Ah!" said Teddy, his eyes brightening at the sight of me. "Hava. Welcome back from your adventures!"

"It's nice to see you, Teddy," I said.

"Skulk," he said.

"Huh?"

His eyes, hazel in a pleasant, lopsided face, brightened further. "I believe a group of foxes is called a *skulk*," he said. "Or an *earth*."

"An earth! As in, an earth of foxes?"

"Yes, though I prefer skulk. Do you have a preference?"

"I—not really?"

He was already on his way, gliding across the courtyard toward the gatehouse, his arms full of manuscripts. Teddy has a printing press in the east city with which he's helping the royal librarian restore books Leck destroyed.

He's also writing a dictionary. In fact, I had a feeling, like the memory of an itch, that there was a word I'd meant to ask Teddy about once. I could remember standing in the bow of the *Monsea*, enjoying the rise and plunge of her beautiful, perfect nose, thinking of a word I wanted to talk to Teddy about. But he was gone now. All of it was gone now.

I wanted to see Linny. So my feet carried me into the library.

118.

LINNY MADE HIMSELF easy to find.

The foyer of the library is huge, with rows of bookshelves reaching so high that ladders run on tracks to access mezzanine levels connected by bridges. Linny was sitting on a bench on one of the mezzanines, reading. I could see him from the doors.

As I moved toward him, he glanced up from his book, saw me, and smiled. It was one of his world-shifting smiles and I stopped for a moment, overcome by confusion. He was sitting on a bench I used to sit on as a child. It's cut from an enormous tree trunk laid on its side, with some of its branches left intact, so that thick, woody protrusions extend from it in places. When I was small, it was easy to pretend to be part of the tree, and watch the entrance. Bitterblue, almost as small as me, came in sometimes with her mother. Other times she came in holding Leck's hand.

At the sight of Linny's increasingly puzzled smile, I forced myself to move toward one of the mezzanine ladders. *Ladder,* I thought, climbing.

"I found a sculpture in this library that your mother must've made, Hava," Linny said as I emerged to his level. "It's beautiful, and so much like your figurine."

Not a good start. I compelled my mouth to speak words. "I haven't seen you since we got here," I said, then heard my accusatory tone.

"Well, I've looked for you," he said, in a voice that contained not annoyance, exactly, but maybe the potential for annoyance.

"I didn't mean it to sound like that," I said. "I'm sorry. I—I've looked for you too. Whenever I come looking for you all, no one's home. It's—disorienting. I guess I'm used to the group."

Linny tilted his head sideways, studying me. "What's wrong?"

I can see Leck below, holding my sister's hand. "I'm tired," I said. "Worried."

"What about?" he said, then added, "Though maybe you can't tell me."

I understood that he meant because I work with the Queen of Monsea, who has secrets. I dropped down beside him on the bench, wishing it weren't true. I wanted to shake the sense that my air and my thoughts and the blood in my veins were made up of Bitterblue's problems, and I had a feeling telling Linny would help. I wished I could reach into my pocket, where I'd tucked Linta's pages, and show him them too. Tell him about LV misremembering ratios, maybe on purpose. Ask him why someone who cares about ahsoken would blow things up.

"It's funny," I said, "because the thing I'd most like to talk to you about really isn't all that secret. But I shouldn't. I'm sorry."

"It's okay."

"I mean, you know this scientist was doing something bad. But what interests me is less *what* she was doing and more *why* she was doing it. She had this other work she really loved, you know?"

"The ahsoken work?"

"Yes. So why did she have to do both?"

"I don't know," said Linny. "Money?"

"Yes," I said, sighing. "Maybe it was money."

"Why do you think she pulls at you so much?" asked Linny.

He was watching me again, but it didn't make me want to hide; it made me want to figure out the answer. "I don't know," I said. "There are times when she just seems—really happy. And I want her to be happy. Even though other times, she does such awful things."

"You're a generous person," said Linny, which almost made me recoil. People keep calling me things I'm not, like generous, and kind.

I dragged myself out of myself, and studied him more closely. He had a big book in his lap, the pages covered with labeled drawings of what looked like ship rigging. "What are you reading?"

He blinked, looking where I was looking. "I'm trying to improve my Lingian," he said.

"Your ship vocabulary, in particular?"

"Yes."

"But you must have a pretty good Lingian ship vocabulary, working on a Monsean ship, right? Don't you speak Lingian with Jacky and Ollie?"

"It's pretty good," he admitted. "But it's more for operations than building, and I've been thinking about taking on some shipbuilding work."

"You have?" I said, amazed by this. "What kind of shipbuilding? Where?"

"Here," he said. "Whatever's on offer."

"Have you built ships before?"

Linny shrugged. "No. But I'm used to having something to do. I'm living in this beautiful castle, eating the queen's food at her expense, with no expectations. I'm going to get bored. And I could use the money."

I wondered then how much I really knew about Linny. Like, I knew some of the things he's learned to do, such as chemistry, archery, riding. Sailing. I knew his even temper and every expression on his face. I had an idea of some of the parts of his past. I knew what he was like when you're stranded with him in the wilderness.

But I didn't know what bored him, or what he needed money for, or what he most liked to do. What he would do if he could do anything. "Does this mean you intend to stay in Bitterblue City for a while?"

"I could," he said, with something in his voice that made confusion rise in my throat. I focused intently on Hope and the kits, who'd formed a clump down below on the library floor. They seemed to be taking a collective nap. I could see one of Moth's long legs sticking out of the pile.

"If I'm building something," he added, with eyes that were considering my face yet again. I could feel their light touch.

Finally I looked back at him too, but I wasn't sure what I was seeing. The features of Linny's face contain a sensitivity I'm pretty sure I'm not capable of, in any part of me. His nose, his mouth, his eyes are more appealing than anything anyone would ever see, looking at me. His hands are broad, with long, calloused fingers, a sailor's hands, but no doubt gentle, whatever they touched. He has a gentleness I could never have. And he could stay for a while, if he was building something.

I had the sense suddenly that even if I'm not sure who Linny is, Linny knows. He's a person entire, who knows what he likes and chooses his occupations. And though he spoke the words "building something" in Dellian, they have the same meaning as the Lingian words Bitterblue used when she talked about "building the world." Both Linny and Bitterblue know what they're here for. If Linny is building ships and Bitterblue is building the entire world, what am I building? Linta? You knew what you were building too. But what am I building? And what am I building it out of? What am I made of?

Also, if Linny is always this physical person, my height, my breadth, gentle and amber-eyed with a face I like to look at—he is *always* that person—what does it mean that my greatest power is to disappear? If I can blend into this bench and become a tree, how can I be anything, to anybody? Can a person be made of nothing?

"Do you ever feel like you don't exist?" I said.

"Oh, Hava," he said, in a different voice. "Do you feel that way?"

Almost without choosing to, I turned into a tree branch.

I heard his intake of breath. Then I felt his hand finding mine, then taking it. I was right: His grip was firm, but also gentle. I glanced at him once, expecting his eyes to be closed, expecting nausea in his face. He was looking right at me, and he didn't look sick.

"There was a time when I felt that way," he said. "It's been years, though."

"Did that lord hurt you?" I asked, almost in a whisper.

"Yes," he said.

I'd hoped for a different answer for Linny, so badly. Love is hope for other people. I swallowed down tears. "Did you have to see him? When you went to visit your mother?"

"He was there," Linny said, "but I didn't have to see him. He knows not to come anywhere near me now."

"Or you'll injure him?"

Linny tucked his chin to his chest. "He's surprisingly easy to injure," he said, "now that I'm grown and hate him. I don't even have to touch him. I just have to show him contempt."

"I see," I said. "Sort of."

"I can explain it better sometime, if you like."

"It doesn't hurt you to talk about it?"

"I don't think it would hurt me to tell *you*."

"Thank you," I said. "*You're* generous." *More generous than I am,* I thought, *ever.*

Somewhere in the course of the conversation, I'd turned myself back into myself. He was still holding my hand—and I his, I suppose. I was confused about what to do about it; did he want me to let go? How would we end it, or wouldn't we end it? Were we stuck on this bench forever now, because of how awkward it would be for either of us to extricate an appendage?

Then he did let my hand go and it was the most natural thing. Not a rejection, not an extrication. Just a gentle easing of pressure, so simple that it inspired me to do the most shocking thing I've ever done in my life: I took his hand back. I don't do things like that. It's the opposite of disappearing. But something came over me.

He responded immediately, holding my hand again. He was watching me and I couldn't quite return that attention; I couldn't know what was in his face just then. But I said, because it pushed itself out, "The king was never easy to injure. I never got to injure him, not even once."

I heard another intake of breath. After a moment, he said, "Hava, do you mean that you knew King Leck personally?"

Too many words were trying to escape. I had the sense that if I tried to say something dismissive to make it all small again, I would crack open, the way my uncle does, but not with guilt: with anger and grief. So much anger and grief that it would make the library explode.

So I took a minute, during which I turned back into a tree.

"Yes," I said, "sort of. Similar to the way I knew a lot of people. In the sense that—I would hide, and spy on them."

"I see," he said. "You spied on King Leck?"

I watched him kill my mother. "I did," I said carefully. "And he hurt me."

"Oh, Hava. I'm sorry." He held my hand tighter. "You don't have to talk about it if you don't want to."

I considered my next words, because I didn't want to say them if I didn't mean them. "I can explain it better sometime," I finally said, "maybe, if you like."

119.

IN THE MIDDLE of the night, I woke to a dream of drowning as the *Monsea* sank, and a sense of swelling cold.

A single ashy log glowed in my fireplace. I dragged myself out of bed, bringing a blanket with me, wearing it like a cape as I built the fire up, thinking, inexplicably, of all the promises I keep making to Linny that I'll certainly break. Like that maybe I'll show him my mother's sculptures. Like that maybe I'll explain about King Leck. How am I ever going to do those things, if I can't even bear them myself?

I lay on the rug while I waited for the new logs to ignite. When they did, their bursts of heat pushed against my skin and my blanket, delicious, safe. Their crackling sounds reminded me of our small, rare fires in the north. When I closed my eyes, I saw bands of green light arch across my eyelids, and I remembered being cold. Always cold, always wet, always hungry. I get a little panicky now, whenever I shiver, or feel the hint of hunger. And I sneak food away after meals, and I pile too many blankets on my bed at night. It's not stealing, to abscond with food from my sister's gigantic kitchens or take the thickest, softest blankets from the linen rooms, but I hide myself while I'm doing it. I don't want people's eyes, and I don't want them to know how we suffered. They can see enough already, in our gaunt faces and loose clothing, our healing skin and ragged hair, the slow shuffle that is Barra's new way of walking. The rest of the truth is ours to keep.

She's angry, Moth had said, while we sat on the steps above the prison. *She's cold.*

I could not bear, somehow, the thought of anyone being cold, especially not anyone from our party. Angry, sure. Miserable with regret, sure. But not cold.

I made a decision.

Then I fell asleep on the floor in front of my fireplace. In the morning, when I woke to a dream of moths, Hope and Moth had found me. They were snoring gently in my arms.

120.

As a known member of the queen's staff who's implicitly recognized as her spy, I'm allowed to visit whomever I want in the prison. The prison master, a woman named Goldie with the incongruous Grace of singing, never asks me my reasons.

She did look puzzled, though, when I stepped into the prison's front office that morning with an armload of blankets and a basket of food.

"Kera, please," I said.

"Of course," she said briskly. "But you know we feed our prisoners and keep the stoves lit, don't you?"

"You may not understand the effects of an ordeal like ours on the body," I said. "Have you heard of the Keepish blue foxes?"

"Indeed," she said. "I encountered a small one in the great courtyard yesterday morning. She asked me, forming words inside my mind in the most extraordinary fashion, why my hair puffs around my head like a storm cloud."

Cornsilk. "Right," I said. "Anyway, they can sense things. One of them told me that Kera's cold."

"You don't say," she said, narrowing one gold and one black eye on me keenly. "Are any of my other prisoners cold?"

"I don't know. She only mentioned Kera."

"These foxes sound useful," she said. "Please come this way."

Kera's cell was a short walk from the entrance, which was a relief to me, because I did not want to be here in these corridors that echoed like the glacier. When we reached Kera, she was sitting in the dark on a wooden block, surrounded by stone walls and a stone floor. She had no window or lamp of her own. Her cell was poorly lit by a single lantern on the wall outside the bars of her cage.

"You," she said at the sight of me, her voice as contemptuous as ever. "What do you want?"

Goldie, producing a large key ring from a pocket attached to a chain at her waist, unlocked the door of the cell, then took the blankets and basket from my arms, carrying them in to Kera. She didn't look inside the basket, didn't even crack the lid open as she set it on Kera's floor, which was fascinating. It had to mean that Bitterblue had ordered Goldie to give me free rein down here.

A guard brought a wooden chair for me, leaving it in the corridor outside the cell. I eyed it doubtfully, because I hadn't meant to stay. But nor had I exactly meant not to; I'd merely obeyed an instinct I guess I've always had, one that draws me to animals in cages.

The image of Hope flashed into my mind then, curled up tight in her crate, smelly, starved, drugged senseless, with infections growing on her skin. Maybe I wanted a conversation after all. At any rate, I would stay long enough to assure Kera that the blankets and food didn't mean I'd stopped hating her.

I waited for Goldie to lock the cell door again, then depart with the guard. We weren't alone. The cells to either side of Kera were occupied, and their residents, both big, bearded men with pale skin and curious faces, had come to lean against their bars and inspect me. I couldn't hide myself from them without also hiding myself from Kera. I sat down, trying to ignore their stares.

Kera, in the meantime, perched stiffly on her wooden block, paying no mind to the colorful blankets now piled on her cot, not even directing a glance of disdain at the basket of food. Her auburn hair, falling down around her shoulders, had lost none of its brightness, nor her voice its aggression. "Well?" she said. "What do you want?"

"One of the foxes told us you were cold," I said. "The queen doesn't like our prisoners to be cold."

"Oh, yes," said Kera sarcastically. "I'm sure our comfort is her first priority."

"Oh, yes," echoed the man to Kera's left in a gravelly voice. "Her first priority." Stone walls divided the cells from each other, so Kera couldn't see her neighbors. But I got the feeling from the easy way she smiled at this that they were becoming friends.

"Who's your benevolent guest, Kera?" said the man to Kera's right, in a high, straining voice that didn't match his size. "There's something funny-looking about her."

"She's thin as a rail," said the left-hand man. "Sitting on that chair like a skeleton."

"Not that," said right-hand in his fluting voice. "One of her eyes is glowing like a fire and the other looks like blood."

"Ah," said the left-hand man, pushing his face harder into the aperture between the bars. "That means she's the queen's Graced spy."

"The one who turns into things?" said right-hand. "Oh, show us!"

"I've seen it," said Kera, cutting in. "It's not very impressive."

"And how do you know her, Kera?" asked left-hand.

"I tried to kill her," said Kera.

"Oh?" said left-hand with a measure of respect. "By what method?"

"I threw her into the sea," Kera said, watching me, her voice different now, far away, as if she was remembering. I was also remembering, not just that moment, but too many other things. Kera attacking the bear that threatened Liel, flying at it with nothing but empty fists. Kera trudging resolutely, as all of us had trudged, hungry, cold, aching, never giving up. Kera being taken away from us by Dellian guards inside King Nash's castle. Kera crying out in anguish, "My daughter will not have a mother who died in a Monsean prison!"

Frustration burst inside me. "Why did you do it, Kera?"

"This again?" she said. "Really, Hava?"

"But couldn't you have made money without hurting Hope?"

"We've been through all of it before," said Kera with rising irritation. "The queen's pet, castle-born, could never understand."

"You're wrong about my life," I said. "While I lived in this castle, King Leck did too. When he died, I left, and when I left I had nothing. I had no one. I was eight. I fended for myself."

"Where was your mother?" said Kera derisively.

"My mother was dead!"

"Your father?"

I swallowed. "He was also dead."

"What a sad story," she said. "Congratulations on your faultless life. I'm sure in your work for the queen, you've never made mistakes or hurt anyone. Or, let me guess—that's different, right, because you only hurt 'bad' people?"

"You put a blue fox in a box in the dark," I said stubbornly. "You starved her and drugged her and ruined her mind. And when I found her, you threw me into the sea."

She stood, her face suddenly blazing with anger. "I am trying to get back to my child," she said. "However many times you ask me, you'll get the same answer." Then she went to her cot and grabbed the top two blankets. Shaking them open, she wrapped them around herself, jerking them tight. She spoke with her back to me. "Why did you come down here, if it was just to say all the same horseshit you've already said?"

It was a good question. Why had I come down here? "You could end up jailed forever!" I said. "Or worse!"

She gave me another irritated, incredulous look. "Do you think I'm unaware of my situation?"

"You created the situation yourself!"

"Hava!" she said sharply. "Haven't you ever followed an instinct to protect yourself, then realized immediately it was a mistake? And now you've hurt people—but it's done? Regrets can't change it. It's done," she said, smacking her hand against her bars.

Inside my mind, the world exploded, and Linta Massera was dead. I fought a bear, then I fought Kera, and Blueberry was dead. My mother was dead.

"It's easy to talk about regrets," I said roughly. "Words are easy. You threw me into the sea."

"Are words easy?" she said. "Do you express your regrets easily, Hava? I'll say it again: I regret what I did. I was scared. I was thinking of Sera, not you. And there's no point talking it over, because all you do is start at the same place and say the same things. You confront me with what I did, as if I didn't know. You ask me why I did it, but I don't think you *want* to understand my answers. You want to be angry and hurt." She stopped and gave me another close look. Then she returned to her woodblock and sat down. "You're not going to make any progress if you won't accept my answers."

"I don't need advice from someone who tried to murder me," I said.

She held up her hands, letting her blankets drop. "All right," she said. "Your choice. Maybe listening to you yell the same horseshit over and over is a fair and just part of my fate."

Kera's fate.

Maybe that's why I came down here: Because I'm struggling with the things people choose to do, and I'm also struggling with their fates. My sister has made changes to her prison in recent years. The cells are clean, the prisoners are uncrowded, their needs are met.

Goldie even sings them lullabies, of all things, and as I sat there, I could smell a mix of cinnamon and cloves. Goldie burns herbs and spices in the stoves to make the air pleasant. I've never been inside a jail in Estill or Sunder, but I'm sure they're not like this.

And yet, it's dark, and Kera is cold, and she'll never see her daughter. Her walls are made of iron bars and stone, and nothing will ever change. I grew up in boxes in the dark. I learned what it was like to wait, and hope, for something that never happened. To suspend myself in a terrible dream, while nothing changed. And then things did change, to something worse.

Leck had cages for the animals he liked to hurt. Well, Bitterblue has cages too.

Kera did what she did. But do I want her to live in a cage?

121.

I PACKED SOME FOOD and went out by myself, throwing another note from my entranceway onto the fire first.

When my feet hit the ground outside the castle, I turned right, toward the west city, almost running. Afraid some clerk would come chasing after me, or Moth, screaming my name.

The west city is a different world from the busy east city. It's the city's edge instead of its middle, and it's quiet, secretive; within its maze of streets, people observe you from dark doorways and ancient shuttered windows, their eyes keen with interest, but offering no information in return.

It's easy to hide in run-down places, easy to blend into broken stone and leaning, ivy-covered timber. Become something's parts. I remember this: I've always headed into the west city when I've wanted to think. I find a garden and crouch in plain sight, using my Grace so no one notices me, idly watching people about their business as my own mind works out its tangles.

Or I do what I did this time: Continue past the city's edges to the place where the buildings give way to broad hills and pale sky.

It's abrupt, the end of the west city. One moment you're passing between tall, close buildings and the next, you're climbing a hardpacked rise of golden grass. The world that seemed small and contained is suddenly vast, with high blue ceilings and a view to forests, then to the mountains that form our borders with Estill and Sunder.

On a clear day, you can see distant farmhouses to the west and south, and the silhouette of a small stone castle crowning one of the highest hills to the north. I know that castle. It'll make a good launching point, maybe, once I've decided where I'm going next. It's square and plain, with one turret overlooking the river beyond. Some noble family lived there a long time ago, some family Leck ruined, but it's been derelict and abandoned at least as long as I've known it. I stayed there for a longish stretch after my mother died, hiding from my father, who was looking for me. Coming back to the city every few days to steal what food I needed, waiting until I could stop shaking and crying and come up with the first of many plans for how to survive, and who to be.

Now, setting out west across the hills, I didn't really do much thinking. I just moved, trying to shake the strange confusion out of my body. Shake Bitterblue's problems out of my body too; return to myself, whatever that meant. I noticed that my feet didn't hurt, nor did my ankle. Hiking with a bag on my back didn't make me tired. A bird caught my eye, a hawk, soaring far above. As I climbed, I began to encounter snow. The first time my boots broke through a hard shell of it and became stuck, I turned back in disgust. I've had enough of that to last a lifetime.

Walking to lower ground, I found a flat, dry rock and sat, looking around at the landscape that should have been familiar but only felt alien, because it was the wrong color. There were no glaciers, no ice; I could see too many trees. I was sweating inside my Keepish furs. When I opened my bag, then pulled out the food I'd brought for myself—buttered bread and cheese, a jar of preserves, a sausage, a slice of cake wrapped in a cloth, a flask of bright, hot Keepish tea—I suddenly burst into tears, bewildered to have such a bounty all for myself; grieving the suffering the survivors of the *Monsea* had endured; and desperately lonely.

I ate, then sat for a bit, my head achy from crying. Curious, I turned myself into a rock the same color and texture as the rock I sat on. Rocklike, I listened to the breeze, and smelled the grass, and watched the sky. I'm not sure why I did it, but it felt better than turning into the prison steps. Out here, it was almost as if I could imagine I was part of the earth.

On my way back to the castle, I paid less attention to the sky and more attention to the ground. That's how I began to notice the patches of flowers pushing their stalks up through cold dirt, unfurling pink and white sails. And where there were flowers, there were butterflies: bright, tiny flashes of yellow, orange, blue, floating on papery wings.

I thought of Moth, who's only ever known winter.

I decided I would come back tomorrow, and invite her.

122.

THE NEXT MORNING, there were no new notes under my door. Maybe I've finally worn Bitterblue down.

I woke Moth carefully, wanting to let Hope sleep. Moth was so excited about joining my adventures, and so manic and rambunctious as we "snuck" out of the castle, that I began to worry that the western hills, when they turned out to be no more than that, hills, would disappoint her.

But of course she loved everything she saw immediately, just as she always does. When we got to the open grass, she began to dash back and forth, overwhelmed by her directional choices.

What's that? she screamed, spotting the distant castle, then bolting toward it.

It's far away! I cried after her. *Much farther than it looks!*

Foxes have excellent depth perception! she screamed, tripping suddenly, spinning through the air in a series of unplanned somersaults, then continuing on as if nothing had happened. I watched her go with that sense again that she might never come back to me.

I love you, Moth, I called after her weakly. *I love you.* She crested the rise of a hill and disappeared down the other side. *I love you.*

I sat on a hump of grassy dirt, not sure what to do. Not sure why I was here; not sure why I ever went anywhere. Wishing I hadn't brought her. And suddenly tired, impatient with this bafflement that seemed to have accompanied me out of the north. I was certain I hadn't been this stupid before. I was like my own mother, empty and useless and numb, mumbling her litany, "I love you, I love you," while someone else's thoughts and ideas fought with her own inside her head. I barely even existed half the time. I couldn't even touch someone unless I turned myself into a thing first, an empty thing.

Suddenly I was furious at my mother. I hated her, for shoving me into closets and making me invisible and denying my existence, then getting herself killed. I scrambled for the bundle of tattered silk inside my pocket, wrenched it out, drew my arm back, and hurled it as hard as I could. As my figurines soared through the air and scattered, I screamed, long and hard.

Then it was over and it was as if it had made no impact whatsoever. The sky pressed its blueness upon me. The hills stretched in every direction, hard and cold. Moth was a dot in the distance, cresting another rise, then disappearing again. I was alone, and my throat hurt, and I was frightened, because I'd thrown my mother's figurines, and now what if I couldn't find them?

I ran after them, trying to remember where I'd seen them fall. It was a long time of scrabbling around on the ground while tears dripped down my face, but then I did begin to turn them up. I guess they're light enough that two of them—the porpoise-girl and the mountain lion–girl—didn't even break through the tangles of grass on which they landed. I found them perched on golden beds of straw, like offerings. And the bear-girl had had the grace to fall into a particularly dark patch of grass. Its flash of white eventually caught my eye.

Of course I couldn't find the bird-girl, my favorite and the one I'm perpetually without. I crawled and groped through the grass, growing increasingly dirty and furious with myself. The time I thought I'd lost it at the bottom of the Winter Sea, it had turned up safely in

Linny's pocket, but that wasn't going to happen this time, and it was my fault, all my fault. A few tiny birds, brown with white bellies—I think they were wrens—hopped around nearby, pecking at the dirt and watching me. I bet they could find it pretty easily. But I couldn't talk to them.

Suddenly, Moth was flying back to me, scattering the wrens. Her excited chatter reached me first, for she'd made it all the way to the castle, climbed in through a broken door, and found a great, long gallery with empty spots on the walls where there'd used to be por-traits, plus a low chandelier with hundreds of half-burnt candles, before her excitement to tell me all about it had sent her back across the hills to me, yelling my name.

It hurt to hear her describing what she'd seen of the castle. Her words brought memories of a darker time slamming into my mind. But I opened myself to it, because I was so relieved to have her back.

What are you doing? she finally demanded, glaring at me as I bum-bled around on my hands and knees, patting at the grass.

I lost something, I said. *This,* I added, sending her a picture of the bird-girl.

She threw herself into the search just as enthusiastically as she throws herself into everything. And after that, it was only a few minutes before she found it for me, camouflaged against a clump of white crocuses growing at the base of a boulder.

It's pretty! she said, poking at it with her nose, then giving it a quick lick. *Is it you, Hava? Why are you turning into a bird?*

My mother made it, I said.

Your mother! she cried, staring up at me in astonishment, her long legs propped around her like stilts. *Isn't Hope-Mother your mother?*

It took a massive effort not to start howling with laughter, or maybe tears. *No,* I said. *Humans have human mothers. My mother was a human.*

Where is she?

She's dead.

Oh. Like Blueberry?

Once again, I fought back tears. *Yes, Moth. Like Blueberry. She was a sculptor. She always sculpted people transforming into ferocious animals, or things that would make them fierce and keep them safe.*

Did your mother have a name? asked Moth, who was still thunderstruck.

Yes. Her name was Bellamew.

What did she look like?

I took a slow breath. *She was tall,* I said, *or at least she seemed so to me when I was a little girl. She was strong, with big arms and broad hands. You need to be strong to be a sculptor.*

Was she white like you or brown like Linny? Or pink like Giddon? Or dark brown like Navi? Or—

She was white like me.

Did she have unmatching eyes like you?

No. Her eyes matched.

Can't you just show her to me? Moth said with a burst of impatience.

I hesitated. *I can show you a memory. It might not be exactly right. It's been many years since she was alive.*

That's okay, said Moth cheerfully. *I want to see!*

Sinking onto the ground beside Moth, I opened my mind to her and sorted through images in my memory, looking for my mother. Myself lying down, curled up, in a chest. Squinting as the lid opened and light flooded in, illuminating the anxious, bewildered face of my mother, who was saying "I love you, I love you" as she reached in and pulled me out, then held me to her; she was cold and shaking. She held me too hard.

Another: Standing in a shadowed corner of our sitting room,

watching my mother sculpt in the light of the glass balcony doors overlooking the courtyard, hearing the tap of her chisel on marble, smelling the dust of broken rock. A sparrow sat on the balcony balustrade, watching her through the glass. "I love you, I love you," she muttered, but she didn't seem to notice me. Half the time, her eyes were closed; she felt the shape of her sculpture with her hands.

Then I stepped out of my shadow because she looked thirsty and I wanted to bring her water and food. When I placed a cup and a plate at the bench at her elbow, she stirred, turned to look at me, fastened eyes on me that were unfocused at first, then became sharp, clear.

"Hava, sweetheart," she said. "How are you?"

"Fine, Mother."

"Step away from the glass," she said, "or use your Grace. Someone might see you."

"Yes, Mother," I said, going back to my corner and waiting for her sculpture to absorb her again, so that she wouldn't notice when I left the room to find a different place in the castle to hide, one where it was strangers who failed to perceive me, instead of my own mother.

Moth was trying to get my attention.

Hava! she shouted. *Hava!*

Yes? I said, struggling back to the present.

Did you bring any food!

Oh. Yes, I said, reaching for the bag on my back. I removed some bread and cheese and broke off a few morsels, placing them on the ground between us. My mind returned to my memories.

Your mother is like Hope-Mother, Moth said.

What? I said, startled, staring at her.

Moth's cheeks were stuffed with bread. She looked like a chipmunk hoarding acorns. *Your mother feels like Hope-Mother. Like she's not really there. Or like her mind is a bubble.*

Oh. Yes, I see.

Are all mothers like that? asked Moth.

No, I don't think so.

Just OUR mothers, she said, seeming pleased by our solidarity.

Yes.

But not us, she added.

Not us? I said, ridiculously reassured by this. *My mind isn't a bubble?*

Of course not, she said. *Your mind is Hava.*

And what does that mean?

She glared at me in outrage. *What do you mean, what does it mean? Don't you know you're Hava?*

Yes, but I'm wondering who you think I am. What kind of person.

YOU'RE HAVA! she shouted. *Can we go back to the castle now and see the bees?*

Yes, of course, I said, suppressing my laughter again, because Moth, at least, was patently herself.

123.

THAT NIGHT, WITH Hope snoozing in my lap and Moth fast asleep on the bed, I translated this:

"LV keeps going out to search for clues about Estillan spies, then comes back a long time later having found nothing. Seeming strangely . . . happy.

"'You're really searching for spies when you go out, aren't you?' I asked. LV's answer: 'What else would I be searching for?' Which isn't an answer. And the weapon procedures continue to fail.

"I wouldn't have believed LV could lie to me. Am I paranoid if I'm beginning to wonder?

"Am I—silly? pathetic?—if it feels like a betrayal?

"Of course not. Why should that be pathetic?

"What is LV doing out there?

"And doesn't LV understand that if I don't satisfy my employer, we'll have to find another laboratory? Another patron? And who would employ me, given the bridges I've now burned?

"Maybe, for the time being, I'll stop depending on LV's memory for anything weapon-related. And maybe we can have an honest conversation about it. I would've thought we were having honest conversations, but, well, who knows. I'm really rather confused."

It took me a while to fall asleep after that.

Linta Massera? I'm trying to summon some sympathy for you

because you felt betrayed by your friend. Maybe even by someone who was more than a friend? Someone who could fill you with confusion, and jealousy. I know those feelings.

And I'm trying not to be a hypocrite, because I've done bad things too. I lie, I sneak, and you're not even the only person I've killed. I've done things for money. When I was younger, I did a lot of things for money, and I didn't always know the consequences. That lord, Danzhol, who tried to kidnap Bitterblue? He gave me money. For all Kera imagines I grew up in the lap of luxury, I had to survive. Maybe you also had to survive. Maybe you felt you couldn't live without your ahsoken work. Maybe you were conflicted.

But it's hard for me to believe that you didn't understand the consequences of the weapon you were building. It's why you asked LV to remember parts of the formula for you, right? So that the complete written instructions of a terrible invention would never exist? Which means you knew.

I hope LV *was* sabotaging your work. You do not get to fund your worthy project with a weapon that could blow up the world.

124.

THE NEXT MORNING, when I opened my door, Bitterblue was in the corridor, glaring at me with her arms crossed. Two guards loomed behind her.

"Remember me?" she said. "The queen?"

Moth bolted down the hall with Hope trotting after her, but I was slow, bleary from a night of wakeful dreams, and Bitterblue wasn't looking too chipper either. In fact, she looked kind of awful. The shadows under her eyes made me wonder if she'd slept at all.

"What's this?" I said. "Were you planning to wait indefinitely outside my door?"

"I just got here," she said. "Adventure communicated with Moth about your timing."

Moth! The traitor. "I see you've figured out his purpose in your administration: spying on *me*."

Bitterblue rubbed her temples. "Sweetie, please. I don't want to fight. And I would love to have your help."

"Well, the queen always gets what she wants."

Bitterblue snorted an incredulous laugh. "Yes, my life is an endless series of indulgences. Would you please collect the pages you've been hoarding, and come with me?"

As we approached her lower offices, a group—a skulk?—of foxes came pouring out of Bitterblue's newly constructed swinging fox door. Owlet, Cornsilk, and Moth streamed past us, with Adventure and Hope bringing up the rear.

Good morning, Hava, Adventure said politely.

Spy, I shot at him.

As you are renowned as the queen's spy, he said, *surely you don't mean that as an insult?*

"What do you want me for?" I asked Bitterblue, ignoring him.

"I'll tell you when we're alone."

Stopping at my feet, Hope touched a paw to my ankle. *Stay with girl,* she said.

Somewhat mollified, I lifted her into my arms and followed Bitterblue into her offices.

It turned out she wanted me for a meeting with Joff.

"Why do you keep granting him audiences?" I said to Bitterblue testily, following her up into her tower.

"Because he keeps asking for them," said Bitterblue, "with a persistence that makes me certain there's something he wants beyond what he says. I want to know what it is."

"Can't you have Po 'accidentally' run into him on the street and ask him questions?"

"Po's gone to Estill with Katsa, to ask Joff's neighbors a few questions."

"Doesn't that seem like an awful lot of trouble, when the man himself is right here?"

"It is a lot of trouble. But it remains awkward for the leaders of the Council, especially my own cousin, to be seen trying to extract information from my foreign guests at my own court," said Bitterblue, sitting down at her desk, glaring at the stacks of paper to either side, then sighing.

"It's going to become exceedingly awkward when you marry one of them, isn't it?"

A small smile touched her lips. "We're still sorting that out."

"What do you mean, you're still sorting it out? You're going to marry him, aren't you?"

"Hava," Bitterblue said, "I'm tired and irritable. I acknowledge it. It's probably making me defensive. But I feel like you're challenging everything I'm saying, almost as a matter of course. Is that true?"

"I don't want to be here," I said.

"All right," she said, putting her hands flat on her desk and focusing her clear gray eyes on me. "Where do you want to be?"

"You look terrible," I said, a headache beginning to form at the base of my skull. "You look like you never sleep and you've hardly put on any weight. And I can tell you have a headache."

"I *have* put on weight," she said. "And I'm tired and worried, but I don't have a headache. I'm fine, Hava. Truly. You can talk to my doctors if you like, or Giddon; they'll tell you I'm fine. I want to know what *you* need."

"No you don't!" I said indignantly. "You want to use me however it suits you!"

"Hava!" she said, her voice finally growing sharp. "I understand that you're angry. You have plenty to be angry about, you always have. But I am not your enemy! If there's something I can do for you that will help you, tell me what it is! Do you want a different job? Different rooms? Do you want to leave?"

"Do you *want* me to leave?" I cried.

"I want you to be happy!" she shouted, then closed her eyes, took a deep breath, and said, "I apologize for shouting. Since we got home, Hava, we seem to be fighting more than before we left. Is there anything I can do?"

Feel better, I thought. *Be less tired and sick-looking. Leave me alone and let me disappear.*

"Why don't you just tell me what you'd like me to do during this interview?" I said shortly.

A strange pain flashed across her face. Disappointment, and worry. Then she said gently, "If you would just stand in one of the windows and be yourself, that would be perfect."

125.

It was a short meeting, and mostly boring as nails. Joff sat in a chair before Bitterblue's desk, crisply enumerating the advantages to a marital alliance between Monsea and Estill as if he were a schoolteacher striking a pointer against a board. Shared resources. A united front against aggressive nations like Sunder. Both northern and southern access to the sea. Guaranteed peace between Estill and Monsea.

I leaned against a window to the side, in Joff's peripheral vision, using my Grace to make myself less noticeable, less distracting. Directing a glower at him anytime he did look my way—being myself, I suppose. Behind me, Hope was in the windowsill, hidden from sight. Hope likes the views of the city bridges.

"As I've made quite clear," said Bitterblue, "we'll have to find another way to ensure that peace. I'm not going to marry you."

"You know that Estill has the potential for a large working army, Lady Queen. Can't you imagine it at your disposal?"

"I find it extraordinary that you continue to imply that our marriage would mean a merging of our nations," said Bitterblue. "You're not a king in Estill, Lord Joff. If we married, Estill would still be Estill and you'd still be a minor Estillan lord. You'd just live farther from the land you're responsible for."

"Possibly," said Joff, "possibly not. Our marriage would raise a lot

496 — KRISTIN CASHORE

of questions—and options—for the lords of Estill who are dissatisfied with the republic that's developed in the wake of our revolution."

Bitterblue's eyebrows shot up. "So, you have delusions of restoring the Estillan monarchy, with you on the throne?"

"Nothing as specific as that, Lady Queen. Merely *questions*."

"Those questions may interest you, but they don't interest me."

"Are you sure you want to turn down the opportunity to have a hand in the future shape of Estill, Lady Queen?"

"I will have a hand," said Bitterblue calmly.

"You refer to your proposed treaty," said Joff. "You want to neuter other nations while your own nation mines its zilfium and probably stockpiles explosive weaponry, despite what you claim. But how will you feel when Estill's survey of our mountains uncovers zilfium of our own? Or when Sunder does, or Wester? If we find zilfium, we can do whatever we like with it."

"All right," said Bitterblue. "I'll marry you."

Joff blinked.

"Just kidding," said Bitterblue. "You're boring me, Joff. Why are you really here? What do you want?"

In my window, I was thinking about Estillans sneaking through the forests around Linta's workshop. "He wants the formulas," I said.

As Joff turned to consider me, a curtain closed in his face, which was interesting.

"The formulas burned," said Bitterblue to Joff.

"He doesn't believe they burned," I said, watching his face grow more and more smooth and even.

"Well, that's rather insulting to Hava," said Bitterblue to Joff. "She risked her life trying to stop those formulas burning."

"Inhaled a lot of smoke," I said.

"Frankly, they're better gone," said Bitterblue, with a tired heaviness to her voice that told me she might actually wish they were gone.

I waited to see what Joff said next. As I glared at him expectantly, shifting in my window, crossing my arms, Hope reached a paw to my back. She climbed her way up my shirt and onto my shoulder, where she perched shakily, then dropped into my embrace.

Joff watched this maneuver with an unchanging expression. "Is that the mother to all the fox kits running around the castle?"

It was an odd thing for him to ask. Something about it made my teeth ache. "Why do you care?"

"They seem to talk to anyone and everyone," he said. "Very surprising. I thought Keepish blue foxes bonded to only one person."

"Let me guess," I said. "One of them asked you why you have stupid hair?"

He frowned at me, then turned a bland expression back to Bitterblue. "Returning to the topic at hand, Lady Queen, I acknowledge that it would be disingenuous to pretend I would refuse an opportunity to acquire formulas for any advantageous technology. But nor would anyone else in this world who cares about progress. I'm here to argue my suit, no more. And though I know you know that I suggest marriage as a practicality rather than as an expression of affection, I am sincerely relieved, given the number of ordeals you plainly endured, that every member of your party made it back alive."

Heartache blossomed inside me. Blueberry. Mart.

And then, as Joff turned his cool eyes back to Hope, it struck me that this was his second time expressing, wrongly, how glad he was that we'd all survived.

Was that interesting? Why did he keep bringing it up? Was he fishing?

For what?

126.

I WAS QUIET AFTER Joff left, thinking.

"Hava?" said Bitterblue, rubbing her braids the way she does when their weight is hurting her. "What do you think? Any insights?"

First my irritation surged, then I just felt tired of my own impulses. It was merely a question. Not a demand, not an imposition or an attack.

"When I accused him of wanting the formulas," I said, "I thought, from his face, that I was right."

"I did too," she said.

"But I got another funny feeling too. I haven't worked it out yet."

Bitterblue said nothing, just watched me from her desk. I held Hope close to my chest, pressing my face into her fur.

"How are you feeling, Hava?" she said. "Now that we've been back a few days?"

"I'm fine," I said automatically.

"Is there anything you need?"

"I need to be left alone," I said. "With my thoughts."

"All right," she said. "Well, thank you for nudging me about the marriage law. Annet came to me yesterday to talk about her wish to resign and return to Winterkeep with Navi, but I was able to show her my progress. I spoke to King Nash about it too, while we were in the Dells. It helps that we can follow their precedent. My new law will open marriage and its benefits to any consenting couple regard-less of gender, as is legal in the Dells, Pikkia, and most of Torla."

I opened my mouth. Closed it. It startles me sometimes that so many laws in Monsea are as simple as Bitterblue deciding to pri-oritize something. And I hadn't truly expected her to prioritize it so soon.

"Will Annet and Navi stay?" I asked.

"They're discussing it."

"I see. I guess I'm a little surprised it's so high on your list, con-sidering everything."

Bitterblue was still watching me closely. "I'm defying a number of conventions in marrying Giddon," she said. "So many people are going to tell me I shouldn't, and I'm going to do it anyway. How can I marry whomever I want, then tell the women who kept us alive in the north that they're not allowed to do the same? How can I say that to any of my people? A large contingent of my office has been making time, and will continue to do so as we sort out the details. I'm going to sign something very soon, today or tomor-row. I've sent messages to the other kingdoms too, giving them the news."

"That's really good," I said, impressed despite myself.

"Frankly," she said, "it's a valuable distraction for those nations whose attention is a bit too intensely focused on Monsea right now. Let them gossip about this for a while, instead of zilfium. I also think it might serve as a bridge to communication with my uncle Ror again. Don't you think he might want to do the same in Lienid, once he considers it? Skye could marry!"

Prince Skye is Ror's sixth son and Po's dearest brother, and he's somewhere on a ship in the eastern Torlan seas right now with his boy-friend. More importantly, I was beginning to understand Bitterblue's urgency better. "You're prioritizing it because it suits *you*," I said. "It's one of the cogs in the wheels while you build the world."

Her mouth became a tight little button. "I would do it regardless," she said. "I should've done it long ago. But haven't you noticed by now that everything I do touches every other thing I do? A queen can do nothing in isolation!"

"Yes, all right," I said, turning away.

"Hang on," she said. "Dinner tonight, if you like? But also, this is for you."

As I turned back, she extended a small, sealed note to me. "Please actually read this one," she said, "instead of burning it or eating it or whatever you've been doing to the others. Okay?"

"Why don't you just tell me what it says?"

"Because ciphers are fun?"

"Right," I said. "Sure. I'll read it if you give me more pages to translate."

I had the feeling that she was holding back a sigh, but she handed me five more pages. I headed for the stairs with Hope in my arms.

Turned back again.

"Bitterblue?"

"Yes?"

I was still thinking about Joff. I was trying to make sense of his interest in Hope, and how it might fit with his interest in the members of our party. "Is Kera's imprisonment generally known?"

"Kera?" said Bitterblue, surprised. "What do you mean?"

"Is it known that one of the survivors of the *Monsea* is in your prison?"

"I assume it's known by our fellow survivors," said Bitterblue, "and Goldie of course, and the prisoners near Kera. I have no reason to think it's known beyond that."

"Okay," I said, continuing toward the stairs.

"Kera," said Bitterblue from behind me, repeating the name as if she were trying to wake from a dream. "I'd nearly forgotten Kera. I should confirm that her trial has been scheduled. I promise I'll do that soon."

I left her offices, wishing I hadn't reminded her.

127.

I HAD A NEW, obscure need to know that all the foxes were well.

Hope? I said, carrying her past Bitterblue's fox door. *Are the babies safe and sound in the castle?*

Yes Moth. Yes Cornsilk. Yes Owlet, she said. *Yes Adventure. No Bir.*

No Bir?

Bir out with Linny.

Oh, I said, suddenly wanting both Bir and Linny.

Moth knows where Bir is, said Hope.

Oh! She does? I said, then called out to her. *Moth?*

Hope called out too, *Moth? Moth? Moth?,* getting into the spirit of the thing so boisterously that when Moth finally rounded a corner and stopped in front of us, breathless and quivering, I wasn't surprised by her irritable tone.

WHAT!!! Moth yelled. *WHAT DO YOU WANT!!!*

Bir, said Hope.

BIR ISN'T HERE AND I WAS VISITING THE BEES! she screamed in outrage.

Bees sting, said Hope mildly. *Toxins. Not safe.*

I WISH THEY WOULD STING YOU! she screamed, then seemed a little ashamed of herself. *Not really,* she added as Cornsilk and Owlet rounded the corner behind her. Adventure arrived next, puffing and groaning like an elderly grandpa who's regretting his offer to mind the grandchildren.

Hava! said Owlet. *Moth showed us your mother!*

I was unprepared for what happened next, both Owlet and Cornsilk bombarding me with my own memories of my mother. They were so excited to share with me, there was so much delight in their knowledge of something personal and dear to me that I was overwhelmed by their love for me, in the same moment they gutted my heart. I found myself kneeling on the cold stone floor while they threw their little bodies into my lap, trying to find purchase around Hope, who was still in my arms. I remembered that I used to hold all of them at once, sleep every night with them tucked against me, share them with Linny while we fought to keep believing we'd find a way home. They'd kept me alive. Caring for them had forced me to go on.

Well, hello, I said to them now. *I love you, Owlet. I love you, Cornsilk. I love you, Hope.* I glanced at Moth, who was still standing before us, exuding the contempt of the eye-rolling teenager who can't believe her family is so embarrassing. *I love you, Moth,* I said, which made her soften, and come to us. *You too, Adventure,* I said, noticing that he was watching us primly.

And you too, Blueberry.

128.

M OTH TOLD ME that Bir told her that Linny builds a ship every day, right under a bridge made of mirrors.

That's Winter Bridge, I said, sighing. Wishing Linny had found employment in the west city instead, away from Leck's stupid bridges.

Are you going there? Moth clamored. *Can I come? Can I come?*

I'm not sure where I'm going, I said. *First I'm going back to my rooms.*

They all came with me, but I left them outside in the corridor prancing around the feet of a couple of bored-looking guards while I hid Linta's pages in my compartment in the floor. I don't need them all watching me doing that, then shouting to strangers in the courtyards that I hide things in my floor. I also broke the seal on Bitterblue's note and deciphered the first of about five lines. She wanted me to come to her rooms tomorrow evening at nine for a secret meeting. Fine. Whatever. I crumpled it up and threw it onto the fire, then opened my door to a tidy row of foxes, waiting for me with glimmering eyes.

Winter Bridge? said Moth. *Bir and Linny?*

We'll see, I said. *Maybe not.* But when my feet hit the ground outside the castle, I turned left, toward the bridges, almost with the sense that my direction wasn't under my own control.

They all insisted on coming with me, every one, even Adventure. It's not how I like to move through the city, but at least I was able to keep an eye on all of them while I thought things through. Hope was the only one who consented to be carried, so we weren't a stealthy group. The kits barreled ahead, then circled back, zooming down every side street, screaming hellos to people, startling horses, tripping pedestrians, an entire earth of foxes spinning around me, their sun. I felt as gigantic and conspicuous as the sun. I changed my eyes and face, I tried to detract the attention of passersby, but it was a good thing this wasn't a spying mission.

Winter Bridge is the bridge farthest from the castle. It's the most mesmerizing bridge, because as you look at it, it changes; it's made of mirrors that reflect the sky and clouds. It's disorienting, because you can see things in it that aren't there. If you stand at its base and look at its piers, you can see yourself.

Under the bridge, we found Linny inside the massive skeleton of a ship that was taking form on the dry docks beside the river. I stared up at the ship in absolute amazement. It had a curved spine that stretched from bow to stern, and ribs attached to the spine perpendicularly to make the frame of the hull. It looked so much like a fish skeleton picked clean on someone's plate that I began to laugh. It was beautiful. The ship beside it was also beautiful, old, weathered, lying on her faded green side while workers repaired her barnacled hull. Above, both ships were reflected in the underside of the bridge, showing me two more ships, with angles on the work being done that I couldn't otherwise see. I wonder if the shipbuilders find that useful.

Linny balanced above us on one of the ship's ribs, holding a hammer, perched as I'd seen him so many times in the *Monsea*'s rigging. A few other people were working on other parts of the ribs, mostly men, though I did see one woman. Linny caught sight of me, pushed his hair out of his eyes, and smiled his smile.

Then the fox kits were climbing and scrambling around Linny

and he also began to laugh. Bir was making his way down to me, leaping from rib to keel to scaffold to the ground, screaming my name. *Hava! Moth showed me your mother!*

Yes, I said, kneeling down to receive him. *I love you, Bir.*

A minute later, Linny joined us. He was gloveless, coatless, smiling wide, smelling of sweat and sawdust. A film of grime smudged his skin all along his collarbone, where he'd pulled his collar open. He looked wonderful.

"Come get some food?" he said.

WE BOUGHT FISH breaded and fried with crispy potatoes, and carried our plates to a section of boardwalk along the river far enough from the shipyard that we could hear ourselves think.

We sat with our boots dangling over water and ate with our fingers; it was delicious. We watched ducks and gulls, cormorants, and one gigantic heron who walked around with big feet at the water's edge. I couldn't keep my eyes off the growing ships. I asked Linny to explain everything about the work he was doing. What were the boards he was attaching to the ribs, lengthwise along the hull?

"Ribbands," he said, switching into Lingian.

"Ribbands," I repeated, liking the unfamiliar word on my tongue. "They band the ribs?"

"Oh," he said, with the light of dawning comprehension. "I didn't make that connection. It's hard, learning all these new words in Lingian."

"It makes me think of ahsoken," I said, switching us back into Dellian again.

"It does?" he said. "The ribbands?"

"The different parts that come together to form a ship," I said, then admitted, "Everything makes me think of ahsoken. I know I'm misapplying it. A ribband is far too big to be an ahsok."

"But it's made of ahsoken," he said, "like everything is. Have you figured out the Lingian word for *ahsoken*?"

"No. I need to find someone to ask. What kind of ship will she be?"

"I'm told she's a silver ship," he said, "designed to carry heavy loads up the river from the queen's silver mines."

"Huh," I said, licking my salty fingers. "Where there's silver, there's zilfium. I wonder if she'll also be a zilfium ship."

"Maybe," said Linny. "I don't know."

I went quiet, sinking into my sister's anxieties, watching the bridge reflect the blue of the sky. Trying to figure out how to approach the topic of Joff with Linny. I wanted to talk it through with someone and the someone happened to be Linny, but there were things I wasn't allowed to tell him. Mainly about the formulas.

"There's a man at court acting too curious about Hope and the foxes," I said. "And the survivors of the *Monsea* in general. I've started to wonder if he could be one of the smugglers who hired Kera to smuggle Hope."

"Oh?" said Linny. "Who?"

"He's an Estillan lord named Joff. He's been trying to marry the queen for ages."

"The queen seems to have other ideas," said Linny, grinning.

"Yeah," I said. "So many people try to marry her that it's barely interesting. But with this guy, it *is* interesting because there's something else going on, and I can't quite put a finger on it. I'm sorry," I said, beginning to get frustrated. "There are parts of it I'm not allowed to tell you. But I saw Joff today, and the way he looked at Hope made me anxious. If he is a fox smuggler, I don't like that he's staying at court, and I don't like how freely the foxes run around the castle."

"Have you warned them?"

"No."

"Maybe you just need to warn them," said Linny. "I mean, they can be pretty silly, but I do think they would understand a warning to stay away from some guy."

I watched the kits for a moment as they raced around us, playing a game that seemed to involve leaping on each other. Adventure sat decorously beside Linny, accepting every morsel of food Linny offered him with a light, careful touch of his teeth. Hope rested in my hood. She clawed her way up to my shoulder now and then, begging for morsels of her own.

"I'm not sure Hope would understand it," I said. "But maybe that's all the more reason to warn the others. Okay.

"Hey, everyone," I said, speaking it aloud as I thought it, so that Linny could hear me too. "Foxes! Hello, everyone. I have a special message."

All the kits stopped mid-tussle, staring at me in amazement. *What special message?* Moth demanded.

"There's a man in the castle who's up to something," I said, "but I haven't figured out what. So I need your help."

What should we do, Hava? yelled Cornsilk. *What should we do?*

"I want you to keep away from him if you see him, and if he asks you any questions, don't answer. Okay? And if he approaches you or tries to talk to you, come tell me right away. And keep a special eye out for Hope, because she might forget the plan."

While I was talking, I opened a picture of Joff to them.

I know him! shouted Cornsilk, who was still frozen in fascination, lying on her back with two feet in the air.

"Have you talked to him?"

I've only said hello! said Cornsilk. *Adventure has told us to only say hello to people like him! Anyway, he's boring! I don't think there's anything going on with him!*

I can find out if there's something going on with him! cried Moth.

"Ah," I said, with a sidelong glance at Linny.

"Better to run a more covert operation," said Linny, with a nonchalant tone similar to the one Adventure uses when manipulating Moth into going to see the bees. "Very hush-hush. We should all just watch him and wait for him to make a mistake, and make sure Hope's okay, then tell Hava. That's how the best spies do it."

The best spies do nothing and then tell Hava? asked Moth skeptically.

"Sure. Ask Adventure," said Linny. "He's the confidant of the queen. He knows all about spies."

While the kits clambered around Adventure, who seemed to enjoy being Very Important, Linny and I waited, glancing at each other.

"Did any of them show you what Joff looks like?" I asked him.

"I'll ask Bir," he said quietly. "And why don't I ask Bir to share his image with the other sailors too? We can all be prepared to fend off his questions."

"Would everyone do that?" I said, my heart rising into my throat.

"Of course."

Hope? I said. *Do you understand that you should stay away from Joff?*

My girl, she said, which wasn't comforting. At least the problem is temporary, since when I leave court, Hope will come with me. I can keep her safe.

All right, said Moth. *We'll do it.*

There was a casualness to her tone that made me a trifle suspicious, but I knew that trying to press my point wouldn't help. *Great,* I said. Then, when they returned to their game, I returned to my salty food.

"Bir tells me Moth says you've been hiking out beyond the city," Linny said.

I glanced at him sharply, wary. "Yes," I said, remembering our clambering search for my bird-girl. "What else did he tell you?"

Linny hesitated. "He showed me some scenes," he said. "Between you and your mother."

Right. My mother hiding me in a chest. My mother sculpting while I hid. Not seeming to know me, but numbly telling me she loved me.

"I'm sorry, Hava," said Linny softly. "I don't think Bir or any of the kits realize that—that you're suffering in those memories."

"But you realized it."

"I didn't understand the memories," he said. "But—I did understand the feeling of them. And also that they were private. I haven't had much luck explaining privacy to Bir, when it comes to how the kits all talk among themselves, or how he talks with me."

I swallowed. "I suppose we can hope they'll learn in time."

"Yes. I'm really sorry."

I was silent for a moment, deciding. "I don't mind you seeing my mother."

"Oh," he said. "Thank you."

"She was usually like that," I said. "Trapped inside her own mind."

"I see," he said. "I suppose—" he said, then stopped.

"What is it, Linny?" I said quietly.

"I was thinking it could be useful," he said, "just like it'll be useful with spreading the word about this Joff guy. A way for you to see my own mother if you wanted, or to tell you things while we're apart, or communicate messages to you in an emergency. Of course, that's supposing they would ever communicate what we asked," he added ruefully, watching Moth climb on top of Owlet and sit down, trying to flatten him with her long limbs while Owlet screamed bloody murder.

It was what I'd expected him to say, because I'd had the same thought. How much easier would it be to open myself to Linny, if I could send the thoughts through the filters of other creatures' minds?

But was that what I wanted? A friend I could never touch for real?

"I've eaten from this fish stand before," I said, speaking with what felt like utter randomness. "It was years ago. I didn't pay."

He considered me for a moment. "Why not?"

I took a breath, feeling a little wild suddenly; frightened. "I stole all my food for years after my mother died. I didn't have a caretaker," I said, with a defensive glare I couldn't help. But Linny looked back at me with no judgment in his face. Only quiet; the quiet that always rests in his face.

"No one knew I existed," I said. "When my mother died, the rooms where we lived were assigned to someone else. So I wandered, and hid, and stole my food."

"But, Hava," he said. "Do you mean you didn't have a place to live? When you were *eight*?"

"I found places."

"But, Hava," he said again. "What do you mean, no one knew you existed?"

"My mother taught me to make myself invisible," I said, "my whole life. She couldn't hide that she was pregnant with me, but when I was born, she pretended I'd died. She hid me, and then I developed a Grace that let me hide myself. That's why I snuck in on people's lessons. I never had teachers of my own, because no one knew I existed. She worked closely with the king," I said, trying to answer the confusion that was growing in his face. "She was the king's favorite artist. She knew what he did to people who interested him. To children. Especially Gracelings. She didn't want him to know I existed. And Leck had power over everyone. He could extract whatever information he wanted from anyone, if he knew to try. So she pretended she didn't have a child. It made her sick all the time, fighting to keep her mind clear so she would remember to keep lying to him. That's what you saw in the memories Bir showed you," I said, becoming conscious, finally, of two things: that I was pressing myself against his side, and that I had turned into a sculpture. A sculpture with tears running down my face. His arms were around me, holding me against his body. He was whispering my name. The foxes were huddled against us as well, all of them, watching me. Moth and Hope had climbed right into my lap, and Adventure was resting one soft paw against my leg.

"I'm sorry," I said.

"For what?"

"For changing," I said, "whenever we touch."

"It's all right," he said, with a hint of something like laughter in his voice. "You don't feel like a sculpture."

"We must be making a scene."

"Oh, who cares. Anyway, you don't need to worry, because *I'm* the one making a scene. Everyone'll think I brought my sculpture to the boardwalk so I could sit there hugging it."

I couldn't help myself; I began to shout with laughter. I was a soggy, choking girl with a lapful of foxes, screaming with merriment, looking like a sculpture. What a mess. *I love you, Hava,* Moth was saying over and over in a worried, high-pitched voice. I lifted her to my heart, kissing her, while Linny held me. His arms were like a blanket binding me in place, safe and strong.

I watched a pair of ships moving slowly up the river. Their sails made me think of wings. Slowly, I turned back into myself.

"Ever since we left the north," I said, "I've been having trouble figuring out who I am."

"Mm," he said, still holding me. "But you can make yourself whatever you want, right?"

"On the outside," I said scornfully. "Not on the inside."

"Mm," he said again. I liked the noises he made, especially when he was making them so close to my ear. Was it safe to admit that to myself?

"The inside is harder," he said. "It takes longer to figure out. But you will."

"How do you know?"

"Because there's beautiful stuff in there," he said, which was no kind of answer, because even if it's true, it has no bearing on what I know about myself.

So why does it make me feel like my heart is a bird, riding on a current of air?

129.

During dinner, Prince Raffin and Bann, the Council leaders and chemists, arrived from the Middluns.

They ambled into Bitterblue's sitting room while we were eating, tall men, tired, disheveled from travel. Bann smiled wide when he saw us. Prince Raffin smiled too, but with the sadness that often sits at the back of his eyes. And Bitterblue jumped up and burst into tears.

"Oh dear," said Raffin, rubbing his pale hair so it stood straight up on his head. "Did that invitation say 'Please come,' or did it say 'Don't come'?"

"'Please come,'" said Bann. "I'm sixty percent sure."

"You sillies," said Bitterblue, snorting through her tears. "I'm just so relieved to see you."

"Uh-oh," said Raffin. "That means you expect us to solve your little problem."

Giddon, rising, wrapped his arms around Raffin while Bitterblue hugged Bann. "Is that what you call it?" Giddon said.

"Have you enjoyed giving us ulcers with your antics in the north?" said Raffin, touching Giddon's scar with one finger, ruffling Giddon's unkempt hair. "Go back to your dinner. You look hungry."

"Hello, Hava," said Bann, giving me a tired grin over Bitterblue's head. He was unshaved, his eyes gray oceans above cheeks rough with stubble.

"Hello," I said, hoping they both knew better than to try to hug me.

"It's good to see you, Hava," said Raffin, his gaze touching my face gently, then dropping down to Hope, who was in my lap, peeking her head up at him over the table. "I take it this is one of the famous blue foxes?"

"Yes," I said. "This is Hope. Moth is usually here too, but she's with the others this evening." *Hope, these are Raffin and Bann.*

Hello, Hope said, rather boldly for her, I thought.

"Great skies," said Raffin. "That's an alarming feeling. Hello back, you gorgeous creature with eyes like your human mother."

"Her—" I began, confused, then realized he meant me.

"Stop hogging her," Raffin said to Bann, leaning over to kiss the top of Bitterblue's head.

"Stop hogging *him*," said Bann, relinquishing Bitterblue, then wrapping his arms around Giddon. "Where's Helda?"

"She's organizing something," said Bitterblue, muffled against Raffin's chest. "We gave her a rush job."

"Where's Katsa and Po?"

"Estill."

"Everyone's favorite vacation destination," said Raffin. "All right, show us these formulas."

"Now?" said Bitterblue. "You just arrived!"

"You know you want to show us," said Raffin, then burst into laughter when Bitterblue pulled the roll of papers out of her pocket. "Have you been carrying them around just in case you meet a chemist on the stair?"

"Too many people want them," she said. "I can't relax when they're out of my sight."

"You should give me whatever's left to translate," I said hastily, with a sudden, panicky sense that I was watching something end. Once those papers pass into the hands of Bann and Raffin, they'll never be mine again.

"I suppose I may as well," said Bitterblue, pulling some pages from the back of the stack and holding them out to me. "There are only a few left anyway."

A few left? I counted. The pages in my hand numbered three. Three! How much could Linta tell me in only three pages?

"All right," said Raffin, "let's take a look."

Bitterblue and Giddon cleared the table and let Raffin and Bann sit down, Giddon bringing them paper, pens, more light. "Ah—ah—ah—" Raffin said in protest when Giddon tried to remove the roast, the soup, the sweet potato pie. "The mind needs nourishment. Sit down and let me teach you a thing or two."

"No thanks," said Giddon, slicing himself about a third of the pie, then going to the sofa with his plate. I joined him, torn between going and staying. I wanted to be alone with my new pages, but I also *needed* to know what Raffin and Bann thought about what they were reading. Hope, who inexplicably seemed to have taken a liking to Bann, decided it for me. She climbed into his lap and sat there as he worked, directing her eyes around the room like little beams of light. I'd never seen her climb into anyone's lap before, other than mine or Linny's.

"I see that Hope is an excellent judge of character," said Raffin, peeking under the table at her. "She went straight for the soothing soul."

"Your soul is soothing," said Bann soothingly.

"A little rumpled of late," said Raffin, touching a pen to his lips, leaving a black smudge there.

"How is your father?" said Bitterblue, standing between them, one hand on either man's shoulder. Beside me, Giddon ate his pie with extra deliberation. Raffin's sickly father is King Randa of the Middluns, the king who used to be Giddon's king. Until he disinherited Giddon, took away his lordship, banished him from the kingdom, and burned his estate to the ground, to punish Giddon for his involvement with the Council.

"Not well," said Raffin crisply. "You would think I'd be pleased for him to suffer, but I find such pleasure empty and uncomfortable, not to mention that in his illness, a great deal of responsibility falls to me." He paused to direct a pointed glance at Giddon. "Maybe you can take pleasure in it, Giddon. That would cheer me."

On the sofa, Giddon really looked like he was trying. He even poked his fork at the air, as if experimenting with how it would feel to stab someone with it. "I think it's a waste of energy," he said.

"See that?" said Raffin. "A king with nothing to offer, not even the satisfaction of vindictive feelings. At least now I'm learning how to build a bomb. Sorry," he said, glancing mournfully at Bitterblue. "I've never told a bomb joke before. I think it falls flat."

Now Bitterblue was wrapping her arms around Raffin's shoulders. "I will always be your friend, Raff," she said; and I knew that in that moment, she was the Queen of Monsea, talking to a man who doesn't ever want to be the King of the Middluns, but will someday.

"Thank the skies for that," he said quietly.

"Have you heard Bitterblue is changing the marriage laws in Monsea?" said Giddon. "Monseans are free to marry whomever they wish."

Quite suddenly, Raffin was trying to blink back tears, and not succeeding. "Forgive me," he said, dabbing his wet face with his sleeve. "I was unprepared."

Bann was also looking a bit blank, and stunned. "Bitterblue," he said. "It's going to be so much easier now for Raff to change that law when he's king. Thank you."

Bitterblue hemmed and hawed, embarrassed. She said something about wishing she'd done it sooner, but I managed to catch her eye before she could say anything to shift their gratitude onto me. I glowered her into silence.

The chemists also subsided into silence, each of them falling to work with a focus that seemed to absorb them completely. Every now and then, Raffin blotted a tear that ran down his face.

"How are you, Hava?" asked Giddon beside me, low-voiced.

"Fine." When he didn't respond, I glanced at him more closely. He'd unearthed a sheaf of papers from somewhere and was studying them grimly over his pie.

"What's wrong?" I said.

"Oh," he said, waving an annoyed hand at the papers. "This is a report from Katsa on the number of soldiers in Estill, and who employs them. Of course, no one's calling them 'soldiers.' They're all the 'private guard' of one lord or another. But why every Estillan lord and all his friends and relations should each have a personal need for thousands of private guards is beyond me, unless they intend to set them on each other—which doesn't seem to be their bent—or unite, and attack someone else."

"How many are there?"

"Some twenty thousand."

"And how many soldiers does Monsea have?"

"Upwards of eleven thousand."

"And the Dells?"

"Thirty thousand."

"Sunder?"

"I'm waiting on that report."

"Has Ror gone home in a huff?"

"No, he's still on our side."

"'Our' meaning Monsea, or meaning the Council?"

Giddon shot me a wry smile, then glanced over at Raffin and Bann, seeming to gauge their levels of preoccupation. "It becomes harder and harder to pretend they're not the same thing," he said quietly. "I think it's inevitable that eventually they will be."

He meant the marriage; but I could tell he didn't want to talk about it in Raffin's and Bann's hearing.

"When are you going to inform your own best friends about what's going on with you two?" I said, feeling contrary.

"Soon," he said. "We told Helda yesterday."

"But—"

"Later," he said warningly.

"This seems like one of those moments when you'd normally call me a brat."

"Later, jewel of perfection."

"There's some entertaining stuff here," said Raffin abstractedly, not looking up from the page he was reading. "Bann? Have you noticed?"

"You mean the places where she's working on an atomic theory?"

"Exactly."

I sat up straight.

"What are you two talking about?" said Bitterblue.

"Have you seen the sections that aren't about the formula at all?" said Raffin.

"I can't tell one part from another," said Bitterblue.

"Well," said Raffin, "it's interesting. Though I'm mostly skipping over it for now, because it's not what you're after."

"Atomic theory?" I said from the sofa, trying to sound blasé. "Is that what it's called in Lingian?"

"Yes," said Raffin, glancing up, holding my eyes. "Though I like your translation very much, Hava. 'Theory of indivisible particles' is exactly right. An indivisible particle is an atom."

Atom, I thought to myself, wanting to tell Linny. *Atom. Ahsok. Moth? Adventure? Where are you? Could you tell Bir to tell Linny?* I wished I could tell Linta Massera herself. *Linta? My friends understand your theory!* "Will you—" I started, then stopped, frightened of my own question. "You won't throw those sections out, will you?"

"Certainly not," said Raffin. "They're far more appealing to me than the formula for a bomb. Can anyone tell me who LV is?"

LV, said Hope helpfully from Bann's lap. *LV.*

"LV?" said Bann, shuffling through his own papers. "I haven't encountered an LV."

" 'Ask LV for the quantity here,' " Raffin read aloud. " 'Ask LV for the ratio of zilfium dust to sulfur.' Seems like your chemist had—an assistant? A companion?"

"A companion like me?" said Bann.

"And maybe a fear of her notebooks being stolen?" said Raffin.

LV, said Hope. *Zilfiumdust.*

"We don't know who LV is," said Bitterblue, "though we intend to find out."

"No matter," said Raffin.

Bitterblue's eyebrows shot up. "Is it really no matter?"

"It will slow us down," said Raffin. "We'll have to experiment. But we can learn the quantities and proportions, as long as we know the ingredients and procedures."

"And *do* you recognize the ingredients and procedures?"

Raffin raised inquiring eyebrows at Bann, who nodded. "The procedures are familiar," said Bann, "or at any rate, I think we can reproduce them. A number of these substances are a mystery to me—"

"But if there's a Keepish speaker you trust?" said Raffin to Bitterblue.

"I have a trustworthy Keepish correspondent who'll know how to translate the names of chemical substances," said Bitterblue.

"You don't need to tell him what it's for," said Raffin. "Just give him a list of the words we need translated."

"*She*," said Bitterblue, with a hint of sourness, "will certainly guess what it's for. She's not stupid."

"Forgive me," said Raffin. "*She*, most definitely *she*. I'm abashed."

"I'll decide whom best to trust," said Bitterblue. "It seems that at least at a glance, you think you'll be able to build these things?"

"I'm sorry, Bitterblue," said Raffin. "Of course, we could run into a stumbling block at any point. But these diagrams are fairly straightforward. I believe that eventually, we will."

Behind the two men, Bitterblue seemed to deflate. She looked across at Giddon with eyes that shone with tears.

Putting his papers aside, Giddon raised a hand that said, *Come.* Bitterblue crossed the room to him and tucked herself beside him, accepting one gigantic bite of sweet potato pie before she closed her eyes and turned to lean against his chest. Giddon's arm came around her. In the moment he lowered his head to kiss her hair, Bann glanced up and saw them.

A softness touched Bann's face. Under the table, he tapped a foot to Raffin's leg, then tilted his head to indicate Giddon, who was now gazing blandly back at them both with the queen tucked around him like he was her pillow, one of her arms quite obviously encircling his waist under his shirt.

Raffin's smile was made of wickedness and light.

"Yes?" said Giddon.

"Oh, nothing," said Raffin innocently. "It's just that sometimes I get the feeling that not all hope is lost."

130.

IN MY ROOMS, with Moth snoozing on the sofa, I stayed up well into the night, translating Linta's last three pages.

LV, said Hope, in my lap. *Ratio. Zilfiumdust.*

Yes, Hope, I said, pushing through Linta's notes.

"LV is out again," Linta wrote, "but I'm feeling more hopeful. We had a good day yesterday, brainstorming about why particles separate and combine. 'Is it loneliness?' LV suggested, which made us laugh, but I do like the idea. It must be attraction that brings particles together, and incompatibility that drives them apart. I mean chemically, of course. Regardless, I might put off the weapons work for a few days, until I have a better read on LV.

"Tomorrow I want to focus on change again. My essential question for a long time has naturally been: What are things? In other words, what are things made of? What are WE made of? But of course the question can be asked a different way, by focusing on events, rather than things. Reactions between attracting and repelling particles. Evolutions, functions, degradations. Everything brings us back to change. What IS change? What changes? What CAUSES change?

"If we focus on change, then—"

Her writing ended, abruptly, in the middle of a sentence.

It had ended, I knew, with a distraction that had caused her to leave her table, allowing me to snatch up her notebooks. Then, soon after, an explosion. Me in a cavern in the ground, broken-boned and choking on dust, and Linta dead. A dramatic change: an ending.

It's hard not to feel all the things that will always be missing from that ending.

131.

I SLEPT FITFULLY, WAKING from a dream of an explosion, the world torn apart, my foxes crying in pain.

But Hope and Moth were sleeping together beside me in our big bed. Fuzzy, soft. Safe, whole. When I moved, Moth's eyes popped open.

Good morning! she said.

Her cheer was a bludgeon. "Good morning," I grumbled.

What will we do today? Where will we go?

I thought you always did whatever you liked, Moth.

I do! she cried indignantly. *Today I like being with you!*

Oh, okay then. I like being with you too.

I know that! she said. *Where will we go? Please, let's go somewhere. Otherwise Adventure says he's going to start arranging lessons for us.*

Lessons? Like school?

Owlet asked about prime numbers, Moth said in a tone of utter disgust. *Owlet likes math. And Adventure got this gleam in his eye and started talking about tutors, and I saw my future spreading out before me, and I thought to myself, no thank you.*

Wait, what? I said, truly shocked. *How does Owlet know about prime numbers? Isn't that a bit advanced?*

He doesn't! Moth shouted. *That's why he asked Adventure!*

But how do any of you even know how to count?!

Foxes are smart! she screamed. *I'm not a baby anymore! Can we please go somewhere!*

Let me wake up, all right? Grown humans can't spring out of bed the way young foxes do.

Yeesh! she yelled.

Can you please tell me how Bir is this morning?

You mean how Linny is? she said. *That's what you really want to know, right? You want to know how Linny is, because you* like *him. You want to* kiss *him.*

I couldn't believe this. I pulled the covers back over my head. *I'm not talking to you again until you're ten years old. I want to know if Bir's okay! And Owlet and Cornsilk!*

They're fine! she said. *Want me to ask Bir if Linny likes you too?*

"No!" I shouted, startling Hope awake. She made a little *brrnnnggg* noise as she popped up, blinking.

I think he does like you, said Moth. *We don't need to ask.*

Great, I said. *I would really love to change the subject now.*

Okay, what do you want to talk about?

I lay quietly for a moment, breathing in and out, still a little lost in that horrible dream. I wanted to go somewhere safe, and be left alone. I wanted to go where I could see birds in the sky.

I turned myself into a cloud, wispy and white. It was strange, to pretend to be a cloud in my own bed. I felt trapped where I didn't belong.

Moth, I said. *Can you tell me how Kera is this morning?*

She closed her bright eyes for a moment, considering. *Kera is far away.*

Yes, maybe she's too far. That's all right.

She's not too far for me, she said scornfully. *I just need you to stop interrupting.*

I lay still, not interrupting.

Oops, said Moth.

What, oops? I said. *What happened?*

She could tell I was trying to get into her mind, said Moth. *She yelled at me. She's all closed up now.*

Oh.

Anyway, there's nothing new with her. She's sad, and worried about that little girl.

On impulse, I said, *Can you show me the little girl?*

It was a mistake, because what she actually showed me was all of Kera's longing for the little girl. All her despair, all her wish that she'd never taken the job that had landed her in prison.

Her feelings were overwhelming, and they reminded me too much of my own mother's pain.

I saw the girl too, Sera, auburn-haired and pale, wriggling and laughing in Kera's arms, and then I saw her eyes and was frightened. One was gray like Kera's and the other was the color of her hair. Kera's child is a Graceling.

Suddenly I hoped very hard that Kera wasn't Estillan, or involved in any way with powerful Estillan lords. Gracelings in Estill are not free. Families try to hide them from the government, but if Graceling children are found, the government takes them, and uses them. And the Estillan government is composed of slippery, selfish, rich men like Lord Joff, men who wouldn't care about the welfare of a child.

132.

I WAS MOVING THROUGH the castle's ground floor shortly thereafter, finding a route to the exit that avoided the pink-floored courtyard, when the inexplicable happened.

It started with Cornsilk and Owlet suddenly coming up behind me, galloping like horses—or, no, I suppose it must've started earlier. It must've begun while I was walking along my careful route, with Moth running circles around me and Hope trotting calmly at my heels. I swear Hope was trotting calmly at my heels, then suddenly Cornsilk and Owlet were thundering on little feet behind me, and when they saw me, they started screaming.

Hava! The bad man took Hope-Mother! The bad man took Hope-Mother!

What! I cried, whipping around, galvanized. *How? Where?*

He called out to her and she went to him. He gave her chocolate. Then he picked her up! He carried her away!

Hope! I cried, reaching for her with my mind. *Hope? Where are you?*

He's taking her upstairs!

Where's Moth?

Moth is following them!

I told Moth to stay away from Joff!

She's being sneaky! shouted Cornsilk. *Hava, come with us! Come see!*

I pulled the knife from my boot, ready. When they ran, I followed.

———————

THE KITS LED me straight into the pink-floored courtyard I've been avoiding, then stopped, craning their little faces up to the glass ceiling.

What are you doing? I cried. *Where is she?*

There, said Cornsilk.

Where?

Wait a second, said Cornsilk. *I'm talking to Moth and Moth's talking to Hope-Mother.*

Everyone should be talking to ME! I yelled.

Stop yelling, Hava, said Owlet. *You're not helping.*

Then suddenly, Hope herself walked onto a balcony above us, on the third floor. She stepped forward and peeked down at us through the vines, eyes bright. She looked completely fine.

My girl, she said, seeing me.

HOPE! I cried.

Why upset, my girl?

Hope, are you okay? Did that man take you?

Just visiting, she said. *Stupid man. Small brains. Chocolate.*

Hope, don't eat his chocolate! There might be something bad in it!

Not bad, said Hope. *Just stupid.* Then she turned and trotted back into the room behind the balcony while I cried out, reaching a hand up as if I could stop her.

"Dardya?" said someone nearby.

Spinning, I found myself face-to-face with Jacky. Jacky! Ollie was grinning behind him.

"What's wrong, dardya?" said Jacky.

"Hope," I said, barely articulate. "She's up there," I said, pointing at the balcony.

"Is she safe?"

"No! That man took her!"

"Well, that's not very high up," said Jacky, measuring the distance to the balcony with his eyes. "Want me to go get her?"

"No! I'm on my way."

"You look like you're on your way to run someone through," he said warily, glancing at the knife in my hand.

"I don't have time for this conversation," I said. "That man has Hope."

I think Hope-Mother is fine, said Cornsilk. *Look, there she is again.*

Once more, Hope trotted onto the balcony and peeked down at us, looking just as calm and disinterested as before.

"I'll get her," said Jacky, then walked to the wall straight under the balcony and braced a foot on a marble protrusion that made a kind of high step.

"Don't be ridiculous. What are you going to do, climb the bare wall? Anyway, you'll be seen!" I hissed at him. "Everyone with rooms on the courtyard will know what we're up to! Joff will grab her and run!"

"But *you* wouldn't be seen," said Ollie, with a bright, sideways grin. "Right? Couldn't you blend into the vines?"

"I'd break my neck!"

"You wouldn't," said Jacky.

"Of course I would!"

"Dardya!" he said. "Look closer." Then he began to point to various protruding parts of the courtyard wall. "It's as easy as climbing steps," he said. "And once you get yourself onto that first balcony, no problem."

And now I did see what he meant, because the walls of this courtyard were in fact not bare or flat; they were ornate, made of carved blocks and swirls that created footholds and, more importantly, handholds. Places where I could grab on to something, use my fingers as hooks. I was panicking, and not seeing the ladder right in front of my face.

I didn't waste time thinking. Usually when I make haphazard decisions in the course of my work, I'm alone without observers, but it wasn't to be helped.

"We'll create diversions if anyone seems curious," said Ollie.

I took off my coat, stuck my knife into my belt, and began to climb.

133.

I CAN NOW SAY that it's not as easy to climb a courtyard wall as it might look from the floor below. Not for me, anyway. I'm sure Jacky would've scrambled up in ten seconds.

For one thing, whenever I caught sight of that floor below, pale pink like watery blood, I remembered looking out at this courtyard as a child. Then I imagined seeing myself out there: a woman using her Grace to blend into hanging vines and courtyard wall designs, but plainly person-shaped, if you knew to look for her.

I needed to stop thinking.

Pretending this was the rigging of the *Monsea*, I made my focus small. The next corner of marble to grasp with my fingers. The next edge on which to balance my foot. Then the next, then the next. My muscles were burning. Don't look down.

What's going on with Hope? I asked Owlet and Cornsilk.

She went inside again, said Cornsilk. *Moth says she's fine.*

You look good, Hava! yelled Owlet, then added, *For a human!*

Are there bees? I asked doubtfully.

Not in this courtyard! Just birds!

I could hear the birds chirping. When one of them flitted across my peripheral vision, I tried to tune it out. My hands reached the base, then the balusters, of the first balcony, which were excellent for grabbing. Relief. Once I'd muscled my way a bit higher, the balcony's balustrade made a nice broad surface for standing on too.

I was pushing myself up the next bit of wall when a child of about six with a crown of puffy blond hair came out onto her balcony and caught the flicker of my movement.

She backed up a step, staring at me with her mouth open. Once someone knows I'm there, once they realize I'm a person, it's hard to unsee me.

"Good morning!" said Ollie below, his attempt at a diversion, but the little girl didn't even seem to hear him.

Tell Ollie to be quiet, I snapped at Cornsilk and Owlet. Then I shifted my appearance slightly so that at the top of the woman-shaped vine-marble-wall-vision she was staring at, she could see my face. Especially my red and copper eyes.

"Not a word," I whispered to her fiercely, clinging to the wall. "Not a sound."

Her eyes grew big as plates. She swallowed, then nodded. She glanced once into the room she'd come from, then positioned herself casually in the doorway, motioning me to continue with the smallest gesture of her hand.

And so I did, until my fingers wrapped around a baluster on Hope's balcony.

Hope? I said, my legs shaking, muscles screaming as I pushed my foot against a marble ridge and brought my face level with her balcony floor. *Hope!*

She trotted out again, sending me a chuckle, then a rush of joy, when she saw me suspended on the wall outside her balcony. *My girl!*

Are you okay? I asked.

Fine.

Are you sleepy? I asked, thinking of the chocolate.

Silly question! Not sleepy.

Will you come with me?

On wall? she said, chuckling again.

Yes, on wall.

Yes, she said, then leaped in an arc through the balusters onto my shoulders, as if it were nothing, not a crazy thing to do, not terrifying, no hard marble two levels down.

My hands and legs, my forearms, my breath were all shaking. *Now hide in my shirt,* I said, holding on while she slid inside my shirt. I began to move. While I was clinging to the wall under Joff's balcony, I heard his quick footsteps above. I froze, grabbing my knife out of my belt.

I waited, ready.

His footsteps receded from the balcony.

I returned my knife to my belt, took a breath, and thought of the *Monsea.*

I continued down.

134.

WHAT DID HE want, Hope? I asked as we descended.

Give me chocolate.

Anything else?

Talk.

Did he ask you questions?

Boring questions.

What questions?

Who Hope is. Where Hope is from.

Who you are? He asked who you are and where you're from?

Yes.

What did you say?

My girl's fox. From my girl's rooms.

What did he say to that?

Stupid fox.

I stopped, suddenly wanting to reverse course. *He told you that you're stupid?*

Brainless fox, she said.

The little girl was still guarding her balcony entrance, trying not to stare as I navigated my way down. Down was awful, really—just as exhausting as up, but with less visibility.

"Thanks," I whispered to her breathlessly, then clenched my jaw and tried to find the right way to express myself to Hope.

You're a very smart fox, Hope. Not brainless. You can even do chemistry, remember? He's wrong.

Doesn't matter, said Hope.

It does *matter.*

My girl missed me, she said. *Came to get me.*

As MY FEET hit the courtyard floor, Moth came skidding through a nearby archway.

HIDE UNDER THE BALCONY, she screeched at me—and apparently at Jacky, Ollie, Cornsilk, and Owlet too, because we all squeezed together under the balcony, barely breathing.

Above us, we heard sharp footsteps, and Joff's voice. "Stupid creature," he said. "Where's she gone?"

Another voice responded, high-pitched, accusatory. "Who are you yelling at, mister?"

"You, there," said Joff. "Did you see anyone? A fox? A person?"

"The courtyard is full of people," said the little girl, as if explaining something obvious to someone not very intelligent. "Sometimes foxes too."

"Near my balcony," Joff clarified impatiently.

"I didn't see anyone."

"Stupid vermin. Maybe she can climb," said Joff.

"What are you even talking about?" said the little girl. "You should go to the infirmary and have your head examined."

"You should stop insulting your elders!"

"You should stop yelling at children on balconies!"

I like that girl, said Moth.

Moth, I said, with more strictness than I meant to convey, but it's hard when you're shaking and beginning to realize you've just done something dangerous. And when you're used to working alone, used to having no one to worry about but yourself. *You promised you would stay away from Joff.*

I did stay away! she said. *I followed from behind!*

Did he see you? I asked. *Did he talk to you?*

She hesitated. *Yes.*

What did he say?

He asked me who my mother was.

My heart rose into my throat, my arms coming around the Hope-lump in my shirt. *Did you answer?*

Yes.

With great effort, I stopped myself from reminding her that she'd agreed not to talk to him. I'm pretty sure she felt the force of my disapproval. *What did you say?*

I told him YOU were our mother, said Moth defiantly. *I should've told him you were our jailer. Or our TORTURER. Or—*

Okay, interrupted Cornsilk. *He's gone.*

135.

First I went to Giddon, because Jacky told me Linny was at his job in the east city. If I can't have Linny to guard Hope for me, my second choice is Giddon.

I burst into his rooms with Hope in my arms and an earth of kits swarming around my feet. "Will you watch them?" I said. "All of them?"

"Good morning to you too," Giddon said from his big chair in the window, barely looking up from the papers he was reading. The librarian's ill-tempered cat, Lovejoy, was in his lap. At the invasion of foxes, Lovejoy popped his head up, a low growl beginning in his throat.

Then Moth made a running leap at Giddon's lap and Lovejoy scrambled away, yowling. Victorious, Moth stood on Giddon's thigh, glaring down at the cowed cat, who was four times her size.

"Moth would make an excellent general," said Giddon, still with his eyes on his papers.

"Don't encourage her," I said. "It's not nice to be a bully."

He shifted his gaze to mine. "Okay, what's going on?"

"Would you keep an eye on all of them for a few minutes, but most especially Hope?"

"I can do that," he said, "as long as it's just a few minutes."

"What do you know about Joff?"

"Joff?" he said. "Plenty. He's one of the first Estillans who approached me and the Council about deposing King Thigpen. I've known him for years."

"Anything about fox smuggling?"

Giddon's face brightened. "No. Really? We've been trying to find something to stick to him. You think he's a fox smuggler?"

"I don't know," I said, "but he just took Hope."

"*Took* her?"

"I got her back," I said, "obviously." Then I crossed to Giddon and handed Hope carefully into his arms. "Can we have Joff followed?"

"You're asking the Council for help with that?" he said with some surprise, balancing Hope and his papers together. "Since when do you work with a team?"

"Well, I can't do it myself while also taking care of all the foxes! The kits are terrible at hiding!"

I'm not! yelled Moth. *I'm a good hider! I'm good at secrets too! You think I'm not, but I am! I would never tell that guy anything secret!*

"Hava," said Giddon, "what's going on? What do you mean, Joff took Hope?"

"I'm not sure what's going on, but if Hope isn't safe when I come back in twenty minutes, I'm going to stab someone."

"I can manage twenty minutes. Why is Moth so upset?"

I helped! yelled Moth. *But Hava is mad at me! It's not fair!*

"Moth is suffering from a guilty conscience," I said crisply, "because she knows she did not do what she was asked."

Giddon's eyes were suddenly mild, and maybe a little amused. "A taste of your own medicine?"

I left the room, but not before giving him a look that could freeze seawater.

136.

My errand took even less time than I'd allotted.

"What's this, no presents?" said Kera, surveying me from behind the bars of her cell. "Not even a lemon?"

"Tell me about Lord Joff," I said.

Kera was wearing one of the blankets I'd given her around her shoulders like a cape, deep purple. At my words, she tightened her fists on the blanket. Then her expression closed.

"I know no one by that name," she said.

"I don't believe you," I said. "Did he hire you to kidnap a pregnant fox?"

"He did not," she said flatly, "and I'm not answering any more questions."

"If he didn't, then someone hired you to bring her to him. Right?"

She stared back at me mutely.

"Kera," I said, "why are you protecting the people who hired you?"

No response.

"Lord Joff is a powerful political figure in Estill," I said. "I would certainly understand your devoted silence if you're an Estillan agent."

Kera made a choked sound. Incredulity crossed her face, but she said nothing.

"I know your daughter is a Graceling," I said. "And I know what someone like Joff would do to her if he found out about her. Are you sure you don't want to talk to me?"

Now Kera's eyes blazed with something desperate and broken. But she turned her back to me and swept to her wooden block.

There, she sat down, refusing to say another word.

137.

When I returned to Giddon's rooms, he hadn't moved, but all the foxes were crowded together in the chair with him, pressed against him and one another.

"Moth and I have been having quite a heart-to-heart," he said.

"Oh? To what end?"

"No particular end," he said. "She's very young, you know. I can tell she admires you. I gather she considers you to be something of an adoptive mother."

I don't think he was trying to make me feel guilty or confused. But I was stung by a small, pointed shame. Moth is very young, it's true, and I'm twenty-one years old. I'm supposed to be the grown-up.

I sought Moth out in the tangle in Giddon's lap, immediately perceiving her little face, glaring golden eyes at me.

I spoke carefully. "Moth was quite helpful when Joff took Hope," I said. "And when he asked her questions, she gave smart answers."

"What an admirable fox," said Giddon.

I felt Moth soften a little, which only made me more confused. How am I supposed to find the balance between encouraging her to be brave, keeping her safe, and stopping her from becoming a bully?

Then I saw the indulgent expression Giddon was aiming at her and rolled my eyes.

"You have a lifelong weakness for bossy girls," I said to him under my breath, which caused him to smile so wide, you would've thought I'd paid him the highest compliment.

"You're coming to Bitterblue's rooms tonight, right?" he said. "Nine o'clock?"

"Yes, all right," I said. "Fine."

His smile, joyous in his too-thin face, was doing something to my heart. I was remembering how in Winterkeep, when I set off the explosion that killed Linta Massera and almost killed me, Giddon, who loves Bitterblue, cats, and apparently fox kits, risked his life climbing down a cliff wall to get to me. He lifted that ladder away from my body with all his strength. He picked me up, groaning and exhausted, and carried me to safety. The truth is that I could scream hateful vitriol at Giddon in the morning, then in the afternoon, go running to him for help, and he would drop everything to help me.

Isn't that the kind of person I'd like to be for Moth?

But how does a person become generous like that?

138.

I NEEDED TO MOVE.

So I went out, in the company of Hope, Moth, Owlet, and Cornsilk, of course. I was glad to be able to keep an eye on them, but also, I'm not sure I could've separated them. The kits were still so excited about Joff taking Hope that they needed to be together.

I wanted to go west, not east—toward solitude, toward hills. But the moment we stepped outside, Cornsilk and Owlet screamed *BIR!* and started racing toward the bridges in search of their brother.

For a moment, Moth stood looking after them with her long legs braced, then shot a rather alarming contemplative expression at me. I had a feeling she was considering bolting off in the opposite direction, just to create a dilemma.

Would you like to come with us to visit Bir, Moth? I said, reaching a hand up to Hope, who was perched on my shoulder. *We'd like your company. But I trust you to take care of yourself if you have other plans.*

You go ahead, she said. *I haven't decided.*

Okay, I said, forcing myself to follow Cornsilk and Owlet. A low, gray sky was releasing a mist of rain that made me think of the falls in the Dellian harbor. When Moth began to trail us, sneaking under the porches of buildings and hiding behind trees, I was relieved almost to exhaustion. I got the sense she imagined herself to be extremely clandestine, so I pretended not to notice.

Moth wants to be spy, said Hope.

A spy? Has she told you so?

Yes. Spy like my girl.

I see, I said, my heart filling with a sadness I couldn't have explained. I don't think it's an occupation that's brought me much joy. After all, spying is forced nonexistence. I want Moth to be surrounded by people, and support.

Spy like Hope, she said.

Like Hope? I said. *Are you a spy, Hope?*

Was spy.

Are you remembering something, Hope? I said. *Do you remember spying?*

Sometimes spy. Sometimes lie.

Like Adventure did, when he was a bonded fox in Winterkeep. I think most bonded foxes in Winterkeep do some spying and lying; their Keepish humans don't appreciate how independent they are.

Who would you spy on, Hope?

She shrugged the question off. *Visit father of babies,* she said.

What? You would spy on the father of the babies?

No! Visit! Walk on ground?

Yes. Hope was beginning to chafe at the constant carrying, but I couldn't put her down. I just couldn't, not until I knew Joff's game, or until we were far, far away from him.

Which meant that maybe it was time to start planning my departure. Where should I go first? South, to the zilfium mines? There was probably useful information-gathering for me there. Or maybe somewhere farther afield? Estill? Sunder? Most of the world was ripe for my kind of spying.

When we got to the shipyard under Mirror Bridge, I waved to Linny, but then I walked on, to a place at the next dock near enough to see him and the teeny bodies of the foxes, but far enough to be alone. I sat against a rock in a patch of dirt, watching seagulls fight above the water, stabbing each other over morsels of food. Whenever people were around, I made myself into part of the rock. My nose was full of the stench of rotting fish, but my mind was strangely empty.

There were no ice blocks in the river, dissolving and releasing their parts. Will I ever stop looking for them?

Walk on ground? said Hope again.

I'm sorry, Hope, I said. *Soon.*

Now? she said a few minutes later.

I'm sorry, Hope.

Chocolate? she asked, with a touch of impatience.

I did at least have some chocolate I could share. While the chocolate occupied her, I pushed my mind to make a decision about where we should go. But I kept getting distracted by the sense that all of my questions led to dead ends. What does Joff want? How much does Kera know? What should Bitterblue do about the weapon? How can I keep Hope safe? How can I best raise Moth?

When the drizzle began to thicken into something that reminded me too much of northern cold, I stood again and worked my way back to the bridges. The kits joined me as I passed the shipyard, even Bir; and then, as we entered the castle, all of them began speaking to me at once.

Adventure wants us! they said.

Why?

We don't know! Something important!

I suspected that in fact, Adventure wanted to divert them from something important. *Adventure!* I shouted.

Must you always shout? came his distant, exasperated voice.

Have the kits told you about Joff taking Hope?

Giddon told me. You might have told me, you know.

You understand that you must keep them safe? I said, ignoring this.
What else do I do, all day long?

All right then, I said, vaguely conscious that I wasn't actually granting anyone permission. The kits were already racing away from me, without a backward glance.

Suppressing a sigh, I moved toward my rooms, Hope in my arms. We entered a narrow corridor that skirted the library.

Visit Bann? Hope said.

"What?" I said out loud, coming to a stop.

Hope visit Bann, she said, with a steel in her manner so unusual that I swallowed my objections, and also shielded my small jealousies from her.

I guess I can't expect Hope to remain attached to my body every moment until either Joff or I leaves town.

OUTSIDE BANN AND Raffin's rooms, I knocked on their door.

It was Bann who answered, then ushered us into a chamber where Prince Raffin sat cross-legged in the middle of the floor, scribbling on a page in his lap. His fingers were smeared with ink and the rug around him was covered with papers. I saw my own translations spread across a nearby table.

"Oh," I said, holding on to Hope with both arms, for comfort. "I see. How's it going?"

"Hava," said Raffin, his eyes lighting up at the sight of me. "You're in my top three favorite people."

"I am?"

"You did a wonderful thing when you rescued this work from that explosion. Bann and I think that some of these experiments in pursuit of an atomic theory might be entirely unique."

"Really?" I said. "What do you mean, unique?"

"It means that these papers are an important contribution to the field!" said Raffin. "And they were almost lost! But you rescued them!"

"Oh," I said again, remembering last night's translations. Linta's abrupt end. "But I killed Linta Massera before she could finish her theory. There's not much more in the pages you haven't seen."

Behind me, Bann made a humphing noise as he closed the door. "There's no such thing as finishing atomic theory, Hava," he said. "There's no finish line. Scientific theories constantly evolve."

"That's right," said Raffin. "They evolve and change and take on new forms—just like atoms do! The drive behind atomic theory is the wish to understand *everything*, Hava. Not just *what* things are made of, but *how*, and *why*. Why do atoms shift and change? How does that change create the stuff of the world? What causes *life*? Linta Massera was never going to finish, and neither will we. Every new thing we learn shows us a hundred new things we don't know. Every answer we find simply shifts us into a new question." He threw his hands into the air. "It's all about movement!"

"Yes," said Bann, who was standing beside me and Hope, watching Raffin's rising enthusiasm with obvious fondness. "Raff's right, Hava."

"Every scientist will always be positioned in the middle of the changing questions," said Raffin. "Never at the end. We're the ones changing the questions, of course, you see? It's our job to move them along."

I thought of a glacier then, crawling across land. I thought of it finally reaching the sea, then breaking into parts. Changing, becoming icebergs, moving away from shore. Floating, cracking. Dissolving into rocks and bones and seawater, shifting into yet other forms.

When I stole those notes, was I helping to move Linta's ideas along?

"Would you ever be willing to make a copy of just the atomic theory parts of her work?" I asked. "For me? Or let me make myself a copy?"

"Oh, absolutely," said Raffin. "I think it should be published as a pamphlet!"

"Though we'll have to figure out how to explain where we found it," said Bann, who was still smiling at Raffin's happiness. "We can't say it was hiding in plain sight amidst a formula for a zilfium weapon."

"Well, we could say it's what I found," I said. "Everyone seems to suspect I didn't destroy what I found in Linta's workshops. Maybe *this* is what I found."

"Indeed," said Bann. "It won't stop anyone bent on finding the formulas, but it might give them something to trip over."

Help Bann, said Hope, who was blinking gold eyes at the large, gentle man beside us. *Chemistry.*

"Right," I said, remembering. "Hope needs a guard."

"Yes," said Bann. "Giddon told us something of what happened."

"She wants to be with you," I said anxiously, "but she doesn't understand her danger. You really need to watch her every moment. If she wants to come back to me, you need to escort her."

"We understand," said Bann. "We won't let Joff anywhere near her, and we won't send her off on her own. Look, Hava." He gestured at their table and floor, at all the papers, at Raffin, who was once more absorbed in something in his lap. "We're a pretty contained unit, and there are guards in the corridor."

"All right," I said. "You'll let me know if anything happens?"

"Of course."

I ATE DINNER by myself in my rooms, worried about the foxes.

Then I brought a piece of cake to my bed and lay there sucking on my fork, thinking about Hope and Bann. Wryly noting that glaciers break off and icebergs dissolve, but my jealousy never seems to change form.

I wondered, would I ever be able to feel that Linta's better work was worth the consequences of her terrible work?

No. I wouldn't. But could I be happy for her better work anyway? Could I help it move along in the world?

Adventure! I shouted. *Is everyone okay?*

For the umpteenth time, don't shout at me! he responded crossly a moment later. *Everyone's fine!*

Even Moth?

Even Moth! We're visiting the bees and talking about mathematics! Joff isn't even in the castle right now!

Well. That was all right then, and maybe the mathematics would bring Moth back to me sooner. And it was warm in my bed, and my tummy was full. My plate on my chest, I began to doze off—then jumped up with a squeal, smearing chocolate icing across the front of my shirt.

You're coming to Bitterblue's rooms tonight, right? Giddon had said.

It was ten minutes after nine o'clock. I was late.

139.

WHEN I BURST into Bitterblue's rooms, Helda, who was standing inside the doors with her arms crossed like a round, haughty guard, took one look at my frosting-covered shirt and said, "Oh, no. That won't do."

"Won't do what?" I said as she dragged me—she dragged me!—down the hall to Bitterblue's bedroom, then flailed around in Bitterblue's gigantic wardrobe, producing a fuchsia scarf and commanding me to put it on.

"I'm not wearing that," I said.

"Oh, yes you are," she said darkly.

"Oh, no I'm not," I said. "It's *pink*. Anyway, what's your problem?"

With a noise of disgust, she threw herself into the wardrobe again and emerged with a scarf of a brownish, coppery hue. "Here," she said. "This one will be pretty with your eyes. I never knew you to be so vain, Hava!"

"I'm not vain!" I said, then submitted while she practically strangled me with the scarf. I've seen Helda make up her mind about something with Bitterblue before, and I've seen Bitterblue try to resist. I do *not* like being ordered around, but it wasn't worth the drama.

Slightly seething, I followed Helda back to the sitting room.

There, I found a bewildering little group: Froggatt and Coran, standing quietly with their hands folded, and Barra sitting in an armchair beside them. The queen's advisers, for a secret meeting? I'd been expecting some Council thing. Raffin and Bann, with Hope, of course. Giddon. Certainly none of the queen's people. Was this a meeting about official Monsean business? Why at this hour, then, and why here?

Anyway, it was nice to see Coran. His work tends to keep him in the infirmary, where I never go. He looked well, more relaxed. Less weighed down by the responsibility of keeping everyone alive.

"Hava," said Barra, with a slow, gentle smile. "How lovely to see you."

"You too," I said in confusion.

"And for such a lovely reason," said Froggatt.

"Is it?" I said, squinting closer at all three of them, wondering if it was possible they were wearing nicer suits than usual. Coran especially struck a sharp figure, all in black, with gleaming gold buttons. "What's going on?"

Barra only smiled again, then indicated the tall windows across the room, where Bitterblue and Giddon stood together with their backs to us, chatting, looking out at the rain. Bitterblue was wearing a dress the color of the inside of a watermelon, slender and elegant and perfectly fitted, as none of her gowns are since we've returned from the north. Giddon had finally gotten a haircut. He wore a dark brown suit I'd never seen before.

All of this was a little peculiar, but nothing rivaled the strangeness of the fact that Bitterblue was wearing the crown.

They turned to face us.

"Oh, good," said Bitterblue, balancing that golden monstrosity atop her head. "Hava's here."

"I'm super confused," I said. "Why are you wearing that ugly thing?"

Bitterblue laughed, throwing her head back enough that the crown began to slide off. "I promise, I'm only wearing it because I have to," she said, catching it, righting it again.

"*Why?*" I said.

"Hava!" said Helda. "Kindly behave as if this is a solemn occasion!"

"Oh, no," said Bitterblue. "Please don't." Then she glided to Helda, stood on tiptoe, grabbed the crown again so it wouldn't fall, and kissed Helda's cheek. Tears were streaming down Helda's face. I realized that Giddon was crying too. Then *Froggatt* began to cry!

"I wonder if we should begin?" said Bitterblue. "I don't know how long the others will be. They had a family dinner—ah!" she cried as the outer doors opened and Annet and Navi slipped inside.

"I'm so sorry, Lady Queen," said Annet. "My mother didn't want us to leave!"

"No apologies necessary. Please come in. Coran?" said Bitterblue.

And I don't know why I was being so obtuse, other than maybe because it diverged so completely from my expectations; and, oh, maybe also because they hadn't *told* me? But it wasn't until Coran began the actual ceremony that I understood that Bitterblue and Giddon were getting married.

140.

IT WAS ONLY my second wedding, the first being Riz and Alzar's, on the *Monsea*. And I wasn't really invited to that one so much as I just happened to be there when it occurred. In all my secret intrusions into other people's lives, somehow I've never encountered a wedding.

Even so, I knew this wasn't like any other wedding I'd ever attend. Because this was Giddon and Bitterblue. My two people. Right? My friend, and my sister.

It was a lot to take in.

Also, I didn't understand what it meant that they were doing this now, in this way. It wasn't going to make sense tomorrow, when the news spread that the Queen of Monsea had married, without announcement or ceremony, a disinherited Middluns ex-lord and Council leader. They'd both seemed to care about the strategy of the thing; well, I couldn't see any strategy here. Also, I felt ambushed. Fifteen minutes ago, I'd been eating cake on my bed.

The ceremony was brief, straightforward. Coran directed Bitterblue and Giddon to speak promises and intentions to each other. When Bitterblue spoke her promises to Giddon, he was crying so much that he had to stop and blow his nose. When Giddon spoke his promises to Bitterblue, he became calm and intent, his voice steady, and Bitterblue went pale and big-eyed, as if she was watching something extraordinary. The entire time, the crown kept sliding off her head, because she's so tiny and he's so tall that she had to crane her neck up to look at him, but the two of them held it on to her head together while Froggatt and Barra giggled—they giggled!—and it was like Bitterblue and Giddon hardly noticed; they didn't care. They were so happy.

I thought about their parts, and how they balance. She's a queen and the richest woman in the world, and he has little to call his own. She is tiny and he's big. She gets seasick and height sick and he's always hearty and well, strong, capable. She's young and he's nine years older. She's sharp and he's warm. She can command armies and sentence people to death, and he's only a well-connected man, with friends who have secret, illegal power, but everything sneaky and hidden, while she reigns from the throne with everyone hearing. She's a genius. And she's been hurt, all her life, badly, and is recovering. He's been hurt too, but it's not the same. His hurt is the size of a man. Her hurt is the size of a kingdom.

He will take care of her, I thought to myself, swallowing my own sudden tears. *She's going to be safe.*

141.

"Do you *EVER* read my notes all the way through, Hava?" Bitterblue asked me afterward, with no rancor. She was sitting beside me on the sofa while the others chatted nearby, and she was far too happy for rancor.

"Not that I can recall."

She laughed, then ate a piece of the beautiful chocolate cake Helda had procured. Everything everyone said was making Bitterblue laugh, then eat cake. The crown was back on its cushion. "I didn't know that," she said. "I'll remember for next time."

"Will you be springing many weddings on me?"

Another laugh. "I signed the new marriage law today," she said. "That's why we waited until today to get married. I'm not sure I could've asked Annet and Navi to come and be happy for us otherwise."

"Oh, well, that explains everything," I said. "I have no more questions."

"Oh, Hava," she said. "We'll still release an official announcement of our engagement. We'll wait for the opportune moment; we'll make it political. And we'll still plan an elaborate wedding. I'll put the stupid crown on again for everyone to see. Maybe with a chin strap this time?"

"That would look absurd," I said.

"And I'll wear a dress with a train as long as the great hall and someone will paint a portrait, and everyone will travel from everywhere to be there. And Giddon will deal with the intense nosiness and speculation of everyone in the Seven Nations, probably forever.

"But in the meantime," she said, "we'll be secretly married, and this little group of people will know."

"But *why?*"

"Because we want to be married," she said. "For us. Not as a part of some carefully timed strategy to ally my kingdom and the Council."

I couldn't make sense of this. "For romance?"

She smiled a little smile that made me feel childish, left out. "I suppose so, yes. Are you angry we told you in a ciphered letter? I thought you would read it, Hava. I thought it would be fun. And I know you've had—well—mixed feelings about me and Giddon. I didn't mean to trick you into coming to our wedding."

I did feel a little tricked. She was right. But I could acknowledge that it wasn't unreasonable for her to have assumed I would read the whole note, especially since I'd told her I would.

As far as the other thing went—well. Maybe it was time to let that go.

"I think it's good that you're together," I said. "I think it's how it should be. It's inevitable. I just didn't like feeling left out."

She reached into a pocket in her watermelon-colored gown then, and pulled out a small ring I'd never seen before. It was gold, in the Lienid style, simple, with a few evenly spaced colored stones. The Lienid wear gold rings that represent all the most important people in their lives. Bitterblue's own fingers are crowded with rings, for her mother, her aunt and uncle, her cousins. In fact, I'd noticed that Bitterblue and Giddon's wedding ceremony *hadn't* included an exchange of rings, and been surprised; then guessed that a gold ring on Giddon's hand would raise suspicions they weren't ready for.

I assumed this was the ring she meant to wear for Giddon. But then she handed it to me.

"I know you're not Lienid," she said quietly. "You don't have to wear it. But you're my sister, and I want you to know I love you."

Punctured, I stared at the little gold circle in my palm. Turning it, I saw that the stones numbered four: one gray stone; one copper stone; another gray stone; then a scarlet stone. Like our eyes.

"You got me a ring for your wedding?" I said.

"I got you a ring because I love you as much as I love anyone," she said. "I wear the same ring now too. Is that okay with you?"

I saw it then, on the littlest finger of her left hand. My vision blurred with tears. "Yes," I said. "Thank you."

"Are you okay, Hava?" said Giddon, lowering himself beside Bitterblue, sliding his arm around her, but his eyes, full of concern, focused on me.

"I'm fine," I said, blinking. "So, what are you, a prince now?"

"That's right," he said, grinning. "Finally something to lord over Po."

"Po's a prince too."

"He's the seventh son of a king," said Giddon. "I'm a much more important prince."

"Good to see you're handling it like a grown-up."

Giddon's smile was incandescent. "No cake?"

"No cake," I said, wanting, suddenly, to go back to my rooms, to get Hope and Moth and lie down with them and think things through. By myself, where it hurt less. "I take it Adventure's distracting the kits for you?"

"Yes," said Bitterblue. "We can't quite count on them to keep our wedding a secret. He volunteered."

"Do Barra and Froggatt know to be careful to guard their minds against Owlet and Cornsilk?"

"Yes. Everyone knows."

"And when will you tell Raffin and Bann?"

Bitterblue and Giddon shared a rueful glance. "We haven't decided," Giddon said.

This surprised me. "Why not?"

"Well, we didn't invite them," Giddon said. "And we did this while Katsa and Po were away. It's hurtful."

Now I was incredulous. "Then why did you do it?"

They held each other's eyes again, longer this time. When Giddon reached out to tuck a strand of hair behind Bitterblue's ear, I felt like I was spying on something not mine.

"It's hard to explain," Bitterblue said. "I still feel the north every morning in my bones, Hava. I look at you and Giddon and I *feel* why you're so thin. I watch Barra getting up and down from his chair, so cheerful, but I see the pain in his face when he doesn't know I'm looking. I see Froggatt's sheer amazement, that he gets to be with his baby. Do you know I cried this evening when Giddon came to me with his hair cut, because now his northern hair is gone?"

"Oh," I said, understanding this viscerally. "I see."

"It's like we're not quite back yet," Bitterblue said. "Not completely."

"As much as we love our friends," Giddon said, "we needed it to be this small group."

"It's the other sailors who feel missing to us," Bitterblue said, "and Ranin, and the foxes. We couldn't invite them, we had to draw a line, because we have too much of a need for secrecy. But can you imagine how any of this would sound to our dearest friends? It's not normal. I'm not sure they'd understand. And honestly, it feels so private, I don't really want to explain it."

I glanced at Bitterblue's mantel then, knowing what I was looking for. Unsurprised when I found it. Not just one but four of Grella's journals stood in a row, propped between a clock and a small globe.

"Yes," I said. "I understand. I feel it too, all the time."

"And do you forgive us for not telling you about our relationship sooner, Hava?" said Bitterblue. "Are you still angry about that?"

I'm not very good at forgiveness. Or gratitude either, or apology. Even Kera has mocked me for it: *Do you express your regrets easily, Hava?* I'm not good at the things humans do to stay attached to each other. I don't want that attachment. Or anyway, that's what I tell myself.

I think it makes me mean.

"You were right," I said.

Bitterblue looked a little puzzled. "For not telling you?"

I breathed a small, unhappy laugh. "No. I mean you were right the other day, and also every other time, when you've told me I'm angry but I turn it on the wrong people. I should be turning it on myself."

"Wait, what?" cried Bitterblue. "Hava, no! That is categorically not what I've *ever* meant!"

"Are you ill, Hava?" said Giddon, in such a voice of anxious wonder that I laughed again. But this time it was different; it cracked my heart open, because I think I really was finally starting to understand.

"You're right," I said. "I'm sorry. I didn't mean that. Is it rude if I leave now? What's the protocol for secret weddings?"

"It wouldn't be rude," said Giddon, "but now we're worried about you."

"Don't worry," I said. "I misspoke. Truly," I said, looking into both of their apprehensive faces. "I misspoke. Congratulations," I said. "I'm really, really happy for you both."

IN THE CORRIDOR, my heart was floating on a wave of grief. A lifetime of anger and grief, a grief so inundating that I needed a moment in a dark corner, to catch my breath.

I was still holding Bitterblue's ring, tight in my palm. I reached into my pocket and tucked it inside the scarf with my figurines, careful not to look at them.

I called out to Hope. *Hope? Are you all right?*

With Bann, she responded drowsily, making me wonder if she was intending not to sleep with me tonight, for the first time ever.

Moth? I called. *Are you okay?*

We're visiting the kitchens! she said, then disappeared from my reach.

I stood in my corner for another minute, thinking about how I haven't once slept alone since the *Monsea* went down. I've always had another body, no matter how small, another soul pressed against mine, keeping me anchored to the earth.

I turned and made my way to the guest apartments.

142.

IT WAS HALF a minute before Linny answered my knock. I might've gone away, but I knew he was in there, because Bir was in there and told me so.

Finally Linny opened the door, his clothes hastily thrown on, his shirt half-open. He blinked at the light. "Hava?"

"You were asleep," I said. "I'm sorry. Go back to bed, I came too late."

"No you didn't," he said, opening the door wider. "Are you okay? Come in."

His fire was roaring and he'd hung his wet clothes on chairs to dry.

"Were you soaked through all day?" I said. "Are you all right?"

"I'm fine."

"Are you sure? You didn't catch a chill?"

"I'm a sailor, Hava," he said, grinning. "I have a high tolerance for wet and cold."

"Still," I said. "You've been through a lot."

Like all the guest apartments, Linny's was composed of one big chamber that served as sitting, dining, and bedroom, with an attached bathing room. I stood in the middle of the rug, rubbing my forehead. Linny's bed was high, the sheets rumpled. While he moved around the room lighting lamps, I isolated the small form of Bir, copper eyes glowing at me from the blankets.

"You were both asleep," I said.

"No, Bir arrived just a minute ago. I take it he was with Adventure and the others."

I carefully guarded my mind against Bir's intrusion, though I don't think he was trying to intrude. *How are your siblings, Bir?*

Fine, he said. *Moth is bossy.*

Is she? I said, trying not to snort.

"Did something happen, Hava?" asked Linny, climbing onto the bed beside Bir. "You seem kind of upset."

"Oh," I said, wanting to lie down so badly that it was almost a form of desperation. I tucked myself into the edge of his small sofa instead, feeling far away from him, and on a different plane. "Yes. Things keep happening."

"Bir told me about Joff and Hope."

"Yes," I said. "I'm sorry, do you mind if we speak Lingian? Or at least if I do? And do you mind if I stretch out on this sofa?"

"We could trade. You can have the bed," he said in Lingian as I swung myself sideways and levered my ankles onto the end of the sofa, which wasn't really long enough for reclining.

"This is fine," I said, switching, with the greatest relief, to my own tongue.

"I'm going to lie down too."

"Okay," I said, considering Linny's ceiling, which was dark with a scattering of silver glitter. "Did you see the aurora borealis while we were in the north?"

"Yes."

We were quiet for a while, just looking at the ceiling.

"Do you miss it?" I asked.

He didn't answer for such a long time that I might've wondered if he'd dozed off, if I hadn't heard the soft scraping of his arm against the sheets as he petted Bir.

"I need to say this part in Dellian," he said. "I can't get it right in Lingian."

"Okay."

"I feel a deep sadness," he said, switching languages, "except there's a sweetness to it. It's almost like a yearning. I don't want to be there or ever feel anything like that again, ever. I don't want to be hungry, frostbitten, or scared. I want to be here right now, having this life. But that experience is a part of me now, and it would hurt if someone tried to take it away. I would tear apart."

"Yes," I said. "I feel all of that too. Except—except the part about wanting to be here."

Again he was quiet, for a long time. "I've worried about that," he finally said.

I propped myself on one elbow, wanting to see him. I watched him watch the ceiling. "About what?"

"I've worried that when you figure out all the things about yourself that you've been trying to figure out," he said, "you'll go away."

I don't know why this made me breathless with surprise. "How did you know to worry about that?"

"Well, bad things happened to you here," he said. "I don't know the details, but maybe it's like the north—it's part of you, but it hurts you."

When I didn't respond, he turned onto his side too, facing me. "I had to leave the place where I got hurt," he said.

"Oh," I said, understanding him. And then beginning to realize that I wasn't sure what it really means—to leave. Leave what?

"Maybe I don't want to be the queen's spy anymore," I said.

His eyebrows rose. The dim light of the lamps was making his skin soft, his mouth soft and sleepy, his clothing and blankets rumpled. It didn't seem like the right moment to be noticing that he was adorable.

"Is there something you'd like to do instead?" he said.

I wanted to lie down on his bed while he lay down next to me, but that's not a profession.

"No," I said. "I don't know."

"Well," he said. "You don't have to know what you want in order to know what you don't want."

"I'm afraid I don't know what I don't want either, not really," I said, sighing, beginning to be exhausted with my own not knowing. None of my questions ever have answers that create new questions; nothing is moving along here.

Linny smiled. Then he started chuckling, with no maliciousness, just humor, and maybe fondness too. He lay back, pulling Bir onto his stomach. While he laughed, Bir bounced around, blinking his copper eyes crossly.

"Hava," Linny said, "you're my favorite."

"Because my problems are so amusing?" I said dryly.

"No," he said, "because you're wonderful. I can't explain it."

"Could I come lie next to you?" I said, barely believing my own words. Then needing to switch us back into Lingian to ensure perfect clarity: "I mean, not in a sex way, just in a companionable way."

He was looking at me seriously now, propped up on his elbow. His amber eyes caught on mine with a softness that made me lean toward him, as if he'd already answered. "Of course," he said. "Climb aboard."

Then he shifted over with Bir, not too far, just far enough to give me space of my own. When I stretched out beside him, the blankets were warm from his body heat.

"Thanks," I said, resuming my perusal of the ceiling.

"Sure."

"How's your ship going?"

"Good," he said. "We finished the last of the ribbands and now we're filling in the rest of the ribs. When you see it next, it'll look a little more seaworthy."

"You're building something," I said.

"Yes."

"Does that mean you'll stay for a while?"

He was quiet again. "Hava," he said, "that partly depends on whether *you* stay for a while."

He said it so matter-of-factly that I wasn't overwhelmed. I lay still, feeling his words. Trying to find the places where they touched my own questions. Maybe bumped them along a little?

"I'm sorry, Hava," he said, his voice blurry with sleep. "I'm really tired."

"I should go," I said, not wanting to go. "I should let you sleep."

"You should stay and sleep right there," he said. "There's plenty of room."

I WOKE FROM a nightmare, gasping, thrashing, confused about where I was.

Then I saw Linny across the room, illuminated in the light of the corridor as he cracked the door open; and then Hope was in my arms. Moth too. Moth landed in the space at my neck and I was still breathing hard, half sobbing.

"Did they startle you, Hava?" came Linny's sleepy voice as he returned to the bed, climbing back in. "They woke me up. They wanted in. Someone called Bann was with them?"

"I—" I couldn't form words.

"Hava?" said Linny. "Are you all right?"

"Nightmare," I said.

"Oh," he said in a different tone, understanding. He shifted

toward me; his arm came around me, and the foxes pressed themselves against us both. He pulled me so close that we fit front to back
like spoons and I remembered sleeping in the north, always against
someone else's warm, safe body.

"Tell me your nightmare," he said, and I wanted to tell him. I
wanted to tell him so badly, but it contained too many secrets, and he
wasn't even entirely awake, not really. His words were slurred behind
me, his arm heavy.

"It was about my father," I whispered.

"Mmm?"

"I'll tell you another time."

"No," he said, seeming to make an effort to wake up. "I'm listening."

Then, while I was trying to figure out how to tell him my nightmare without revealing my entire life, I felt something harden against
my bottom, then grow bigger and harder. While I was trying to
switch to figuring out what to say about *that*, Linny came awake,
noticed it too, uttered a Dellian swear, and flipped onto his stomach.

"Hava," he said. "I'm sorry."

"It's okay," I said. "I know you're half-asleep."

"But I'm really sorry," he said, with something in his voice that
startled me, and turned me around to face him. He sounded like he
was almost crying.

"Linny!" I said, my hand reaching to his hair, his forehead. His
cheeks were wet. "Linny, are you crying? You didn't hurt me. Why
are you so upset?"

"I don't want you to think I'm excited by your pain," he said. "I'm
not. It's because of *you*, because of liking *you*."

There is a lord in the western Dells I'm going to find someday,
and tie up. And undress, and burn with a poker, over and over again.

"I understand," I said. "Shh, Linny. It's okay."

"But did I frighten you?"

"No. You didn't! Linny, my body does things too when we touch. I turn into things, or I get confused about things—"

"But you don't push your wants on to me!"

"I'm not sure that's true," I said. "And anyway, I didn't feel like you were pushing."

He was watching me now as my hand stroked his hair and face, his shoulder and back. His eyes were dark pools, intent with listening. And I noticed that I was still me. Not a sculpture or a tree, me, as real as the curve of his cheekbone under my thumb, as real as the hardness he'd pressed against me. And I guess maybe it was strange that it hadn't bothered me. Wasn't that strange? Mightn't I have expected something like that to alarm me, or make me angry? But it hadn't. This is Linny. I know he has a penis, I've seen it before when he's washed in the sea, on the *Monsea*. I know how penises work, or don't work; I've seen plenty of that too. I know the difference between someone pushy and someone half-asleep who takes it away as soon as he realizes what he's doing, as I'd known Linny, in his gentleness, would do.

Anyway, I hadn't minded the feeling of it.

"Wanting is confusing for me," I said. "I don't think it happens to me like it does to other people. I've watched people do sexual things. I've seen the way it takes them. And I have an imagination, I have yearnings sometimes too. But it's like yearning to be a bird. It's like yearning for something that exists only on the moon."

He turned onto his side again slightly, so he could face me. Then he reached a hand out and brushed my hair out of my face, just exactly how Giddon had done to Bitterblue earlier.

"I understand that," he said.

"You do?"

"Yes."

It meant a lot that he understood. And still, I wasn't sure that I myself understood it. I grasped for a way to get closer to it so that I could explain better. "I feel like with a lot of things in my life, every step I take is slow," I said. "Like, glacially slow. I do a thing. Then I can't do the next thing until I understand the thing I just did. Sometimes that takes me a long time. And I never know where the things will take me next."

"You're very articulate about how confused you are," he said, which made me laugh.

"If so, that's new."

"You don't have to change," he said.

"But I want to be less confused!"

"Hava," he said. "I didn't upset you?"

"No. You didn't."

"I'm ready for your nightmare if you still want to tell me."

I was quiet again, lowering myself down onto my back. Trying to find a glitter of stars on the ceiling, a sparkle caught in the glow of the real stars outside the window. But the ceiling was dark.

I wanted to tell him my nightmare. I wanted Linny to understand the reason I'm mean sometimes, or ungenerous, or distant or cold. I wanted him to understand that it isn't because he isn't wonderful. I needed him to know he's wonderful.

"Are the foxes asleep?" I asked.

Linny located them, snoozing gently in a tangle on his far side. Bir's snore was a faint whistle. "Asleep," he said.

I took a long breath. "What if I told you a secret you couldn't tell anyone, ever, for the rest of your life?"

Linny was quiet too. Then he reached out and took my hand. "A secret of the queen's?"

"No. This one's mine."

"I can keep your secret, Hava."

What does it mean that I believed him?

Holding his hand very tight, I said the words that scare me more than anything. "King Leck was my father. The queen is my half sister. Hardly anyone knows, and I need it to stay that way, because I don't want to be part of the royal court. I don't want anything to do with the kind of work my sister has to do and I can't bear anyone speculating about my place in the succession."

"Oh," said Linny on a breath of surprise. Holding my hand to his chest. "That's a big secret, Hava."

"Will you tell it?"

"I'll never tell anyone."

I wanted some light then, to see his face clearly, but there was no light. Turning onto my side, I touched his hairline, his cheek, trying to absorb his sincerity. I touched his mouth.

"There's more," I said.

"Yes," he whispered.

"My mother hid me from him so he wouldn't know I lived. And then one day he burst in on us and saw me. After that, he knew, and soon after, he killed her. He killed her because of me, to punish her. I saw it, I was there. He broke her neck. Sometimes I see it in my dreams."

At my faltering breath, Linny had pulled me against his chest. I spoke those words, words I've never spoken aloud to anyone before, with his heart thumping steady against my face. I closed my eyes and gave myself to that rhythm, I let him stroke my hair, my back. My only job was to breathe, my breaths a melody fitting into the percussion of his body.

"I want you to know why I'm angry," I said. "I want you to know why I get mean. The anger inside me is too big. If I look at it too close, I feel too much grief to survive."

"Oh, Hava," he said, and I could hear that he was crying. He was crying for me.

"I've never told anyone I saw it happen."

"I'll never tell anyone," he said.

I guess I was exhausted after that, because I sank into a profound sleep.

143.

IN THE MORNING, I woke to birdsong, and a pale sky still clinging to one western star.

The foxes slept between me and Linny. His back was to me, shoulders rising and falling with even breaths. Linny, who knows my secrets. I wanted to touch him, but I didn't want to wake him. I kept my hands to myself.

Very close to my face, Hope opened her eyes. Their brightness was beautiful, like burnished suns. She gazed straight at me.

Seven, she said.

Seven?

Seven. Point three.

What? I said. *Have you been talking about math with Adventure and the kits, Hope?*

Ratio, she said. *Seven point three. To one.*

That's a ratio? Seven point three to one?

Zilfium dust, she said. *To sulfur. To chocolate?* she added, with a rumble of amusement. *Joke. No chocolate.*

Did Bann tell you that ratio?

No.

He didn't? I said, confused.

No.

Did Raffin?

No.

Okay. Who told you that ratio? Did you make it up?

She considered my question for a while, her gold eyes unwavering. *Linta,* she said.

I blinked. Then rubbed my eyes, trying to wake up. Propping myself on one elbow, I petted her fur, watching her, trying to read something in her face, anything that would make sense of the new, strange hum inside my head. But foxes have inscrutable faces.

Linta? I finally said. *Linta Massera told you that ratio?*

Linta, she said.

Hope, I said as the hum began to grow louder. *Are you* sure *that Linta Massera told you that ratio?*

Linta? she said. *Don't tell Linta ratio. Tell Bann. Trust Bann. Bann won't make people burn.*

She tucked her head down, nestling her face against Moth's side, while I stared at her, my mind scrambling around my rising disbelief. Memories were bumping against me now, like icebergs. Like how she'd told me that in her previous life, she'd sometimes spied, sometimes lied, sometimes visited the father of the babies in the forest. Meanwhile, Linta Massera had complained that LV kept going out to spy, then coming back oddly happy. "I wouldn't have believed LV could lie to me," Linta wrote.

Was that because in Winterkeep, humans believe their bonded blue foxes never lie?

Also, she remembered a barn. She remembered the sea, and trees. She remembered so little, but what she remembered matched. And her playfulness matched. She didn't have LV's mind, she couldn't make cognitive leaps. But she told chocolate jokes. And she'd known my star nail was copper, then remembered the chemical formula for removing its tarnish. And she sat in my lap whenever I did my translations, proudly telling me that she was a chemist.

And then I thought about Joff, who'd snatched her. Kera, who'd inexplicably kidnapped her. Bitterblue, who was certain we needed to locate LV, because LV was a person everyone would want. Hope, whom everyone kept taking. And who'd just told me a ratio, then told me not to tell Linta.

I couldn't believe it. And I should have believed it. I should've known. I'm ashamed of myself for not realizing it was possible. For limiting my own views of who she could be.

Hope, I said as tears began to run down my face. *Are you LV?*

She lifted her glowing eyes to me again. *Hope chemist,* she said.

I understood then that she might never be able to tell me. That some people, if I told them, might never accept it. That they would want proof, which we might never be able to give.

I didn't need proof. I decided then whom I believed.

Yes, Hope, I said. *You are.*

I wiped my tears, then reached a hand over the foxes to Linny. "Linny," I said, shaking him. "Wake up."

144.

First I explained it to Linny. All of it, including the weapon formulas that the Estillans wanted and that Raffin and Bann were even now deciphering for Monsea—all of it that I'd been so careful not to tell him before. I needed to tell him. Too bad what anyone else will think of that.

"If I'm right," I said, "then Hope was bonded to Linta Massera, the chemist who invented the zilfium weapon. I think that's why Estillans kidnapped her. They think she knows how to build zilfium explosives."

"They do?" said Linny, stunned. *"Hope?"*

"She didn't always have these cognitive limitations," I said. "Foxes are smart. Owlet is already asking to be taught advanced mathematics."

"But then why did they drug her?"

I was trying to work it out. "Well, they believe the common knowledge that a Keepish fox can only bond to one person at a time. Maybe they couldn't risk her bonding to the wrong person."

"Such as the sailor they hired to convey her," said Linny. "Kera."

"So they drugged her," I said. "But they used too much of a bad drug."

"Why didn't this envoy guy transport her himself?"

I shrugged. "Maybe he's not the person they wanted her to bond to either. Maybe they had someone specific they wanted to get her to—I don't know anything about Estillan scientists. Or maybe they wanted to hire someone who could sail with the Monsean queen's party, and spy on us. I wonder if they always wanted LV," I muttered, thinking of the person Linta had believed was snooping around her workshop. "Or if they really wanted Linta—and then she died."

"Or the notebooks, and then you stole them," said Linny.

Either of which would mean that what happened to Hope is partly my doing, I thought grimly. And now Hope was still in danger. If she really knew the proportion of zilfium dust to sulfur, if that had really surfaced through some hole in her memory, it meant she could come out with any of the other information she'd once known. Or anyway, Joff would certainly think it meant that. As long as Hope might have formula facts in her head, she was in danger.

The foxes sat between us on the bed. Moth and Bir seemed to understand what was going on; they seemed to find it quite interesting. Hope, in contrast, was alternately watching us incuriously and dozing.

If all of this is true, I thought to myself, *Hope's real name, her Keepish name, can be abbreviated as LV.* And Hope had probably been there, somewhere, the day I stole Linta's notebooks and set off that explosion. She might've been hiding in the trees or the barn, with the future father of the babies. She might've even seen me that day, known me, before we met on the *Monsea.*

I could've killed her.

I did kill her bonded person.

And then they stole her.

And her own memory of all of it is gone.

"I'd better go," I said. "I need to make a plan."

145.

I DID MAKE A plan. Just not the way Bitterblue or Giddon or any of them might have chosen.

First I wrote a note to Bitterblue, which I delivered to her offices, handing it to a clerk.

Next I packed some food.

Then I went into the western hills with Hope.

146.

THE SKY ABOVE the western hills was a weak blue, piled with clouds that looked like walls of ice. Mountains, and glaciers. A world up there that I knew, but couldn't reach.

I put Hope down, letting her walk, much to her relief. We began to climb the hills, our destination that far-off castle. I had a memory of a skinny, plain girl with dishwater hair and eyes of scarlet and copper, sitting in an empty hall before a cold fireplace, trying to work out all the answers. If I went back to that spot, could I find her there?

What I found, after a more tiring hike than I remembered, was a ruined building weathered from wind and water and almost stripped of memories, just as pilferers had stripped the glass panes from the windows. The curtains were bleached and tattered, the floors filthy. The castle was a cave, rotting in the places where the rain had blown in.

In the long gallery, a family of squirrels nested in the remains of an upholstered chair.

Smelly, said Hope.

Yes, I agreed. Everything reeked.

Girl look for something?

Yes.

What?

I'm not sure, Hope.

Slime? she said, stepping delicately around a crack in the floor that oozed a green substance so dark, it was almost black. *Bones?* she said, touching her nose to a little bundle of bones some creature had knitted into a nest.

Something from a long time ago, Hope, I said.

Stone? she said, stopping in front of the room's biggest fireplace.

I joined her, remembering.

A man and a woman, nearly life-sized, are carved into each side of this fireplace. When I was a child, I would sit before them, imagining them as someone's parents. Not mine; I couldn't quite stretch my imagination that far. But someone's.

"We must get this fire going," the father would say, his voice gruff, "so the children will be warm."

"We must light the candles in the chandelier and make a plot to kill the king," the mother would respond, her voice as clear as a violin's song.

Today I waited for them to say something, but my imagination was empty. I noticed that they were exactly as I remembered them, straight-backed and proud. Their stone edges were sharp as ever.

Stone survives, I said, *much longer than other things.*

My girl? said Hope.

I thought of a boulder, picked up by a glacier, dragged across land, then released by an iceberg. I thought of it riding the iceberg while the iceberg melts, then finally dropping into the sea. Then pushed and pummeled by seawater, its stone edges smoothing down over time, changing, but slowly, ever so slowly. *The ahsoken that make stone are strong,* I thought, *and stable. Is that right, Linta? Is that the right way to think about it?*

I touched my pants pocket, where my figurines bulged. Then I pulled them out and knelt. I opened the scarf and Bitterblue's ring fell out. Carefully, I returned the ring to my pocket, then spread the figurines across my lap where Hope could see them too.

My mother made these for me, I said.

Mother? said Hope.

Yes, I said. *My mother.* She'd once made me keepsakes out of stone. They'd lasted through the reign of a cruel and destructive king, my father. They'd lasted through shipwreck and a desperate trudge. They would probably last through whatever future was coming to Monsea.

And yet my mother's own thoughts had not been allowed to last from one day to the next. Every time she'd come back from the king, mind-fogged and lost, she'd had to build herself up again from nothing. She'd sculpted me in stone, because to my mother, a sculptor, stone was the thing that lasts longest. She'd wanted me to last, more than anything.

I did last, Mother, I thought as tears fell onto my figurines. *You wouldn't believe the things I've survived. You taught me to last. But I don't feel strong, like stone. I feel stuck, like stone. Like a thing that barely changes, no matter what it bumps against. I'm so, so angry,* I thought, beginning to gasp through my tears. *I have an anger for the king so massive and so deep that I can hardly breathe. He hurt you, and he killed you, and now he's gone, and I can't hurt him. I will never forgive him. I can't bear the pain of what happened to you, Mother. It's like I'm drowning. The sadness is too great.*

Girl is breathing, said Hope.

She'd startled me. Dripping with snot and tears, I stared at her over my figurines. *Are you listening to my thoughts, Hope?*

Girl told them to me. Girl isn't drowning. Girl breathing.

I feel like I'm drowning.

Girl's lungs full of air. Expanding.

I took a long, deep breath, paying attention to my lungs filling with air.

See? she said. *Hope right.*

I tried to imagine the inside of Hope's mind then. Hope's life, her past, her language, her relationships, an entire world of chemistry, all of those parts of her trapped behind a thick, scarred web of damage that I'll never be able to undo. Kera caused that damage.

Didn't she?

Yes. Maybe she caused it by accident, because she didn't know the harm the medicines would do. And maybe she caused it because an Estillan with a secret purpose hired her to cause it. She did it to get her daughter back. I believe that now. I suppose I've believed it for a long time. But it doesn't alter the fact that Hope's mind is damaged, and Kera caused it.

And she also threw me into the sea, with Hope in my coat. If it weren't for a hook and a harness; if it weren't for a knobby porthole; if it weren't for Linny and Jacky deciding to help me even though they had every reason at the time to hate me, Hope and I would be corpses picked over by fish right now, frozen on the floor of the Brumal Sea. That was Kera's fault. And I was still angry about it.

So, why didn't I want her to suffer?

Well. I did want her to suffer, a little. I was fine with her standing in the shame of what she'd done, feeling its pall. I wanted her to feel regret.

But I didn't want her to die in a prison—to live or die in a cage. And I didn't want her never to see her daughter again either. I couldn't figure how those results would make anything better.

Why? Why wouldn't revenge make things better?

I think I saw then the difference between my anger toward my father and my anger toward Kera. It was like watching two icebergs separate, after moving together for a very long time. One was enormous, the size of an island; so enormous that I'd been standing atop it my entire life and never realized it was dragging me away from myself.

The other was a regular iceberg. Not small, because icebergs aren't small; but not bottomless either. Contained within a definable space. Able to be seen all at once, if I was willing to dive into the cold, and look at it from below.

Was I willing to dive? What would that mean? Could I look at one anger, without being overwhelmed by all the others?

I wonder if angers can connect to each other, if you're not careful. I wonder if they combine, and feed one another, strengthen each other, make each individual anger bigger than it's supposed to be?

That seems dangerous. It seems like something to look out for, in a life of perils.

On the floor of the ruined castle, with Hope watching, I touched each of my figurines in order. Mountain lion–girl. Bear-girl. Porpoise-girl. Bird-girl, my habpva, my seasparrow. I ran a finger over their faces, recognizing each one. Each was me, changing.

Then, in my heart, I focused. I found the place where I'd hooked my anger toward Kera into my bottomless anger toward my father. I pushed. Creaking and groaning, they cracked apart.

When they did, I saw what I needed. I saw what would change things, so that I could let the smaller anger begin to go.

147.

It was fairly easy to arrange.

First, I went to Goldie in the prison.

"Has anyone visited Kera?" I asked her.

"No one but you," she said gravely.

"Well, if anyone comes to visit her," I said, "I want you to stall them. Make it clear that they can see her in a few days, but first they need to schedule an appointment. They need paperwork, whatever. Then I want you to tell me about it straightaway."

"Clear enough," said Goldie, matter-of-fact as always.

Next I went looking for Giddon, who wasn't in his rooms or Bitterblue's. Eventually, I found him in the queen's tower. I could hear him having an animated conversation with Bitterblue—it sounded like an argument—as I climbed the spiral staircase. But when I stepped into the room, they broke off, staring.

"What?" I said.

"Hava," said Giddon, looking a little pale. "Nice to see you."

"Giddon," I said, "I need Joff to learn Kera's in the prison. Can you arrange that? Gracefully? I need it to fall into the conversation naturally. He can't know he's being manipulated."

"That won't be a problem," said Giddon. "It's what the Council does. But what's this about, Hava?"

"I have a lot to tell you," I said, conscious of the soft weight of

Hope against my back, where she was snoozing in my hood. Safe, for the moment. "I think I know who LV is. I think it's Hope."

"Hope?" repeated Giddon, his eyes widening with astonishment. "Hope, the fox?"

"Bitterblue," I said, turning to my sister, who'd propped her elbows on her desk and was burying her face in her hands. "Bitterblue? What's wrong? Why are you two being weird?"

"Nothing is wrong," said Bitterblue evenly.

"What's happened?" I said. "Just tell me."

"Well," said Bitterblue, raising steely eyes to mine, "you left me a note saying you needed some space and you were leaving. So we thought you were gone. But now you're back, aren't you? So nothing's wrong."

I stared at her, incredulous. "Did you think I was leaving forever?"

"Well, you didn't specify, did you?" said Bitterblue, her voice rising. "You've never left me a note like that, ever! And last night you made some dire statements!"

"I just wanted to let you know I was taking some time to myself! You're always so annoyed when I leave the castle without saying!"

"Hava!" cried Bitterblue—then, with that single shriek, caught Giddon's eye. She coughed, seeming to gather herself. "Thank you," she said carefully. "That was considerate."

"You two seem awfully stressed out, for newlyweds," I said, a statement I immediately regretted, because they both instantly began beaming at each other like brainless loons. "I have more business to discuss."

"Yes?" said Bitterblue, casting her luminous smile upon me. "What is it?"

"I need more help from the Council," I said, "and I need help from the Monsean throne."

148.

I ASKED GOLDIE TO bring Kera into a separate, private room in the prison. I needed to talk to her alone, out of the hearing of her neighbors.

I wasn't prepared for what I found in the room's corner, touched by flickering light: a sculpture of my mother's, which I didn't remember and had never seen.

It was a man in ragged clothing with his eyes upraised, one hand reaching for the sky. His face was tight with exhaustion, but his eyes were full of hope. He wasn't transforming. He was just a man. But I knew he was a Bellamew, as certainly as I would've recognized my mother's voice. And I remembered then that she hadn't started sculpting transformations until I was born, and settled into my Grace.

"You're stuck in here," I said to the sculpture. "Why are they keeping you in here? Are you supposed to be inspiring to the prisoners? Give them fortitude while they die of loneliness, or something?" Then I did a thing I keep doing recently: I used my Grace, even though there was no one there to use it on. I reached one hand up, raised my eyes, and made myself into a mirror of the sculpture, just to see what it felt like. I think it's a kind of test. A way to assess how I feel.

It helped. Pretending to be that sculpture, I felt how trapped he was, and I knew I'd made the right choice about what I was about to do.

I turned my back to it and sat at the table, myself again.

Then the door opened and Goldie ushered Kera in. When Kera saw me, she hardened her face into a mask. She was wearing shackles at her wrists and ankles that clunked as she sat, and no blanket cape this time. She looked thin, and worn, and cold.

"You're not leaving me alone with this maniac, are you?" she asked Goldie.

"There will be guards outside the door," said Goldie. "They'll hear you if you yell." Then she flicked a warning look at me that clearly said *Don't you dare*, and left the room.

"Well?" said Kera sharply. "What do you want?"

"We're freeing you," I said.

"What?"

"The Council's going to help you return to your daughter. You are Estillan, right?"

"Is this a trick to get me to talk?" said Kera, staring at me in patent disbelief.

"Assuming you're Estillan, or otherwise from a nation where Gracelings are the property of the government," I said, "the Council will offer you and your family whatever assistance you need, including safe passage back to Monsea if you prefer. You'll have to work out your family drama yourself, though," I added. "And you'll have to tell Giddon the truth about where your daughter is. The Council can't help you if you're not open."

Kera's eyes shone with something that seemed an attempt at insolence, but it was a failed attempt. Really, she just looked frightened. "Why should I believe you?"

"Because we can't help you otherwise."

Scorn burned in her eyes. "I thought you thought I was some sort of political operative."

"I was afraid you might be," I admitted. "But I never really thought you were."

She considered me for another beat, the fear in her face beginning to shift into something more frightening to me: hope. "What do I have to do?"

"You're right that there's something I want you to do."

"Well, obviously," she said. "And then what? You'll pull this dream out from under me?"

"It's not a deal," I said. "You'll get the Council's help regardless of whether you do what I ask. But I'm asking you to do it as a kindness to me and Hope."

"Why would I do you a kindness?" she cried.

"To fix what's broken between us," I said.

149.

IT WASN'T JOFF who made an appointment to see Kera, but a man named Enni.

Enni produced Monsean papers, claiming to be Kera's cousin from Hawkery. But when Kera met with me and Giddon to talk about him, she told us she's never even been to Hawkery.

"The people who hired me told me to pretend to come from there," she said, "because few people know it well." She spoke emotionlessly; Kera seemed intent on answering all our questions in the flattest voice possible. But in the back of her eyes, I could see the flicker of hope she kept trying to suppress.

"Did the people who hired you mention this Enni person?" Giddon asked her.

"They never told me anyone's name except Joff," said Kera. "They told me that when I got to Monsea, an Estillan man named Joff would find me, ask me a few questions, and collect the fox. He was supposed to pay me too. They didn't tell me he was a lord."

"What was he meant to ask you questions about?"

"I was supposed to keep my eyes and ears open on the ship," she said.

"Spy?"

"They didn't use that word," she said in a hard voice. "Nor did they give me the slightest indication of what information they were looking for. Or even who I was supposed to be focusing on, though I assumed that since it was the queen's ship, they were interested in the queen."

"Okay," said Giddon. "Can you describe who hired you?"

She took a small breath. Giddon never runs out of questions. "There were a few men who approached me in Ledra Harbor," she said. "All pale, like Monseans and Estillans. They seemed to be glad I was Estillan, so I assumed they were too, but I don't actually know. They brought me to a meeting with another man who acted like he was in charge. He was little, with pink skin and orange hair."

Giddon gave me an even look across the table. Kera was describing Lord Cobal, the Estillan envoy to Winterkeep, and the man who tried to broker the Estillan deal for Linta Massera's zilfium weapons.

It proved nothing we don't already know about Estill. But it's satisfying when puzzle pieces fall into place.

When Enni met with Kera in the prison, I was in the room too, hidden. I'd always planned to be there, but circumstances made it easier than it might otherwise have been. If it's routine for the prison's private meeting room to contain one sculpture, why shouldn't it contain two?

We sat Enni with his back to me, so I could relax my Grace whenever he wasn't looking. This meant that Kera could see me, which made me worry she'd give me away.

I should've had faith in her hard head. Though we prepared her with dozens of instructions, really all we ever needed to do was tell her to be herself. The moment she entered the room and saw Enni waiting, she was on the attack. She began lambasting him before Goldie had even shut the door.

"You're not my cousin," Kera spat at him. "I've never seen you before. Why should I talk to you?"

"Sh!" said Enni harshly, indicating the place where Goldie had just been. "Are you trying to get me jailed too?"

"Why would I care what happens to you?"

"You have no interest in the welfare of your employer?" said Enni, who had a whiny voice that fit perfectly somehow with Joff's coldness. He looked a little like Joff too, tall and icy-eyed, sharp in his features, though his hair was darker. I wondered if they were related.

"You're not my employer," said Kera flatly.

"I'm his representative."

"Then maybe you'd like to explain what you plan to do for me," she said, "now that I'm in prison on your behalf and my money's at the bottom of the Winter Sea?"

"Where's the fox?" said Enni.

"Maybe you'd like to explain why you promised me the other half of the money on delivery," said Kera, "if you never meant me to deliver her?"

"Of course we meant you to deliver her," said Enni impatiently. "Where is she?"

"She's dead!" shouted Kera. "Where do you think she is? The drug you gave me killed her!"

THAT WAS IT. That was what I'd needed from Kera; that was all.

She filled in the details for Enni, pretending to answer his questions unwillingly. She yelled about the fox's pregnancy, how it and the drugs had been too much for the fox's little body. She yelled about having to feed a hive (her word) of baby fox parasites (her word) from the milk of a goat as she stumbled through a barren wilderness, because their mother was dead. She yelled about tossing the fox's corpse into the ocean north of Pikkia, and with it, the fortune she'd been promised. Where was her fortune? She screamed at Enni, demanding an explanation for why a fox was worth so much trouble in the first place, and who was going to take the trouble now to care about *her*?

There was one question I badly hoped Enni would ask, and he did. Who is the adult female fox at court who's attached to Hava, the queen's Graced assistant?

"So I need to explain to you why the queen would acquire a fox for her spy?" Kera said scornfully. "That fox pretends to be stupid, just like Hava pretends to be stupid. In the meantime, she gets into everything. I hope the two of them together decide to take an interest in *you*."

She did a good job. Her anger was vicious, and she never looked at me once, but it spread through me like kindness, because Enni seemed to believe her. If Enni believed her, and if Joff believes Enni, then Hope will be safe.

I don't think she did it with kindness. I don't know. Maybe she did. I doubt I'll ever be able to see inside Kera to all her parts. It doesn't matter. I didn't need her feelings to change. I just needed her to choose to do the things I asked her to do.

The ocean began to carry that iceberg away.

AFTER THE MEETING, Goldie released Kera straight into Giddon's care, for they were wasting no time. Giddon was bringing Kera to the town on Estill's northern shore where Kera's from, and where she hopes to find her daughter, Sera, and her husband's family.

"Thank you, Kera," I said to her.

When she frowned at me, I understood her frown, because I could still see that look in her eyes, the disbelief. The fear that this was going to turn out to be some sort of trap. I understand that instinct. You learn it, in a life of too many traps.

When I turned away, her question hit my back. "Why are you doing this?"

I took a long breath, trying to think of how to answer. *Love is hope for other people,* I thought, but didn't say.

"I did it for a little girl," I finally said, letting her assume I meant her daughter. And I did mean Sera, of course, partly. But there's another heartbroken little girl who would've wanted me to give Sera her mother back.

150.

My next conversation was more difficult.

I went to Bitterblue in her tower. I found her at her desk, scribbling something furiously, her body coiled over the paper, tight as a spring. I watched her for a moment, waiting for her to notice me in the doorway. She rubbed at her braids, in that way that always starts a dull ache in my own head.

Finally she came out of her preoccupation and glanced my way. "Oh!" she said, her face brightening at the sight of me. "Hava. Come in."

"I'm sorry for sending your secret husband away," I said, stepping into the soft light of her windows.

Her smile was rueful. "This is probably the hundredth time Giddon has gone away since I met him. I knew what I was signing up for."

"What are you writing?" I said. "You look pretty intense."

"It's an argument."

"With whom?"

"Myself," she said. "As a sort of preparation, so I'm ready with the right words when I have a massive series of arguments with other people."

"Do you practice your arguments in writing ahead of time?" I said, struck by this. "Do you practice your arguments with *me*? Is that why you're so successful at being bossy?"

"I think that's because I'm a monarch," she said, snorting. "But I do practice sometimes, if I know I'm going to be facing pushback from my people."

"So? What are you expecting pushback about?"

Bitterblue placed her pen down neatly beside her papers. She tilted her head, considering me with those big gray eyes. I've always loved the clarity of Bitterblue's eyes. You can look right into her through her eyes, and know if she's in pain, and see how much she cares about everything.

"Remember how I was going to make everyone sign a promise not to build explosive weapons," she said, "then sign it myself, then secretly build them anyway?"

"Yes."

"I'm considering a different plan."

"Okay," I said. "What plan?"

"Honesty."

It was a concerning word. "What do you mean?"

"What if I told the truth?" she said. "What if I told all the nations that in addition to having most of the world's zilfium, I have the formulas? And that I also have the means to understand them? That I have powerful allies in the Dells, Lienid, and probably very soon, the Middluns, because one of these days, Randa's going to die. And that I'm about to formalize an alliance with the Council, by engaging myself to one of its leaders."

"Okay," I said. "All of this sounds a little aggressive."

"But what if I was honest about building the weapons too?"

Now I was beginning to be seriously alarmed. "Tell Estill and Sunder you're stockpiling zilfium explosives, 'just in case'?" I said. "Won't that make them even more determined to have zilfium weapons of their own?"

"No, silly," said Bitterblue. "I meant, what if I move forward with the treaty as planned, but after I sign it and say I won't build them either, I *don't* build them?"

"You mean you wouldn't stockpile them?" I said. "Is that safe?"

"I want to live in a world where the simplest way to be safe from explosive weapons is not to build explosive weapons in the first place. Is that so outrageous?"

"But do you really expect the other signers not to be trying to build the explosives?"

"No," she said. "But Monsea and the Council have the resources to figure out what other nations are doing. And don't forget, I still have most of the known zilfium."

"Hm," I said, understanding why she was expecting pushback, and even more worried now. On the day Estill shows up at her border with twenty thousand soldiers, I want my sister to be sitting atop a mountain of explosives. I want her to blast Estill into the sky. Of course, I also want her to be able to be honest and not build explosives, if that's what nourishes her heart. And of course I want fewer bombs generally. But not if it gets her killed.

It came back to me again then, the explosion, and my fall into the earth. The pain in my broken ankle, my broken torso. My fear of being left to die in that cavern slowly, all alone. Linta Massera? You were already dead at that point. And when it comes down to it, I'm not sorry I stopped you. You were doing something too terrible to be allowed to continue. But I am sorry that all the other parts of you had to die too. Maybe I shouldn't be. Maybe I should condemn you completely, forever. But I don't.

I remember something else from the time I spent trapped. I remember Bitterblue's voice, calling down from above. I remember how inconsolable she was, terrified that I was stranded in a place where she wouldn't be able to reach me. And I remember that even in that moment, my own pain began to shift into the wish to comfort her pain.

I lose myself in that wish. I disappear. Suddenly Bitterblue is there, and I am gone. It's not her fault. It's my whole thing, right? I disappear from myself. It's a way of being I got stuck inside, a long time ago.

I've been thinking about how to get unstuck. Even if it hurts.

"There's something I need," I said.

I could tell she sensed that I was changing the subject. Her eyes narrowed on me. When she saw the tear making a track down my face, she went still.

"What do you need, Hava?" she said.

"I need some time away," I said. "Some space."

I could feel it, the instant when understanding touched her and her sorrow bloomed. She looked into her hands and turned one of the rings on her fingers. My ring. I touched my pocket, where I keep mine safe with my figurines.

"I don't think you mean just for a morning or a day," she said.

"No."

"Well, Hava," she said. "The truth is that you've always taken time and space when you've wanted it. What's changed is that you've begun telling me. And though I'll miss you terribly, it makes me happy that you trust me enough to let me know."

She didn't seem happy. She had started to cry. I could feel it in my own throat. But as she turned her face up to me she was also smiling, and the smile was real.

It occurred to me at that moment to think of myself, my whole life even, as a ship. If my life is a ship, then the things I'm most scared of and want most are at the top of the foremast, on the highest platform in the rigging. Maybe leaving my sister and setting out on my own is up there. Maybe Linny is. Maybe my own clearest feelings—mine, all mine, no one else's—are up there too. I can meet myself up there.

I also have parts down below, keeping me balanced on the skin of the sea. Giddon is my ballast. Hope and Moth are my spine and my ribbands. And Bitterblue is my anchor. She always will be; she's not going to break free.

"I'll return," I said.

"That's the best news of all," she said. "What will you do?"

I took a breath, remembering the feeling of the wind at my back.

"I'd like to try being a sailor," I said.

151.

ANNET SAYS IT'S not as unusual as you might think, for sailors who've been shipwrecked to sail again.

"The *Monsea* sank because first we lost an anchor," she said, "then a storm pushed us into shallow waters. Also because we were in uncharted territory. What's the likelihood of all those circumstances converging again? Especially now, sailing to Wester, at the start of summer? Are you ready for some warm rain? Won't that be blissful compared to snow, habpva?"

I've missed standing on the deck of a ship with Annet and Navi, being called that name.

Our ship is a barque. She's a lot like a barquentine, but not exactly like. Similar in length to the *Monsea*, and three-masted, but the fore-mast and the mainmast carry square-rigged sails and only the aftermost mast is rigged fore-and-aft.

Do I sound more and more like I know what I'm talking about? The front and middle masts carry square sails that drop down from above. The back mast carries triangle sails that we raise from below, with lines I know the names of. And she's beautiful, she's so, so completely beautiful with the wind in her sails. She's tried and true; she has barnacles clinging to her once-crimson hull that's been burnished by sun and sea into something more weathered. Annet bought her from a wine merchant in Monport, on behalf of the queen. Bitterblue wanted to rename her something boring, but Annet and Navi both cried out in alarm that it was bad luck to rename a ship.

I was relieved, because her name is the *Fledgling*.

"Silly name for a ship that's sailed many seas," said Bitterblue, but I like to imagine a grown bird that's only just now learning to fly.

I'M THE LOWEST-RANKING sailor on the *Fledgling*, even lower than Ollie, who's eight years younger than me. When we left Monsea, Annet and Navi, once again our captain and first mate, were afraid I was going to have an insubordination problem.

And okay, maybe it's true that too often, I want to know *why* I'm supposed to do something before doing it. But I do what I'm told, because as the lowest-ranking sailor, I'm the person who cares for the animals and I take most of my daily orders from the cook.

And guess who the cook is? Liel. Liel has returned to us. He has a leg made of wood. He has pain, and balance problems. But he swears his balance is better on the ship than on land.

And Ladybug, who's a giant now, makes him laugh. Ladybug is bigger than his shipmates Bir and Moth, and on track to grow bigger than Hope soon. He still has those spots on his shoulders. He's also an unparalleled food thief, which is completely unnecessary since Liel spoils him rotten. At least he shares his spoils, or at any rate, he's as cowed by Moth as anyone, and Moth commands him to share. While we work together in the galley, Liel and I are designing a series of exercises for Moth on the topic of How to Be a Kinder Tyrant. I do think there's hope.

Speaking of Hope, she came out with her Keepish name the other morning. It always seems to be morning when she remembers things. I open my eyes to the roll of the ship and the sight of her watching me with her thoughtful, gold gaze, and then she'll say something monumental, delivering it as if it's as insignificant as which socks I should wear that day.

Luta Voma, she said.

What? I said, confused.

LV, she said. *Linta.*

Linta? Ahsoken?

LV! Luta Voma!

I was trying to wake up, trying to form thoughts around why the words *luta voma* should be dropping into my consciousness with a splash of what sleepily felt like surprise.

Isn't luta voma *a Keepish expression for hope?* I finally managed.

No, she said. *Tova voma is hope.*

But isn't it almost *a Keepish expression for hope?*

Luta voma is something else, she said. *Trust.*

So, your prior name was Trust and your new name is Hope? I said. *Isn't that a strange coincidence, that they're so similar?*

No, she said. *Girl tried many names before Hope agreed. Remember? Before, Hope liked Luta Voma. Now, Hope likes Hope.*

It made me wonder, wish, that something essential remains, no matter how much we are hurt.

WE'RE BRINGING TRINA clockwise around the Royal Continent to northern Wester.

It's a secret mission, and a lot of our sailors double as guards and soldiers. We'll take her to all the parts of Wester rumored to have zilfium, and sneak her wherever she needs to go to determine for the queen if it's true. I expect my Grace will be useful.

We'll do the same with a small corner of Nander where zilfium rumors have sprung up, though Nander's not the enemy Wester is likely to be. And then, at King Ror's invitation, we'll sail to Lienid, which is a mountainous island and which may take Trina some time to explore. I expect the rest of us will explore it too. Ollie wants us to meet his family and Moth heard something about a castle on a cliff and now she wants to see it. Probably she wants to pretend she's its queen.

I mostly stay out of the way of the sailors I don't know, though I bunk with three of the women and some of them aren't too shy to talk to me. They know who I am. They always balk a little at my eyes. Maybe my reputation protects me? Maybe it makes my experience as a subordinate more comfortable than it otherwise would be? Jacky certainly likes to tell me so, at least once a day.

Trina is different. I don't consider myself subordinate to her, and I don't consider her my friend. But we interact civilly enough, I suppose, at meals and on deck. I notice myself not wanting her to learn any private things about me, because what if then she was able to look inside me and find those parts of me, like Linta observing ahsoken? What if she can find thoughts and feelings? I don't think she can, but it crosses my mind. And then I start thinking about my own Grace. A Grace isn't always what you think it is, even your own. My mother told me my Grace was hiding, because she wanted me to *live*. But my Grace is other things too.

I'm not sure what yet. But I'm using it more when I'm alone, to turn into whatever I want to try the feeling of. Water. The aurora borealis. A part of the ship. Sometimes when I'm in the rigging, I give myself gigantic wings that lie flat against my back, ready to unfurl, and I don't really care if anyone sees me. Maybe that's why some of the sailors don't seem to know what to say to me. Whatever. I like it. It makes me feel like I'm figuring something out. If people can see me, then it makes me feel like I'm saying something. Like, something about myself.

Anyway. Linny says a ship throws people together. He says I'll find the way to be Trina's companion in time. Then someday, decades from now, I'll pass her on the street somewhere, and when she looks at me, I don't know what she'll see. But when I look at her, I'll see the sails taut with wind behind her and the bright water beyond.

"So, Princess Dardya?" said Jacky when I sat down to dinner. "Why did you just take a hammer to the top of the foremast?"

I guess I should've known that Jacky would notice my mast-top carpentry—though he'd make a terrible spy, despite his nosiness. He talks too much.

"A memorial to the *Monsea*," I said.

"What memorial?"

"Look for it yourself next time you're up there."

"You're such a dardya," he said, with no malice. I thought he might enjoy the scavenger hunt that would lead him to a teeny, tiny copper star embedded in the mast.

I shoveled my dinner into my mouth, sitting in the nook of Linny's arm. Around me, Ozul and Ollie chatted with a few of the sailors I don't know well. Jacky quipped. Linny chuckled, then asked me if I wanted seconds. I shook my head, because I didn't want him to remove his arm.

Gradually, the others left, returning to their work. The cook's assistant is always the last to eat. It's often me and Linny at the end, alone in the salon.

His nose brushed my neck. As the ship climbed a wave, I relaxed against him, but didn't turn. Listened to his quiet words as he told me about his day, asked me about mine. When he smiled, I felt his lips on my skin.

We are moving; we're not stuck. But we're taking this more slowly than anyone ever has. We're thinking about now, not where we're going. We're paying attention to what we're building. That's the way we choose.

"You do actually want seconds, don't you?" he said.

"Yes."

While he went to fill my plate, I sat at the edge of my seat with my eyes closed, feeling the ship's roll. It's never the same from wave to wave. There are always surprises. Why do I find that exhilarating?

I ate the seconds Linny brought me, then we sat together until the bell rang to signal the watch change. That meant Linny had to go, but I was free.

The days are long on this voyage. The sun sets late. I went up to lie in one of the lifeboats, where Hope and Moth found me after a time. We chatted, and looked for birds. As the clouds turned to puffs of pink and orange, they left me in search of Ladybug and Bir.

I stayed there on my back, turning briefly into one of the sunset clouds. It felt like flying. I lay there for a while, watching the white sails above me catch the wind and propel our ship across the changing sky.

CAST OF CHARACTERS

ADVENTURE: A Keepish blue fox devoted to Queen Bitterblue.

ALZAR: A sailor on the *Monsea*. The wife of Riz. Kamassarian.

ANNET: The captain of the *Monsea*. Monsean.

ASHEN: The mother of Bitterblue and the previous Queen of Monsea. She was married to King Leck. Lienid. Deceased.

BANN: One of the leaders of the Council. A scientist and the companion of Prince Raffin. From the Middluns.

BARRA: An adviser to Queen Bitterblue. Monsean.

BELLAMEW: A sculptor in the time of King Leck. The mother of Hava. Monsean. Deceased.

BIR: A blue fox kit with coppery eyes, named after Lady Bir (Fire) of the Dells.

BITTERBLUE: The Queen of Monsea. Secretly Hava's half sister. A cousin of Prince Po. Of Monsean and Lienid lineage.

BLUEBERRY: A blue fox kit with a round, dark blue nose.

BRIGAN (BRIGANDELL): A Dellian prince. The retired commander of the Dellian King's Army. The husband of Lady Fire and a brother of King Nash of the Dells.

604 — KRISTIN CASHORE

BRITTABO: The infant daughter of Froggatt and Fralla. A Graceling (though her Grace is unknown). Monsean.

COBAL: The Estillan envoy to Winterkeep.

CORAN: An adviser and doctor to Queen Bitterblue. Monsean.

CORNSILK: A blue fox kit with big, silky ears.

ENNI: A man in Monsea claiming to be Kera's cousin.

FIRE (OR, IN DELLIAN, BIR): A Dellian lady who is half human, half Dellian monster. Her hair is scarlet, pink, and silver and she can communicate telepathically. She is the wife of Prince Brigan and a sister-in-law of King Nash of the Dells.

FRALLA: A woman who lives at the Monsean court. The wife of Froggatt and mother of Brittabo. Monsean.

FROGGATT: Queen Bitterblue's foremost adviser. The husband of Fralla and father of Brittabo. Monsean.

GIDDON: One of the leaders of the Council. A dispossessed Middluns lord and a friend of Hava and Queen Bitterblue.

GOLDIE: The prison master at the Monsean court. A Graceling Graced with singing. Monsean, though she grew up in Lienid.

GRELLA: A mountain climber and explorer who died in a mountain pass between Monsea and Sunder that is now called Grella's Pass. Monsean. Deceased.

HAVA: A spy for Queen Bitterblue and secretly Bitterblue's half sister. The daughter of the sculptor Bellamew. A Graceling Graced with the ability to change what people see when they look at her. Monsean.

HELDA: The caretaker of Queen Bitterblue's domestic affairs and her spymaster. From the Middluns.

HOLT: A retired member of Queen Bitterblue's royal guard. An uncle to Hava and brother to Bellamew. A Graceling with the Grace of strength. Monsean.

HOPE: A Keepish blue fox devoted to Hava.

JACKY: A sailor on the *Monsea*. Monsean.

JOFF: A lord from southern Estill who wants to marry Queen Bitterblue.

KATSA: The founder of the Council. A friend and mentor of Queen Bitterblue. The companion of Prince Po. The niece of King Randa and cousin of Prince Raffin. A Graceling Graced with survival. From the Middluns.

KERA: The first mate on the *Monsea*. Monsean.

LADYBUG: A blue fox kit with a dark spot on each shoulder blade.

LECK: The previous King of Monsea. The father of Queen Bitterblue and secretly of Hava. A psychopath. A Graceling Graced with the ability to tell lies that people believe. Deceased.

LIEL: The cook on the *Monsea*. Monsean.

LINNY: A sailor on the *Monsea*. Dellian.

LINTA MASSERA: A chemist who invented an explosive zilfium weapon. Keepish. Deceased.

LISA: A sailor on the *Monsea*. Keepish.

LOVEJOY: An elderly cat living in Queen Bitterblue's castle in the care of the royal librarian.

LV: A colleague and confidant of chemist Linta Massera. Assumed to be Keepish.

MART: One of Queen Bitterblue's guards and a sailor on the *Monsea*. Monsean.

MOTH: A blue fox kit with long legs and floppy paws.

NASH (NASHDELL): The King of the Dells.

NAVI: The second mate on the *Monsea*. Keepish.

NOA: A sailor on the *Monsea*. Keepish.

OLLIE (OLIVAN): A sailor on the *Monsea*. Lienid.

OWLET: A blue fox kit with a squat head and pointy ears.

OZUL: A sailor on the *Monsea*. Keepish.

PO: One of the leaders of the Council. A Lienid prince, the seventh son of King Ror. A cousin of Queen Bitterblue. The companion of Lady Katsa. A Graceling with the Grace of sensing thoughts and physicality relating to him.

RAFFIN: One of the leaders of the Council. A Middluns prince and the heir to his father, King Randa. A scientist and the companion of Bann.

RANDA: The King of the Middluns. The father of Prince Raffin and uncle of Lady Katsa.

RANIN: One of Queen Bitterblue's guards and a sailor on the *Monsea*. Monsean.

RIZ: A sailor on the *Monsea*. The husband of Alzar. Kamassarian.

ROR: The King of Lienid. The father of Prince Po and uncle of Queen Bitterblue.

ROSIE: A pig on the *Monsea*.

SERA: Kera's daughter. A Graceling.

SORIT: A sailor on the *Monsea*. Keepish.

TEDDY: A member of Queen Bitterblue's Ministry of Education. Monsean.

TRINA: A Graceling Graced with finding things, currently assisting the Council. Originally Estillan, she escaped to Monsea with Giddon's help.

TULIP: A cat on the *Monsea* in the care of Liel the cook.

ACKNOWLEDGMENTS

IN OCTOBER 2018, I spent two-plus weeks on a tall ship called the *Antigua*, sailing around the northwest shores of Spitsbergen in the Svalbard Archipelago as part of an artist residency known as The Arctic Circle. It was one of the most spectacular experiences of my life and largely inspired this book, which I began plotting during the journey and began writing immediately upon my return. The *Monsea* is modeled on the *Antigua*, the most beautiful structure I've ever had the privilege of calling my home. We sailed and hiked among glaciers; saw beluga whales, walruses, Arctic foxes, seals; learned how to set the sails and climb the mast; and I was permitted to lie on my back in the zodiac boats while other people worked, simply because "that's what I needed to do for my art." It was that kind of residency: The staff worked extremely hard to provide us with the experiences we needed for our various artistic projects, while keeping us safe in an Arctic landscape. Heartfelt thanks to our kickass guides, who answered all our questions about the land, glaciers, weather, wildlife, history, etc. while guarding us from polar bears: Sarah Gerats, Emma Hoette, Kristin Jæger Wexsahl, and Åshild Gåsvatn Rye. (The Norwegian name Åshild is pronounced a little like "Ozul." A known Norwegian name would be out of place in *Seasparrow*, but on the day Åshild found my lost phone on the ice and saved me and everyone a great deal of trouble, I decided to find some small way to write her into my book!) Thanks to our captain, Mario Czok; our first mate, Marijn Achterkamp; and our second mate, Annet Achterkamp, who has a blond ponytail and glasses and inspired my captain. (Sorry, Mario and Marijn, but in my world, Annet's in charge!) Thanks to our cook, Piet Litjens, and crewmembers Alex Renes, Janine Jungermann, and Jana Maxová. Thanks to my wonderful co-passengers, whose own artistic projects thrilled and inspired me. Thanks to Nemo (who happens to be a dog). Thanks to Aaron O'Connor and everyone at The Arctic Circle program who offered me this indescribable, inexpressible experience. I've done my best to describe and express parts of it with *Seasparrow*.

Thank you to my editor, Andrew Karre, who asked all the best questions, saw all the connections, and—in a rather miraculous way that I still haven't quite figured out—created the perfect mental space for me to do the work I needed to do. It's a privilege to work with you, Andrew.

Thank you to my agent, Faye Bender, always and ever, for being my tireless champion and support and also my friend.

Thank you to my excellent publisher at Dutton, Julie Strauss-Gabel. Thank you to Melissa Faulner, Natalie Vielkind, and Rob Farren. Thank you to Regina Castillo, copyeditor extraordinaire. Thank you to Jen Loja, Elyse Marshall, Emily Romero, Felicia Frazier, Debra Polansky, and the entire team at Penguin Young Readers Group who care for my books with such energy and skill. Reader, this book wouldn't be in your hands without this team. Please turn to the Credits page to see the names of these incredible people!

Thank you to Anna Booth, Jessica Jenkins, and Theresa Evangelista for your beautiful art and design work. Thank you to Kuri Huang for this gorgeous cover (and all my new Penguin Random House covers). Thank you to Ian Schoenherr, who created this book's frontispiece, endpapers, chapter spots, maps, and diagram of the *Monsea*, all of which make me tizzy with happiness.

It's a thrill to see my books sailing off into other parts of the world. I'm endlessly grateful to my foreign publishers. Thank you to my co-agents who make my foreign editions possible: Lora Fountain (western Europe), Ia Atterholm (Scandinavia), Annelie Geissler (Germany), Milena Kaplarevic (eastern Europe), and Gray Tan and Clare Chi (China and Taiwan).

A number of careful, thoughtful, honest, trustworthy people served as early readers for *Seasparrow*. Thank you so much to Catherine Cashore, Dorothy Cashore, Laura Chandra, E. K. Johnston, Jamie Pittel, Marie Rutkoski, and Shiri Weinbaum Sondheimer for caring about Hava and helping me shift her story in the directions it needed to go.

As I wrote this book, many friends, colleagues, and helpers assisted me with questions, answers, and suggestions, or allowed me to talk things through and/or whine. Heartfelt thanks to Judy Blundell, Laura Chandra, Eve Goldfarb, Sarah Hamburg, Deb Heiligman, Marthe Jocelyn, Barb Kerley, Emily Michelson, Betsy Partridge, Margo Rabb, Marie Rutkoski, Natalie Standiford, and Rebecca Stead. Extra special thanks to Kevin Lin, who listened as I talked things through every night at dinner for approximately three years.

My books involve a fair amount of research, this book more so than most. In my attempts to breathe life into Hava's story, I researched, in no particular order: the makeup of explosives; the history of chemistry, especially atomic theory and the discovery of early elements; ships, sailing, and shipbuilding; anchors specifically; hypothermia (again! I have yet to write a book for which I don't need to reacquaint myself with the particulars of hypothermia!); and most especially, shipwreck and polar survival stories. These latter are such incredible reads that I'd like to mention a few of the books that most influenced me: *In the Kingdom of Ice* by Hampton Sides; *Island of the Lost* by Joan Druett; *The Ice Balloon* by Alec Wilkinson; and *Shipwreck at the Bottom of the World* by Jennifer Armstrong.

Finally, my husband is such a treasure in my life, such a support, and such a boon to my work that I must thank him twice. Thank you, Kevin Lin.

CREDITS

DUTTON BOOKS AND PENGUIN YOUNG READERS GROUP

ART AND DESIGN
Anna Booth
Jessica Jenkins

CONTRACTS
Anton Abrahamsen

COPYEDITORS AND PROOFREADERS
Regina Castillo
Rob Farren

EDITOR
Andrew Karre

MANAGING EDITOR
Natalie Vielkind

MARKETING
James Akinaka
Christina Colangelo
Alex Garber
Brianna Lockhart
Danielle Presley
Emily Romero
Felicity Vallence

PRODUCTION MANAGER
Vanessa Robles

PUBLICITY
Elyse Marshall

PUBLISHER
Julie Strauss-Gabel

PUBLISHING MANAGER
Melissa Faulner

SUBSIDIARY RIGHTS
Micah Hecht

SALES
Susie Albert
Jill Bailey
Andrea Baird
Maggie Brennan
Trevor Bundy
Nicole Davies
Tina Deniker
John Dennany
Cletus Durkin

Eliana Ferreri
Drew Fulton
Felicia Frazier
Sheila Hennessey
Todd Jones
Doni Kay
Steve Kent
Mary McGrath
Debra Polansky
Colleen Conway Ramos
Mary Raymond
Jennifer Ridgway
Judy Samuels
Nicole White
Allan Winebarger
Dawn Zahorik

SCHOOL AND LIBRARY MARKETING AND PROMOTION
Venessa Carson
Judith Huerta
Carmela Iaria
Trevor Ingerson
Summer Ogata
Megan Parker
Rachel Wease

LISTENING LIBRARY

Linda Korn
Rebecca Waugh

THE BOOK GROUP

Faye Bender
DJ Kim